T. J. MARTINSON

THE REIGN
OF THE
KINGFISHER

FLATIRON
BOOKS
NEW YORK

THE REIGN OF THE KINGFISHER. Copyright © 2019 by T. J. Martinson. All rights reserved. Printed in the United States of America. For information, address Flatiron Books, 175 Fifth Avenue, New York, N.Y. 10010.

www.flatironbooks.com

Designed by Jonathan Bennett

Library of Congress Cataloging-in-Publication Data

Names: Martinson, T. J., author.
Title: The reign of the Kingfisher : a novel / T. J. Martinson.
Description: First edition. | New York : Flatiron Books, 2019.
Identifiers: LCCN 2018030160| ISBN 9781250170217 (hardcover) |
    ISBN 9781250170224 (ebook)
Subjects: LCSH: Superheroes—Fiction. | GSAFD: Suspense fiction.
Classification: LCC PS3613.A7876 R45 2019 | DDC 813/.6—dc23
LC record available at https://lccn.loc.gov/2018030160

Our books may be purchased in bulk for promotional, educational, or business use. Please contact your local bookseller or the Macmillan Corporate and Premium Sales Department at 1-800-221-7945, extension 5442, or by email at MacmillanSpecialMarkets@macmillan.com.

First Edition: March 2019

10 9 8 7 6 5 4 3 2 1

For Mary Martinson

PROLOGUE

HERE IN THE BLACK-LIGHT NIGHT of another endless Chicago winter is a boy walking home later than he ought to be. The streets are barren, unrecognizable. Streetlights flicker a dull orange. Yesterday's snow falls like ash from the rooftops with each gust of wind.

It's December 1983. The end of the beginning of a new decade.

The boy moves in a skip-step, unaware of the blistering cold, the empty streets, the faltering lights, the whistling wind, the new decade. He tucks his pointed chin into his zipped-up coat and feels his breath thaw his frozen lips.

Somewhere out from the brick tenements and the cars on blocks, he hears his mother's voice asking him just where on God's green earth he has been all day. He's been hearing it all night. He answers her out loud, practicing for the moment itself, as he cuts into an alleyway to make up time. "When Portia's dad came to pick her up after the Bulls game, I forgot to ask him for a ride, and I couldn't call you because all the pay phones were used up or busted. Wires all tangled, cut loose, hanging from the wall. So I took the bus back to Halsted and walked the rest the way."

It was all true, or most of it. But at this time of night, coming home without notice, the truth didn't count for much.

He crosses the street and cuts into another alley.

"You should have seen Reggie Theus, Mom, you should have seen him move. Might as well have been out there all alone."

To which his mother will say something about gangs and drive-bys and pedophiles and psychopaths and crack addicts—her litany of midnight dangers—but these things are impossible to take seriously on a night like this. A blanket of stars is suspended above the humming web of power lines running slantwise and longways over the tenement rooftops. Pulsing red lights of jet planes and satellites spinning, spinning, through space. He would walk like this all night if he could. He would tread each city block, hands in his pockets jangling sixty cents change, maybe stopping off outside of Portia's apartment to try and get her attention without waking her father.

He would wait for her face in the window.

As he steps into another alleyway, a car passes behind him in the street. A white Lincoln Continental moving in a slow, slick crawl. He feels the heavy weight of a stare coming from behind the tinted windows, which are darker than the night itself. He freezes, midstep. Every muscle in his body contracts and holds. He becomes aware of the way the streetlights are spaced along the street and he sees that he is between them, shadowed, and so he doesn't move and maybe prays for the car to pass him by.

The engine picks up and the car pulls away, hesitantly. He waits until it turns a corner down the street and he listens until he hears nothing but the sound of his own heart, beating wild like a rabbit trapped in his chest.

The street is empty again but he no longer feels alone.

He takes off running, bounding over potholes and piled bags of trash. He's got three more blocks to go before he reaches his building, but why is he just now worried about that? This is the same night that Portia laid a delicate, clandestine, don't-tell-your-mother hand on his lap while Reggie Theus sunk six outside buckets like it wasn't anything. He is invincible.

He reaches the mouth of the alley just as headlights crawl up on his left. It's the same Lincoln Continental, drifting malevolently beneath streetlights. He steps back into the shadow of the alley and presses himself against the wall, and he hears the engine settle into a steady whine as the car floats down the street, predatory. The passenger-side door opens and the car stops. A man steps out and his body unfolds. He wears a leather jacket that shines. Each crease and wave of the fabric ripples as he walks. He wears sunglasses in the moonlight. His hair is kept in a neat afro, recently trimmed. His shoes are snakeskin, and the color shifts from iridescent green to purple to black as he walks.

The man brings one hand from his pocket and holds it out, his fingers curling inward to say, "Come here."

The boy is unable to do anything but to nod and to follow. He tells himself in a meek, compromising voice that if this man wanted to kill him he would have done it already. He tries to look confident and brave. He tells himself to breathe in deep and jut his chest out like a man, but he feels his shoulders falling inward and his head turning down. He is withdrawing, diminishing with every scattered heartbeat.

The snow still falls, but he hears his mother's voice, softer now, like she's calling out to him from behind a closing door.

"How old are you?" the man asks in a lacquered voice.

"Thirteen."

"Thirteen. What are you doing walking around here at one o'clock in the morning, Mr. Thirteen?"

"I was at the Bulls game."

"You were at the Bulls game?"

"Yes, sir."

"Who won, then?"

"Bulls."

He spits on the ground and twists his face. "What was the score?"

"Eighty-eight to eighty-three."

"They play the Bucks, right?"

"Yes, sir."

The man laughs sharply and stops. He studies the alley walls. "I fucking hate the Bucks, Mr. Thirteen. Hate them to hell."

"Yes, sir."

"Hey." The man steps forward. "Come on now, look up at me."

He looks up and meets the man's gaze. It is insistent, maybe halfway kind. His jaw muscles flex before he breaks into a smile as if he'd been holding it in. "You don't have to talk to me like I'm your pastor or your daddy, all right? What's the matter, Mr. Thirteen? You're looking scared. What's going on? You scared of me?"

The boy shrugs and sniffs. He feels the cold for the first time and he shivers.

"You're scared of me. I can tell it. I can see it. Look, you don't need to go and get scared. I saw you back there." He points in the direction of the street behind the boy. "My friend is driving and I see a kid and I think to myself, 'It's late. No thirteen-year-old kid ought to be walking around here so late.' I asked my friend to pull up to see if you'd like a ride. That's all that's happening here. A helping hand to a kid. Thirteen years old."

"Thank you, but I'll just walk."

"Kid your age oughtn't be walking this late. You say you're thirteen."

"I am."

"Oughtn't be walking so late."

"I'm just three blocks away."

"Whole lot can happen in three blocks. Believe me when I say I seen it all."

"Like what?" he asks, voice cocked in pathetic defiance.

The man raises his eyebrows, amused. "There are people here, Mr. Thirteen, people who just want to do bad. They don't care if you just saw the Bulls play and they don't even care if the Bulls whooped up on the fucking miserable Bucks. They just want to hurt you. They like hurting people. It makes them feel good to hurt people."

The man stands with his legs spaced and his arms behind his back, a military posture. The boy isn't satisfied with the answer, too much left undefined, but he doesn't press it any further. He doesn't have a choice.

"Let's get going, Mr. Thirteen." He points to the car behind him, coughing up a long tendril of exhaust, same color as the clouds gathering over the rooftops.

The boy consents with a slow nod and the man walks ahead of him, holding the back seat door open and gesturing inside. The leather interior is warm and smells like cigarette smoke. Menthol. There is a woman seated next to him on the other side of the seat, her head turned away. Her hair is red, the glowing of embers in a dying fire. The man gets in the passenger seat and gestures to the driver, a large and varicose man whose catcher-mitt hands dwarf the steering wheel. "This is my buddy, Olander," the man says, getting comfortable in the leather seat, pulling at his jacket.

Olander nods, breathing heavy. His eyes are sleepy and bloodshot. His head is bald and wrinkles of skin fold over his shirt collar.

"And that thing of beauty next to you, kid, that's Miss May. Miss May, the woman with the heart of gold." He smiles in the rearview, a half-hid grin. "Ain't that right, Miss May? You got a heart of gold on you, don't you? Maybe you should say hello to our guest, Miss May."

She doesn't turn away from the window, but she raises a hand and curls a single finger through a stray strand of hair, and the boy watches this cryptic motion as though it could unlock every mystery he's ever encountered in his thirteen years of living.

R&B music filters through the radio in half-static frequency. It somehow matches the longing pitch of this night, the flicker of a distant streetlight.

The interior of the car is polished and immaculate, the color of ice cream fresh and glistening in a bowl. There is a woman's ivory hairbrush at the boy's feet on the floorboards. He resists the sudden urge to pick it up and hold it in his hands, to run his fingers through the teeth for a stray hair to examine in the streetlight.

The man turns the rearview mirror away from Olander so that he can keep an eye on the boy. His eyes float in the reflective surface. Snow begins to fall outside, scattered and lazy.

"Where does he live?" Olander asks, his voice a hushed baritone.

"Where do you live, Mr. Thirteen?"

"West Lincoln Apartments. Just down that way."

"West Lincoln Apartments," the man repeats, propping his feet up on the dash. His leather shoes reflect his face, his eyes moving back and forth between Miss May and the boy in imprecise intervals, lingering on her for moments that seem to pause and hold.

Miss May wears a shiny skirt, like a disco ball. She wears a tank top that cuts off just above her belly button. She has tattoos that writhe on her skin. On her shoulder blade, a cartoon duck the boy recognizes but cannot name. She does not have a coat with her and the boy wonders how she could survive without a coat while standing outside on the street on a night like this. Because he knows what she is. He doesn't have a name for it and he doesn't understand the exact nature of it, but he knows as well as he has to what she is. And he can't pull his eyes from her.

Her hair is long and curled tightly into springs that bounce when the car turns.

"I don't want to work with the Mustang guy anymore," Miss May says, her voice rattling from the window, hollowing out. "The guy with the Mustang. No more, no thanks."

No one says anything.

"Did you hear me, Richie? I said no more guy with the Mustang."

"What'd he do?" Richie asks without turning around. "Did he do something to you?"

"What does it matter what he did? I didn't like him. End of story."

"It matters because he paid for something and if he did something else, I guess I'd consider it theft of some sort."

"It wasn't like that."

"What happened, then?"

"I didn't like him. End of story. Give him to someone else. I don't want any more of him."

"They're not all Prince Charming, May. Not all of them can be Mr. Hotshot. You know this."

"He must have been seventy years old. Had an oxygen tube. It clicked and clicked. Distracting as all hell."

"Since when do you care? What's gotten into you?"

"He was rude and nasty, too. I don't need that sort of stuff in my life right now. I got enough going on without that sort of nastiness."

"Smoke one and relax." He passes a soft pack behind his shoulder to her. "You've had a long night. So have I. So have we. So has everyone else in this shit-show city. All of us tired and griping."

She takes two cigarettes from the pack and throws it back up front. She takes one cigarette in each hand and offers one to the boy, who stares at it, trying to make sense of the offering. He finally shakes his head and she shrugs, stuffing the extra cigarette behind her ear and lighting the other. When she strikes her lighter, he can see her face in the orange glow. She is older than he thought she would be, maybe his mom's age or a little bit younger. She holds her cigarette between her thumb and her forefinger the way he's seen other kids hold joints. She's beautiful. She exhales smoke into the space between the two of them, as if to cloud his line of sight. He thinks he sees her smile before the smoke masks her.

Olander pilots the Lincoln slowly through the snow-littered street. They sit without speaking. The car's heat blasts through the vents. The back of Olander's head sprouts pear-shaped droplets of sweat. His breathing is loud. They are two blocks away from his apartment.

Then there is a crashing noise. Unannounced. The crush of metal. So loud that it can't be real. The car jerks and spins across the snowy street, and the boy falls against the window and May presses against him, her hair falling in his face. The car finally comes to a rest and they are quiet. Ears ringing. The snow has picked up, falling in a dense curtain, rendering the outside world invisible.

"What the fuck was that?" Richie asks.

"I don't know," Olander answers, his hands still gripping the wheel. "I don't know, Richie."

May sits back up. She still has the cigarette between her fingers and she takes a long drag.

"You two all right?" Richie asks, turning around.

May nods. So does the boy.

"Far-out shit," Richie says, and then he starts to laugh. "I thought we were going to fall right off the earth. Down, down, down."

The driver's-side door suddenly swings open and Olander's body is pulled out into the snow flurry. One single motion. It happens so fast that no one responds, the remaining three simply staring at the open door, the thick falling snow now drifting into the warm leather interior.

On the radio, someone sings, *I'll be true to only you.*

A piercing cry, high and shrill. The oxygen empties out of the car. The boy moves as close as he can to the window, trying to peer through the snow, his face against the glass, but all he can see is white. He grips the leather seat to steady himself.

Another cry, the same pitch, but this time it takes shape into a word and it is the voice of Olander screaming, "Richie."

Richie stares wide-eyed out the open driver's door, then reaches behind his back and removes a polished six-shooter. He counts to himself, "Three, two," and then he throws open his door and jumps out. The door slams shut behind him.

From the lessening curtain of snow the boy sees shapes, defined by rough contours, shifting suddenly to nothingness. He sees movement, but movement is all he is sure of.

The boy tries to listen to what is going on outside the car but his heart pounds loudly in his ears and the wind howls. Blues riffs crackle from the radio. The streetlights illuminate the snow in flashing intervals, giving the impression that time has broken, pausing and then lunging forward. He tries to count the seconds.

He hears a voice, Richie's, scream, "No!"

A face careens from the snow and smacks with a heavy thud against the boy's window. He jumps back with a shriek. The features of the face are distorted against the glass. After a moment, he can tell that it is Olander. The large man's tired countenance is replaced with a gaping mouth, split-lips, and a twisted, bleeding nose. Three of his teeth are chipped and one is missing. He looks to be gasping for one last breath, which fogs the window. His crazed eyes spin lazily in their sockets and he looks to the boy in a way that is desperate and scared, but in the next moment he is jerked back into the swirl of snow, disappearing like a magic act.

May sits next to him, smoking patiently on her cigarette.

The boy frantically pushes down on the locks on the doors that he can reach, his palsied hands fumbling. He feels sick. Streaks of Olander's blood cover his window like paint from a brush.

The snow parts momentarily. He sees a man, much taller than Richie and much thinner than Olander, his skin and his clothes the same midnight shade, standing pin straight against the brick wall like he's waiting for a ride. His face is covered and then he's gone, the snow resuming its torrential fall, but his image burns brightly in the boy's mind.

Something thunders atop the hood of the idling car and rolls off. The car shakes under the tumultuous weight.

On the radio, a trumpet angles up along an arpeggio.

A few seconds pass. The boy thinks of getting out of the car and running as fast as he can, but his ears still ring with Richie's bloodcurdling scream and his eyes still ache with Olander's bloodied face, pulpy and broken against the glass. He breathes like he's just run a mile and he feels like he has. Every muscle of his body is tied up in knots and he wants only to fall asleep in his bed.

A shadow passes over the window, the unmistakable outline of a man. The boy closes his eyes and pulls his knees to his chest, wrapping his arms around them, as if to hold himself together.

"Are you happy?" May shouts, her voice echoing from the car windows. At first the boy thinks she is talking to him, but then she adds, "I know you're out there. I know you can hear me. You can hear everything, can't you? Can't you?"

Her voice grows louder with every syllable, shaking with rage. She pounds on her window with her fist. Dull thumps, dead in the air.

"Are you happy now?" her voice strains. "Is this what you wanted?"

She pauses as if there will be a reply, but it doesn't come.

"I never want to see you again. Never." Miss May's voice falls slightly, but it is still loud enough to somehow echo in this small space. "You're a monster and I hope that's all you see when you look in the mirror forever, for as long as you live. A fucking monster."

She falls back into her seat and covers her eyes with a hand. Then she says, much softer, "Kid, I'm going to go check on Richie and Olander. Stay right here."

She shuts the door behind her and he watches her for as long as he can until the snow picks up once more. When he can't see her any longer, he listens. He places his ear against the window, his breath fogging the glass. He hears snow crunching under footsteps back to the car. When the door opens, it's Miss May. She sits back down in the back seat and withdraws the second cigarette from behind her ear and lights it.

"They're gone," she says flatly. "He took them away somewhere."

He nods as if this makes sense. He stares down at his hands again. His vision blurs and his eyes burn with tears he won't allow to fall.

"Are you going to be all right to walk the rest of the way home?"

Then the tears come. At first, they're silent, dripping down his cheek in long streaks, but in a moment it's his entire body shaking, and he's making noises he's never heard himself make. She scoots next to him and pats his back, scratching lightly up and down his spine with her long, manicured fingernails, and after a minute or two he's calm.

"I'll walk you home. You need to get home. Someone will be worried about you."

"I don't want to go outside," he whispers.

"You're safe. He wouldn't hurt you. Besides, he's gone now. I promise."

He shakes his head.

"Kid," she says in a gentler voice, "it's OK to be scared. But be brave, too."

She grabs his hand and he follows her out of her door. A thin layer of snow drifts in whorls across the street. When he takes a few steps from the car, he turns and sees that it had skidded longer than he had thought. The front-left side of the car is smashed, the broken headlight dangling like an eye out of socket.

"Come on," May says, squeezing his hand and walking him down the street.

She wears heels that leave her feet exposed to the freshly fallen snow. Her long pale legs appear blue and he isn't sure if this is the reflection of light from the snow or if she is freezing. He thinks it may be both.

"My apartment is that one over there." He points at the next block over, at a rust-colored building whose windows are dark except for one window on the fifth floor, his kitchen window. He knows his mother is seated at the table, her hair in curlers, her head in her hands, waiting for him.

May leads him to the concrete stoop and lets go of his hand. "Maybe you don't tell anyone about this," she says, not looking at him but at the direction they had come from. "Maybe just keep it to yourself. A secret of ours, OK?"

"OK."

She lingers for just a second, and then she turns around and heads back. He stands entirely still, waiting for an answer to a question he isn't sure of, and watches her walking down the street, dissolving with each step, harder and harder to make out, until he catches only glimpses of her outline here and there, until finally she is gone.

1 THE VIDEO

MARCUS WATERS WOKE SLOWLY to the tinny ringing of his cell phone—a digitized marimba that erupted into the room. The emerald numbers on his nightstand clock read 5:04 A.M. and a crosswind entered the cracked bedroom window, carrying with it the smell of the neighbor's lilac bush and last night's whispering rain.

He answered and heard breathing on the line while he rolled over across the startlingly cool empty half of a king-sized bed.

"Is this Marcus Waters?"

"Who is this?"

"Lt. James Conrad calling from the Chicago Police Department."

"What is this about?" Marcus asked, hearing the panic in his own voice before he felt it melting across his skin.

"Sorry to disturb you, Mr. Waters. I was told to contact you and ask that you come down to the station." The voice ran through scripted lines, pausing between sentences. "We are simply hoping that you may be able to answer some questions for us."

"Is my family OK?"

"I was told to tell you that this does not, so far as we know, directly involve your family."

"What is it about, then?"

"I was told to tell you that we received something that we'd like you to take a look at."

"Can you please tell me something that you weren't told to tell me?"

"Honestly, Mr. Waters," the officer said as he broke into a thick down-state drawl, a stew of vowels, "I'm just the guy who was told to make the phone call. I got no fucking clue what's going on down here. It's nuts."

Marcus heard in the background phones ringing and voices shouting out orders.

"When do I need to come in?"

"We sent a squad car to pick you up. It should be arriving shortly."

"I just woke up. I still need to shower."

"I was told to tell you that it is a time-sensitive matter. Keep an eye out for your police escort."

He rose from bed and changed as quickly as he could into khaki chinos and a starch-white collared shirt. The motions of dressing before the day had yet begun felt vaguely calming, intimately familiar. A pantomime of his life before retirement several years ago, back when he would rise like a saint from the dead at four in the morning, silently so as not to wake his sleeping wife, who, if woken, bolted upright with the blankets clutched in her fists, her beautiful black-woven hair matted down her cheeks. Cherrywood eyes piercing the darkness in silent reproach.

Old habits being what they were, he tried to be quiet as he pulled his socks over his bare feet, even though there was no one left in the house he might disturb.

He found his old leather shoulder bag in the back of the closet, covered by a collection of wing tip shoes he'd not worn in years. He regarded the bag for a few moments before shrugging and throwing it over his shoulder. Through this simple motion, he sensed the years condensing into a single point like a star collapsing. He felt like a journalist again. Not just a retired journalist, but a red-blooded, red-eyed journalist, waking up before the sun to chase the day ahead.

He pulled the curtain from his living room window. No cop car. No nothing. The street was empty. He paced flat-footedly along the hallway where pictures of his family hung in intervals, arranged in chronological order. With each step he took, another picture, another year. The faces aged like some static tribute to time itself. As he reached the end of the hallway, the pictures contained a large, growing family—babies, children, adults, and at the center, two old wizened faces that Marcus only ever recognized when he leaned in close, his nose brushing against the glass—

himself and his late wife, Denise. Their faces seemed to look back at him like strangers, half-aware of his probing stare.

He arrived at the last picture of the family as a whole. It had been taken two years ago, just a matter of weeks before his wife's death. In it, everyone wore pastel-colored T-shirts that his youngest daughter, Lisa, carefully coordinated. Lisa had tortured herself over color gradients and bodily arrangements—Marcus openly adored his daughter's obsession with details. In the picture, the family was arranged in front of a gazebo, smiling brightly. Denise stood behind Marcus, who was seated in front of them all in the position of the patriarch. She gripped her husband's shoulders.

He shuffled back down the hallway and peered out of the window. A cruiser idled in the street, looking vaguely otherworldly with the siren off but the lights flashing red and blue.

As soon as Marcus sat down in the passenger seat, the driver said, "I'll tell you right now, all I know is that about half an hour ago, the station was deathly quiet as it ever is this late into the night, and then everything went apeshit. Haywire, bedlam. All that."

He pulled out into the street and turned the flashing lights off.

The driver was a young black cop with a trim beard through which peered an ear-to-ear smile even as he spoke of total chaos. He wore suspenders over a too-tight white collared shirt. He introduced himself as Detective Jeremiah Combs and insisted that Marcus call him Jeremiah.

"You're a detective?" Marcus asked warily.

"Don't worry." Jeremiah smiled. "Only reason I'm the one taking you in is because it's all hands on deck right now. I'm happy to do it, though. Feels almost good to be back in a patrol car. Keeps me humble."

Over the cruiser's radio, a woman's voice fed numbers through the decaying frequency. Jeremiah put his lips to the radio and said, "Mr. Waters and I are en route." He set the radio back down.

The street, awash in headlights, was empty. Ghostly. No soul in sight save for the few cats that had escaped their homes for the night, wandering the suburban jungle in long strides, their luminescent eyes tracking the police car from indeterminable distances.

"No, I don't know what the situation is down at the station," Jeremiah said, responding to a question Marcus hadn't asked. He spoke with a South-Side affectation, each word blending into the next. "I saw some unfamiliar faces before I left, which makes me think they were feds or some other agency personnel. FBI, by the look of it. They all come in wearing suits, even though it was three or four in the morning. Their hair is perfect. They whisper into their cell phones. Supposed to be all inconspicuous, but you can spot them a mile away. Like, who are they trying to kid, you know?"

Marcus hummed, too tired and too confused to muster a coherent response.

They joined the highway. The city skyline emerged from the indigo pulp of clouds and smog. The beacons at the top of the skyscrapers pulsed white and red, warding off air traffic and hypnotizing the city's insomniacs at their windows.

"So are you from Chicago originally?" Jeremiah asked, though the time for small talk seemed to have passed already.

"South Side."

"Yeah? Me too. Which part?"

"Englewood."

"Englewood?" Jeremiah repeated.

"The very same."

Jeremiah's eyes danced between Marcus's moon-pale skin, his cardigan with tweed elbow patches, the Italian leather shoulder bag, his pleated chino pants.

"Guess we're just two peas in a pod." Jeremiah smiled.

Marcus understood Jeremiah's suspicion, but it was true that he had spent his early childhood years with his single mother in a government-subsidized building directly in the brick-and-mortar heart of Chicago's South Side. It was also true that when Marcus was six years old, his mother had met and promptly fallen in love with a philosophy professor from Northwestern, Corn Wallace, who frequented the university hospital she worked at due to his type-one diabetes. After the marriage, Marcus and his mother moved into Corn's spacious home in the north suburbs, where Marcus grew up watching *The Twilight Zone,* reading his stepfather's collection of Proust, and playing padded street hockey in the cul-de-sac.

Jeremiah pulled off the exit and maneuvered the car at a high, throttling speed beneath the skeletal belly of the L, Lake Michigan visible through the spaces between buildings, the barges and skiffs gliding along its surface. Marcus looked for a single person in sight on the sidewalks or in a window, but there wasn't anyone. The engine roared and echoed and bounced from the buildings that stood still on either side of the street.

Jeremiah led Marcus through the crowded halls of the precinct, sidestepping throngs of uniformed officers walking shoulder to shoulder. Phones rang in chorus. A conglomeration of musk colognes hung stagnant in the air. Commands were shouted from everywhere, muddled and lost.

At the end of the hall, they arrived at a corner office, the hallway windows obscured by blinds. Marcus read the name on the door: Police Chief Gregory Stetson.

A low groan rose like bile from Marcus's throat.

Jeremiah knocked on the door and it swung open immediately. Stetson stood in the open space in a pressed suit, a fresh crew cut, his cartoonish-wide shoulders filling the doorframe. A hairbrush mustache covered his upper lip. He dismissed Jeremiah with a nod and turned back to Marcus.

"Thank you, Mr. Waters, for coming on such short notice," Stetson said, smiling in an aggregate of hostility and hospitality. "I'd introduce myself, but I think that would be largely unnecessary and"—he pretended to search for the word that was already loaded in the chamber—"a little *outlandish*, wouldn't you say?"

He held out a calloused, fleshy hand.

When Stetson had been appointed police chief fifteen years ago, Marcus had covered the story with a few strong word choices, *outlandish* among them. Stetson's career had always been something of an anomaly. He'd spent only a couple short years as an officer before being promoted to homicide detective—the youngest in CPD history. When he was appointed police chief just seven years later—again, the youngest in CPD history—none of Marcus's police contacts would offer a good reason for the promotion, though they also refused to condemn their new boss on the record. Off the record was another matter entirely. Unable to go to print with his suspicions, however, Marcus settled on calling the mayor's appointment of Gregory Stetson to police chief "outlandish." It had seemed like the only appropriate word at the time. Even so, Marcus regretted it now.

"Happy to be here," Marcus said, submitting to the unrelenting grip of Stetson's handshake. He felt the bones in his hand bend.

After what felt like too long, Stetson released Marcus's hand and motioned for him to take a seat in front of his desk. A football signed by the '85 Bears was buried beneath a ziggurat of file folders and, at its base, half-drunk cups of coffee, their Styrofoam rims lip-stained an antique sepia. In the corner of the room, a taxidermy bobcat was in midleap, claws raised.

"Before getting into this," Stetson said, leaning back into his leather chair, "I trust that you, Mr. Waters, understand that whatever is revealed to you in this office remains in this office?"

"Yes," Marcus said.

Stetson bit down on a pen cap and raised his eyebrows. "I hope you'll forgive me for being skeptical, because I know that you retired from the press corps a few years back, but I also happen to know about the book you published last year after retirement. So I'm going to say it one more time. Everything that I am about to tell you and show you is strictly off the record. You are here as a consultant. Do you understand that?"

Marcus nodded.

"And frankly," Stetson continued, "if you were to leave here with the sensitive information I am about to show and go tip off one of your old cronies at the *Inquisitor* or go and start writing a follow-up book to the previous one, well, I would take that very seriously. By seriously, I mean prosecution. This is a very sensitive matter. Are we understanding each other?" Stetson asked.

"Yes." He tried not to flinch.

"Very good." Stetson rapped his knuckles on his desk. "You ever heard of the Liber-teens?"

"The who?"

"The Liber-teens. They're a group of computer hackers—excuse me, *hacktivists*—based here in Chicago, or so we think. But I didn't bring you down here to talk about them. I was just curious."

Stetson turned his computer monitor around. A video program was already opened, the screen frozen, black.

"We received the following video as a zip file attached to an email at approximately three in the morning. I'd like you to take a look."

"Who sent it?"

"The email address is disposable from one of those email generator sites. Anonymous, or so I'm told. Tracing it would be near impossible.

Even with a warrant, we're not sure if we could make heads or tails. Any other burning questions before we get started here?"

Marcus shook his head.

Stetson pressed play and sat back, turning his chair to look out over the crossword grid streets below. With his back turned, he said, "This is where I advise you to hold on to your breakfast."

Pixels flooded the screen, sharpening gradually as seconds clicked forward. Coughing came through the computer speakers. The pixels finally smoothed together in a sweep of black and blue to form coherent images. A light swinging gently from a ceiling like a hypnotist's pocket watch, casting oblong shadows across a room, the concrete walls of which were covered with metal racks. The time stamp at the corner of the screen gave the day's date, fifteen minutes after midnight.

A man stood in the frame, his head cocked to his shoulder, with a curious stare into the camera. A pistol shined at his hip. He wore a black jumpsuit that fit him like excess skin, wrinkling around his knees, hanging from his body in folds. His face appeared twisted and pale, but when he leaned farther into the light, Marcus saw that he was in fact wearing a mask—glassy and translucent. It was formed in the watery likeness of a man. Pointed nose, broad forehead, wide jaw. The only trace of color in the mask was the lips, which were painted a bright, vibrant pink. After an uncertain pause, the man reached out and adjusted the video camera before stepping out of frame.

There was a whimper and a cry, muted. And then the man reentered the frame pulling an office chair and in it a hostage bound by ropes. A burlap sack covered his head, but a low, muffled scream struggled from his throat as he fought against the ropes. The masked man's breath was heavy and labored. Either exhausted or exhilarated, or maybe even both. He stepped behind the camera and adjusted it so that it faced the hostage in the office chair, and he reemerged on-screen. He came closer and knelt down, his face filling the screen. It felt as though he were looking directly into Stetson's office and into Marcus's waiting eyes. He reached offscreen and held something up in front of the lens. It took a moment for the picture to adjust, but once it did, it was clear that the gunman was holding a book. Marcus recognized it immediately.

On its cover a black-and-white photograph of a massive crowd, taken from somewhere far above, bodies filling every single breadth of space.

Atop the photograph the title: *Halcyon Days: The Reign of the Kingfisher*. Beneath the title and beneath the photograph, in much smaller type, was the name of the author: Marcus Waters.

"When the Kingfisher died thirty years ago, we gave him a funeral." The masked man's voice was digitally modulated in an affectless drone that flattened the vowels. A voice scrambler. He pointed at the cover photograph with a gloved finger and then turned to address the camera. "This photograph was taken on that day. Look at all those people. Thousands strong. They are mourning him. This whole city mourned him. Chicago wore black and the citizens gathered at Promontory Point. Do you remember this, those of you who were there?"

The masked man set the book down and stepped back from the camera until he stood next to the office chair and its prisoner. He rocked back and forth.

"It was January of 1984 and we stood in quiet formation as the mayor spread the ashes across a frozen Lake Michigan. We listened to those bagpipes and we watched them spread the ashes around the ice until they dispersed. The mayor stood in front of a microphone and he said some nice things about heroes, about hope. And when it was finally over, everyone shuffled back home through the cold."

He cleared his throat and the hostage in the chair twisted desperately beneath the ropes.

"The next year, the crime rate not only rose, but it rose exponentially. The Kingfisher left behind a vacuum that criminals were all too happy to fill. The police ignored it and the rest of us could do nothing to stop it. And to this day, here we are, living in one of the most dangerous cities in America. Even the world. A city where dozens of people die every weekend. The anonymous dozens. Stray bullets passing through windows, doors. Children shot on their way to school in the morning. Children with their backpacks on their shoulders, walking the streets they know. And still. And still."

He breathed in and out, in and out, as though waiting for the irregular rhythm of his breath to take on some meaning.

"Here is the uncomfortable truth. None of it needed to happen. The body pulled out of the Chicago River that night in 1984, which the police claimed to be the Kingfisher, was not actually the Kingfisher. The police knew this, of course, because they helped the Kingfisher fake his death and desert this city. They knew the consequences, but they did so anyway, because they do not care about us, just like the Kingfisher does not care about us. It's about time we recognize this. All of us."

He picked up the camera. It shook in his hands and the image blurred. When it steadied, he panned over two remaining hostages, both of whom were bound to office chairs, masked by burlap sacks. The gunman set the camera back down where it had been and again stood in the center of the frame next to the hostage he had brought forth. With a flourish, the gunman removed the mask from the hostage's head. An older man, his bald head dripping with sweat. His teeth bared against a rope tied around his head and digging into his mouth.

The gunman stepped back and raised the pistol to the hostage's head.

"No," Marcus whispered. "No."

The gunman continued, "To the chief of the Chicago Police Department, Gregory Stetson, if you wish to exonerate yourself and the rest of your force of this charge, I urge you to release the medical examiner's report conducted on the body you later claimed to be the Kingfisher. The very same report that you and your predecessors, oddly enough, have never released to the public. These hostages at my disposal are scared, and they should be scared. Because they are temporary. There will be others, as many as necessary. Because every second that passes that the report is not released is a second in which they may die. Just so."

He pulled back the hammer of the pistol and it clicked like a plaything.

He pushed the barrel of the gun against the hostage's temple. The hostage closed his eyes while the gunman adjusted his feet like a batter at the plate. He was still for a moment, so still that it appeared as though the video had frozen, but then there was a static eruption of sound. It came somehow off-tempo, premature. Marcus jumped in his seat. The prisoner's body slumped sideways, a spray of blood and brain matter freckling the wall. The man pushed the chair out of the frame. He turned back to the camera and knelt, slowly, his masked face once again filling the screen.

The camera shook and went still, frozen on the pale, indelible, nightmarish grin.

There was a depth to Marcus's sudden numbness, as though he could plunge into it and never fully return. The floor shifted beneath him. The walls seemed to expand and implode with each breath struggling out of his lungs, all of his surroundings receding into a narrow, dark tunnel.

"What else happens?" Marcus asked, his voice hollow. He fought a wave of nausea. "What else happens in the video?"

"Nothing. That's it."

"No demands?"

"Just the ME report," Stetson said.

"Christ." Marcus laid his forehead in his hands. It felt cold, slicked with sweat. His throat felt dry. "He has others. Other hostages."

Stetson gave him a moment's pause with a look on his face that nearly resembled something like empathy. But it lasted for only a brief second before he shook it off. Stetson's cell phone chimed on his hip. He unclipped it from its plastic holster and read the message.

"Shit." Stetson sighed, putting his phone back into his belt. "The video was uploaded online. Thanks for coming down, but I've got to be going, assuming you don't have any idea who the gunman is."

Marcus wasn't listening. "Play the video back. When he takes the mask off the hostage. Let me see it again."

"What?"

"Please. Just do it."

Stetson sat back down and replayed the video from the moment the gunman pulled the burlap mask from the hostage's head. But this time, instead of centering on the gunman, Marcus focused entirely on the hostage. He leaned in closer to the computer screen, his nose nearly touching the image. He waited for the hostage's face to change, for the hostage to shift into someone he had never seen before, for the sickness welling in his gut to dissolve. But none of this happened.

"I know that man," Marcus whispered. "The hostage. I interviewed him for the book."

"Who is he?" Stetson asked, straightening in his chair.

Marcus could not look away from the screen. "His name is Walter Williams."

"Why did you interview him?" Stetson asked.

"The Kingfisher saved his life."

2 SHALLOW FOOTPRINTS

WREN LAY AWAKE AT FIVE in the morning, two hours before she had to leave for work. She was deliriously, out-of-body tired, but she couldn't sleep due to a wave of rapturous shouts descending from overhead like water leaking through the floorboards.

Her upstairs neighbor watched porn through a stack of amplifiers, or at least that was what it sounded like. A lot of porn. An unending chorus of moans roughly shaped into ecstatic obscenities. During the day, you could tune it out, relegate it to the background noise of the city. But in the rosy-fingered hours of dawn, with nothing but a box fan humming in the window, there was nowhere to hide from it.

She used to pound on the ceiling with a broomstick in protest, but this didn't do anything. It never did. In fact, she had never actually seen her upstairs neighbor, but that wasn't a huge surprise. Wren only left the apartment to go to work at the bowling alley or go grocery shopping, and even then, she walked with her head down.

When she pictured her upstairs neighbor watching porn, she imagined some bipedal Jabba the Hutt, his fleshy, greenish body splayed across a sunken couch. She often considered quickly hacking into his computer and torching his hard drive or at least turning down the volume of his speakers, but she knew she wouldn't ever go through with it. He wasn't hurting anyone.

It was simply sad, not malicious.

After she finally came to grips with the fact that sleep was not coming for her anytime soon, she rolled off her egg-crate mattress and stumbled into the living room where she found Parker, her quasi-girlfriend—they had mutually agreed to eschew nominalizing their relationship—sitting cross-legged on their couch. Parker did Web design from home, which allowed her to work through the night and sleep at random points throughout the day. At this early hour, wide-eyed and focused, she glowed blue in the light of her laptop.

Parker didn't so much as look up at Wren shuffling past. Her head bobbed in rhythm to the music blasting through her headphones and spilling out into the room as one hand pulled mindlessly on one of her lip rings while the other ostensibly wrote a line of code. Wren noticed that Parker's hair was different this morning. It was braided, dyed a dark shade of lavender. Yesterday it had been neon green. Every few days it was different, and every time a different Parker emerged from the bathroom drying her hair with a hand towel.

Parker had offered, on more than one occasion, to dye Wren's hair. Or, in Parker's words, "give you an edge." But Wren politely declined. She preferred to keep her hair the same dirty blond and cut it with a pair of kitchen scissors, just above the ears. It was easier to manage, which is to say she didn't have to manage it at all.

In the kitchen, Wren dug a stray granola bar from the back of the pantry.

"Jesus Mary Miyazaki," Parker said in the living room.

Wren poked her head around the wall and saw Parker staring slack-jawed at her screen.

Parker muttered, "Holy shit."

Wren detected in her voice a tremble that didn't belong there. Not from her, at least.

"What is it?" Wren asked.

Parker didn't answer.

"What is it?" she said louder.

"Get your laptop."

"Why?"

"You need to get on the message boards right now."

Wren hurried back into her room and retrieved a laptop from her desk. She brought it with her into the living room and logged in to the message boards they had been using for the past two weeks. Lately, everyone was getting paranoid about sticking around on one server for too long, even if they were encrypted for members only. Their collective paranoia had a definite genesis. It had begun last year after the FBI brought down the group HydraLulz through spying on the group's online communications. In response, the Liber-teens relocated their private message boards every couple weeks. And whatever data they left in their wake were shallow footprints in the snow, gone before you knew it.

Wren scrolled through the most recent thread titled "Video." There was rarely this much message board traffic among the Liber-teens at six in the morning.

"I don't see what people are talking about. A video? What's going on?" Wren asked.

"Hold on," Parker muttered, her fingers clicking away at her keyboard. "I'm trying to get a working link. It keeps getting taken down."

Finally, someone else posted a working link to the video. Wren clicked and then watched, smiling in disbelief at the amateur clumsiness of the video—the labored breathing, the digitized voice, the awkward pauses, the way the polished gun made the man appear off-balanced in the frame. The constructed quality of it all. The man even wore a Liber-teen mask—a translucent likeness of Robespierre. She immediately thought it must be a joke, something in the vein of the nihilistic humor found in the dark corners of the internet, filmed by some kid looking to troll the Liber-teens or maybe fishing for an invitation to join.

And then the gunshot.

The blood and slump of body.

There was nothing constructed about it. She could practically feel the bullet, a hot ember burrowing down into her brain.

A feverish chill clawed beneath her skin.

"Jesus," she whispered.

Parker didn't look up from her computer. "So fucked up."

Wren went back to the busy thread and typed, *Who made this?* The words popped up alongside her handle, /MonsieurRamboz/.

—It was just released on YouTube a few minutes ago.
—Prepare for a fucking witch trial, everybody. You know they'll blame us.

—They?

—Who the fuck is the Kingfisher?

—Jesus Christ. Did you guys watch that video?

—It isn't real, right?

—He said he has more hostages. We need to do something. We can get that ME report.

—You seriously don't know who the Kingfisher is?

—They?

—Anyone can order our Robespierre mask online.

—The KF was some sort of superhero or whatever the hell.

—This is going to be fucking anarchy.

—We clearly had nothing to do with this.

—No way in hell we could hack the CPD computer network. That's a no way.

—It can't be real. You can tell by the pixilation. It's a fake.

—He wasn't a superhero. He was a vigilante.

—What's the stream quality? Can someone run it through and get a count?

—It's not a fake.

—You can tell by the pixilation.

—Are you fucking kidding? We could totally hack their network.

—What's the difference between a vigilante and superhero?

—That's a fake video. I can tell.

—Vigilantes die.

Upstairs, the pornographic delirium reached a crescendo. Shouts, screams, intimating intense pain and pleasure, sustaining for what felt like whole minutes. With the ecstasy from overhead combined with the images from the video lingering in her mind, Wren felt more than a little sick, enough for the room to bend each time she blinked. She hoped that if she held her eyes closed long enough, the whole world might collapse into a dream.

Wren's phone began ringing. She jumped and clutched at her heart, as if holding it inside her chest against its will. It was only her alarm.

"You have to work today?" Parker asked, though it sounded more like an accusation.

"I work every day."

"You need to call in sick, then. You can't go skipping off right now. Just call in sick."

"I already called in once this week."

"You work at a bowling alley," Parker scoffed. "It's not the fucking White House. They'll be fine without you. We just got a fucking atomic bomb dropped on our fucking heads. We'll be dealing with this all fucking day. The FBI is going to be on our asses like never before. And can you imagine all the shit this will get us on the forums?"

Wren deferred her gaze and picked at a loose piece of carpet on the floor. "That's what you're worried about? Someone died in that video. And there were other hostages."

"What are we supposed to do about that?"

"Are you serious right now?"

"Yes I am. You're thinking emotionally, not logically. We can't do anything about those hostages. What we *can* do something about is the fact that this asshole with a gun is trying to blame us for this."

"We could try to find him."

"How do you propose we do that, Wren? I'd love to hear how exactly you think that is possible."

"I don't know, but we could try. Or we could try to find the hostages. We could search missing persons databases. If we got a name, we could get a phone number, hack into the SS7 and get a location."

"That's ridiculous."

"Why?"

"This just happened. What are the chances the hostages are reported missing? Besides, do you really think those people have their phones on them? Whoever did this isn't stupid, Wren."

Wren wasn't sure it was hopeless, but she understood it was next-to-impossible. "Are you sure we're not to blame for this?"

Parker's posture stiffened. "What are you trying to say?"

"I don't know."

"We didn't do this, Wren."

"How do you know that?"

"You're kidding, right?"

"I'm just saying. We don't know the other Liber-teens. Not personally, at least. We don't know for a fact that a Liber-teen didn't do this. We couldn't know."

"Jesus. None of us did this. This isn't what we do. You know that. Or at least I thought you did."

"But that guy is wearing our mask."

"That's why we have to clear our name. You can order that mask online for fifteen dollars. It isn't hard to get."

"You're not listening to me," Wren was surprised to hear her voice rising, even if it was slight. "Even if a Liber-teen didn't do this, what if we inspired it? That hostage, the others—"

"That's not our problem," Parker interrupted. "There's no use in worrying about that. About them. Right now our problem is that pretty soon everyone is going to start blaming us for this because that asshole is wearing our mask. And I don't need to explain to you why that is a major fucking problem. So just stick around while we figure it out. Please."

"I can't. I have to catch the L for work. I'll be back this afternoon."

"Jesus." Parker shook her head and reabsorbed herself in her computer screen, picking at her lip ring. "Look, I know you think I'm being insensitive or something. And maybe I am. But we can't do anything to help those hostages, Wren. That's the reality of the situation."

Wren chewed her fingernail, which was already waning to her cuticle. "We could analyze the video. We could try to match descriptions from the missing persons database." She regarded Parker's doubting smile. "I know it's a long shot, but we could do it."

"Disregarding the 'long shot' quality of that plan, it would require time we don't have, Wren. You know as well as I do that the FBI is probably already focusing all of their attention on us right now because of this. If we get arrested because of this shit, who will be left to watch over the systems of power that landed us in this fucking mess? You know I'm right. And you need to be here to help us dig our way out of this hole."

"I have to go to work. I'll bring my laptop with me. I'll be on the message boards."

"Whatever." Parker flapped her hand in dismissal. "If you're going to leave, just leave."

As Wren passed by Parker on her way to the bathroom, Parker reached out and grabbed her gently by the arm.

"I'm sorry. I know this bothers you, all of this," Parker said. "It bothers me, too. But this isn't the right time to be acting on feelings. We need to be realistic and logical, and we need to cover our asses before we can even think about doing anything else."

Wren didn't say anything. Parker squeezed her arm, lightly, tenderly.

"We have to look after ourselves before we can help anyone else. That's just the way the world works, Wren."

"Is it, though?"

"Don't shoot the messenger." Parker smiled. It was a smile that either welcomed a kiss or threatened a slap, so Wren chose to let it be. It was too early in the day to decrypt Parker's intentions.

3 JUDGE OF MAN

EVERY MORNING LUCINDA TILLMAN RUNS. Sometimes with the wind, sometimes against it. She runs along Lake Michigan with the other runners who acclimate to the powdery grayscale of predawn with specially designed clothes meant to capture and reflect the stare of oncoming headlights. They run with their keys and wallets in their socks or fanny packs that bounce with each forward stride. They run as individuals without any sort of predictable formation and speak only in a vernacular of grunts and nods and half-waves, and at various paces they begin to spread out across the Western shore of the lake, squinting as the sun rises over their shoulders, breathing in through their noses and out through their mouths.

Her running shoes are old and worn and they emit a soft sigh each time they hit the ground.

The other runners along the lake shine iridescent in their neon windbreakers and chartreuse sneakers, buzzing points of electricity against stony, cloud-beaten Lake Michigan. But Tillman wears black sweats, black shoes. And she runs fast, faster than most, and sometimes she runs like this for thirty minutes, an hour, or several hours. A near-sprint. She runs until she feels like her lungs might collapse, her heart might give out, the world might dissolve and fall away. And then she stops, sits down cross-legged wherever she is, waits for her breath, and runs back even faster in the direction she came from.

Tillman stood at her apartment door fishing the apartment key from her ankle socks. Behind the door, she heard Al Green crooning on the record player and this meant her father was awake. Sure enough, she found him sitting like a museum statue in the recliner by the window. He was wearing the same pajamas she had bought him for Christmas four years ago even though she had bought him a new pair every year since. They were stacked in the closet like a drunken pyramid.

The record player lazily spun at her father's side. His eyes were closed and he opened only one of them when she walked in the door.

"Where were you?" he asked.

"I went for a run," she answered, just as she did every morning.

"Where?"

"The lake."

"Why?"

"Exercise."

"I know this," he said. "I am not stupid."

"It's going to be hot today. Hot and humid. I could feel it."

"Always hot. Because conditioner unit"—he pointed to the air conditioner in the window—"blows hotter air inside."

"No it doesn't," she said, unlacing her shoes. "It's a new air conditioner, Dad."

"I know it when I feel it. I am not an idiot."

She left him sitting in his recliner, and as she passed him she thought he looked smaller today than he had yesterday. Yesterday she had thought this as well. This didn't make her observation any less true, but it comforted her on some level to know that, at the very least, she was noticing his gradual dissolution. She wondered if someday in the as-of-yet distant future she might come home to find nothing more than the mere suggestion of her father, the man having fully collapsed into himself.

He called after her in the kitchen. "What time you come home from work today?"

She pretended not to hear him.

In the kitchen, she made a protein shake. She added honey to the frothy mix and stirred. It tasted like sidewalk chalk and dirt and brown-mushy banana. And honey. What she couldn't choke down in a single swig she brought with her into the living room. She sat on the couch next to her father and turned on the television for the morning news. The news anchor competed with Al Green in the small, dimly lit space.

"Turn it off," her father protested. "I have my music."

She turned up the volume on the remote.

"—the gunman then proceeds to demand the release of the medical examiner's report, which our producers were able to confirm has, in fact, never been released to the public. Until the ME report is released, the gunman says, he will kill again. This threat is all the more ominous considering that the gunman claims to have more hostages. We are still waiting on a statement from the police department, but for the time being, we are going to show a clip of the video right now for those of you who have not already seen it online. Even though we have edited the footage to remove most of the graphic imagery, we want to caution that particularly sensitive viewers, such as young children, may want to leave the room at this point."

"Dad," Tillman said. "Are you seeing this?"

One eye struggled open. Al Green hit a high note and simply hung there.

"I do not see what's happening," he said, but watched anyway as the grainy video played. When it was over, the camera returned to the news anchor, clearly improvising as he went along, waiting for his producers to speak into his ear. Tillman turned down the volume until only a whisper escaped the speakers. In the near-silence, her fingers flexed into a fist.

There is something unimaginably cruel and small, Tillman thought, about filming the murder of someone and then sharing it with the watching world. This is a specter haunting the twenty-first century, the unspoken hunger for these once-unspeakable things. She imagined her final moment on earth replayed a million times for everyone but herself.

"That man said the Kingfisher is still alive?" her father asked with a temerity she wasn't used to hearing from him.

"That's what you take away from that?" she asked sharply, and immediately wished she hadn't.

Her father closed his eyes again, knitted his hands together, and rested them atop his stomach. He made a low sound in his throat, a grated rumble.

"Dad?" she asked.

He smiled, breathing loudly. "It would be nice," he said finally, without opening his eyes.

"What?"

"It would be nice if the Kingfisher is alive today. But he is not. He is dead. You want to know how I know? I know because he would not leave us like he did if he was alive. That man on the television, he is crazy. He is a crazy person with stupid ideas."

"You missed the point," Tillman said. "That man killed someone. He put the video on the internet. He has other hostages and he's going to kill them. And then he's going to show the whole world again."

Her father shrugged, a gesture that seemed to require great effort. "People die each day, Lucy. It's very little new. So maybe we see it sometimes. Maybe we don't. It does not mean anything if I see it on my television or I do not."

She shook her head, readying her possible rebuttals. But she reminded herself of the most useful advice her mother had ever gifted her: *Your father likes arguing more than anyone likes making a point.*

Tillman collapsed on the couch next to her father's chair. Her head felt heavy. She dug her palms into her eyes, trying to erase the face of the hostage the moment before the gun fired. He had stared at the camera. Into the camera. Into the millions of waiting eyes. His lips quivering, eyes wild. Like nothing you've ever seen unless, of course, you've seen it, in which case you instantly recall every other time you've been so unfortunate as to witness that indelible moment of primal terror, a life on the brink of ending. That moment when a life is staring back at you, begging without words.

She looked up. She was not back there. She was here.

"I think," her father said. He waved a finger, about to mark his point, eyes still closed. "I think that if you remembered the Kingfisher, you would also think it nice for the Kingfisher to be alive today. But you do not remember. You were very little. Maybe that is truth. If the Kingfisher could be alive, you would know. He would clean up the dirty streets. It would make your job much more easy. When do you work today?"

"We've talked about this," she said, just as she did every morning. "I'm not going into work today."

"But they need you today," he said, his voice falling back into the fog of his crippling mind. With a shaking finger, he tapped his temple and let it rest there. "My smart daughter. My strong daughter. They need you."

"I'm not going into work today," she said again, but this time louder. Not for her father to hear, but for herself to hear.

Lucinda Tillman was in middle school when the first Kingfisher story broke. She attended St. Mary's Academy, a private school for girls nestled due south of Logan Square. The other girls she hung around were mostly other first-generation immigrants from Puerto Rico or the Dominican Republic, which meant that Tillman, whose parents were Haitian, was free to observe but not much else. The other girls brought to school newspapers they purchased with money their parents gave them for lunch. They sat outside before the class bell rang, turning through the pages. Their interest in the Kingfisher, so far as Tillman could tell, derived not from the city's collective fascination with this man, but from the romantic ideal of a true-to-life superhero who, so far as anyone knew, lacked the quintessential love interest. There was an opening and they were looking to fill it.

"What do you think he looks like?" asked one of the girls.

"Dark," replied another. "And handsome."

"*Very* handsome."

"And tall."

"*Very* tall."

"And strong."

"*Very* strong."

The nuns at school discouraged the girls from reading about the Kingfisher. To them, the mythic Kingfisher existed on a diametrically opposed plane to the other names they prayed to. They confiscated the newspapers and tore them up in long, exaggerated motions, faces twisted into disgust. They burned them in trash cans with sulfur matches that stunk up the room. Sister Frances made each confiscation a sort of ritual, turning slowly from the orange flames in the trash can to deliver a spontaneous and improvised catechism.

It is not man's job to punish his fellow man. Leave this to the Creator Eternal. Only God, and God alone, can judge mankind.

The day that the Kingfisher's death was announced in the newspapers, Tillman was in the ninth grade. She heard the news from the girl who sold her individual cigarettes in the alleyway before school. Sister Frances gave the announcement over the PA system and amid the static and the steel-frequency, Tillman was surprised to hear the sadness that permeated Sister Frances's uncharacteristically quiet voice as she reminded the students that only God, and God alone, could judge mankind. She said a prayer, lost in the static of the intercom.

On her way home from school, Tillman bought one of the few remaining copies of the day's *Inquisitor* from a street vendor. The front page was the article written by Marcus Waters. It was titled "The Kingfisher Dies." When her parents arrived home from work, they listened solemnly as she translated the article into Creole. Although they both spoke proficient English, they preferred the familiarity of their first language. It was a small comfort, which might have been necessary now more than ever.

A captain of a shipping barge passing through the Chicago River had spotted a body under a bridge and called it in. Cops pulled the body from the water. It had been burnt horribly. Shot and stabbed and carved. Mutilated. After what the article called "extensive testing," police officials and the county coroner determined that it was indeed the enigmatic Kingfisher. No suspects, no further evidence, no justice. Just several hundred words brittle against paper.

Her mother cried. Her father delivered some Creole variation of "no good goes unpunished." But she herself watched the two of them, stone-faced and unimpressed, smelling vaguely of the menthol cigarette she had smoked on her way home.

Her father turned on the television. *Happy Days*. They watched through the night. Tillman pretended to laugh when the audience laughed.

The following morning, her father decided to send a letter to the journalist Marcus Waters. It was a sympathy letter of sorts. Though her father had never met Marcus Waters, he nonetheless felt close to him after reading every last word of the Kingfisher articles for nearly five years—or rather, having his daughter translate and read to him these articles. Perhaps it was appropriate then that he also had his daughter write the letter as he dictated it to her in his native tongue.

And all these years later, though the rest of the four pages were completely lost to memory, she could still remember the closing line of the letter, and when she remembered it she remembered it in her father's drag-and-glide voice: "I am sorry you lost your friend, because he was also my friend. He was all our friend and he did good things and I miss him, too."

4 PRO BONO

AFTER LEAVING STETSON'S OFFICE, Marcus found Jeremiah waiting outside the door, staring down at his phone. He was watching the video, eyes inches away from the small screen on which Marcus saw the same sickening mask. Miniaturized, but no less imposing. When Jeremiah looked up, he stared straight through Marcus and into Stetson's office, lips pressed together so tightly they disappeared.

"Someone will meet you outside at the car, Mr. Waters," Jeremiah said flatly and pushed past him to walk through Stetson's open door. Before Jeremiah shut the door behind him, Marcus heard Stetson ask what the hell he was doing barging in like that.

A telephone ringing, and then another, and then another. All of them in a floundering rhythm.

Marcus shuffle-footed down the hall like a last-call drunk, feeling completely lost in almost every sense of the word. The floor seemed to shift with each uncertain step.

Walter Williams. Walter Williams. No matter how much he tried to focus on the physical world in front of him, the name echoed in his head.

A flurry of uniformed officers scurried around him in a half run toward the motor pool. He assumed they were going after the other people whose names Marcus had given Stetson just a few minutes before—the other two people who were with Walter the night the Kingfisher saved him. Or at least he hoped that's what the police were doing. After Marcus gave the names, Stetson thanked him and said, "So you think this gunman is rounding up people that the Kingfisher saved?"

"I don't know. But I know that was Walter Williams."

"The Kingfisher saved a lot of people, Marcus. So why are you worried about these two guys?"

"Because they were there with Walter that night."

Stetson nodded. "But you didn't use their real names in your book, right? I'm just trying to understand how someone could have known about it."

"I don't know." Marcus shrugged. "There were other people there that night. I don't know how many. The story may have gotten around. I don't know."

Stetson thought about this for a moment and nodded. "I'll see that someone does a welfare check on them." Marcus thought he had heard a thin trace of skepticism in Stetson's voice that seemed much less thin in hindsight.

But to Marcus it was simply beyond the realm of coincidence that the hostage in the video happened to be Walter Williams and that there were exactly two other hostages shown in the video. And besides, Marcus wasn't sure he believed in coincidences. There was something lurking in the word—a faith in neatness behind the chaos of life—that Marcus absolutely despised after sixty-eight years of living.

It was a few weeks after his wife's death that Marcus decided to brush off the old files—kept in an aquamarine filing cabinet in his closet—and write the book he had always told himself he would one day write. He imagined it as the culmination of a career he had recently left behind. He got in touch with some old contacts, but he mostly planned on using the stories and interviews he had collected during his time reporting on the Kingfisher thirty years prior. Word must have spread, as it often does, and as he was finishing up his manuscript, he received an unexpected phone call from someone who began the conversation by saying that the Kingfisher had saved him and two others. Even over the phone, the man's voice sounded desperate to convince Marcus that the story he had to tell was true, but Marcus remained dubious. And rightfully so. Those who claimed similar stories had contacted him back during the Kingfisher years. The Kingfisher had saved them, they said. He'd even met with several of them.

They told stories of a man who, at the exact right moment, had descended from the heavens to shield them from a bullet, a man who emerged from the earth to whisk them away from an attacker. Whether or not their stories were fabricated or even just exaggerated, Marcus wasn't one to say, but he couldn't print these single-sourced stories and still call himself a journalist.

And it was with this same trepidation that Marcus agreed to meet Walter for coffee. Walter had just gotten off from work. He was wearing hospital scrubs, said he was a nurse in the ICU at Mercy. He had a smile, unfaltering, that seemed carved into his face. But when Marcus asked him to tell his story about the Kingfisher, Walter's smile vanished. "First things first, I don't want you using my name or anything. I had to work like hell to get out of that past life and get to where I am today. Are we good on that?"

"If you don't want me to, I won't use your name. No problem."

After just a few moments into Walter's story, Marcus had no doubts that it was true. The structure and details of Walter's story aligned neatly with just about every other verified Kingfisher story he had heard whistling through the cracked teeth of dozens upon dozens of criminals lying in their hospital beds, handcuffed to the railing.

It was 1983. Walter was twenty years old and working as a runner for a major drug distributor on the South-Side circuit by the name of Lawrence Tressy. One night, Lawrence was supplying Walter and two other runners when the Kingfisher burst through the back door of the house.

"That door was triple-locked," Walter said, blowing at the rim of a cup of coffee. "I know that because I was the one who locked it. Three bolts. Lawrence was paranoid like that. But then—I don't even know—the door just flew from its hinges. It's unreal, Mr. Waters. It's hard to describe. Like one moment we're just hanging out, some girls are dancing in the next room, Lawrence is dividing the supply. Next moment the door pounds open—no, it *shoots* open. And in walks the Kingfisher. We knew it was the Kingfisher, all of us, because we'd all read about him in the paper— your articles, actually. We knew he was tall, big, and freakishly strong. And this dude was tall, big, and freakishly strong. Who else could have knocked open that door like it was nothing? The girls were scared out of their minds and went running and screaming out the front door. So you know, it was just myself, the two other runners, and Lawrence. Lawrence tells us to kill the *motherfucker*—that's his word, not mine. Us runners pulled our guns and we just start shooting. I was scared halfway to death, if I'm being honest, but I'm still firing that gun like my life depends on it. Because in my head, it does. We empty our clips into the man. And the whole time, he's just standing there in the open doorway. Like it isn't anything. And the moment our clips are empty, Lawrence grabs his own piece from his waistband." Walter pantomimed the movement, swinging an invisible gun around the coffee shop. "Of course I'm thinking he's going to get some shots at the Kingfisher, but instead he aims it at us." He pointed the invisible gun at Marcus's forehead, his finger hovering over an assumed trigger. "He tells the Kingfisher that if he makes a move, he's going to kill us three. It doesn't seem like much of a threat, right? We're thinking the Kingfisher is here to kill us anyway, so what does it matter if Lawrence pulls the trigger? But then, and here's the thing, Mr. Waters, the Kingfisher bolts across the room—faster than I could even describe— and he has Lawrence by his throat. Lawrence drops the gun, of course. The Kingfisher squeezes Lawrence's throat until his whole body goes limp and he lets him drop to the floor. It all happened in twenty seconds or less. The whole thing. From the moment he walked in the door until the moment he dropped Lawrence. Twenty seconds or less. I swear."

Walter said that when it was over, when the Kingfisher had evidently decided he was finished, he picked up their boss's unconscious body and threw it across the room, where it splintered the kitchen table. He looked at the three runners standing stunned before him. They held their emptied guns limp at their sides, awaiting whatever hell had crossed their patch of universe tonight. And then he walked out of the house and disappeared into the night without a sound. This, according to Walter, was an act of mercy.

He had saved them twice that night, Walter observed. Once when he stopped their boss from killing them. Twice when he stopped himself from killing them.

"What happened to Lawrence Tressy?" Marcus asked.

"He died," Walter said mechanically. "Died from the attack. Internal injuries, they said later." His expression grew somber, as though a shadow were slowly passing through him. "Lawrence was a bad man. I'm not saying that he deserved to die like that, but it's true—he wasn't a good man." He paused, picked his coffee back up, and took a drink. "But yeah, that's all that happened that night. That's it. That's all of it."

Marcus waited until he was sure Walter was finished, because he thought he saw some other thought forming on Walter's lips, but it didn't come. "Did you get a look at the Kingfisher's face?"

"Do you think I was worried about getting a look at his face?" Walter laughed dryly. "I was just trying not to piss myself. I'd shot him, Marcus. And he'd just stood there. He could have killed me without a second thought. But he didn't."

Marcus had heard variations of this before. The Kingfisher was evidently bulletproof. He assumed the Kingfisher had invested heavily in Kevlar during his years on the streets. That was the only possible explanation. "Do you think you might be able to give me the names of the other two men you were with that night? I believe your story, but it would still be useful to corroborate your version of events."

"I've lost touch with them, so I'm not even sure if they're still around. But I guess I could give you their names, so long as you don't tell them I gave you their names and you don't use their names in your book. I doubt they'd talk to you, though. I'd be surprised if they did. We're all older now, maybe wiser, but we still got that street-smart paranoia, you know? That doesn't exactly go away with age."

"So then why did you reach out to me?"

Walter's smile briefly returned. "Call it a favor for a friend."

"A friend? Who?"

"Doesn't matter. But listen, I want you to keep something in mind when you write this story, Mr. Waters. A lot of people, especially where I'm from, didn't see the Kingfisher the way the rest of this city did, the way that a lot of folks like yourself saw him. The Kingfisher wasn't a hero to a lot of folks who look like myself. He was a villain. This dude beating the hell out of petty criminals—most of them just trying to make a living in a society that didn't offer them many other options—and leaving them for the CPD to put in jail when he could have just as easily gone and beat some white-collars on the North Side who were committing bigger crimes than we were."

"What are you getting at?"

Walter thought about it for a moment, selecting his words with care.

"I like to think our society is evolving past the Kingfisher's idea of what justice looks like. I hope you'll keep that in mind when you write your book." Walter paused, his eyes seemed to trace a thought. "But I also recognize that the Kingfisher could have beat me, killed me, or done whatever to me that night, but he didn't. He saved me from himself. That doesn't make him a hero, of course. I'm not sure what it means, to be honest. Maybe there doesn't have to be a name for it." Walter shrugged, leaned back in his seat. "After that night, I knew I had to get out of the game, and I did. I'm thankful to him for that, if only that. I'm one of the lucky ones."

One of the lucky ones.

Marcus remembered when it was over, thanking Walter for meeting with him and Walter said he was happy to do it and Marcus could see that he meant it. Walter looked lighter, easier, smiling into the sun. A freer man than the one who had walked in the door. Exorcised of whatever demon lurked in that story he'd carried inside him for so long. They shook hands in the parking lot and Marcus assumed that was the last time he would ever see Walter Williams.

Marcus exited the precinct and walked into the garage where Jeremiah had parked the car just an hour earlier. But it looked different, as though rearranged by the morning sunlight pouring over the concrete railings. The fresh air—or at least as fresh as metropolitan Chicago could supply—did something to clear Marcus's junk-drawer head as he waited by the remaining fleet of vehicles for whoever was to give him a ride back to his suburban home.

He spent his idling moments looking out over the railing. Daytime clusters of traffic jostling for position, car horns, the smell of diesel trailing lost big-rigs wandering through downtown like whales through an inlet. Early morning passersby clutching coffees to their chests. All of it appeared orchestrated, as though these objects and actors had rehearsed this same scene for months to perfect it for an audience of one.

He hadn't realized how much he missed the city.

Marcus heard footsteps behind him. He turned around to see Jeremiah exiting the precinct, his hands stuffed in his pockets, shoulders flaring against his suspenders. The smile plastered to his face that morning had flatlined into a razor's edge.

"Weren't you going to speak with Stetson about something?" Marcus asked.

"There's no such thing as speaking with Stetson," Jeremiah grunted. "He talks and you listen. And apparently I've been assigned to keep an eye on you," he said, nearing a car and waving Marcus to follow. "A psychopath killing people out there and looks like I'll be your loyal escort."

"I'm sorry," Marcus said, unsure, feeling guilty without much reason. "I could catch a cab back home. It's really fine. You should be out there. You should be out there finding whoever is doing this."

Stetson had told Marcus he was assigning a patrol car to him, just as a safety protocol. Stetson's voice still echoed in his mind. "I sincerely doubt you're in any danger. If he wanted to hurt you personally, he would have gone after you first, I should think." Marcus had searched for any small trace of comfort in this thought but found none.

"Boss's orders." Jeremiah threw open the driver's-side door with a huff. "Let's at least get going. Last thing I need right now is to be sitting in traffic with my thumb up my ass."

They sat in traffic. Jeremiah turned up the AC and leaned his head against the window. He tapped his fingers against the wheel impatiently.

"So you're *that* Marcus Waters?" Jeremiah asked, staring ahead at taillights.

"Excuse me?"

"You're the journalist from way back then. The guy who wrote that Kingfisher book."

"Yes."

Jeremiah nodded slowly. "I didn't even put that together." He adjusted himself in his seat, laid on his horn. A medley of horns answered him. Jeremiah rolled down his window just enough to expel a few choice words. He settled back into his seat. "Guess it makes sense Stetson would call you in, then. That video and all."

"Guess so."

"So maybe you can tell me something. Anything. Because when I talked to him, Stetson was feeding me pure bullshit."

"He seemed to think it's a hacker group. The Liber-teens? I guess they wear the same mask as the gunman."

Jeremiah snorted. "Hackers. Computer geeks. Doing something like this? No way. He probably doesn't even have a plan to look for the other hostages if he's just taking aim at some pimple-faced kids living in their parents' basements."

"I really don't know. I gave him some names to check on. But I guess he didn't seem all that optimistic."

Jeremiah cocked his head. "You gave him names? Of who?"

"He didn't tell you?"

"Tell me what?"

"The hostage killed in the video was someone I interviewed for my book. Someone saved by the Kingfisher back then. There were two others with him that same night."

"Jesus," Jeremiah whispered.

"But like I said, I told Stetson, and I gave him some other names. He said he'd look into it."

"*Look into it.*" Jeremiah laughed mirthlessly. "My God, Stetson really is a useless fucking prick sometimes. He's got just about every single officer running around doing godknows, while his detectives run his petty little errands instead of looking for those people. No offense, Mr. Waters. But for real, what in the actual fuck am I doing here babysitting you? Seriously, though. That man," Jeremiah shouted at the precinct already four blocks behind them, "doesn't have an ounce of common sense in that giant-fucking-empty head."

A stiff silence passed through the car, even with the chorus of horns and engines ricocheting between the buildings growing up alongside them. Jeremiah took a deep breath and released his tight grip on the wheel.

"But he's the boss, so . . ." Jeremiah said, casting a glance at Marcus.

"Don't worry. I don't care for him much either."

"Good." He laid on his horn again. "You know what, I forgot I was driving a cruiser. It's been a while." He reached forward and flipped the siren on. The traffic in front of them slowly, slowly inched forward, begrudgingly, to the side of the road, until a path was cleared down the middle of the street.

"This job's not always so bad," Jeremiah said as he pulled forward, gladly returning several obscene gestures. He laid on the gas, engine whining, taking sharp turns just for the hell of it. A smile returned to his face as he launched the cruiser across a congested intersection.

"I really should have known it was *you* in my car today," Jeremiah said, smacking the steering wheel with his palm. He had fully returned to his previous, cheery-no-matter-what self. "I can't believe I didn't put it together. You know, your name is still tossed around the precinct every so often. You have a good reputation there. You were one of the good reporters. The new police reporters at the *Inquisitor*, the younger ones, they don't have the same respect for the badge. You know what I mean? They don't even call or stop by. They just shoot us emails. Three, four sentence emails. Looking for quotes. Can you believe?"

"I figured as much. It explains the recent drop in quality."

Jeremiah nodded deeply. "Who was your main contact at the station?"

"He was way before your time. Long gone."

"Dead?"

"Retired. Maybe he's dead, too. I don't know. I interviewed him for the book a few years ago, but we haven't really kept in touch."

"What's his name?"

"Paul Wroblewski."

Jeremiah shrugged. "Yeah, I don't recognize it."

"Didn't expect you to."

During the Kingfisher years, Paul Wroblewski and Marcus had met once a week at a rust-and-concrete bar near Fullerton under simple conditions: Marcus bought the drinks and Paul shared inside information that he preferred calling privileged instead of confidential for liability purposes. Paul had been the one to first tell Marcus about the bizarre vigilante activity occurring around the South Side. He slid some photographs across the table. A man mangled in a back alley. His cheekbones crushed, an eye out of socket, blood pouring from his nose. Paul explained that there had been a few of these by now, all of them following the same pattern. They were dangerous offenders. This one—Paul pointed at the photograph—even had a warrant out for his arrest for killing an officer. But the real mystery: no one had stepped forward to collect the bounty. More than anything, this was what mystified Paul. His strength as a detective—or his weakness, depending on who you asked—was that he saw people as bodies in possession of motivations and desires and impulses. The rest was skin and bone.

"Been a few of them now." Paul nodded at the photograph in Marcus's hands. "Wanted criminals, worst of the worst, showing up around the city like human origami. And whoever is doing it, they're doing it pro bono," Paul said, his voice slick and even a little proto-Italian, though his mother and his father hailed from Poland. "It makes no fucking sense."

Marcus felt sick when he looked at the photograph, but that didn't stop him from staring at it for the better part of the hour they spent together, most of which was occupied by Paul as he hinted to Marcus that although the police were technically investigating whoever it was behind this, it was a formality more than anything.

"I'll tell you this much about whoever is doing this," Paul said, lowering his voice, stabbing the photograph in front of him with a finger. "He deserves a fucking medal. That's what he deserves. If I ever ran into him, you can be goddamn certain I wouldn't reach for my cuffs. I'd reach for his hand, buy him a drink. Man's doing God's work out there. Bless his stupid soul."

Marcus, these thirty years later, wondered if Paul Wroblewski was still alive, still drinking in some dingy bar, still blessing stupid souls.

Jeremiah was quiet for the rest of the ride into the suburbs. He turned on the radio to a pop station. After one song, the DJ began reading a news bulletin detailing the recently released video. Jeremiah turned quickly to an oldies station, shook his head, and gripped the wheel so tightly his knuckles seemed poised to rip through his skin.

But Marcus paid little attention to any of this. He was trying to remember the last thing Walter Williams had said to him before they parted ways to their respective vehicles. Whatever it had been, it was insignificant. Just a triviality passed between two fledgling acquaintances. But maybe whatever it was he'd said—a "thank you so much for meeting with me" or even just "take care"—would contain in itself some scrap of subtext that would relieve Marcus of the guilt he felt spreading throughout his bloodstream.

Marcus didn't realize they had pulled in to his driveway until Jeremiah put the car in park.

"Are you all right, Mr. Waters?"

"I'm fine."

"I'm sorry about what I said earlier," Jeremiah said. "I'm happy to be looking out for you. It's an honor, really. I was a kid when you were writing those articles, and they meant a lot to me. It's probably why I'm here doing what I'm doing, if I'm being honest."

"No, you were right," Marcus said, shrugging off the compliment. "You should be out there."

Jeremiah waved it off. "How about you go try to catch some shut-eye? You had an early morning. I'll keep the crazies away."

"No, I'm serious," Marcus said, fixing his stare to Jeremiah. "Stetson made it sound like he's going after the Liber-teens, or whatever they're called. When I told him about the other two people who may possibly be hostages, he took the names, but like you said, I don't know if he's serious about it. But these two guys really ought to be someone's concern, because even if they're safe, they may know something. Someone needs to find them and talk to them."

"I wish like hell I could go after them," Jeremiah said. "Really, I do. You have no idea. But I can't just disobey orders. I was told to stay here with you and make sure you're safe. So that's what I have to do. May not be the best use of my time, but I can't do anything about it."

Marcus recognized in Jeremiah a resoluteness that wasn't going to change no matter how long he waited or pleaded. Marcus was briefly reminded that the good cops could be almost as maddening as the bad ones. There was nothing left for Marcus to do but smile and thank Jeremiah for the ride before emerging into the heat of the climbing sun. He slowly lowered himself to pick up the day's *Inquisitor*, which the paperboy had an uncanny gift of throwing directly into his freshly planted and mulched verbenas.

He was unlocking the front door when Jeremiah called out after him, "Mr. Waters."

Marcus turned around.

Jeremiah was standing with one foot on the driveway, the other inside the car. His head turned shoulder-to-shoulder, voice lowering.

"If you're serious about what you said, I think I might know someone who can help." He smiled into the sunlight.

"Are you sure?"

"Give me the names and I'll see what I can do."

5 TINFOIL BIRDS

TILLMAN LIFTED HERSELF through the kitchen window and out onto the fire escape. She lived on the sixth floor of a narrow apartment building that seemed, at least when she looked down at the alley below, to gently sway.

She pulled a pack of Camels from her sports bra and struggled to light her cigarette in the wind. Once it was lit, she took an enormous drag, the paper crackling. She turned and looked through the window to make sure her father was still seated in his recliner, listening to Al Green and staring at the ceiling.

One of life's many cruel ironies was that cigarettes tasted so much better after a long run. The death-drive at its finest.

When her father had moved in three months ago, just days after her mother's funeral, she blurted out that she had quit smoking. She wasn't sure why she'd said it, given that it wasn't true at all. The words had evidently formed themselves without her consent. She had been carrying a box of his clothes into the apartment. He was sitting in the recliner. She saw him seated in her small apartment, diminished and embarrassed, occupying this unfamiliar space, and she simply blurted out that she had quit smoking. He smiled and said he was glad for that. And then she knew why she had told him the lie—to give the man some small, false peace that she couldn't otherwise offer.

It had been an easy lie to maintain back when she was still working.

She'd smoke on her way to the station, smoke on patrol, and smoke on her way home. She never had to worry about her father smelling it on her because—and here was another one of life's cruel ironies—four decades of chain-smoking had disintegrated completely his sense of taste and smell. The only thing he could remotely taste, or so he said, were Hershey's Kisses, which he ate by the handful. He kept the tin wrappers and made little sculptures of birds, which he kept in the junk drawer where he said they belonged.

But lately it was hard to find excuses to get out of the apartment. She didn't have the money for unnecessary errands, and there wasn't anywhere else she really had to be. So she resorted to a few quick breaks on the fire escape, her head on a swivel, the city bending and swaying beneath her feet as the nicotine rushed to her head.

Her phone vibrated in her pocket. The caller ID read: Jeremiah Combs.

She looked back into the window, saw her father unchanged, and looked back to the phone. She ignored the call. She didn't have anything to say to Jeremiah.

She leaned against the iron railing, took another deep drag, and felt her phone ringing again. Jeremiah Combs. She didn't answer. Jeremiah Combs, again.

He was nothing if not insistent. Always had been.

She stared at the phone for a moment before answering. "Yeah?"

"I've been trying to call you."

Jeremiah had a way of always sounding distantly amiable, the sort of tone that, from a friendly stranger, had maybe once been endearing, but was now unbearable. It made her wince, grit her teeth.

"Are you busy?" he asked.

"Why?"

"Can you please just answer my question?"

"I have a few minutes to spare."

"You seen the news?"

"What about it?"

"Please just answer me."

"I've seen it. Must be pretty busy today down there."

"Yeah, well, I wouldn't know."

She heard the anticipatory edge in his voice, inviting her to ask him why. But she didn't.

"Yeah," he continued, "Stetson put me on escort."

"Babysitting? Must have pissed him off."

"Maybe. I'm just parked out in a driveway right now."

"Sorry to hear it."

"It's actually all right. It's for someone you might remember."

She didn't say anything.

"Marcus Waters," he said. "You know, the journalist. The Kingfisher reporter. I remember you talking once about how your dad practically worshipped him."

"I never said that."

"Something like that."

"What do you want, Jeremiah?"

Her cigarette had burned down nearly to the filter, enough for a small hit, but she took a large one anyway. It burnt her lips. If nothing else, she thought, cigarettes taught you to relish the moment of pain that accompanied the inevitable end of all good things.

"How are you doing with everything?"

"I'm fine."

"We miss you down here. I hope you know that. We talk about you. What happened to you wasn't fair."

"Don't."

"I'm serious."

"Since when do detectives reminisce about disgraced beat cops?"

"Come on, Tilly. Cut it out. Wallowing isn't a good look on you."

She sighed loud enough for him to hear through the phone. "I can't imagine Stetson wants you, or anybody else for that matter, talking to me."

"He's got enough to worry about right now. Speaking of which"—his voice notched down a register—"I might need your help with something. Only if you're interested."

"What, you need another babysitter?"

"No, listen. I need you to look into something for me. I'd do it myself, but well, I'm stuck here. Thumb in my ass."

Tillman flicked her cashed cigarette down into the alley and watched it spin out of sight. She looked inside the window and saw her father snoozing with a newspaper folded across his chest. She brought the phone back to her mouth. "What is it?"

Jeremiah explained the situation to her. Marcus Waters knew the hostage in the video. For Marcus's book—which Tillman had actually given her father for Christmas last year; she had read him a few pages, but he ended up falling asleep and the book, to this day, lay forgotten on his nightstand—Marcus had interviewed the hostage in question. The King-fisher had evidently saved him one night those many years ago. And from that same night, there were two others the Kingfisher had saved.

"And Waters told Stetson all of this?" she asked.

"That's what he said."

"Then why isn't it being reported?"

"I don't know. Maybe Stetson is trying to keep it quiet, but Mr. Waters is worried that Stetson may not be going after the other two names. He said that Stetson seems most interested in locating the Liber-teens."

"You're fucking kidding me." She laughed. "Those kids have nothing to do with this. They don't need to kill someone to get their point across. They can do that with a few strokes of the keyboard. The Liber-teen mask was a diversion. It's fucking obvious."

"You're preaching to the choir, Tilly. But I'm not calling to talk about the Liber-teens. I'm calling about the other people Mr. Waters interviewed for the book. He's worried they might be in danger. I know I'm putting you in a bad position. If you don't want to help with this, I'm not going to throw stones. I mean, like I said, I would do it myself, but—"

"If Stetson found out, you'd lose your head. Maybe your job, too."

"Right."

"Give me the names."

Jeremiah sighed through the phone. "Before you agree, I need to point out to you that if Stetson finds out you are doing this, he'll go apeshit. Not to mention, Stetson may already be sending people to check up on them. It'd be bad news if you ran into a familiar face out there."

"You and I both know that's not going to happen," she said. "He wants the arrest. That's all he cares about. All he's ever cared about."

"I'm just saying. If he finds out you were there."

"Fuck Stetson. I don't care if he finds out."

"Look, I want your help. But I also happen to care about you. You and I both know you tend to cannonball into things. So think this through completely. You could be taken off administrative leave any day. But if you do this, you're blowing your nose at Stetson. If he finds out you were out on the field, well," he mumbled, "you know what he'd do."

"Send me the names," she said. "And put in a call for the addresses while you're at it."

"Are you sure about this?"

"Ask me that one more time, I swear to God."

She heard Jeremiah laugh on the other end. She could picture him as he did so, his head pressed against the headrest. She nearly smiled.

"If you get a chance," she said, "come check up on my dad while I'm out. He should be OK while I'm gone, but just do it anyway. He's gotten used to someone being around."

"Will do. I owe you one, Tilly."

"Don't call me that," she said.

"Does your dad still eat those Hershey's Kisses? I could pick some up at the CVS on my way."

But she was already hanging up the phone.

6 THIN LINES

WREN HAD HER LAPTOP OPEN on the counter next to the cash register, but she quickly stashed it when her boss, Fester, leaned out from the office door at the end of the alley. He did this every hour—poking out like a cuckoo clock, scoping out his domain, and then disappearing back inside his office, where he would remain until about five o'clock, when he would then emerge, sit at the bar, and pound Bud Lights into something resembling oblivion.

She had spent the first hour of her shift running the gunman's video through a digital enhancement program—Pixie, still in Beta—developed by a fellow Liber-teen who went by the name of TrotskiiResort. With Pixie, she was able to select certain coordinates of the video and enhance the collection of granular pixels. The resulting image wasn't crystal clear, but it was better than nothing. Wren watched the enlarged face of the hostage as the gunman held a gun to his head. She took a screenshot of his face, trying not to look at his moving, trembling lips. She stopped the video before the gunshot. There wasn't any point in watching his death again.

That living body, that beating heart. Reduced to sheer matter in the space of a second. It was chilling enough to numb. She didn't have the time to feel numb.

As she parsed the image, it occurred to Wren—though not for the first time—that in some alternate reality she could have worked cyber security for the FBI or NSA, a hacker with the blessing of the United States government. She could work to protect information vital to national security, launch full-out cyberattacks at hostile governments in retaliation. She knew her skill set well enough to know she would be a vital asset, which was to say she knew—though she wasn't one to brag, the Midwestern curse—that she was better than any single cybersecurity expert working for the government. She dreamt up algorithms in the shower and wrote code in her dreams. But she'd never work for the government, even if the pay were better than a part-time bowling alley job. She'd never work for anyone who told her what to protect, what to take, and who to attack. She was not a mercenary. She was a watcher of the watchers, and this was an identity she had adopted with complete comfort before today.

The bowling alley this morning was empty, with the notable exception of two day-drunk college boys—likely prolonging last night's revelries—shouting each time the ball collided with the pins. Spare, strike, split, scream. To make it worse, she had recognized one of them when he stumbled through the door, though he clearly hadn't recognized her. She had been in a class with him during her brief, yet fateful semester at the University of Chicago several years ago. It was the same class in which she'd met Parker.

Wren had been seated in the front row of Introduction to Informatics. The professor—a hunched black man who wagged his finger like a dying metronome—stood in front of a clean chalkboard, lecturing about the impending effects of the Big Data Revolution.

"If you live long enough," he said, in a doleful voice escaping unmoving lips, "every single one of you sitting here today will die a collection of numbers and come back the same."

A girl seated next to Wren—Corvette-red hair, a VIVA LA ATARI T-shirt, typing madly on her laptop—whispered, "If you and I are coming back as numbers, Professor Father Time up there is coming back as Roman numerals."

Wren laughed, and the professor paused his lecture to settle a punitive gaze on her.

"Sorry," she whispered.

The girl seated next to her smirked, and turned back to her laptop, where Wren saw her typing out a line of code. A tattoo of the pigeon from

Neil Gaiman's *The Sandman* adorned her wrist, and each movement of her fingers against the keys gave the bird the illusion of flight.

A more sentimental person than Wren might have called it love at first sight.

The college boys at the end of the alley loudly celebrated a strike. She turned back to her laptop, in order to dissociate herself from the television that hung by a few fraying wires on top of the shoe rack. The news stations had finally gotten to the execution video and had begun to dissect it for their audience with a gluttonous glee. The newscaster jittered in his seat. He said, "At this point, a lot of speculation, and perhaps now we'll have some answers. We're going live to a press conference where Police Chief Gregory Stetson is speaking."

The camera cut to a broad-shouldered man standing at a podium outside, staring down at a few loose sheets of paper. The voice that found its way through the dense mustache was brusque, as though he were hurrying through the platitudes written before him—"the people of Chicago are strong and resolved and will not be shaken by malicious attempts to incite panic." He assured the gaggle of reporters that the suspect's claims about the Kingfisher were wholly false, the words of a "deranged individual." He added, as an accentuated footnote, "Regarding the ideologies and affiliations with criminal groups alluded to in the suspect's statement, specifically the Liber-teen hacktivist collective, we simply do not have enough evidence for such speculation at this time, but with the cooperation of the FBI, we are actively investigating any and all leads into their involvement."

She took a much-needed breath and opened the Liber-teen forum. The latest thread was titled "Vote?" She scrolled back through the conversation to find that they were considering whether or not they would launch an offensive against the Chicago Police Department.

—If they won't release the ME report, we'll take it from them! There are lives at stake.
—They're not going to release it. We have to take it.
—Fucking anarchy. I love it ☺
—This is why we exist. To balance corrupted modes of justice. Why wait?
—By helping a murderer?

—This isn't the way to bring about anarchy.

—They ALREADY THINK WE'RE BEHIND THE FUCKING VIDEO!
   Why give them more reason to think that?

—Sorry, I know this isn't the right thread for this, but does
   anyone have a link to the Beta of *SkullKrushers 2*? Heard it's
   fucking dope.

—So we get the file and then what?

—We RELEASE IT! We don't need to do anything else. We let
   the PEOPLE decide what happens next.

—"Anarchy is the only slight glimmer of hope."

—Did you seriously just quote fucking Mick Jagger?

—Hacking the report gives the asshole with the gun a reason to
   stop shooting people. That's reason enough.

—And let's all remember that this is a police force that consistently
   brutalizes their minority citizens without penalty. They don't
   deserve our deference.

—http://doomsdayportalgames.com/skullkrushers2beta

—There's not going to be anything in the report.

—This isn't about the ME report. This is about showing the CPD
   that we are going to hold them accountable. No more secrecy.
   No more lies. They don't care who lives and dies.

—Who gives a SHIT about the Kingfisher anyways?

—The Kingfisher was a badass. Real-life Superman. Ubermensch.

—We could use the Kingfisher right about now.

—The Kingfisher sucks ass.

—The Kingfisher = harbinger of Reagan's fascist/neoliberal
   drug war.

—We've wanted to shine a light on the police in this city for a
   while now. This is our chance.

—Anarchy, bitches.

—In case you somehow missed it, we're the number one
   trending topic on Twitter and Facebook right now. Pretty cool!

—*SkullKrushers2* sucks, don't waste your time.

Wren added her voice to the conversation, *I can't believe we're even debating whether or not we advance the cause of a deranged sadist. This is not who we are. This is not our territory. What the fuck?*

And with that, she closed out of the tab and returned to Pixie, where she refocused the coordinates in the precise moment that the gunman displayed the hostages. There were two of them. But even with enhancement, it was nearly impossible to discern much else. Sacks covered each of their heads. Their torsos and legs were hidden beneath ropes binding them to chairs. The only parts of their bodies that were exposed were their hands. She took screenshots of each hostage's hands, shadowed though they were. When she was finished, she viewed them one by one. By her best judgment, one remaining hostage was black. The other she couldn't quite tell, but she enhanced the image another time and discerned a ring adorning one of the left hand's slim fingers. An engagement ring, maybe. A woman. What this meant for identifying the hostage, Wren wasn't sure. But it was something. And that was more than she'd had before.

Just then, the bells above the glass door chirped and a woman walked in, her head casting shoulder to shoulder like she was expecting someone. As the door closed, it ushered in the smell of rain threatening to fall. The woman appeared to be older, midsixties. She moved weightlessly and effortlessly through the space, as though gliding a fraction of an inch above the unvacuumed carpet. Her apple-red, dyed hair fell in neat ringlets to her neck, curling just above the unbuttoned collar of her floral-print blouse. She wore a sequined miniskirt that changed color with every step under the overhead lights, while a cigarette burned in her hand, the smoke wrapping around it like a glove.

Wren watched the woman walking toward her like a celebrity along some empty red carpet. The woman placed her purse on the counter and rooted inside of it, discarding crumpled receipts, condoms, hard-candy wrappers, and loose change in search of something. She stacked wadded dollar bills alongside emptied gum wrappers, cursing silently, her lips forming four-letter words and releasing them with the crisp menthol that oozed from her mouth.

Wren cleared her throat. "Can't smoke in here. Sorry."

She nodded and brought the cigarette to her lips and left it there, using both hands to go through the purse.

"Are you here to bowl?"

She stopped her digging suddenly, running a hand through her hair, gray at the roots. "What's the point in buying a cell phone if you can't ever find it?" She huffed and turned around, looking out over the desolate lanes, her eyes squinting in the smoke. "I haven't been here in godknows how long. Place has really gone to shit. I used to come in here when I was younger." She remained looking out at the pins and the blank, suspended screens. The drunken college boys high-fiving for no evident reason. She pointed at a wall behind a pool table. "See the picture hanging there—a mirror, I think it is."

"Yes."

The woman leaned back onto the counter and craned her head, her chin touching her shoulder.

"That's where I got felt-up for the first time. Swear to God it's true."

Wren nodded, with the sudden image of a faceless man, holding a piece of this woman—her breast—disembodied, cradled in his cupped hand.

"You don't ever forget it, do you? First hands that aren't your own, covered in teenage sweat. Wandering over you like you're some porcelain doll. Like you might break at the slightest touch. It's only later they learn that you don't break. That's where the trouble starts, doesn't it?" She took a long, long drag, until Wren thought she might suck the whole cigarette down in a single breath, but finally she released. "No, you don't forget it. And then you come back to where it happened. Years later. And you feel it again. Like you're walking back to where it all began." She coughed into an open palm. "It's fixing to storm outside. Hope you have yourself an umbrella."

Wren saw from the corner of her eye the college boys looking at the woman. One of them, the one she knew, pantomimed fellatio with a clutched fist to the delirious amusement of his friend.

The woman didn't seem to notice. She looked down at a silver watch, loosely wrapping her toothpick-wrist. "I'm guessing that's the boss's office?" she said, pointing to Fester's closed door with his name printed on a wooden placard.

"Yes."

"All right. Well, back to work, then." She slung her purse over her shoulder and walked off sure-footed in her heels, her sequined skirt catching all the light from the room and reflecting it all in a sort of radiance around her. She knocked on Fester's door and it opened wide enough for her narrow body to pass through before shutting.

Wren looked down at the pile of old papers and receipts the woman had left on the counter. She withdrew a folded business card. It read: MISS MAY PIECEWORK. A phone number in fine print at the bottom.

She looked out over the lanes and saw the two college kids in a sort of huddle. They were looking back at Wren. Frozen in laughter, teeth bared to the dim and unchanging lights. She wanted to beat them with a bowling pin, but instead she turned back to her laptop. She studied the image of the ringed finger for a moment, and then she pulled up the Chicago missing persons directory. An array of thumbnailed faces stared back at her. There were hundreds—men, women, children. Even after she filtered her search for women, she wasn't sure how she should proceed. When she clicked on a picture, there was listed the missing person's name, their last known location, their birth date, and their physical description. There was nothing about recent engagements.

A half hour later, Fester's door opened just wide enough for the woman to emerge. She looked no different than before, but she carried herself with more precision, a certain measure to each step she took atop the geometric carpet.

As she walked past the counter, she caught sight of the television hanging from its frayed wire. The woman squinted to make out the caption on the news channel: THE KINGFISHER BACK FROM THE DEAD? A group of four commentators gathered around a table appeared to be arguing over the question with considerable enthusiasm.

The woman touched a hand to her lips, where it remained.

"Do you want me to turn it up?" Wren asked.

Her voice seemed to surprise the woman. "No, no," the woman said in a soft voice that didn't seem to come from her at all. She laid a hand on the counter as if steadying herself. "I ought to get going before the rain comes."

The bell above the door called out and she was gone.

In her absence, Wren heard footsteps approaching from the other side and she turned to see the college boys standing before her. They both wore polo shirts, pastel shorts, Nike socks, dock shoes. They laid their bowling shoes down on the counter, having finished their game. But they lingered about still, each of them halfheartedly fighting a stupid, drunk grin.

"You were that girl that was in my Introduction to Informatics class a few years ago, right?" asked the one she knew. As soon as he spoke, his name came back to her immediately: Nikolas Wilson. He had been a sports science major, or some other equally facile discipline, and he must have arrived at Introduction to Informatics as an ill-advised elective course. He didn't know anything about informatics, but that didn't stop him from speaking over everyone in the class, including the professor. But so far as Wren could tell, being a man in this world meant you could talk as loudly as you liked about things you didn't know anything about and the world was more or less obliged to listen, nod, and maybe even agree.

Wren collected their shoes.

"Did you hear me?" Nikolas asked with a wolfish grin, leaning across the counter. His hair was buzzed on the sides, but neatly coiffed on top. Or, as Parker called it, "the proto-fascist alt-right haircut du jour." Nikolas repeated himself, "You were in that class, right? You were some sort of awesome coder or something."

She nodded with reluctance. Nikolas's friend nudged him with an elbow, a peevish sidekick's grin slopped across his sun-red, liquor-stained face.

"So can I ask you something?" Nikolas asked. He didn't wait for a reply, which was just as well. "I heard you dropped out because you ran off with that other girl who was in our class. That one with the weird fucking hair. The real bitchy one. I heard you two moved in together after that semester. Is that true?"

What was true was that they hadn't even waited until the end of the semester. Parker had arrived breathless at Wren's dorm room one night, too excited to even speak. So instead, she'd pointed at her laptop screen. The enigmatic Liber-teens had posted a cipher, an open invitation for anyone who could meander its labyrinth of puzzles involving data encryption, Byzantine art history, Nicomachean ethics, continental philosophy, geopolitics, Russian literature, Japanese popular culture, and chess. There was also what Wren had considered a music appreciation segment in which a song by My Bloody Valentine played through the speakers. It was followed by the question: *Did you like that music? Yes or no?* They worked through the night, and woke in the morning to separate invitations to join the group under the condition of total and complete anonymity. Several days later, after splitting a twelve-pack of PBR and two joints each, they had decided to drop out. Why spend four years preparing for the world, when, with the Liber-teens, they had an opportunity to have a tangible effect on the exact same world? Why study information systems and code from a textbook when the entire world was little more than a series of ones and zeros constantly rearranging?

And at some point in those indeterminable hours, Parker had turned to Wren, holding out a joint. "This is the Manifest Destiny of the twenty-first century."

"A shitty apartment and a bag of weed?" Wren said.

"And the whole world at your fingertips," Parker said, reaching out her hand, running her fingers lightly across Wren's cheek.

But Wren wasn't about to tell Nikolas—beer-glazed blue eyes—any of this, so instead she turned around and sprayed the racks of shoes with a disinfectant. A cloud of aerosol billowing into her face. Acerbic, but also halfway sweet.

"Hey, I asked you a question," Nikolas said behind her, his voice climbing. "And you should answer. It's rude otherwise. Did you go become a lesbian with that bitchy girl or not? Were you a lesbian before or did she make you become one?"

She took a rag to a rack of bowling balls, polishing their surfaces with quick, tight spirals.

"Jesus, fine," Nikolas said, each word more slurred than the last. "Ignore me. Just trying to have a friendly conversation. I guess you can chat with that nasty ginger grandma prostitute in here earlier, but you're too good to talk with me?"

His friend wasn't laughing anymore. The humor of the moment was quickly replaced with something else: a sudden and silent stiffness. Wren heard his friend whisper to him that they should leave. But Nikolas pushed him away. He laid his knuckles on the counter and leaned over the wooden countertop, his shoulder pressed into the Bud Light tap handle, releasing a spray of suds.

She wasn't looking at him, but she could sense him just the same with a greater clarity than her eyes might otherwise allow. She felt him drawing from his small lexicon for something that would capture whatever fury lay behind his glassy eyes.

"Lesbo bitch shining bowling balls for minimum wage too good to talk with an old friend," he pronounced as though reading a newspaper headline, and pushed off the counter, sauntering off in long and leaning strides.

His friend turned around apologetically while steadying his drunken counterpart, who kept his eyes trained to her like a guided missile.

She could see herself through his eyes—a girl in baggy denim jeans, kitchen-scissors haircut, growing smaller and smaller, staring at the earth somewhere below the carpet and concrete and dirt and bedrock until the bell above the door chirped and she disappeared from his line of sight altogether.

She took her laptop back out and opened an IP-cloaking software and a password decryption algorithm—both of which she and Parker had recently developed—and hacked into Nikolas Wilson's university bursar account, then withdrew his checking and savings account routing numbers, along with his cell phone number. Three minutes later, his accumulated eleven thousand dollars and fifty-seven cents had been *reinvested* to a women's shelter four blocks away. But just for good measure, she also hacked into his iCloud account. From there, she sifted through concert photos—Incubus, the Goo Goo Dolls, Dave Matthews Band, and every other shitty band imaginable—until she found what she was looking for, what she instinctively knew would be there.

She sent all of Nik's contacts a blurry picture of his grotesquely discolored genitalia—one of many he had taken, actually—onto which she overlaid a loud, pink-colored text: *SHINE MY BALLS?*

When it was over, she wondered if it had been a mistake. He would know it was her, but then again, he had no way of proving it and he wasn't quite stupid enough to seek revenge. He had deserved what came to him. But whoever the hostages were, they didn't deserve what could come to them. It was that simple, single difference that meant everything. She turned back to the missing persons directory, staring at the faces that passed her screen.

7 MAY 1979

OFFICER GREGORY STETSON was a practical man who prayed to a practical God and set practical goals—marry Mindy, buy a nice house together, have a kid or two, lease a shining American-made car, get a promotion to detective, retire somewhere perpetually warm, and die at an old age surrounded by those he loved. And he saw the world as a practical object willing to dispense with these things if he worked hard enough. The world was his for the taking, so to speak.

He had met Mindy in a bar a few weeks back. After a few too many drinks, he had decided he was in love with her, the brunette ashing her cigarette on the bar floor. He beat her in a game of darts, talked some shit, and she punched him in the shoulder. Harder than he would have expected. Hard enough that it hurt. He'd told her she had just assaulted a police officer, a man of the law. She held out her hands, stepping closer to him. "Guess you'll have to handcuff me." Later that same night, he still felt the shape and kiss of her knuckles on his shoulder as he lay awake next to her in his one-bedroom Woodlawn apartment.

The radio crackled on his shoulder. "Adam Thirteen, code five."

Stetson grabbed the radio before dispatch had even finished the sentence. "Thirteen, code five, go ahead."

"Officer located on corner of 51st and 52nd reports finding suspect with outstanding warrant. Requests immediate backup."

"Copy and confirm."

And then he was not thinking about Mindy anymore, a nice house, an American-made car—all of his attention narrowed like a noose around a single duty. He was a cop. A cop assisting another cop in the city he loved more dearly than he loved life itself. And all things considered, he happened to love life very much.

Stetson spotted an unmarked cruiser in front of a foreclosed home on 51st. As he exited his patrol car, he found that the officer he was here to assist was in fact a detective. What a detective was doing out here, alone and at this time of night, was beyond him. And Detective Paul Wroblewski, no less.

Detective Wroblewski had what might charitably be called a "reputation." Less charitably, Wroblewski was a raging alcoholic, a two-bit homicide detective, and an all-around prickly dick. But a detective is a detective, and a first impression is a first impression, so Stetson held out a hand. Wroblewski regarded Stetson's hand as though it were a space-object fallen to earth as he reached instead into his pocket for a loose cigarette.

"Got a call for a code five," Stetson said, retracting his outstretched hand and thumbing his belt. "Where's the suspect?"

Even in the dark of night, Stetson saw that Wroblewski's eyes were wide and dilated, as though trying to take in the whole world all at once. His lips and fingers quivered as he laid a cigarette gently between them. He was drunk. That much was obvious. But Stetson had seen Wroblewski drunk before—talking at a high volume in the precinct, cursing at anyone that passed him. This was something more than drunk.

Wroblewski patted his pockets for his matchbook, the cigarette hanging from his mouth. He didn't seem to remember the cigarette was there, because when he opened his mouth to answer, it fell out onto the sidewalk. He picked it up and withdrew a flap of matches from his breast pocket. With a quivering hand, he tried striking a match, but the flame was dead on arrival.

"Are you OK, sir?"

"What's your name?" Wroblewski asked, a deep rattle in his throat. He threw the bum match to the ground and tried to light another.

"Officer Stetson."

"*Officer* is a funny first name. You have a Zippo on you, Mr. Officer?"

"No, sir."

"Don't smoke?"

"No, sir."

"Mm," Wroblewski hummed, finally getting a good light on a match, the flame contouring the soft and indistinct edges of his alcohol-swollen face. "You should. It helps."

"So where's the code five?" Stetson asked again.

"Well, Mr. Officer, that's the thing." Wroblewski exhaled a plume of smoke. He seemed to relax a touch, stretching his neck to scan the stars. "That's why I wanted some backup here."

"Why?"

"He's dead. The code five. Dead as dead."

Stetson maintained a professional calm. "You neutralized him?"

"No, no, no." Wroblewski waved it off. A heaving drag, exhaling between fits of trembling laughter. "Jesus, *neutralize*. Listen to yourself."

"What is it, then?"

"Honestly, kid? I got no fucking clue. I just want to make sure I'm not losing my damned mind. Thought I'd get a second pair of eyes. But understand, maybe you don't tell the guys back at the station what you're about to see. Not yet, OK? Call it liability or whatever-the-hell. Call it a secret we maybe share for the time being. Are we understood?"

A detective is a detective. Stetson nodded. "Where is he?"

"This way." Wroblewski led him through the gate of a chain fence, around the foreclosed home, past dusty and dark windows. Fireflies illuminated the night, appearing and reappearing, a hundred points of scattered light. A charcoal grill lay upended in the backyard, overtaken by a jungle of uncut grass. They entered into a gravel alley at the edge of the lawn. Wroblewski turned in to the alley, a cloud of smoke in his wake, slowing his surprisingly spry step to allow Stetson to catch up.

"I've been trying to run down this guy for a while now," Wroblewski said over his shoulder in a hushed voice. "One month back, he shoots a gas station employee. Wasn't fatal, but the employee is all sorts of messed up. Paralyzed, breathing tubes, crying family. A nasty scene."

"So what happened to the perpetrator?" There was a naked, sheared Barbie doll buried in the dirt to her neck. Stetson fought the inexplicable impulse to pull it from the ground and instead stepped over it.

"*Perpetrator?* My God. Well, the *perpetrator* gets charged, but the shit-for-brains judge lets the scum pay bail. Of course, he doesn't show up to his hearing. All the while, I've been reaching out to his family. They want to see him behind bars more than I do, but they have no clue where he is. So I get a call tonight from the guy's mother. I can't understand a single fucking word she's trying to say, she's crying so much. Finally, she makes out something about how her son is at her house, so I'm thinking, 'OK, the dumb fuck came back home.' I haul ass down here, ready to call for backup and put the guy in cuffs, and then the mom comes running outside and points me right over here."

Wroblewski reached out and pointed at a shadowy mass in the middle of the alley. Its edges undefined, refusing to sharpen into focus even as Stetson stood over it. It was only when he knelt down that he could make out the texture of skin, a shining pool of stagnant blood.

Stetson had seen dead bodies. Two or three. Gunshot victims, all of them. But the body before him now was not a dead body as he had known them. It was a tangle of vaguely human elements arranged into an unholy creation. Legs, arms, head, neck. Twisted and broken and re-assembled. If God created humankind, He Himself would not have recognized this as His own.

"Don't touch him," Wroblewski said behind him and Stetson wondered why the hell he would even think to touch it. Or him. Or whatever the hell this was he was looking at.

And then, without warning, Stetson felt himself retch. Vomit shot from his stomach like a bullet. He tried to hide it with a cough, but this sped the inevitable collapse. He fell onto his hands and turned inside out. After the contents of his stomach passed his lips, embarrassment followed.

But Wroblewski didn't seem to notice or care about Stetson's vomiting. He was staring fixedly at the thing before him.

"I'm glad you see it, too, Mr. Officer." Wroblewski's voice was quiet. "Thought I'd lost my goddamned mind." His lit cigarette fell from his open lips and smoldered there between his shoes. Half-smoked. "It just doesn't make any fucking sense. Never seen anything quite like it."

And later that night, which was actually early morning, Officer Gregory Stetson arrived home to his empty apartment, changed into his pajamas, brushed his teeth, said a prayer, and then fell asleep in his twin-sized bed and dreamt of hell and the secrets that escape it.

8 PETER RICHARDS

IT WAS MIDMORNING, nearly noon, but it already felt like midnight. Marcus boiled water in the kitchen, brewed a cup of coffee in his French press, and lowered himself and a coffee mug slowly, slowly into his recliner.

He'd written the names down for Jeremiah on a napkin, the same way Walter Williams had written down the names of the other two for Marcus those years ago. It felt appropriate, dragging the pen across the delicate fabric in long and careful cursive.

And now the situation was out of his hands. He had done all that he could do and then some.

Marcus had purchased tomato seeds yesterday to plant in his garden today, but that would require energy he couldn't muster. Instead, he drank his coffee and opened the day's *Inquisitor*. The paper had clearly gone to the printers before the video had been released. The headline—HUNDREDS PROTEST STATE BUDGET CUTS TO PUBLIC SCHOOLS—felt pleasantly innocuous, given the world that had erupted in the hours since the printers ran. He turned to the crossword puzzle at the back of the paper and withdrew a pencil from the breast pocket of his shirt. He had never done crossword puzzles prior to retirement, but since that day, he had completed each of the *Inquisitor*'s crossword puzzles as best he could.

He considered crossword puzzles to be a sort of exit exam, a probing into the insignificant events that crop up in the span of sixty, seventy, eighty years of rambling along the surface of earth. Names of dead or dying celebrities, breeds of dogs, songs you used to sing over the roaring engine of a car they now call classic.

His cell phone began ringing in his pocket. He withdrew it warily. The caller ID simply read: New York, NY.

"Hello, Mr. Waters. First, let me begin by saying I'm an enormous admirer of yours."

"Who is this?"

"This is Jack Thomas with the *New York Times*, and I'm just calling in regards to the video that was recently uploaded to the internet. Are you aware of it?"

He mumbled a quick goodbye and hung up the phone. Then the dam broke. The little device began to convulse endlessly in the palm of his hand. The caller ID identified the area codes as the phone calls piled up: Los Angeles, California; Washington, D.C.; St. Louis, Missouri. He watched them with numb interest as the words and locations piled atop each other in the digital display. One obsequious voice message after another.

News vans, jockeying for position, rolled up and down his street and Marcus watched them from behind the curtain. Reporters hung out of passenger-side windows, squinting at the squat suburban home, microphones protruding from their manicured hands. Jeremiah stood in the driveway, warding off these unwanted guests, flapping his hand at the passing vans as though shooing fruit flies from a bowl of two-week-old oranges.

Marcus sat at the window for a while, unblinking, and stared into the street where the vans kept coming, an endless procession. He just hoped the passing news crews wouldn't air any footage of his home. His verbenas hadn't bloomed the way the way he'd hoped they would. Half-closed bulbs sprouted atop bent stems. He feared that this made his entire home— limestone, vines crawling along the corners—look vaguely Gothic, a midsummer's haunted house.

His cell phone continued to ring unceasingly. He turned it off.

And then his landline phone rang on the wall. He thought at first that it was just another journalist who had been clever enough to check the white pages, but this seemed highly unlikely, seeing as how none of this new generation of bushy-tailed reporters seemed to know that landlines had ever existed. Then he thought, with some panic, that it could be one of his children who hadn't been able to reach him on his cell.

He rose slowly from the recliner and picked it up.

"Hello?" he asked cautiously.

"Hello?" A morose voice wandered from the phone as though it were lost, surprised to find a voice on the other end. "Marcus?"

"Speaking. Who is this?"

"Oh, good." A heavy sigh. "Marcus, it's Peter. Peter Richards." And then he added, in an almost cheery inflection, "Do you remember me?"

"Peter?" He laughed, equal parts disbelief and relief—his landline was safe for the time being. "My God. Of course I remember you."

"Good. That's good. What are you doing right now?"

Marcus looked down at the crossword puzzle in his other hand. "Why?"

"I need to talk to you."

Several months into his coverage of the Kingfisher, Marcus had written almost a dozen articles. Every single one had headlined. And each headline seemed to grow in size until nearly the entire front page consisted of bold, elongated letters you could read from across the street.

The newspapers were so ubiquitous that Marcus gradually forgot that the name on every front page—the Kingfisher—was a name Marcus had created for the man. After all, it wasn't as though the Kingfisher had ever called himself by this name. Based on his conversations with criminals who had survived their encounters with the man, the Kingfisher didn't say much at all, if anything. When Marcus wrote his first story on the mystery vigilante of Chicago, his editor demanded he have a name. "This isn't just some backstreet do-gooder vigilante you're describing," his editor said—an overweight man with perpetual sweat lining his lips that he licked after each utterance. "This guy is something else. Give him a name, Marcus. Something sexy. Something dark. Yeah. Sexy and dark. And mysterious, too. Sexy and dark and mysterious."

Marcus had half an hour before deadline, a half hour to name the vigilante whom he knew almost nothing about. Witnesses were few and described little more than a shape swooping down from the dark to grab criminals like unsuspecting prey. He remembered his stepfather, Corn Wallace—tenured philosophy professor and part-time amateur ornithologist—who obsessed over kingfishers, birds native to Southeast Asia. The image of the kingfisher itself was neither sexy nor dark nor mysterious. It was brightly colored, small, fragile in appearance. But its beauty was deceptive. The kingfisher was quick, reclusive, fiercely territorial, and a dangerously efficient hunter. Not to mention that the name kingfisher itself sounded royal, stately, and above all, superlative. The king of fishers. Deadline approached, and Marcus defined his career in a few strokes of his typewriter. The next day, the Kingfisher was a name passing through the city's collective lips.

Call it sensationalism. The *Inquisitor*'s competitors sure did. But Marcus never felt the sting of this accusation. The articles he wrote were written with care, skill, integrity, devotion, and attention to detail. So what if Marcus gave the vigilante a colorful name? And so what if his editor added a few exclamation marks to the headline?

He began to notice the newspapers everywhere he went. The obvious places, sure—the newsstands, the gutters, and folded on café tables and bathroom stalls. But at other times, he saw them floating like tumbleweed down the street, sometimes never quite touching the ground, but simply gliding as though possessing a mind of their own—a sense of direction, a desire for destination.

Inevitably, a fraction of the enthusiastic attention directed toward the Kingfisher was redirected toward himself. Whereas the Kingfisher existed solely in the shadows, a peripheral figure of the imagination, Marcus Waters was a concrete presence—a man in a coffee shop, walking the sidewalks, dropping a dollar for a trombone player on Michigan Avenue. He received calls throughout the day from other newspapers for verification and quotes. He received notification of his nomination to journalism prizes that he hadn't ever heard of before. He was invited to talk shows and charity dinners hosted by the Chicago elite. The mayor invited him to play golf and Marcus accepted, only to wish he hadn't. He hated golf almost as much as he hated the mayor.

He received hundreds of letters each week from the public, their tone ranging from racist to elegiac to profane to prophetic. "I know who the Kingfisher is," wrote one, "because he is all of us as one central body, one life force raised to the physical dimension. He is God come to earth in all of our blood."

It was around this time of public attention that Marcus Waters first met

Peter Richards, who arrived unannounced at Marcus's office one morning, not bothering to knock. When Peter closed the office door behind him, Marcus first noticed the starchy hue of his skin, the reddish shock of hair left unkempt, dangling to his eyebrows. Behind it all, a trace of refinement. Boarding-school posture. He stared at his feet, and Marcus followed his gaze to a worn, dirty pair of Converse shoes.

He spoke in a scratchy whisper. "Mr. Waters, my name is Peter Richards, and I have something you need to see."

Marcus opened his mouth to ask him, as kindly as he could, to get out of his office.

"I only ask that you take a look at it," Peter interrupted preemptively. "If you aren't interested in what I have to show you, I'll leave. I don't mean to bother you. I know I showed up out of nowhere. But I tried calling, and you didn't answer. So here I am."

Everything about this kid was strangely incongruous. His voice wavered between audible and inaudible. His build suggested he was a teenager, but the corners of his eyes sprouted wrinkles. He carried himself with a pained self-awareness, as though always silently apologizing for the space he occupied at any given moment. He was endearing in some inexplicable way.

Peter set the box on Marcus's desk, knocking off a miniature grandfather clock in doing so. It chimed when it hit the floor. Peter apologized under his breath, reaching into the box with nervous hands. He withdrew what appeared to be a sculpture of some sort, oblong and amorphous. He handed it to Marcus gently. It was made of plaster. That was the only observation Marcus could make. He turned it over in his hands curiously.

"What is this?" he asked.

"It's a mold."

"Of what?"

"A footprint," Peter said, reaching out and turning the mold over in Marcus's hands. He pointed to a deep impression, filled with crisscrossing lines. "That's the Kingfisher's footprint."

The print itself was large, perhaps a size fifteen. At the bottom, there were treads, those of a boot. Marcus traced them with a finger and then looked at Peter, meeting his insistent, unyieldingly sincere gaze.

"Sure it's not Bigfoot's?" Marcus asked.

Peter's already diminutive posture grew somehow smaller. A wheezing breath through his nose, as if Marcus had not said a word and instead had punched him in the stomach. His face darkened from pale white to sickly gray. "I'm sorry, I thought you might be interested in viewing it," he said, reaching sheepishly to take back the mold.

But Marcus didn't let go. "Where did you say you got this?"

Peter explained that he lived on 33rd Street where, two weeks before, the police had found yet another wanted criminal beaten, bound, and barely alive. Marcus remembered reporting on it: a man with a warrant for killing a rival gang member was found in critical condition. Peter continued to explain that he had watched the police from his window and after they left he went down to the street with an idea. Earlier in the evening, a construction crew had poured concrete in the adjacent alley. Sure enough, he found three footprints leading into the alleyway. Two were partials, one was complete.

"So you made this yourself?" Marcus asked.

"Yes."

"Why?"

Peter shrugged. "I wanted to show it to you."

Marcus brought the mold closer and studied every contour, looking for any indication that it was not real, but it appeared to be a legitimate print. That it was the Kingfisher's print, he remained highly doubtful.

"How would you even know this is his? It's not like you saw him stepping into the alley, right?"

Peter mumbled something softly and then, louder, said, "Whose else could it be? It's huge. It was in the exact alley the cops found the criminal."

"I can't do anything with this." Marcus shrugged, handing it back to him. "That's not to say I don't believe what you're saying. It's just unverifiable. That's all."

A few days after his discovery of the footprint, Peter bought a police scanner and a Polaroid camera. On nights when he didn't have anything better to do, which was every night, he listened to the transmissions. Whenever a call came through that someone had reported a person bound on the sidewalk, he raced there on his bike. On the rare occasion that he beat the police to the scene, he began taking photographs of the criminal lying crippled and unconscious on the sidewalk. Sometimes, he later confessed to Marcus, they would come to consciousness while he was hovering over them, camera flashing. He said they would scream or cry at him to help them—they would threaten to kill him or they would tell him they had a family, a daughter, a son. They would stare into his eyes, hopeful for some small mercy. He said he ignored them, all of them. No matter what they said, no matter how they plead, no matter how they begged, he only took their picture and left before the cops descended on the site.

Marcus struggled to imagine it—this reticent, shame-faced kid who couldn't even meet Marcus's gaze somehow finding the brazen nerve to ignore sirens roaring down the street while he framed a bloodied face in a viewfinder. In fact, he wouldn't have believed it if Peter hadn't dropped by his office, wordlessly laying on the desk an arrangement of glossy photographs. They were actually incredible. Breathtaking in the literal sense of the word. The lighting was often naturally stark and dramatic, like a still from a film noir. Peter's framing was bizarre—sometimes the criminal was positioned on a diagonal vector, surrounded by negative space. Marcus wasn't sure in which direction the photographs were meant to be regarded, or if it even mattered.

He arranged with his editor at the *Inquisitor* to pay Peter on a photo-by-photo basis. When Marcus began running his stories alongside the photographs, paper sales skyrocketed even further. Even so, Peter never once shopped his photographs to the many competing newspapers, any of which would have offered him more money than the *Inquisitor* could afford. Marcus brought this up with Peter once out of curiosity.

"Why are you bringing these to me and not someone else? You're not stupid. You could get double what we're paying you from the *Tribune*. So why not go there?"

"Because you don't work at the *Tribune*."

"Then why me?"

"The Kingfisher trusts you to tell his story." Peter smiled. "I want to help you do that."

"And how do you know the Kingfisher trusts me? I've never so much as seen him."

He shrugged. "Because he hasn't stopped you."

9 OCCURRENCE

THE CHECK ENGINE LIGHT was on in Tillman's SUV, the glowing orange outline of an engine in some begging despair. She ignored it just as she had for the past month.

At all times, she kept it unlocked and parked outside her apartment, a purgatory of residential parking, in the hopes that some hurried thief would steal it. Insurance money was better than a busted-up vehicle she hardly ever drove anyway.

She opened the GPS on her phone and input the nearest of the two addresses Jeremiah had sent her. It was just a couple of miles south. The other one was in South Bend, Indiana, and she figured it would be wise to see if the car could make it three miles before she took it across state lines.

The car broke from the curb with a scraping yawn. An unshod horse whining across the road.

Before she'd left, she'd made her father a tuna fish sandwich. This would keep him occupied for at least an hour, seeing as how he spent most of the time studying the sandwich for imperfections, which he would announce into an empty room. But still, he ate the same tuna fish sandwich every day—had always eaten the same tuna fish sandwich every day. That tuna fish sandwich was a microcosm of the man who fussily ate it. He had immigrated to America as an architect when he was twenty-two years old. This was immediately after he had married her mother back in Haiti. For a short while, he worked for a small Chicago architectural firm in a position that was barely above that of an intern, and he quickly realized that there was little room for him to advance. It had nothing to do with qualifications; it had everything to do with being a black immigrant. To provide for his young family, he'd quit to work for the CTA, where he drove a bus, a job he'd rarely spoke of even when he had still been working. But Tillman imagined that he had enjoyed it, all things considered. It was steady, unchanging—both adjectives he considered to be the highest virtues. She could picture her father sitting on the elevated seat, steering wheel under his unyielding grip, circumnavigating Chicago with an impassive expression, staring out into the street. The sole consistent variable of an always evolving ecosystem. He brought tuna sandwiches in tin foil for his lunch breaks and he continued to eat them straight through retirement. How many presidents had come and gone while her father had eaten a single tuna sandwich for lunch?

She turned down the street, headed in the direction of Lake Shore Drive. Her GPS assured her—in a robotic woman's condescending voice—that Tillman would arrive at her location in seven minutes. She settled into her seat, feeling the cool kiss of the pistol in her waistband against her skin.

Her father would chastise her for having to use a GPS. He would tell her that the streets are not that complicated to navigate if you just pay attention.

The day her mother died, Tillman hurried through the hospital sliding doors. Her police uniform, combined with her frenzied sweep of her surroundings, elicited several curious, worried stares from the waiting room. Her father followed after her in his slow, unhurried pace. They had taken a cab to the hospital. All the way, her father asked her what had happened, where they were going, why they were in a cab. She told him she didn't know. But she did.

"There's been an occurrence," the doctor said to her when Tillman and her father found him standing in the hall, surrounded by nurses. Tillman told her father to go sit down in the waiting room while she spoke with the doctor.

Whenever she looked back on that nightmarish day, the detail that bothered her most was the doctor's use of the word *occurrence* because, as a name for what had happened, it was horribly inadequate, yet appro-priately banal in a way that made her physically ill. For countless nights afterward, whenever the word passed through her soundless mind, it seemed to jeer at her.

Occurrence. Occurrence. Occurrence.

Her mother had been shot three times. Once in the back, along the base of her spine, once in the right leg, and once in the chest. She would later bleed out during surgery. But she had not been the only one to die. Two other people were killed, three others wounded. The only common de-nominator between the victims was that they happened to be standing in line at a pharmacy on State Street, waiting on their prescriptions, when a man entered the lobby. He carried an assault rifle under his leather duster. He pointed it and immediately opened fire.

She arrived on the scene just moments after paramedics hurried the victims to the hospital. She kept the crowd on the street at bay while a forensics team hauled in their equipment. She hadn't known at the time that her mother was one of the victims en route to the hospital until she received the call from the doctor close to an hour later.

"There's been an occurrence."

There was a video of the whole thing captured on the security cam-eras. They would later play it on the nightly news over and over again until the beginning and end of the video bled into each other. The whole scene quick and quiet and granular and withholding. An occurrence for the world to watch. Her mother's sloped posture in the bottom left of the screen, grainy and soft. The glass doors sliding open, a shape emerging, noiseless chaos ensuing. Her mother's body spasmed gracefully, or so Till-man liked to think, and fell gently to the ground while lights flickered and shapes held still. Tillman watched the video on repeat. She memo-rized every detail, but what haunted her the most was not the visual of her mother collapsing beneath a bullet, but rather the moment when the shooter stopped firing. He stood about for a moment with bodies scat-tered around him and simply turned around. It was so casual, this mo-tion, as though he were resuming his day without interruption. And he exited the building into some anonymous oblivion where no one would ever find him.

And every time she watched the man exit those sliding doors, she prayed the next frame that she had seen a thousand times would reassemble into something that made sense—the man falling to his knees in remorse, the man shooting himself in the head, the man grabbed by a long-dead vigilante and thrown into traffic—but instead he simply walked away just as he had done a thousand times before. Justice deferred in the sunlight of an otherwise unextraordinary afternoon.

Her mother was in surgery all day. A few other cops dropped by to offer condolences and then lingered about uncertainly, all of them unsure of what else to say, how soon they could leave. Jeremiah brought her coffee and brought her father a bag of Hershey's Kisses. Jeremiah sat next to her, held her unfeeling hand. He didn't say a word, and she was thankful for this. Her father began peeling the Hershey's Kisses, shaping the foil into the likenesses of birds. He gave one to Tillman and one to Jeremiah. Jeremiah thanked him, pretending to make the bird fly, which made her father smile.

But for the most part, her father seemed lost in the hours in the waiting room, only occasionally leaning over to ask her when they were leaving this place. And Tillman could only manage to pat his hand and tell him they would leave soon. She wanted to tell him what had happened, why they were here. But his mind and memory were both deteriorating, and she had no control over what stuck and what slipped away. Maybe it was better this way.

By midnight, the doctor emerged from surgery. She rushed up to meet him. But before he even spoke a word, she knew as well as she had to that she was not going to leave the hospital with her mother.

When Tillman and her father entered the room, her mother's body was still hooked up to machines. Her dark skin appeared not lighter, but somehow thinner, as if one stray finger could peel her flesh from her face and reveal the skeleton beneath. But even worse, her hair was wild, unkempt. Her mother had always prided herself in her perfect presentation. Tillman tried to fix her mother's hair, coaxing it to lie flat against the pillow. She tried to remember the last conversation she'd had with her mother. It was a phone call the day before. Her mother often called once a day with some sort of complaint, often philosophical in nature, and thus completely outside of either of their control.

"Young kids on the upstairs, they have the music on loud. They think that they own the whole world, so they play their music so loud I cannot even think."

An occurrence.

Tillman sat next to her father in the hospital room and held his hand. He looked at his wife, stone-faced. His lips were trembling, as they sometimes did when he was straining for a lost thought. He simply stared. She wasn't sure if this was just her father being her father or if this was her new father, the one who spoke in monosyllables and listened to Al Green all day on a record player. And for a brief moment she envied him for the disease that removed him from the dull and dark hospital room and inserted him somewhere else. Somewhere far away, untouched and unanchored and drifting out to sea while squinting at a foggy shore.

Tillman parked the SUV down the block from the apartment building her GPS had led her to. She swiped her debit card through the electronic meter and added an hour. Longer than necessary, she hoped.

The man she was looking for was named Jeffrey Jenkins, but, according to Marcus Waters via Jeremiah, he went by the name of Penny.

"*Penny* like the coin," Jeremiah had said over the phone after he'd given her the addresses.

"Thanks for the clarification," she'd said.

From what Marcus had told Jeremiah, Penny had been a drug runner for some kingpin back in the '80s. The Kingfisher had busted up the guy, somehow saving Penny in the process. The details were unclear to Tillman, but then again, the details didn't matter for what she was doing. Either Penny was safe or he wasn't safe at all. It was a fairly binary situation she was entering.

Penny's apartment building was on the liminal orbit of the Back of the Yards. The building was rust-red, squatting into the earth. The inside of the building smelled like piss and bleach and vomit and Pine-Sol. Forest green walls, forest green carpet. Tillman passed up a flight of stairs and found apartment twelve—Penny's apartment—in the middle of the hall.

She knocked on the door, leaning in close to listen for footsteps or any other sign of life, but all she heard were the sounds of fighting coming from apartment thirteen. A man and a woman exchanging hostilities with the bored inflections of two people who did this sort of thing every day. A daily ritual of stabbing words into each other's skin like daggers.

Tillman raised her hand to knock again, but she heard the dead bolt turn. The door cracked open as far as the chain anchored to the wall would allow. A face appeared in the narrow void—a Latino man, lips held in a skeptical slant. He was young, maybe twenty or so. A tattoo of an eagle peeked out of his T-shirt, wings out, as though taking flight from his neck. His disheveled, bed-head hair shined in the light of a half-opened window behind him.

"What?" he asked.

She began to recite the reflexive identification of a police officer, but she stopped herself right away. An ex–drug runner, or maybe even a current drug runner, doesn't exactly seek out the company of police officers, and those with whom they surround themselves abide by a similar logic. Even if the person knocking is not technically a police officer. "I'm looking for Jeffrey Jenkins."

"You got the wrong place."

"Penny. I'm looking for Penny."

"Wrong place," he said and shut the door.

The dead bolt turned back into place.

Tillman knocked again. "Penny is in danger," she spoke into the door. "I need to talk to him."

A pause, followed by the slide of the dead bolt. Again, the door opened as far as the chain would allow.

"What kind of danger?" the guy asked. He spoke with a veneer of disinterest, but beneath it Tillman saw, or at least heard, a scant trace of something else.

"Is Penny home?"

He continued to study Tillman. His lips pursed, eyes darting back into the room. "You a cop?"

"I just need to speak with Penny."

"I asked if you were a cop," the guy said.

"I'm not a cop. I'm just looking for Penny."

The guy smiled, then nodded, his entire demeanor softening. "I didn't think you were, but you know what it is."

"Where is Penny?"

"What sort of trouble he get himself into this time?"

"I didn't say trouble. I said danger."

"Fine. What sort of danger?"

Tillman looked around the hall. No one, save for the voices of the arguing couple, who seemed to be acquiescing into apologies now. But still she felt vulnerable. "Can I come in?"

"If he owes you money, I'm not paying. You can take that up with him."

"He doesn't owe me money. I just need to speak with him."

"Well, he's not here."

"Then maybe you can tell me where I can find him. It's important."

The guy shut the door. Tillman thought it was for good this time. But then she heard the chain sliding off the door. The door reopened to the guy walking into the apartment, waving over his shoulder for Tillman to enter. "Close the door behind you," he called out. "And lock it, please. Lunatics in this building. They smell an open door."

The apartment reeked with the heavy dusk of cheap weed. A homemade gravity bong on the kitchen counter next to a half-pot of coffee. Tabloid magazines stacked like slanting obelisks. The TV was on in the living room, Jerry Springer offering his final thoughts on a woman who'd married her ex-husband's ex-step-brother's ex-fiancé. The guy plopped down on the couch and turned the volume down a notch or two. Tillman stood in the living room next to the TV. She didn't want to sit. Sitting invited a conversation, conversations took time, and time right now was a precious commodity. He caught her eyeing the bong on the counter.

"You want a hit or something? I'll key you up."

"No, thanks. Where's Penny?"

"I told you, he's not here," he replied.

The door into the bedroom was open. An unmade bed, sheets twisted and dripping to the floor.

"What's your name?" she asked.

"Ibrahim. Are you Penny's girlfriend or something?"

"No," Tillman said. She wasn't sure what she was in relation to Penny, or any of this, for that matter. "I know some people who are worried about him. I said I'd check up on him. It's a favor to a friend."

"A friend of Penny's?"

"Sure."

He stood up, lazily made his way to the water bong. "Now I know you're lying to me. Penny doesn't have friends. He's only got people he owes money to. That's probably who sent you looking for him. Paulina's always telling Penny they are going to come looking for him one of these days. They are going to send people like you to remind him. But Penny doesn't listen to her. Penny doesn't listen to anybody but Penny."

"Who's Paulina?"

"Penny's daughter," Ibrahim said before taking a long hit from the bong. He straightened up, releasing the smoke in a thin tendril. "But she's my girl. My *fiancée*." He pronounced the word with pride.

"So you and your fiancée live here with Penny?"

"No, no, no," coughing up the last of his hit. He pounded his chest and cleared his throat. "You got that backwards. *We* don't live with Penny. Penny lives with *us*. We're the ones who give him a place to stay. I got a full-time job working interstate construction. I make good money doing hard work. Bust my fucking body for a paycheck. But Penny? The man can't keep a job more than a few days. Paulina begs me to let him stay with us. I tell her, sure, a few days can't hurt. He's been living here for years now. You ever met Penny yourself?"

"No."

"That's good. He's like herpes. You can't get rid of him. You just have to hope he doesn't flare up." He smiled, pleased with the accuracy of his metaphor.

"Has Penny been here today?"

"No. But that's nothing new. He comes and goes. Probably spent the night facedown on a curb. But look, if he owes you or your boss some money, all I'm asking is you don't come around here looking for it. Penny's hardly ever here anyway. Shake him down somewhere else, OK? Don't kill the guy, but feel free to rough him up. Just don't do it here. This is my place."

"I'm not collecting."

"Yeah, yeah." He smiled. "You're worried he's in danger."

"Where's Paulina?"

"I don't know."

"I promise you I'm not looking to hurt her. Or Penny. I really need you to tell me the truth."

Ibrahim shook his head, scratched his stubble-lined cheek. "I'm telling you the truth. I don't know where she is. I'm betting Paulina met him last night for a drink at Lucky's. She always comes home right after work, but she didn't last night. But, see, Penny's always begging her to come have a drink with him. Probably felt it was time to give the devil his due, get him off her back for a while."

"You haven't heard from her at all today?"

"No. I been texting her all morning, but she hasn't said anything. Her phone probably died at the bar. She never charges it. Drives me fucking crazy."

Tillman nodded warily. "Do you think you could tell me where Lucky's is?"

"How about you tell me what's really going on?" he asked, apparently after sensing something wrong, some latent fear coming to life. "I don't like all these questions if I don't know what the fuck you're talking about. You keep talking about danger this and danger that. Just tell me what the hell is going on."

Tillman briefly debated what to share, what to withhold. But she ultimately decided she would share what little she knew, in hopes that he knew something she didn't know.

"Did you see the video that was released this morning?" Tillman asked. "The one about the Kingfisher?"

"On Twitter, sure. Why?"

"Did you recognize the hostage killed in the video?"

He seemed to think about this deeply, retracing the pixelated images. He was becoming more panicked, fidgeting with his fingers, as though playing some invisible instrument in his lap. His red, glazed eyes danced in their sockets. "No. I don't think so. Why? What's going on?"

"Are you aware that Penny used to run drugs? Maybe he still does?"

"He doesn't do that anymore. Or at least I don't think he does. Why does it matter?"

"The man killed in the video used to work with Penny. Years and years ago. They both were apparently saved by the Kingfisher."

"The fuck are you talking about?" he asked, not waiting for an answer. He smiled disbelievingly. "Penny never said anything about that. And trust me, Penny would have said something if he'd run into the Kingfisher. He'd never shut up about it. I can guarantee it."

"I don't care about the Kingfisher," Tillman said. "I care about finding Penny. Just because Penny's"—she searched for the word—"*associate* was a hostage doesn't mean that Penny is, too, but I just want to make sure he's safe. When did you last see them?"

"Them?"

"Penny and Paulina."

"Hold up. You think Paulina is in danger, too?"

"I'm just trying to cover bases. When did you last see them?"

"All right. I saw Penny,"—he thought about it for a while—"maybe two days ago. He came home to change clothes and take a shower and then he went back to Lucky's. And I saw Paulina yesterday morning. Before she left for work."

"Where does she work?"

"Mercy Hospital." And he added, proudly, "She's a CNA. Just got her degree."

"What time did her shift end last night?"

"She worked a twelve, so about nine, I guess." Ibrahim seemed to ball up, constricting against the weight of these questions, the subtext lingering beneath them. He was grabbing his hair with white knuckles, maybe just to hold on to something. "Are you trying to tell me that whoever killed that guy might kill Penny? He might have my girl, too?"

"I'm not saying that. Just being cautious is all."

Ibrahim nodded, breathing out deeply.

"I need some things from you," she said. "I need Penny's cell phone number, along with your fiancée's. I might try to get in touch with them myself. And while you're at it, give me some names of people I might want to talk to in order to get in touch with Penny. But if I were you, I'd also start trying to track them down yourself, because I have to go check up on someone else after this."

As he jotted down phone numbers and names on the back of an envelope, Tillman was suddenly reminded of a question she had meant to ask, more out of personal curiosity than anything else. "I take it the police haven't stopped by here today looking for Penny?"

Ibrahim shook his head, still scribbling. "Should I call them?"

"May not be a bad idea," she said. She wasn't at all surprised the cops hadn't shown up, but she wished she were. This only confirmed what she had already known—Stetson wasn't looking for the hostages. Or even if he was, he wasn't looking all that hard. "If you get in touch with the police, I'd just ask that you keep my visit between us."

He nodded automatically. "Sure."

Tillman left her number with him. But before she could leave, he

grabbed her elbow. She pulled away, but only to turn and find him looking at her with a pained expression, begging and unassuming. "Be straight
with me. Do you think Paulina is in trouble? I know you don't know for
sure, but just tell me what you think."

She ignored the question. Any answer could only lead to unnecessary
pain. "Give me a call if you find them," Tillman said over her shoulder as
she shut the door behind her.

She exited out into the hallway, which had fallen silent, save for the distant tremors of a subwoofer several stories overhead blasting techno
music. She took her phone from her pocket and texted Jeremiah an up-
date, as per his request: *No Penny. Talked to daughter's fiancé. Said he
hadn't seen either of them since yesterday.* And then she sent another: *No
cops dropped by. Going to check on Bedford.*

As she passed down the stairwell and back out onto the street, the sky
was drab with the cloak of a soon-to-be thunderstorm. She entered the
next address into her GPS and lit a cigarette. It felt magnificent to smoke
out in the open once again, instead of hiding on her fire escape from her
father. She nearly felt like a cop again. But as soon as she felt this, she
pushed the thought away. She wasn't a cop. Not right now and maybe not
anymore. She was a citizen doing what the cops should have been doing.

She got a reply from Jeremiah as she started the SUV: *Fucking Stetson.*
Followed by: *Keep me updated. Be careful with Bedford. Dude's got a long
rap sheet. I've got a bad feeling.*

10 QUEEN CLEOPATRA AND ANNABELLE LEE

WHEN WREN RETURNED TO THE APARTMENT after her shift at the bowling alley, Parker was seated in the same spot and same position as that morning—hunched over the couch, her laptop on her knees. The only change in the surroundings was a half-eaten Bowl-O'-Noodles between Parker's crossed legs. She stared into her laptop and acknowledged Wren's arrival with only a grunt. Either Parker was still upset with her for leaving that morning or she was too engrossed in her work. Or she was simply being herself. Parker had never been what Wren might call an "emotive" person, and she had learned that trying to read Parker's various and inscrutable emotional states was a certain brand of torture not worth the effort. Not like that ever stopped her, though.

Wren passed directly to their bedroom, where she stripped down to her underwear and lay down on the egg-crate mattress. The box fan hummed lazily in the window, joining the cadence of rain tapping at the glass.

She wanted to smoke a joint, or a few of them, but it was Parker's week to buy weed and she always procrastinated on these things.

"Guess today's a granny panty sort of day?"

Wren saw Parker leaning against the doorway, studying Wren's beige and ill-fitting underwear. Parker had a way of smirking without a detectable movement of her lips. It was a talent she brandished often.

"Shut up." Wren smiled. "It's a million degrees in here."

Parker cleared a space on the mattress and sat down beside Wren.

"I don't know if you saw this or not," she said. "I'm guessing you were busy doing whatever exactly it was that you do at that shitty bowling alley. But I wanted to let you know that the rest of us voted." She paused. "We're going to hack the CPD servers for the ME report. Tonight."

"Did you say *our* move?"

"We're a group, Wren. We voted."

"For a collective of anarchists, I'm a little confused by the sudden democratic logic."

"I know you don't want to do this." Parker spoke calmly, but without so much as a trace of apology. "We all know you're against it. You made yourself pretty clear on the thread. Very clear, actually. But still, we want your help. We *need* your help. We won't get within a mile of their servers without you. You know that. We need decryption. We need you."

Wren stared at her fingernail as though she had found something intensely interesting beneath it, but she still felt the weight of Parker's gaze.

"Are you going to say anything?" Parker asked. "We need you, Wren. Don't overthink this. We don't have time for you to overthink."

"I don't know," Wren mumbled. "It's just that I think we're making a huge mistake. We can't give that gunman what he wants. It's wrong."

"We would be saving those other hostages. How is it that wrong?"

"Because. It just is."

"Not good enough. Tell me how."

"When death becomes a means to an end"—she paused, searching for her thoughts—"there's no way back from that. We become just like them. Just like the gunman. Just like the police. We'd be compromising our morals and ethics and codes just to protect ourselves."

"We're not just protecting *ourselves*. We're protecting those hostages." Parker's rebuttals were always crisp, delivered with a confidence difficult to see beyond. "Because the police aren't doing it. They could deliver the ME report and put an end to this, but they aren't. They won't. They're going to let innocent people die just because they won't release some stupid file? If that's the case, someone needs to intervene, and we're the only ones capable of it. But we need your help."

It was only mid-afternoon, but Wren wanted to take a shower and feel the day slide from her skin, pool around her ankles, swirl down the drain, and flush out into the reservoir of everyone else's yesterday.

Parker reclined on the mattress. "We can't change the fact that someone died. It's tragic and sick. It fucking sucks. All of us agree on that. And we've condemned the video as a group on all of our social media accounts. But the truth is if the police won't find a way to fix this, then we need to be the ones to protect this city, to save those other hostages. We need to put an end to this. And the only way we can is to take the ME report. But it's going to be hard, even with all of us. The FBI is going to be monitoring the CPD servers like hawks. But we need to do it."

"Do what? Assist a murderer?"

Wren expected Parker to become angry, but she didn't. In fact, she only moved closer. "Here's how I see it. We can either sit back and allow the cops to decide what the public gets to see, which will result in who-knows-how-many more deaths, or we can take that report from them and put an end to this fucking violence. Neither option is perfect, obviously, but if we don't act at all, that's even worse. It's like what Marx says—"

"Oh God, please don't bring Marx into this."

She ignored Wren. "He says that morality evolves. The only thing that matters is the pursuit of the greater good. *This*"—she gestured around at nothing in particular, the closed space between them, the open space above them—"is the greater good. We'll still catch some shit for doing it, but it's for the best."

The rain quickened outside. A thunderclap long and far away, an echo of itself.

"You're pretending like the rest of the Liber-teens care about those hostages, Parker. You know they don't. They only care about taking down the police. They want anarchy. They don't care how it comes about. They just want to see it happen so that they can take credit for it. You know I'm right."

"So what?" Parker laughed dryly. "Intentions are useless. It's the end result that matters."

"You're contradicting yourself."

"I'm allowed to. It's the twenty-first century. We're living in new history. The whole thing is a fucking contradiction." She breathed in deeply, then lay down on the mattress with a long sigh. Her shirt crawled up her ribs. Her pierced belly button shined like a fishing lure in Wren's periphery. "Oh, before I forget." Parker nudged Wren and handed her a neatly rolled joint. "I called Bronze Eagle a few hours ago," she said, referencing Jack, their diabetic drug dealer who liked to use code names for himself and his clients. "He dropped off some supply. Said it's a new shipment. Supposed to be pretty good. But you know him. He doesn't even smoke the stuff. Makes him more paranoid than he already is."

Wren feared that taking the joint from Parker might be mistaken as a concession, so she refused until Parker said, "Relax, it isn't a bribe. Just take it. It's my week."

Wren lit the joint lying down. She passed it as she held the heavy smoke in her lungs.

"What was Jack's code name for you today?" Wren exhaled.

"Queen Cleopatra," Parker said, suppressing a smile. "When he got here he was looking around for you. I think he likes you, by the way. He asked where Annabelle Lee was. Tried to step inside the apartment and take a look around. Like he thought you were hiding around the corner."

"Annabelle Lee? Seriously?"

"I know. I was surprised he's literate, too. At least he's got that going for him."

Wren nodded as she exhaled a thick plume of smoke that hung delicately over the tips of their noses as they stared at the weathered ceiling.

"I thought it was a good name for you, actually. Annabelle Lee," she repeated, hanging on the name. "Oh, and he wore a trench coat. Like, a flasher's trench coat. I think he figured it made him look nondescript."

"Did you say anything about it?"

"I told him he looked like a flasher."

"That's good. He needed to hear that."

Back and forth they passed the smoldering joint until each inhalation burned the tips of their fingertips and tongues. Wren cracked open her window that faced a neighboring brick wall and threw the roach outside. It tumbled down the side of the building, a spinning orange ember, until it disappeared altogether.

"What if we could do something else?" Wren asked.

"About what?"

"I was putting the gunman's video through Pixie at work today, and I saw that one of the hostages has an engagement ring. Or at least I think it's an engagement ring. I was trying to match that woman hostage with women from the missing persons database. I'm still trying to narrow it down, but if we can get the list small enough, we could probably give the names to the police."

Parker groaned.

"Or, if we get the list small enough, we could even do it ourselves. We could get into their cell records like we did a few months ago with that congressman's aide. Where they've been, where they are. We might be able to identify and locate her that way."

Wren realized for the first time how close together their bodies were positioned. Their arms were touching. Parker's skin felt warm and electric. Wren's was goose-bumped, cold.

"Look, I'll help you try to identify your mystery woman if you agree to help with the ME hack later tonight," Parker said. "I think it'll be impossible to identify her, though. Not to mention that the FBI is probably trying to do the same exact thing."

"We're better than they are."

"I know that." Parker inched closer to Wren, then reached her arm beneath Wren's back and pulled her closer.

Wren felt her body relax, a disentangling of figurative and literal knots.

"Have I ever told you about when I came out to my parents?" Parker asked. She turned her head to meet Wren's semi-stoned, sea-squall gaze. Maybe it was the pot, but Parker's voice sounded far away, though not so far away that Wren didn't want to reach out and touch it, hold the words in her fingers like water. "My father, he told me, 'You have to do what you hope is the best.' It's sort of a beautiful thing to say, I think. Don't you?"

Wren shrugged. Even though she was lying down, her shoulders felt impossibly heavy.

"I know you, Wren." Parker said, her voice lower now. Close enough that Wren could feel her breath on her face. "And you know me. You know that I love how much you feel. You feel things deep down. But sometimes that can blind you. It messes with your judgment." Parker let a silent moment pass. "Is it weird if I say I'm actually really turned on by those granny panties?"

"Shut up."

Parker ran her fingers down Wren's thigh. "I'm deadly serious."

Wren pushed it away, playfully. She felt high. Her eyes were heavy, unfocused, struggling to make out the shapes and colors of Parker's face hovering above her own, shadowed and backlit by the desk lamp. Gentler than usual, gentler than ever. A frozen moment, crystallized and permanent. Parker's neon hair draped over Wren's face, and then her face coming closer and closer still. Lips parted, eyes closed. A kiss so soft Wren wasn't even sure it had happened at all.

"We're planning to execute the hack around nine o'clock," Parker said. "That's when we have the best shot at infiltrating their network." And then she added, consulting her phone for the time, "That gives us four hours to identify your mystery woman. Let's get to it."

Wren put on a pair of sweatpants and pulled her laptop out of her bag while Parker fetched her own. She sat back down on the mattress and waited for Parker. The fan spun in the rain-freckled window. A siren called out from far away, far enough to ignore, but Wren listened anyway. And she allowed herself, briefly, to slip into the high-pitched cry of a city drowning in its own miserable beauty and beautiful misery.

11 D-I-N

A TRIO OF MEN older than Marcus sat at the counter of the diner, marking their words with knotted fingers, their bombastic argument rising above the radio in the kitchen, which was broadcasting news coverage of the video from the morning. One of the men said in a voice meant for everyone to hear, "They're here somewhere among us. Sleeper cells of Mohammed."

The front windows of the diner were divided into four panels, with letters painted in thick, dripping red on each panel: D-I-N and then on the final panel: ER. The bottoms of each letter bled down to the window frame, and it had always been this way ever since the first day he'd walked past on the sidewalk, though this was the first time he had actually gone inside. Peter was the one to suggest it over the phone. Like so much of the city, this diner never seemed to Marcus like an actual place—a business where short-order cooks hollered out commands, where people spent a micro-fraction of their lives chewing an Italian beef sandwich. It seemed more like adjustable scenery, a one-dimensional movie-studio construction, where if you opened the door there wouldn't be anything beyond but a black, unlit space. But here he was, sitting in a booth, nursing a tepid cup of coffee and trying to peer through the glass panels for Peter to appear.

He had been hesitant to make the trip back into the city for the second time in one day. He was tired enough already, and he had a feeling like tomorrow might be longer. But he wasn't sure he'd ever get another chance to find out what had happened to Peter Richards.

After the Kingfisher died, Peter stopped dropping by the office altogether, and Marcus had no way of contacting him. He almost missed Peter's sporadic visits—welcomed distractions from his fifteen-, sixteen-hour workdays. In Peter, Marcus had found someone who understood the significance of what they were both doing, even though neither of them could articulate this significance in any coherent way. And it was surely because of this shared, ineffable understanding that Peter stopped visiting Marcus after the Kingfisher died. The only common bond between them was scattered in ashes across a frozen Lake Michigan.

When he began planning the book, he wanted to interview Peter. He looked up his name in the Chicago white pages, then sent a typewritten letter to every single Peter Richards he found. He had no reason to think that Peter was still in Chicago except that he knew he was. Peter Richards was the sort of person so fully engrained in the texture of this place that Marcus suspected he would literally dissolve if he were to step outside the city limits. After he sent the letters, Marcus awaited a response. Nothing. He was surprised at how much he was surprised.

He checked his watch. A quarter after four. The waitress came by to top off his coffee. She asked if he was expecting someone else, and he nodded, though he was beginning to wonder if Peter would show up at all.

The after-work crowd began shuffling in, ravenous and wild-eyed from long staring contests with computer monitors, their necks stiff from nodding in agreement with one another from across some oblong cherrywood table.

He envied them. When Marcus had returned from the north suburbs to the city for college, he found that nearly everyone he encountered carried with them a certain confidence of place that he himself no longer possessed. At best he could only ever mimic the effortless poise of a man smoking a cigarette out in the deep-bone cold of Chicago. He felt like every other living being out there in the expansive beyond, every wino passed out slumped in corners and every car passing by on the freeways, could see that he was too soft for the hard texture of this city. A tourist in citizen's clothes. Their eyes traced him and held him and disregarded him all in a single, weary blink.

He kept his eyes trained on the door, waiting for Peter, and when an ambling man with a heavy limp stopped next to the table, he did not immediately register his presence.

"Marcus," the man said.

Marcus looked up and couldn't catch the disbelieving sigh that crept from his mouth. Time had twisted Peter into a boardwalk caricature of himself. His once pin-straight posture had atrophied into a hunch, a sort of permanent shrug. His short, graying hair was retreating up his scalp. Fresh razor scars pockmarked his neck, his jawline. He wore a dirty brown turtleneck to cover what he could. It was Peter, Marcus knew, but not Peter as he had known him. This was someone else entirely, at least in appearance.

And Marcus feared Peter was thinking the same about him.

"Peter." Marcus swallowed, tried to offer a smile. "It's good to see you. It's been a minute."

Peter said, "You look more than a little shocked."

Marcus was relieved to hear that Peter's voice still possessed a childlike inflection, amazed to hear multisyllable words escaping his mouth.

"I didn't recognize you at first. That's all. Please, take a seat."

Peter lowered himself—slowly, gently—in the booth across from Marcus. Peter sighed once he was seated, slicking a few stray hairs from his forehead. "I'm not maybe as nimble as you remember." He patted his leg, as though this were the only surprise. "I normally use a cane. I would have used it to come here, but I'm self-conscious of it, I guess. It makes me feel conspicuous."

"Why would I care if you have a cane?"

"I'm fine without it for the most part. I just ignore the stares. Limping man on the sidewalk."

"I hardly noticed it."

"The thing I always liked about you, Marcus, is that you never lied to me. Don't start now."

"So then what happened?" Marcus pointed at Peter's leg.

"Had an accident some years ago," he said, his eyes shifting throughout the diner, taking it in piece by piece. "Doctors said I wouldn't ever walk again."

"And here you are."

"And here I am," he agreed, with a wavering smile. "To hell with those white coats."

Marcus noticed the measured space between them, comfortable and halfway familiar, the glossed table reflecting their changed faces.

"I was in a body cast for weeks." He removed his silverware from its napkin and studied the spoon as though it were an unearthed artifact. "I couldn't so much as turn my head. I had to lie there staring up. Only thing in sight was the crack along my hospital ceiling." Peter laughed. "It's really not all that funny, but to this day, I have dreams where I'm laying there in the hospital bed and the crack widens. Like I'm underground, frozen, and I can't move. It just all falls, the floor gives way, and then I wake up. Sweating and screaming and tumbling."

"I'm so sorry, Peter. That sounds horrible."

He shrugged it off. "It's better now. You survive these things."

"What are you up to these days?"

Peter hesitated and then smiled. "I'm a valet at a hotel garage. Parking cars that cost more than what I make in two years. Not exactly the dream, but it's something."

"Something's better than nothing." Marcus cringed at his platitude, but Peter didn't seem to be listening anyway. His roving eyes landed on his hands, where he tore at the straw wrapper with obsessive dedication. Marcus was glad to see that the years had not succeeded in changing this small part of Peter. The sudden singularity of focus, the dedicated thrust of attention into whatever task he had assigned undue meaning.

"How about you, Marcus? How are you?"

"I'm doing pretty well. I retired a few years ago—I don't know if you know that or not."

"I know," Peter said. "I noticed when your name stopped popping up in the *Inquisitor*. I canceled my subscription shortly after. It's just not the same as what it used to be. But you probably know that already. How's retirement?"

"It's a nice change of pace. I'm getting a lot of reading done. My kids bring the grandkids by about once a month or so. Other than that, I work in my garden. I relax."

"Really?"

"What?"

"I'm trying to imagine you relaxing, especially in a garden. I can't quite picture it."

Marcus smiled. "Relaxing may not be the right word for it. I guess I just try to take it easy these days. My wife passed a couple years ago, so things are quiet around the Waters residence. I try to respect that quiet with my own sort of quiet."

"But you also wrote the book, of course," Peter said. "The Kingfisher book."

"I did." Marcus nodded slowly, reminding himself that Peter was not the sort to offer condolences, even for a deceased spouse. "I sent you a letter, tried to get ahold of you for an interview, but I couldn't seem to get in touch. I at least would have liked to send you a copy."

"I read it," Peter said, still picking at the straw wrapper.

"Are you going to make me ask you what you thought?"

"It was good, Marcus." His eyes fixed on the small, balled-up particulates of the wrapper. "It was really good. I read it once and then again. Felt like I was back there. Back then. Felt like nothing had ever happened. Years hollowed out in the pages. Really good."

A grin flickered like a candle flame across Peter's face. Marcus was glad to see the effort at least, even if Peter was full of shit, which Marcus was almost certain he was.

"You don't have to say that if you don't mean it. I wouldn't care. You can tell me what you really think."

"I thought it had its issues."

Marcus was surprised at how much he did, in fact, care. "Like what?"

"I think your nostalgia for those years painted the Kingfisher a simple sort of way."

"I'm not nostalgic—"

"Don't get me wrong, Marcus. You accomplished what you set out to do. You covered how the Kingfisher did a whole lot of good for this city, lowering the crime rate and all. But he wasn't perfect. You know that as well as I do. He was—well—he was complicated."

"How do you mean?"

"For one thing, he killed some criminals who would have otherwise gotten five or ten years in prison."

"I mentioned that in the book."

"I know you did. But you didn't contextualize it." Peter began to animate, looking more and more like the Peter Marcus he had once known. "The fascinating thing about the Kingfisher was that he was fallible and made mistakes. No one knew why he was doing what he did. You made him out to be a superhero, but superheroes are horribly boring. Superheroes have unassailable motives. They fight unquestionably evil villains. They always win." Peter's thought seemed to drift away, but he snapped to attention. "No, the Kingfisher wasn't a superhero. He was much more than that. He was a mystery."

"I never once called him a superhero. I never used that word."

"You didn't, no." Peter paused, deflating with a breath. "But then again, you didn't have to."

The waitress came to the table and poured two coffees. Marcus placed his hand atop the mug and let the heat soak into his palm. "Why'd you call me today, Peter?"

Peter sighed. He shifted nervously in his seat and swept the pieces of wrapper into his hand and held them there. "I saw the video."

"You and the rest of the world."

"What the hell is happening, Marcus?" Peter shook his head, a vacancy in his eyes. "It feels like I woke up to a nightmare. A nightmare thirty years old."

"I know the feeling. I even got called down to the police department this morning. Doesn't seem real."

"Why'd they call you down there?"

"Police Chief Stetson wanted to talk. That's all. He asked me if I knew anything and if I'd ever heard of that particular conspiracy. That the police helped fake the Kingfisher's death and whatnot."

"What did you say?"

"What do you think? It was the first time I've heard anything like that. Total lunacy."

Peter nodded, his hands wrapped around his mug. "Lunacy is the right word for it. Anyone who knows anything about the Kingfisher knows that he's long gone."

"But now I have a policeman in my driveway, because they're worried I may be in danger. Just to come here I had to assure them I was coming back soon. And the cop had to stay there, seeing as how news vans are rolling up and down my street." Marcus felt the words burn as they came rapidly off his tongue. "There are journalists calling me nonstop. They all want to know if I think he could still be alive, and I can hear in their voice that they want him to still be alive. Not because they care about the Kingfisher, but because it would be a guaranteed three days' worth of material. They're not even asking about the hostages or the man who died. They just want to talk about the Kingfisher. They want to talk about the gunman. They'll squeeze every last ounce of intrigue from the story and then move on. It didn't used to be like that, you know. We saw things to the end. We covered the whole story." He stabbed his fingertip on the placemat as a punctuation mark.

Marcus felt embarrassed at this show of emotion, so he tried to smile, to play it all off. "It's just crazy," he said, shrugging. "It's making me crazy, too, I guess."

Peter stared into his coffee. "I just don't get it, Marcus. What's happening out there is evil. Pure evil. Makes me wish he really were still around. We could use him now more than ever. Even if it were just for a day."

They were quiet for a few moments. Uncomfortably so. Peter turned in his seat to follow Marcus's gaze outside, where storm clouds began to gather, the street shaded an industrial monochrome, gunmetal gray. Toxins, pollutants, and vapor rising off the lake.

"I'm guessing you didn't just want to meet with me to tell me you saw the video," Marcus said, cutting through whatever pretense still lingered between them. "So what's on your mind?"

Peter took a long drink of his coffee, some inner struggle playing out in a series of palsied twitches across his face. "That hostage in the video, Marcus. That hostage."

"What about him?"

"I know you interviewed him for the book." Peter said with glassy, downcast eyes. "Walter Williams."

Marcus lowered his voice and leaned across the table. "How do you know that?"

"Because I was the one that told Walter to call you. Three years ago or whenever it was, I was the one that gave him your number, Marcus."

"How did you know Walter?" Marcus stared back at him, struggling to make sense. "How did you even know I was writing the book?"

Peter sat back in his seat, crossed his arms, and then promptly unfolded them. He looked around at the other diners and then back at Marcus. "I got your letter a few years ago. About the book, the interview you wanted. I'm sorry I didn't respond. I just—I didn't want to get back into all that. I just didn't want to. I hope you can understand." He paused, took a deep breath. "But back then, back when I was still chasing the Kingfisher and taking those photographs, I showed up on a scene and met Walter Williams. It was after the same incident you wrote about for your book."

"You can't be serious."

But Peter continued. "Walter was the one who called the station after the Kingfisher beat the hell out of his boss—I don't remember the guy's name. Some major distributor operating nearly everything south of Halsted. But when the call came through dispatch, I caught it on my police scanner. I was down there in just a couple minutes. It wasn't far from where I was living."

"And you talked to Walter?"

"Just"—Peter held out a hand, which trembled like a tuning fork—"just listen, OK? When I arrived on the scene, I came through a busted back door just as the other guys were making scarce before the cops came. But Walter—he was sitting on the kitchen floor, keeping his boss's pulse, trying to keep him conscious. The kitchen was wrecked. Bullet casings everywhere. The kitchen table broken. I asked Walter what the hell had happened. I don't know why, but he started to tell me the whole thing. Like he was in a confessional or something. I tried to ask him some questions about it, and he gave me a few answers, but he was focused on keeping his boss alive."

"Why didn't you tell me about that night after it happened? I would have been able to write a story on it then."

"Walter asked me not to tell anybody. He begged me not to take pictures and not to tell anyone about it. I told him I wouldn't, and I guess I meant it. I couldn't bring myself to take a single photo."

"Why?"

Peter shrugged, looking over his shoulder at the wall. He bit his lip and then turned back. "He was scared, Marcus. Even after it was over. He was scared like I've never seen anyone be scared."

"Of what?"

Peter opened his hands, shrugged. "Anything, everything. He was probably worried that night would catch up to him one way or another. And now I guess it did."

Marcus rested his head in his hands. He imagined Walter Williams, standing in a bullet-stained room speaking with Peter Richards—the both of them thirty years younger. Marcus imagined the look on Walter's stunned face as it might have appeared to Peter, and it was the same face he had seen on the video. Vacant, sweating, pleading, and knowing. And perhaps Walter had known, those thirty years ago. Perhaps that night—staring down the barrel of Lawrence Tressy's gun, standing just feet away from the Kingfisher—he anticipated his death so thoroughly he caught an actual glimpse. Tied to a chair, staring into a camera, screaming into a rope between his teeth. Perhaps he had seen it and immediately dismissed it, because what else could he do?

"But here's the thing." Peter blinked rapidly, withdrawing deeper and deeper into memory. "I ran into him some years later. Walter. He was working at the hospital I was at after my accident. He'd cleaned himself up, gotten a nursing degree. Took me a while on the pain medication, but I eventually recognized him from that night. And he said he recognized me, too. We got to talking. Sort of like old friends. It sounds weird, but that's how it felt. Like we'd been through something together, the two of us." He wiped the corner of his eye with his thumb, catching a tear that hadn't fallen.

"Did you talk about that night with him?"

"Not really. He didn't like talking about it. We mostly talked about other things. Little things. He liked football, always wanted to talk about the Bears. He'd bring me milkshakes after his shift and we'd sit in that room. Me, staring up at the ceiling, and Walter feeding me a milkshake through a straw." Peter paused, his voice drifting, sliding from his teeth. "So when I got your letter a few years ago, I got ahold of Walter. I told him to call you and give you the details about that night. Figured I owed you that much."

"He didn't mention you when he and I met."

"I asked him not to. I'm sorry, Marcus, but I really just didn't want any part in all that. I hope you understand."

Marcus struggled to comprehend everything he was hearing. But what he struggled with the most was that Peter had been avoiding participating in the book. Of all the people Marcus had planned to interview a few years ago, he had assumed Peter would have been the most eager to tell his story.

"Anyway," Peter said, a rattle in his throat. He cleared it. "When I saw the video this morning, I knew right away this is all my fault. I shouldn't have told Walter to call you. I shouldn't have done that. It was stupid, Marcus." His voice was rising steadily, enough to attract the attention of nearby diners. "It was so fucking stupid. If I hadn't showed up that night or if I hadn't told him to call you maybe none of this would have happened." His eyes were blurry beneath a cloud of stagnant tears.

"This is not your fault," Marcus said sternly. "Forget the hypotheticals, Peter. They don't matter. You didn't do anything wrong. You couldn't have known."

Peter reached for a coffee-stained napkin and brought it to his eyes. "You asked me why I wanted to meet with you," he said, steadying his voice. "I didn't ask you here to talk about Walter. I would have just carried that guilt to my grave. But I'm worried about someone else who might be in danger. Someone that the Kingfisher may have saved."

"One of the other runners from that night? I've been worried about them, too."

Peter shook his head. "No, someone else. Someone who may have been very close to the Kingfisher."

"What do you mean 'close'? Who is it?"

"I'd rather show you."

"Show me?"

"Yeah. Do you mind taking a walk?"

"To where?"

"It isn't terribly far from here," Peter said, turning over his shoulder and looking out the window where the slate-gray clouds gathered like shadows. Thunder rolled outside. A lazy, lasting drawl across the misty hologram of a heavily trafficked street. "Did you bring an umbrella?"

Luckily, Marcus had brought an umbrella. He and Peter shared it as they exited the diner to the street, where a ghosting rain fell in intermittent sweeps.

It was early evening, but it may as well have been twilight. The same sort of dreamlike saturation to the surroundings. The indistinct edges of distant buildings blending into a one-dimensional tapestry. The living blur of a crowded sidewalk.

A group of school children passed before them in a cloud of light mist kicked up by passing cars. They wore checkered uniforms, black backpacks. They jostled quietly, shepherded by a Catholic nun who stood at the center of their formation like a tower, eyes swiveling along her periphery in a state of constant suspicion. Marcus assumed she was marching them to a cathedral down the block, one of those old structures that looked as though it were an extension of the earth itself, shaped by human hands.

"Can you at least tell me where we're going?" Marcus asked as they waited for the light to cross the intersection.

Peter didn't answer.

The rain continued to fall like a veil from which shapes of cars and bodies emerged slowly and never fully, ephemeral and atomized. An L thundered from down the street, screeching and squealing.

Marcus's doctor had told him a few years ago that he was developing arthritis in his knees and his elbows and even gave him some medicine to take each morning, but at the time Marcus considered arthritis to be one of those shadow diagnoses that drifts over a shifting pool of symptoms, a synonym for the body's gradual entropy. Now he felt the arthritis fully, a dull ache seeping through his skin and bones.

Peter walked a full step ahead of Marcus, turning his head over his shoulder once every so often, as though to make sure he was still there. Marcus saw for the first time the full extent of Peter's limp. His left foot never fully cleared the pavement and dragged with each labored step forward.

"It's just a few blocks away, really," Peter said each time they crossed another intersection. Tourists bumbled past on the sidewalks, trying to escape the rain. Their faces hid and shadowed beneath visors and baseball caps; on their shirts, ink drawings of the Sears Tower sprouted from the skyline in wispy strokes. They watched a limping Peter move toward them with expressions of amusement and pity intertwined into a grimace. Peter shrunk to fit through narrow openings between bodies.

"Let me get us a cab, Peter. This can't be good for your leg."

"No, no. We're close. Just a few blocks more. Just give me a second." He massaged his back with his fingers and stretched carefully, as if any sudden movement would snap him in half.

"We've been walking for a half hour."

"We're close."

They moved farther south, crossing the southern branch of the river. The sidewalks and streets thinned into husks of a metropolis, sparsely populated with a few evening wanderers in the distance. The bricks of the homes they passed became less and less pronounced until soon they were wandering through run-down concrete tenements on the edge of

Englewood, Marcus's childhood home. Prairie grass grew up miraculously from the sidewalk in long, heaving stalks. Kids screamed and chased after one another through alleyways, some barefoot, smiling at the cool cusp of a chilled rain falling on their foreheads. Marcus tried to orient himself, to recall where he was in relation to his childhood as though navigating through someone else's memory. But he felt lost. In every possible sense of the word. A tourist in citizen's clothes.

Peter turned sharply to a tenement building and walked up a concrete stoop. He swiveled around and made sure that Marcus had followed.

"This is it," he said, waving him up. His mouth opened and closed like a hooked fish as he caught his breath.

Inside the building, a stale smell of sawdust, vomit, pot smoke. Cellophane sheets hung at random, billowing in unseen drafts, revealing walls halfway torn down. Rusty nails littered the floor. The numbers on each apartment door followed an illogical arithmetic, scattered at random. 3, 15, 1, 28. The hallway was devoid of human presence save their own.

"It looks condemned," Marcus said. "Are you sure we can be in here?"

Peter shrugged and continued to the end of the hall. He stood before a door on the left side and waited until Marcus stood next to him. Peter was still catching his breath. His chest heaved. Sweat poured from his forehead. He massaged his limp leg with both hands.

"I never told you this, Marcus, but I traced the Kingfisher here once," he said in a whisper, half-apologetic. "I heard on the scanner that someone had reported seeing a man running on the rooftops along 64th. I was just a block away at the time, so I grabbed my bike and pedaled like hell. I arrived probably just a few minutes after the call."

"What'd you do?"

"I just stood out in the street out there." He pointed through the walls at the street beyond. "I wasn't sure if I'd missed him or if he'd gone somewhere else entirely. But I knew it was the Kingfisher that I was looking for. Who else would be running along the rooftops at midnight? And that's when I heard this sound. Loud. Really loud. Like two cymbals crashing together. So I followed the sound into an alley and saw a human-sized dent in a dumpster."

"When was this?"

Peter ignored the interruption. "All around the dumpster were footprints in the snow. The same size footprints from the mold I showed you once. I ran after the footprints, tracking them. The footprints led to another alley and disappeared beneath a window that leads into this apartment right here." He pointed at the door in front of him. "I knocked on the door. A woman answered. She asked me what I wanted, so I asked her if she had seen anyone around her apartment, but she said she was alone. I didn't know what to say, because we both knew she was lying. I could see it, and she wasn't trying to hide it. So I just sort of stood there until she closed the door on me."

"Why didn't you tell me after it happened?" Marcus asked. "I would have looked into it with you."

Peter stared at the apartment as though trying to see beyond not only the wooden door itself, but also the years that separated him from that night. "I planned on coming back here to look for him myself. I didn't think you'd be interested unless I had some sort of hard evidence."

Marcus wanted to take issue with this claim, but it wasn't worth it. "Did you ever come back?"

He nodded, "Almost every night."

"For how long?"

He shrugged. "Doesn't really matter. The woman who was living here never answered the door again."

"Who lives in the apartment now?" Marcus asked.

From down the hall, mariachi music began blasting through blown-out speakers.

"No one's home." Peter shook his head. "Not anymore. About ten years ago, I started to do some digging into who all had lived in this apartment. I pulled records, but the record-keeping on government housing is a shit-show. The last person to have a name on a lease here was a guy who I tracked to a graveyard in Southlawn. He may have moved in sometime after the woman I saw that night, or maybe even before. Hard to say."

"Did you ever find out who she was?"

"A few years back, I finally got in touch with the landlord and asked if he could give me a name, but he didn't know it. He was able to confirm that a woman lived here at the time that it happened. Red hair, just like I remember. I remember him implying that she was some sort of prostitute. Said she got creative when her rent came up short. That's about all he could say. I asked him if he ever saw a guy coming in through the window, but he didn't. Didn't seem too happy to hear that there might have been an additional tenant who wasn't paying rent."

A kid walked into the building and moved toward them as if he didn't see them, which maybe he didn't. Pressed pants, headphones slung around his neck like an ornament. Loud music spilled from his headphones and into the walls. Hip-hop, unmeasured beats and double-timed rhythm. He entered a door in the middle of the hall and shut it, locking it behind him.

"So you were still looking into the woman's identity just a few years ago?" Marcus asked, softer now. As though the walls were leaning in to listen. "Why?"

An expression crossed Peter's face, some sort of pained tremor. Marcus couldn't tell if it was his back, his leg, or something else altogether.

"I just wanted to know what I missed that day," he said quietly. "That's the only reason. I came so close once. I spent years living in that one moment, in the time it took that woman to close the door on me. I needed to know what I had missed, what she had known. But obviously, it didn't work out. So"—he held up his palms and gestured at the door—"here we are, I guess."

Marcus leaned against the wall and stared at the closed door before him. A breeze passed through the hall, the cellophane curtains rising, particulates of sawdust skittering across the bare cement floor. Peter slid against the wall into a crouching position, grimacing as he did so. With his free hand, he began to massage the small of his back.

Marcus imagined the Kingfisher—a moving shadow he had never seen—wandering this unlit shadowed space. He imagined the Kingfisher lying in a bed just beyond this door, listening to the hollow reverb of sirens from across the river, and maybe removing himself from whoever it was he was lying next to—lover or otherwise—walking out from this very hallway, and setting out into the night.

"What are we doing here, Peter?"

He wasn't sure Peter heard him, and he nearly forgot what he'd asked by the time Peter responded.

"We're here because he brought me here." Peter sighed contentedly, as if he'd said something that had pleasantly surprised him. "And whoever that woman was behind that door, she must have known the Kingfisher. She must have known him, Marcus. And if that guy in the video is killing people the Kingfisher saved, people whose names were never reported, he knows more about the Kingfisher than most people. Maybe even more than you and I. And for whatever reason, he believes the Kingfisher is still alive, and he's trying to taunt him. He's trying to draw him out of hiding." Peter stood up and moved in shuffling steps toward the building's exit. "We need to find her. The woman who lived here. We need to find her before he does."

"What if he's already found her?"

"I don't think he has."

"Why?"

"Because I think he would have shown her if he had her. If he thinks the Kingfisher is alive, he would have known she was important to him. And if he somehow knew about Walter, well, there's no reason to think he doesn't know about this woman."

"What about the other men who were with Walter that night? They're probably in danger, too."

"I know that," Peter said. "But what happens if he's already taken them? Who is he going to take next?"

12 JUNE 1981

OFFICER GREGORY STETSON thrived on the graveyard shift. The other cops complained about pulling midnight patrol—cruising through the streets bone-weary while the sky shifted from bleak nothingness to the Easter-egg strata of dawn—but these were the same cops who complained about everything.

Give those guys a Holy Bible, and they'll tell you the print is too small.

But what they didn't seem to recognize was that Chicago at twilight was a different world. A better world. When the tourists finally retreated back into their swanky hotels, when the hawkers packed up their wares, when the children acquiesced to their mother's calls for bed, Stetson was left with little more than static shadows on the sidewalks, and a sudden and real sense of the nothingness that surrounded him as he drove past the same old drunks prostrate in the gutters, muttering promises to themselves that tomorrow—*yes, tomorrow*—they would wake in the comfort of their beds next to someone who forgave them.

It was magical, all of it. And at this time of night, it was all for him.

He checked the time on the dash. Nearly three o'clock. Right now, Mindy would be asleep in their home in Chicago Heights, and she would be curled in the sheets as she chased whatever dreams came her way tonight. And when he was done with his shift, he would be home just in time to kiss his wife's sleeping head and lie next to her until her alarm clock sounded just fifteen minutes later. But this was enough. Mindy didn't complain. She understood that these things, these late nights, were investments in the future he dreamt of every waking day. She was good that way.

Stetson spotted something that did not belong, a spindly figure on the sidewalk. His headlights refracted from her ghost-pale arms sprouting from a tube top, the sequins on her skirt. Like a walking disco ball, this woman. Her bright red hair was curled in tight ringlets that jostled and bounced. He slowed down and drew the cruiser close to the curb, and he saw that her heels dangled in her left hand. In her right hand, she held a cigarette.

She turned over her shoulder, squinting in the headlights, and then turned back around. Uninterested.

He pulled up next to her and cranked the passenger-side window down. "Busy night?"

"I'm almost home, Officer," she said, striding forward in an easy glide.

He eased off the brake pedal to keep up with her. He called out the window, "Didn't answer my question."

"Have a good night, Officer." She waved.

"Shouldn't be walking home this late all by yourself. Don't you have a man to look after you?" He let the question hang out to dry before adding, "Maybe a pimp somewhere nearby?"

"I'm just a girl walking home. You don't know where I've been and you don't know where it is I'm going. Best we keep it that way. For your sake."

She was walking faster now. He tapped the accelerator to keep up with her.

"Tell you what." He leaned across the passenger seat as he drove. "I'm guessing if I search you, I find some serious cash," he said. "That might fill in the gaps for me as to where exactly you've been. It's what we might call *evidence*."

She laughed as she continued marching up the street, her heels clacking at her side. "You don't want to do that, Officer."

"And why is that, sweetheart?"

"It'd be a big mistake on your end."

"That so?"

She nodded, took a drag, kept walking.

He threw the car into park and got out, slamming the door shut behind him. "Get up against the wall," he said, pointing at the concrete side of a grocery store whose doors were shuttered with iron gates.

She sighed a cloud of smoke from her nostrils and put out the cigarette beneath her bare foot. "You sure about this? You still got a chance to turn tail and get the hell out of here. If you're not as dumb as you look, I'd suggest you do so. Never know who might be listening in."

"Up against the wall," he said louder. "I don't think your pimp is coming to your rescue anytime soon."

She laughed without making a sound as she folded her arms behind her back. He gripped her shoulders, pushed her closer to the wall, and began patting her down. His hands lingered over the fabric of her skirt. He dug his fingers into her narrow pockets and withdrew only a condom wrapper that he let fall to the sidewalk.

"If you're looking for the cash, you'll want to look up there, Officer." She nodded at her breasts and turned over her shoulder to face him directly. "In the bra. Don't you dare linger. That would be the end of you."

There was a challenge in her stare.

He reached over her shoulder, between her breasts. His fingers folded over a wad of cash. He withdrew it and held the fold of bills against the light. Fives and tens, the usual suspects. Crumpled and warm with sweat.

"Oh my God, would you look at that?" She did a little schoolgirl giggle. "You found my grocery money."

"This'll buy you a whole lot of groceries. What about the drugs?" he asked, looking back at the street, which remained empty. "I know some of your johns probably like to pay with dope. You don't tell me where you keep it, I'll have to look around myself."

"No drugs."

"Bullshit."

"Don't do this to yourself, Officer."

"I'm going to conduct a search."

"Yeah, you'll conduct a search all right."

"It's called being a good cop."

"And that's called an oxymoron. And that's what you are. An oxymoron."

He thrust her against the brick, one hand passing over her skirt while the other held her neck, the ligaments like harp strings in his fingers. "Tell me where you keep the dope," he breathed into her ear.

She whispered something, her voice muted by his fingers around her throat. He relaxed his grip enough for her to speak. "Don't make me do this to you," she said.

He tightened his grip again and pushed her face against the wall, his free hand checking her waistband for dope, his fingers grazing her bare and cold skin. He felt her pull away beneath him, breaking out of his grasp. He clutched at her tighter but it was too late. Her body twisted beneath his, a powerful torque of her hips, followed by blinding pain as she leveled a knee directly into his groin. His world went black and quiet and he collapsed to his knees. Coughing, whispering, praying to the sidewalk just below him, strands of spit dripping from the corners of his mouth as the known world spun around him like hands on a dizzied clock.

He regained his footing with lung-heaving coughs. "You just made a big mistake."

Surprisingly, she had not run. She stood before him, smiling. "I was about to say the same to you." She cupped her hands around her mouth and shouted, "Help!"

He grabbed her arms and jerked them violently behind her back. He heard a hollow pop—one or both of her shoulders having dislocated from the socket. A scream and cry escaped her clenched teeth. He slapped his handcuffs around her upended wrists, clicking the cuffs as tightly as he could until the metal bit into the skin. He pushed her forward, opened the back door of the cruiser, and jammed her into the back seat.

He looked out over the empty street. He gathered a few calming breaths before rounding the hood and lowering himself into the driver's seat. The station was only four blocks away. He would hover over her as she went through processing. All the street whores stuck to the same script. Their arresting officer tried to get *handsy* with them, they said. And when she would level this particular claim against him, he would laugh and nod at whatever poor soul was sitting at the front desk, and they would understand that this was just another lie among the countless lies they had heard already from the denizens of this otherwise wonderful city. And when she said it, it really would be a lie. Because he had only been doing his job. He was looking for money obtained illegally, he was searching for illegal drugs in the usual places. He was doing his job. He was a good cop.

"You sure fucked up," she said from the back seat in a sort of dazed singsong, a trilling laugh. "Yes, you sure fucked up."

"You can tell whatever story you want to tell," Stetson said, meeting her face in the rearview mirror. She was smiling back at him, head tilted. "But no matter what you say, doesn't change the fact you resisted arrest and assaulted an officer. You'll regret those theatrics when you're sitting in a cell. That'll give you some time to maybe reconsider your life decisions."

In response, she offered only noiseless laughter intermixed with pained whimpers as she shifted in the seat. "You're out of your fucking head if you think we're going to the station," she said between breaths before falling suddenly silent. She whispered, "Listen."

Stetson was just about to put the car in drive when a whistling came from the rooftops overhead. High-pitched, but expanding to a loud rushing wind and then growing into a roar. His first and only thought was of classroom lectures on Soviet missiles, the way they fall faster than sound can travel. So fast that death finds you first. And then came a crash. An impact against the sidewalk that shook the entire street. Stetson saw dust billowing from the broken concrete, wrapping around a dark shape at the center. But as the dust slowly cleared, the shape was gone.

"Took you long enough," the woman said from the back seat. Stetson understood, slowly, that she wasn't speaking to him.

His white knuckles gripped the steering wheel. He peeled one shaking hand off the wheel, fumbling with the keys in the ignition.

"Hey, Good Cop, you want some good advice?" the woman asked in a low voice. "Beg. He hates when they beg. Says it drives him crazy. He can't sleep at night when they beg."

A second. A silence. A footstep. By the time he understood who it was outside of the car, it was too late.

He had fucked up.

The driver's-side door exploded from its hinges, and Stetson saw it spin through the air like a Frisbee, colliding against a building across the street and chipping the brick wall. And then there were hands, rough and calloused, gripping his neck, lifting him easily from the car, dangling him over the sidewalk.

He leveled kicks at the shadowed man before him, but he felt his toes bend backward against this immovable force. So he grasped at the fingers tightening around his neck—each one hard and cold as stone—and tried to pry them away with all the strength he could summon, but they did not budge. They only constricted. Tighter and tighter. Stetson's vision went dark, the world narrowing into a single point somewhere beyond his reach.

"You shouldn't be here," the man said. His was a deep voice, but hollow. An echo of itself. Stetson prayed this voice—a distant bomb blast rising from a subaltern cave—wouldn't be the last thing he ever heard.

"Please," he managed to whisper, spit falling from his lips. "Please don't. Please. I beg you."

And then there was only empty space as he was thrown across the street. Sprawling, spinning, weightless. He collided with the pavement, a blur of arms and legs and grunts and cracked bones.

He rolled to a stop on the asphalt. There was a dull pain in his side that transformed immediately into an agony unlike anything he had known. A dagger digging deeper and deeper through his skin and tissue with each unlikely breath. He had broken a rib. Maybe two or three. With a hand, he felt the disconnected bones pressed against his skin like fingers meeting his own.

He lay motionless on his back. The night sky. Constellations, spinning, spinning. Circling like vultures waiting to descend.

He heard the thud of boots approaching. "You will let her go."

Stetson tried to stand, rising so far as his knees. But the rush of pain in his side knocked him back down. He fought tooth and nail for each poisoned breath. He tasted blood in his mouth.

"Let her go," the man was able to shout without raising his voice above a whisper.

"Who are you?" Stetson wheezed. But he already knew.

"Just let her go."

Stetson grasped for the ground beneath him, his fingernails scraping against the concrete. He tried, once more, to rise to his feet. And this time he did, fighting through the fire burning and spreading in his side. And through his watery gaze, Stetson saw him. A shadowed figure. The man from the newspapers, his name passed in exultant and clandestine whispers through the precinct. The Kingfisher.

He was not the giant that Stetson had pictured, but he was even more imposing than Stetson could possibly have imagined. Hulking shoulders, fists clenched, breathing from his nose like a rodeo bull. Stetson squinted to make out the man's face, but he couldn't. His features withdrew further the harder Stetson looked.

Stetson clutched more tightly at his ribs. He thought of Mindy asleep in their bed in their three-bedroom home where he would curl against her in the spare light of another morning and she would rise and he would sleep, just so, for those minutes in a state of unconscious togetherness, their dreams joined, momentarily, in the lax space between them.

Stetson looked at the cruiser. He saw the woman's face in the back seat, pressed against the window. She was smiling like she was watching her favorite movie in the back row of an empty theater.

"Why are you doing this for her?" Stetson asked.

"Just let her go."

"She's a street whore."

"Say that again."

"Since when do you save criminals?"

"She's not a criminal." The man stepped forward as though to grab Stetson, hurl him once more or otherwise snap his neck, but he stopped himself.

Stetson did not flinch. The pain and the delirium cohabitating Stetson's semi-broken body was all-consuming. "You love her? Is that what this is? Or is she just something to keep you warm?"

"Stop talking," the man said, his voice bending the space between them. "Just let her go right now."

"I'll tell you what," Stetson said, straightening up. Each word welcomed a fresh wave of torturous pain, but he forced himself to stand even taller, to look this shadowed man directly in his face the way his father had taught him to look into the face of fear. "I won't ever bother her again. And I'll even make sure no one at the precinct ever bothers her again. But only if we understand each other."

The man remained fixed. Waiting.

"I respect what you do," Stetson said. "We all do, all of us cops. Everyone in this city, except the low-down shit-bags you kick the shit out of."

"What do you want?" he asked sharply.

"I want you and I." Stetson gestured at the indeterminable space separating them. "I want us to work together. We can help each other. You know this."

"What do you mean?"

"I mean we help each other." He pretended to smile. "I have access that you need. I have information you want. You're looking for some bad guys to rough up? You must spend a lot of time looking around for the worst of the worst. The filth of Chicago. Well, shit, I can get my hands on a whole lot of names for you. More names than you'll know what to do with."

The Kingfisher shook his head, laughing. "I don't need your help."

"You don't understand. In the eyes of the law, you're a criminal. A vigilante. Most of us don't care because we see what you're doing, but others are playing by the book. I could keep them away."

"I'm not worried about them."

"What about your *friend* over there?" Stetson raised a weak arm and pointed at the woman, her face pressed against the car window. "Girl like that in her profession—it's a tough road. You going to rough up every cop that stops her? No, you can't do that since I'm guessing you have enough enemies as it is. Last thing you'd want is the cops on your back, not to mention hers."

The Kingfisher glanced back at the cruiser and then back at Stetson. He took a step forward. "Are you threatening her?"

"No," Stetson said, holding up his hands. "I'm just stating facts. But maybe if we work together, we can rearrange the facts a little bit. Maybe I make sure no one from the department gives her any more hassle and no one gives you hassle. Everyone wins."

"And what do you want from me?"

"Don't worry about me." Stetson clutched his ribs tighter. Cold sweat lined his lips. "I want what you want. I want to put away dangerous people. I want to help you."

To Stetson's surprise, the man laughed at this. Like a bass drum kicking in an empty room. "I knew you were full of shit."

"No, listen," Stetson said, clutching tighter at his side, trying to hold himself together. "You and I, we're cut from the same cloth. We love this city. I know you do. And me, I love this city more than life itself. I want to see it become what I know it can be. And I know you want that, too. Because we're cut from the same cloth."

"You don't know me."

"Christ," Stetson laughed, which made him wince, coughing between words. "This whole city knows you. But I know you better than they do."

"You don't know me," he insisted, louder this time. "Stop saying you do."

"We're cut from the same goddamned cloth. You and I, we care. We care about protecting those we love." Stetson nodded at the woman's face pressed ghostly against the glass, hanging on every muted word beyond her reach. Her eyes danced between the two of them. "See," Stetson said, daring a step forward. The Kingfisher didn't move. "You could have just taken her by now. You could have beaten me into the dirt. You could have ripped that back door and thrown it to the moon and back, but you didn't do it. Because you know that you need us, the police. Because you care about doing good. And you could use someone like me. You and I, we can do more good together than we can do alone. We can do something for this city for once. Something important. Something good."

Stetson saw the shadowed figure shift his step, weighing the proposition. "Why should I trust anything you're telling me? How do I know you're not setting me up?"

"Setting you up?" Stetson managed a pained smile. "Setting you up for what, exactly? Who in the hell could possibly hurt you? Who would ever want to try?" And then he added, lowering his voice into a register that seemed to him sincere, "I'll let her go. No questions asked. And you and I, we do something great. Because we care about this city. Because we're the good guys."

Stetson stepped forward on shaking legs and outstretched a hand.

But the man was looking at the back seat of the cruiser, his fingers rapidly curling and uncurling into fists. Stetson eyed them nervously, these weapons of war. From behind the cruiser window, the woman was looking back at the man. She touched her forehead to the glass and smiled at him, only him. And dawn was bleeding into the sky.

The man's fingers slowly relaxed.

He turned back to Stetson and took his hand, which Stetson hadn't realized he was still holding out.

"Now let her go," the man said. "And don't ever bother her again."

13 A CASTLE WITHIN A CASTLE

SHAFTS OF THE DAY'S LAST HOURS of light speared flakes of dust hanging frozen in the air. Wren and Parker sat next to each other on the mattress, both of them hunched over their laptops. Parker had approximated the height of the woman hostage, judging by the dimensions of the office chair, to be between five foot three and five foot five. In the meantime, Wren had created a makeshift algorithm to sort through the missing persons database. She input the height range, and the already-narrowed list narrowed to fifteen names. It was still too many, but it was close.

"We don't even know the woman in that video was reported missing." Parker rubbed her eyes. "It's not even been twenty-four hours, right? Would the cops post her info in that time?"

"We don't know how long she's been missing. We don't know much of anything."

"That's the problem, Wren. We don't know much of anything." Parker leaned back on the mattress, stretching her back against the wall. From overhead came the sounds of their upstairs neighbor's porn. A man exhaling nonsensical sounds while a woman shouted the name of God like some desert prophet. "Honestly," Parker said, "your—our—best bet is to get into each of the fifteen women's phones. We need their locations. You could do that easily. An SS7 hack. That's right up your alley."

"What would that accomplish?" Wren said, her voice soft but sharpened.

"Getting their locations wouldn't do anything. The gunman could be keeping her anywhere."

"You could search their individual metadata?"

"For what?" Wren asked, louder than she meant to. "You think the gunman was sending them pictures before he abducted them? You think he was texting them?"

"I'm just trying to help."

"I know," Wren sighed.

Both of their cell phones chimed at once. Parker pulled her phone from her bra. Her eyes widened and she brought the phone closer to her face. "Oh, fuck," she whispered.

"What is it?"

"We need to get on the forum."

"You said you'd help me identify the hostage. We're not finished."

"There's another video, Wren."

Someone had posted a link on the latest thread titled: "Second video." It led to a YouTube page where the user who had uploaded it had written in the description: THIS IS NOT MY VIDEO. FOUND IT ON REDDIT. ORIGINAL VIDEO DELETED. DON'T ARREST ME FBI PLZ N THANKS ☺

The upstairs porn stopped abruptly. And for the first time Wren could remember, the city lurking outside their bedroom window was silent. As though the entire world had stopped its spinning, bating its celestial breath.

Wren watched the video from behind the curtain of her fingers. But Parker leaned in close, observing each detail. It was the gunman. He stood perfectly still, head cocked to his shoulder. His Liber-teen mask shined in the swinging light overhead. Before him, another hostage struggled in an office chair. The gunman ripped the burlap sack from the hostage's head, revealing a Latino man. He had a black eye, and dried blood covered his nose, his jaw. His head rolled on his shoulders. Beaten to the cusp of consciousness. The gunman grabbed the man's thinning hair and held his head upright to face the camera.

"Turn it off," Wren whispered. "Please. We don't need to see this."

But Parker either didn't hear or didn't care. She only leaned in closer.

The gunman reached for his pistol, off camera, and brought it to the man's head. He held it there, pressed it tightly against the man's head.

And the whole time, the man's eyes opened and shut, opened and shut. His lips kept moving, without sound. For a moment, his briefly opened eyes landed directly on the camera, and he held Wren's relenting stare, as though he were looking into this exact room, speaking inaudibly to only her. Wren wanted to touch the screen, run her fingers across his serene and sweating face, and provide him with some false assurance that he was not alone.

"His time is running out," the gunman said in his digitally modulated growl. "I have waited patiently for you to turn over the medical examiner's report, Gregory Stetson. But still you have not done so, and I, along with the rest of the city, am growing impatient. We deserve to know what you have been hiding. And this man deserves not to die. You, Gregory Stetson, have until midnight to turn over the report and save his life. If you do not, he will die, and others will follow. Their blood is on your hands."

The gunman leaned forward, reaching out to the camera. He knocked it over on its side. The sideways frame showed the other hostage, bound to her chair. Twisting against the ropes. And the screen went dark.

Wren watched that black screen, waiting for it resolve into something she could forget.

"Fuck," Wren said. And then louder, "Fuck. Fuck. Fuck." She stood up, pacing the room, knotting her hair around her knuckles.

"Hey." Parker stood and grabbed Wren by the shoulders, her fingertips warm against Wren's cold skin. "That hostage still has a chance. We can help."

"It doesn't matter what we do. He'll kill him. And then he'll kill her."

"Not if he gets the ME report. That's all he wants. You heard him. We can save both of those hostages."

Wren broke away from Parker's hold and leaned against the wall. Her legs felt numb. She slid to the ground, put her head between her knees.

The box fan in the window whined into the room. Its oscillation was infuriating. It was all Wren could hear. It grew louder and louder. Wren leaned over and ripped it from the window frame. She threw it across the room.

Parker squatted in front of her, grabbing her face. She waited until Wren returned her stare to speak. "We need to act right now. The police aren't going to bend. That man in that video is going to die if we don't do something. So will the woman you are looking for. We need to act."

"Just please stop talking," Wren said.

She closed her eyes, but saw only the hostage's face materializing in the total dark. Bruised and bloodied. Shifting dimensions, disappearing and reappearing. His eyes rolling around in his head, as though searching the dark for something or anything, someone or anyone.

Wren opened her eyes. Parker was still there in front of Wren, her warm hands pressed against her cheeks.

Wren nodded. "OK."

"Good. I'll get everyone mobilized on the forum. They should be ready to go in soon, though."

"No, let's go right now." Wren stood up shakily. She sat down on the mattress with her laptop.

"What?"

"Do we have network range info for the CPD network?"

"JackoByte did recon on all that earlier, but—"

"Send it to me."

"Just give me a fucking second, Wren." Parker opened her laptop. "I need to let everyone know we're going in now."

"No," Wren said sternly. "Don't."

"Don't what?"

"Don't tell them. Let's do this just you and I."

Parker stopped typing, faced Wren with a look that vacillated between disbelief and laughter. "Are you still stoned?" Parker asked. "It would be suicide to do this hack with just two people. The FBI cybersecurity team is going to be patrolling the servers now more than ever. We need all hands on deck, and we still have time to gather everyone."

"This isn't about time."

"Then maybe you could tell me what this is about then, because I'm at a total fucking loss over here."

"I would just be more comfortable if it was you and I," Wren said, hearing her words trail off into the promise of some further explanation, which she struggled to offer. "We don't know who the other Liber-teens are. It's not impossible that someone . . ." But she didn't finish her thought.

If ever a stare could possess enough energy to burn skin, Parker's did so now. "You think a Liber-teen has something to do with this?" Wren tried to shrug, but only managed to lift her eyebrows.

"I can't believe this." Parker shook her head, biting her lip.

"If a Liber-teen is behind the video, then that person could be using us to hack into the CPD computers. Who knows what they would take once we're inside? We may just be their Trojan horse, Parker. They would have unlimited access to insane amounts of data on not only the police, but also citizens. Don't you understand how dangerous that would be?"

"You're being so fucking paranoid, Wren."

"Maybe I am. But who cares? Let's do this together. Let's hack the CPD servers and take the Kingfisher file and only the Kingfisher file. We'll do exactly what the Liber-teens voted to do, but just ourselves."

Parker was shaking her head. "You're not fucking listening—we can't do it ourselves. The FBI is anticipating an attack. They'll have the network protected like a fucking castle within a castle. The Kingfisher files were probably already buried deep. They'll be deeper now. The FBI isn't fucking around here, Wren."

"We're better than they are."

"I know, but—"

"Just send me the recon info. We have some time to test their firewalls and see what we're up against. Let's not waste any more time."

"You really think we can do it?" Parker's skin glowed iridescent blue in the light from her laptop. Wren wondered if, were she to reach out and touch her finger to Parker's skin, her fingers might meet nothing but the electric glow.

"Yes. We can do it."

"This is reckless as hell," Parker said, a smile warming on her face, or at least something resembling a smile. "But I'd be lying if I said I didn't kind of love it." She turned back to her laptop. "All right. I just sent you the network range info. According to JackoByte's recon, the CPD last updated their servers a month ago. But obviously, the feds will have done some remodeling recently. We can poke around for a soft spot, but I'm guessing we'll have to jackhammer the firewalls. It'll sound the alarm. But once we're inside, that's your game, because the file is going to be stashed beneath layers of encryption. I can hopefully volley some attacks to keep the system distracted, but not for very long. Assuming we even manage to get through the firewall, I'd give us about a two-minute window to get the shit and get out. Any more than that, and we're fish in a federal barrel. That means you'll need your decryption algorithms on hand and ready to deploy for when we're inside. Obviously you'll have to adapt them, but we don't need you wasting time writing code. You'll have two minutes total, not a second more."

"That's fine," Wren said. "I can do that."

Parker leaned over and kissed her—deeply, shortly, infinitely. "Look at us. The twenty-first century's Bonnie and Clyde." She touched Wren's jaw and dragged her thumb across her lips.

"That's not the greatest metaphor."

"Shut up. If we pull this off, we'll be legends. Now let's show these assholes who's really in control."

14 GUN DRAWN

THE AREA OF INDIANA where Baxter Bedford lived, though just a short sprint south of the same Lake Michigan that Tillman ran alongside every morning, felt like a different world altogether. All cornfields and silos. Sun setting overhead in no apparent hurry. Rusted tractors parked in driveways next to modest farmhouses with blue-painted windowsills.

Something torn from another century and placed abruptly within this disinterested millennium.

Her phone's GPS directed her down a gravel road and into a prairie surrounded by run-down town houses that were scattered on either side. On the perimeter of the prairie grass, far in the distance, enormous smoke stacks spewed forth clouds of white smoke that glowed eerily in the pastel clouds, diffusing into the air.

Bedford's address was at the end of the gravel road. A gray-yellow, jaundiced building, windows dark. The architectural equivalent of a dying breath. She double-checked the address, the numbers on the mailbox. She had arrived.

She parked a few doors down and scanned the rest of the street. There was no one in sight. Just two or three basketball hoops hung precipitously over gravel driveways. In front of each town house, grass grew knee-high and, with each breeze, it lapped like ocean waves.

She checked her phone. A text from Jeremiah from an hour before.

Second video released. Demands ME report, says he'll kill another hostage by midnight. Sending you a link.

She read the message again, wanting to feel surprised, shocked, disgusted. But all she felt was the absence of feeling. Jeremiah texted her a final time—a link to the second video. Her thumb hovered over it, but remained there, unable or unwilling to make contact, to make it real.

Tillman got out of her car and approached the front door, practicing the script she had prepared. "Sorry to bother you, but I'm just wondering—"

But before she could even reach the front step, an enormous, rasping bark erupted behind the door. A dog jumping and clawing, rattling the hinges, alarming whoever was inside the home to Tillman's presence.

Pure reflex, she drew the gun from behind her back, trying to keep it shielded out of sight behind her thigh.

As quickly as it began, the barking stopped, but she could sense someone behind the door. A waiting presence. She was aware of herself being watched in the last light of day. She considered turning around slowly and calmly, walking—no, running—back to the SUV. She could put this all behind her, watch it fade in her rearview, disappear into the literal sunset. She could be back in Chicago in two hours. She could write this off as some fever dream.

But instead she called out in a cool, tempered voice, "Hello?"

She felt her gun cold in her shaking hands.

"I'm sorry to bother you." She swallowed. "I'm passing through with a few questions."

She knew it wasn't the right thing to say. Knew it as she said it. She tried to collect herself, push the panic welling in her gut down into her concrete feet. She turned and looked around at the other buildings for someone in case this went south, but there was no one. She felt suddenly vulnerable, alone, and it came through in her voice.

"Mr. Bedford?" she called out.

From behind the door, a brassy voice. "Put the gun down." Like a voice from the heavens reaching down from parted clouds.

Her fingers curled tightly around the pistol's grip until it felt like an extension of her skin. She could not have put it down even if she wanted to.

The voice said, "Toss that gun over here, take a step back, and get down flat on your stomach. Don't make me wait."

She remained frozen, hundreds of instincts colliding all at once. They told her—a symphony—to remain calm, to panic, to run, to stay, to shoot, to beg, to fall to the ground and kiss the sleeping earth.

"The gun," he said. "Toss it over here now."

But she didn't. She raised her weapon to the door.

"Come out with your hands up," she shouted.

A sudden shift in the world, an electric current running through the air, the fast release of adrenaline into her veins like ice water.

Click.

She dove away from the door. A loud gunshot entered the evening and hung there. Deafening static rang in both ears as she collapsed to the grass, rolling onto a knee and swinging her gun at the door, which now sported a bullet hole at eye level. From inside the house she heard loud, ungainly footsteps running up a flight of stairs. She regained her footing and charged at the door, lowering her shoulder.

The door swung back on its hinges.

Gun at hand, she swept inside the doorway. To her left, a messy yellow kitchen with dirty dishes piled in the sink, fast-food wrappers on the counter. To her right, a living room with a couch and nothing else. Walls bare, cream white. Newspapers gathered in random, slanting stacks. A stairway directly in front of her. She stepped inside to follow after him, whoever this really was, but at that moment she heard heavy galloping from the hall, claws clicking against linoleum. And with her gun cocked and pointed, she saw from her periphery the figure of an enormous, hulking dog bounding toward her, teeth bared. She stepped back and grasped for the door handle, pulling it closed behind her. Even though she had busted the lock when she kicked in the door, the door miraculously shut. She felt the dog throw itself against the wooden barrier. Barking, scratching, howling.

She rushed to the side of the town house, lowering into a crouch as she passed unlit windows. In the backyard, rusted lawn furniture was scattered about the overgrown and unkempt lawn. With her back to the siding, Tillman craned her neck to peek into the back window. A bedroom—messy sheets atop a twin-sized mattress. But she saw no other movement. Whoever it was inside, he was upstairs.

She took one hand from the gun and patted her pockets for her phone, but she felt nothing. She cursed herself under her breath.

She breathed in through her nose, tried to calm down. Her mind raced through her remaining options, chief among them making her way back to the SUV long enough to call the local police station for emergency assistance. She did not deliberate for long. After a few steadying seconds, she was running back to the front of the house. Her back to the wall, gun raised and ready.

She took off from the protection of the house at a dead sprint, focusing all of her attention on the SUV, its promise of safety, as she glided over the lawn in long strides. The wind whistled in her ears.

Midway to the SUV, a voice rang out from a window overhead. "Stop now or I shoot." It possessed a textural grit and confidence of the moment that brought her to a dead stop. She raised her hands above her head and began to turn around in slow, deliberate steps.

"No, don't move," he called out. "Drop your gun and stay right there. I'll kill you right now if you move another inch. Don't test me."

She let the gun fall from her fingers and closed her eyes. Curiously, she wasn't afraid; she was only wondering what would it feel like. Death. Would it happen very fast or very slowly? So slowly that she would have time to realize how slowly it was occurring? An occurrence here and not here, there and then.

But there was no bullet through her chest. Just the same hardened voice, now laced with annoyance. "What the fuck are you doing rolling up on me like this?" the man called out. "Who are you?"

She began to turn her head to answer, but the man in the window made a halting noise, a chain-gun stutter in his throat.

"My name is Officer Lucinda Tillman," she said.

"Officer?" He sounded surprised.

"I'm with the Chicago Police Department." It was a lie, but with a gun aimed at her back, she felt justified. Her only remaining hope was that he wouldn't kill a police officer.

"Chicago? What in God's name are you doing out here? Running up on me like that?"

He sounded more confused than upset, though he was undoubtedly upset.

"Welfare check. We have reason to believe you might be in danger."

"So you roll up here with your gun in hand?"

She repeated herself. "It's just a simple welfare check. We're checking up on you. That's all."

He didn't say anything. In the air, she could taste and smell the industrial smog from the liminal smokestacks on the dark horizon. It was musty, oxidized. Like licking a frying pan.

"Well, looks like I'm just fine. So you can leave."

She considered it. Turning the keys, driving off into the sunset while the adrenaline waned and a waxing moon rose. Arriving back in Chicago in time to drop by the bar that Penny supposedly frequented—Lucky's—with time to spare to get home and take her father to his bed. But at what cost?

"I need to speak with you," she said. "Ask you a few questions. I won't take much of your time."

"You want to talk?" he laughed. "You just rolled up on me with a gun drawn. Doesn't put me in a talkative mood. How about you show me some identification, Officer."

"I don't have it with me."

"Well, then," he said. "How about I call the real police? Let them sort through this."

"It's about the Kingfisher," she announced, and only after she said it did she realize the risk she was taking. She continued. "I have some questions I need answered from you, Mr. Bedford. That's all."

The pause that followed lasted long enough for her arms to begin to ache as she held them upright.

"Turn around," he said.

She saw a .30-06 rifle barrel protruding from a window on the upper floor. She felt its insistent stare on her gut.

"A few minutes, Mr. Bedford. That's all I need."

"I don't think you're exactly in the position to be making demands," he said.

"Please."

"You said this is about the Kingfisher? I can't imagine what the hell is so important about all that."

"Then let me explain."

Slowly, the rifle disappeared from the window ledge. "Stay right where you are." She heard footsteps descending creaking stairs, and a few moments later the front door opened to Baxter Bedford studying the busted lock, the bullet hole. "Jesus Almighty. This is a brand new door."

15 .EXE

IT'S ALL MUSIC AND RHYTHM, improvised algorithms and premeditated scripts. The atonal patterns of network chatter, keyboards clacking. It's magic in each stroke of your finger. Entire worlds imagined and forgotten, created and destroyed. Wren is reminded during hacks of the descriptive truth of the word *cyberspace*. Ordinarily, the impact of the word eludes her, its stunning banality in the twenty-first century. But during a hack, she realizes that it perfectly describes the digital world, a physical dimension of cybernetic architecture coexisting not-so-peacefully beneath the holographic veneer of everyday life.

She hears Parker, vaguely, a voice submerging to meet Wren at whatever depth to which she has descended. "Holy shit. We're inside. You've got two minutes. Not a second longer. In and out, Wren."

And the rest of the world—the physical world of trains, lovers holding lovers' hands, and buildings grown from the earth—is something Wren remembers only in theory as real numbers scroll through her open eyes. This is the only world that matters, that ever mattered, that ever will matter. A landscape of information, corollaries, data—this is the physical world refined into the purest possible version of itself. And before Wren now are files, listed in haphazard and nonsensical orders. There are layers of firewalls accompanying each file, and her steeled fingers move on their own as she pushes deeper, digging into the center of something so vast and layered she realizes it was hidden for a reason. Some leviathan caged in the depths.

"A minute and a half, Wren."

She passes through the interior of the network, marveling at the ordained chaos of the numbers, the sequences, the purposeful mess before her eyes. Whoever had done this had done so recently, masterfully. It is almost beautiful, the bedlam before her unblinking eyes.

"A minute. Get the file and get the fuck out."

This should frighten her, but nothing frightened her in cyberspace. She runs decryption on the files, but they remain obdurately inaccessible. They must have been locked down several times over. To open any of them, she would have to perform individual decryption, but there isn't time for that.

"Forty-five seconds, Wren."

She is able to organize the spread of coded files by their updates. She locates the five most recently updated files and ran manual decryption through her improvised algorithm. It's a last-ditch effort, but so is everything else.

"Thirty seconds."

The files rearrange before her. Wren opens an archived file. At the top of the page she locates the words *ME Report #24447* and retrieves the file without a second thought.

"Fifteen seconds. Get out, Wren. File or no file. Just get the hell out."

But she notices another file, updated at the same time as the previous one. She opens it. It is a letter. The subject line reads: "Detective Gregory Stetson Inquiry." She does do not know what it is, but it is hers now.

"Five seconds, we're done. Get the fuck out, Wren."

She backs quickly out of the server like a body floating from the pressured depths to the surface of a storm. Fingers moving against the keys, separate from her body. And cyberspace dissipates into a dream, and there is only the physical world before her now, all shape and sound, blur and dream.

She is back in her quiet apartment, joined to her flesh and bones, seated cross-legged on a couch next to a cracked window. Staring ahead. Rubbing her tired and disbelieving eyes. Waiting for the room, the walls, the face of the woman she loved whom she believed or trusted or hoped was looking back at her, to sharpen into something she could call focus.

"Jesus Christ." Parker lay back on the mattress. She was breathing as though she'd just run a marathon. "I can't believe we actually got in. It doesn't even matter that we didn't get the file, that was some seriously impressive shit."

"I got it."

Parker shot up. "You're shitting me, right?"

The room was still distorted around Wren. As if the world around her were melting like a Dali painting. She felt detached from it all, an observer from another time, another dimension. A spectator to the end of something.

"I got it," she repeated.

"Oh my God." Parker laughed. She stood up and punched the air in front of her in celebration. "The others aren't going to believe this shit. We just single-handedly kicked the entire FBI cybersecurity team in the balls. This is the stuff of legend. Holy shit. I can't believe it."

"I got it."

"You're a freak, Wren. A beautiful fucking freak."

"I got it."

Parker pulled Wren into her, her hands running along her spine, pulling at her skin. But Wren didn't feel it, any of it. Because when she closed her eyes, she was somewhere else entirely. A dream world of numbers, a world of codes and algorithms—things that don't change, things that you can always control. Images were passing by that couldn't be real, only simulations, but she reached a hand out and found her fingers meeting warm skin, something real, something here in front of her.

16 "UNKNOWN"

MARCUS WATERS WAS KNEELING in his garden, plucking weeds, or at least what looked like weeds in the light from the half-moon. He hadn't thought to change out of his chinos and his collared shirt, both of which were now covered in topsoil. But he didn't notice this. He focused all of his attention on the small green sprouts alongside his tomatoes, his cucumbers. It felt almost good to invest his attention fully in this mindless and unnecessary task.

After parting ways with Peter, Marcus had arrived home to a cascade of news vans lingering about his street. As he pulled in to his driveway, passing Jeremiah's cruiser, the vans broke formation. Reporters and cameramen jumped from sliding doors like paratroopers from the belly of a plane, microphones extended for a sound bite. "Mr. Waters, did you see the latest video?" Another, "Mr. Waters, do you believe the Kingfisher is still alive?" Another, "Mr. Waters, do you think Gregory Stetson should release the ME report?" As the garage door shut behind him, he heard Jeremiah shouting at the hungry masses, "Get back. Nope, nope. Get back. I swear to God, get back."

He immediately turned on his television. Another video, this time depicting a hostage Marcus didn't recognize, but he hadn't expected to. It could be Jeffrey Jenkins, Baxter Bedford, or some other poor soul altogether. But whoever he was, he was still alive, for the time being. And that was something, a small something. He thought of what Peter had revealed to him—the mystery woman who might have known the Kingfisher. But whoever she was, Marcus had no way of finding her. There was nothing to be done.

So he had turned off his television, gone to his garden, knelt in the dirt, and begun plucking weeds. Or at least what looked like weeds. A half-moon risen. A day ending.

After his legs began to ache, he returned inside and drank a glass of water. He searched his refrigerator for a beer. He wasn't much of a drinker, never had quite gotten used to the taste. But he wasn't concerned about the taste right now.

He found a Budweiser his son had left behind after his most recent visit. He sat down in the living room, the chilled glass bottle pressed into his dirty palm, and opened his never-to-be-finished crossword. He stared at the clues and tried to remember characters from television shows he had never seen, song lyrics he had never heard.

He didn't realize his television was on until a fanfare of trumpets announced more breaking news. Marcus gripped the bottle tighter.

The newscaster spoke hurriedly, off-prompter. "We have just found out that the supposed ME report of the Kingfisher has been released through the Liber-teen Twitter account just minutes ago. Right now, we are attempting to verify the authenticity of this document, and we are awaiting a statement from police spokespersons, but we have decided to show it, with the understanding that it has not yet been verified. We ask that our viewers keep this in mind."

The television broadcast an image of the document. Marcus turned up the volume, as though this would sharpen his eyesight. But from the first, blurry glance, it looked like the few other ME reports he had seen before. He noticed the Cook County insignia at the top of the typewritten page. At the very least, it bore the signs of legitimacy.

The newscaster said, "Notice at the top of the page, the date matches with the date the Kingfisher's body was reported found in the Chicago River—January 4, 1984. And here in the middle of the page, where the medical examiner of Cook Country was prompted to write out a cause of death and a manner of death. The cause of death referring, I'm told, to how the person died, and the manner of death being whether or not it was a homicide, a suicide, et cetera. You can see that next to each item the medical examiner wrote—and this is of particular interest, considering recent claims from the Chicago police chief—*Unknown*. Again, we are not able to verify this document at this time, but if this is in fact the actual ME report of the body claimed to be the Kingfisher, it may contradict previous statements made by the police. We are still waiting for their response to this latest development."

Marcus dug his phone from his pocket. He wanted to call his daughter, Lisa. He wanted to hear her voice, soft and unchanged, through the speaker. He wanted to ask her mundane questions that would fill the moment unfurling before him.

"And here," the reporter continued, "at the bottom of the report. It's very hard to see, but at the bottom of the page, it appears as though the examiner jotted down a few notes. It appears that he wrote—I'm struggling to read the handwriting—it appears that he wrote, 'Chemical burn compromises tox reports. Null. Dental negative. Physical build resembles anecdotal descriptions of K.F. No possible identification available.' That's quite a lot to take in, and we'll have an expert analysis as soon as possible, but in the meantime, we're going to go to a quick commercial break. Stay tuned for up-to-the-minute analysis of this potentially enormous development in this ongoing story. We'll be especially interested to see if the release of this document brings an end to the horrible violence we have been witnesses to."

Marcus opened his phone to call Lisa—her eighth-octave voice would bring him back to earth—but as he did so, he saw on his phone an email notification. The subject line read: STETSON INVESTIGATION FILE—IMPORTANT. The sender's address was just a string of numbers attached to an email server he didn't recognize. The email had no opening salutation, no greeting aside from a wash of blank space, followed by the words: *I'm sorry Mr. Waters, but I didn't know who else to send this to. You are the only one who I will send this to at all. I only ask that you not share how you received it. Do what you think is best.* Attached to the email was a pdf file, which Marcus opened with a clumsy finger. He was still getting used to technologies that answered to his fumbling touch.

Marcus held the phone close to his face as he used his fingers to zoom in on the document. It was a photocopied letter, originally written on a typewriter. The top of the letter was dated 1983:

Dear Chief Gonzalez,

Several detectives of the Chicago Police Department have become increasingly concerned about one of our colleagues' possible collusion with a wanted criminal actor--the vigilante heretofore known as "The Kingfisher." We have reason to suspect that this colleague is not only assisting "The Kingfisher" in his illegal activities, but also benefitting professionally from this unlawful and unethical partnership.

The colleague in question is Detective Gregory Stetson. Prior to and during Det. Stetson's time as a homicide detective, Det. Stetson has been the arresting officer for at least two-dozen criminals reportedly incapacitated originally by "The Kingfisher," whom the Chicago Police Department has identified as a criminal actor in regards to his vigilantism. This far outpaces other officers' arrests of criminals who were reportedly incapacitated by "The Kingfisher." This seems to us more than circumstantial.

Moreover, we are concerned that Det. Stetson's possible communication with "The Kingfisher" has been not only condoned by various officials within the Chicago Police Department, but in fact encouraged and rewarded with his promotion to CPD Detective. Due to the above concerns, we fear that Det. Stetson is willfully withholding his knowledge of "The Kingfisher"--identity, whereabouts, etc.--as well as his personal involvement with "The Kingfisher." We write to you today to request a formal investigation into Det. Stetson's ties with "The Kingfisher." We understand the complex nature of this request, but we are acting on the interest of the integrity of the Chicago Police Department, and we hope that you will respond in kind.

The letter was signed by a number of detectives, none of whom Marcus recognized, except for one: Paul Wroblewski. Marcus's old contact at the station.

He stared blankly at his phone, the words of the letter melding into an amorphous clump the more he parsed through each sentence. He found himself distracted by the most banal of details: Why did the detectives who wrote the letter put quotations around the Kingfisher's name? What distance did these marks provide and from what?

He had always assumed it was something of an open secret that the police, Stetson included, had cooperated in some capacity with the Kingfisher—how else could the Kingfisher know of all the wanted criminals in the city? But that the Kingfisher had cooperated solely with Stetson was a different matter altogether. It was true that Stetson had gladly taken credit for the most of the arrests that the Kingfisher provided, but that certainly didn't mean that he had been working with the Kingfisher. It was equally plausible that Stetson's disproportionate arrest rate was a result of his unflagging ambition. As an officer and then as a homicide detective, Stetson had a reputation of working around the clock—hitting the streets and establishing contacts. He was far and away the most hardworking cop Marcus had ever encountered on the police beat. It hadn't ever seemed strange to Marcus that Stetson would be the one to bring in most of the criminals the Kingfisher had left in his wake. And on the rare occasion that Marcus had managed to pull a quote from Stetson about any of these arrests, Stetson had deftly avoided acknowledging the Kingfisher at all. Marcus had always assumed this was purely an act of self-interest—Stetson's meteoric rise in the department ran parallel to his arrest rate, which he could not afford to share with a criminal vigilante.

Even so, if it was true that Stetson had cooperated directly with the Kingfisher—well, Marcus didn't know what it meant. It was clear how Stetson would have benefitted from the partnership, but what the hell would the Kingfisher have wanted from Stetson?

It was the Liber-teens who had sent him this document, Marcus knew. They must have taken this file when they hacked the ME report. But if they were trying to insinuate some larger conspiracy with this letter concerning Stetson, why not make it public? And why send it to just him? He wasn't a journalist anymore. There were working journalists who would gnash their teeth, claw their skin at the opportunity to report this information. Whoever had sent this to him, what did they expect him to do about it?

These questions tangled into knots the harder he pulled. But still he pulled.

The newscaster returned from commercial and shuffled papers on his desk. "We have reached out to the Liber-teens via their social media accounts for a statement, but have not yet received a reply. Obviously, this release of the possible medical examiner's report raises many questions and concerns regarding the Liber-teens' involvement with the video released this morning, but it answers almost no questions until we are able to verify its authenticity. We simply are unable to say what it means at this time."

And as if in response, Marcus spoke out loud to an empty room in answer to a question unasked. "It doesn't mean anything."

If there was one thing Marcus knew from a career in journalism, it was that there were a hundred explanations for every mystery, every lie, every half-truth. The inconclusive ME report, a letter indicting Stetson, the Liber-teens, the Kingfisher himself. Anyone could shape and rearrange coincidence into some grand narrative that was halfway believable and halfway comforting in a world whose only order was chaos, a back-alley gambler with blank-faced dice.

They showed the ME report on the television once more. The scratchy handwriting—*Unknown . . . No possible identification.* And that was when Marcus remembered a detail from his reporting: Stetson had been the first on scene after the call had come through about a body floating down the Chicago River. It had never struck Marcus as strange before, though perhaps it should have. Stetson was a homicide detective at the time. What the hell was he doing responding to that call before anyone else? Had he simply been close by? And if so, why?

And it was Stetson to whom Marcus had spoken that same night for the story on the death of the Kingfisher. "It's him," Stetson said over the phone, his voice predictably neutral and calm. "A positive identification. We've matched him based on witness reports." It had seemed inevitable at the moment, entirely procedural, as though confirming something Marcus had already known, or at least thought he had known.

Now, here, these many years and lifetimes later, some unspoken word bypassed Marcus's faculty of reason and entered directly into his bloodstream. The way others might say they felt the voice of God at midnight, a vibration in their soul. But the only word that escaped his lips was, "Shit." He savored the flavor of the word. He had forgotten how easily a simple, four-letter word could capture otherwise unspeakable emotions.

Something was going on, he begrudgingly admitted to himself. And if even a fraction of what he had just seen were true, Stetson was at the center of it.

The television pundit spoke to a group of panelists. A man with a blue pocket square and shock-white teeth said, "The problem seems to me two-fold: you have a transparency failure on the part of Chicago police leadership, which is heightened by a very competent, albeit sinister, attack conducted by a shadow group of anarchists. The police are easy targets—they are held to precise standards: to serve and protect the citizens of Chicago. If those duties are questioned or challenged, then the whole house of cards falls apart. That is why the criminal anarchists have the advantage—the expectation is that they answer to no one, and in this way they are beyond reproach."

Marcus went to his front door. No news vans in sight, probably called to some other location to cover the latest development.

There was just the sun already set and the fingernail curve of the climbing moon. And Jeremiah seemed to study it, sitting on the trunk of the cruiser, elbows on his knees. It reminded Marcus of a child waiting for his mother or his father to pick him up from school, the same languid patience for something that might or might not come.

He whistled for Jeremiah's attention and waved him inside again.

"What's up?" Jeremiah entered through the door. Judging by his expression, Marcus figured he must have looked as haggard as he felt. "Are you OK?"

Marcus dug his hands into his pockets. He gestured over his shoulder.

Jeremiah's eyes landed on the television, where another pundit said, "This ME report adds a frightening amount of credence to the man's claims in those horrific videos." Jeremiah's expression didn't change as he watched for a few moments, but his shoulders slackened as he shifted his weight, leaning against the entryway.

"Holy shit. Stetson actually released it?"

"No. It was the Liber-teens," Marcus said. "Not sure if it's real. But it sure looks like it might be. They hacked it."

Jeremiah scratched his neck, swearing beneath his breath. "Those kids have no idea what they're doing. This isn't going to fix anything. This is going to fuck everything up."

"Do you have a minute to come in and talk?" Marcus asked.

Jeremiah nodded at the bottle in Marcus's hand. "You got another one of those?"

"Afraid not. How about coffee?"

"I won't get much sleep anyway. Sure."

Marcus led Jeremiah into the kitchen and pulled out a chair for him to sit at the table. Jeremiah collapsed with a wordless sigh. A five o'clock shadow covered his clenched jaw. "Long day keeps getting longer."

Marcus poured water into his kettle and laid it on the stove.

"So did you get a good look at the ME report?" Jeremiah asked.

"More or less."

"What did you think?"

He removed the French press from the cupboard and poured coffee grounds into the cylindrical base. "The coroner wrote that he couldn't positively identify the body. There were some other inconsistencies with what Stetson has said, too."

"And you think it was a real report? Not some fake?"

"Looked real to me. But I'm no expert."

"Jesus," Jeremiah said. "Stetson's going to have a hell of a time explaining that away tomorrow."

"That's what I was hoping to talk with you about."

"What?"

"Stetson."

"Stetson," Jeremiah repeated, as though it were not a name but a slur. "What about him?"

"What do you know about him? His career, I mean."

"I'm betting you know more about that than I do. You've known him longer."

Marcus turned on his stovetop, centered the kettle, and sat across from Jeremiah at the table. "Just tell me whatever you know."

"Well." Jeremiah rubbed his face, as though summoning insight from his skin. "Assuming I'm off-record and we're being honest here, he's a gaping asshole."

"Care to expound on that?"

"Man's got a head thicker than concrete. He doesn't listen to anyone. Except maybe the mayor, I guess. But even then, not really. He plays everyone like those little puppets on strings—you know, the goofy Pinocchio things—"

"Marionettes."

"Right. Marionettes. I mean, the whole department is pretty much the Stetson show. Acts like everyone beneath him, which is just about everyone in this city so far as I can tell, is always in the way of his spotlight. Not to mention he acts like we don't know what the hell we're doing. He treats us detectives like we're kindergartners with badges and deadly weapons. Doesn't give us an inch of rope. Word I'm looking for is *micromanage*. Breathes down our fucking necks like you wouldn't believe. Everything has to go through Stetson, doesn't matter what it is."

Nothing Marcus didn't already know. "I'm curious what you know about Stetson before he was police chief. When he was an officer and a detective."

"That was long before my time."

"But I'm guessing word gets around. These things travel. Are there any veteran detectives who talk about all that?"

Jeremiah thought about it and smiled. He seemed to be enjoying the shit-talking. "Yeah, there's a few on the force who were around back then. Maybe two or three. I don't interact with them all that much, but I know they hate Stetson. But so do most of us, so it doesn't seem all that strange to me."

"What do the older detectives say about Stetson?"

"They say all sorts of stuff about him. Like he's a neurotic asshole, a bureaucrat, a con man. You know, that sort of stuff."

"A con man?" Marcus tried to rein in his piqued interest. "Any idea why they'd say that?"

"Like I said, I don't talk to them too much, at least not about old history. But that's just one of those things they say. They say all sorts of things, though, those older guys on the force. I don't give it too much weight, personally."

"Why?"

"Don't get me wrong, I'm not fond of Stetson, but I get the sense that the older guys hate him out of simple jealousy. You know as well as I do that Stetson leapfrogged up the chain of command when he was appointed chief. Some of the brass he passed along the way weren't too pleased." Jeremiah smiled, perhaps at the image of his superiors shaking with rage. "What are you asking about Stetson for?"

Marcus glanced at Jeremiah's expectant posture, his insistently curious gaze, anticipating a benign answer to a simple question.

Do what you think is best.

"I'm going to ask you to look at something, with the understanding that you tell no one else, at least for now."

"What are we talking about here? You have a lead?"

"I'm not sure."

"Let me take a look."

Marcus pulled up the letter on his phone. "I don't think this needs much context." He slid it across the table to Jeremiah, who held it up to his face. His lips moved silently as he passed through the words.

The kettle began whistling over the stove. Marcus stood up and prepared the coffee while Jeremiah read the letter, with the occasional grunt or click of his tongue. Finally, after a minute, Jeremiah looked up with a blank expression and slid the phone across the table.

"Where'd you get this?" Jeremiah asked.

"Anonymous source," Marcus said, pouring the steaming water into the press.

"Probably the same kids who took the ME report."

"I wouldn't know. You recognize any of the names of the detectives who signed the letter?"

Jeremiah nodded. He reclined in his chair, folded his arms, and craned his head to the ceiling. He let out a heavy sigh. "There's already talk of protests tonight against the police. When this letter gets out, it's going to be mayhem. Torches and pitchforks."

"I don't think it will get out. Whoever sent it said they were only sharing it with me."

Jeremiah leaned forward as if he had misheard. "Why the hell would they do that? Those kids could destroy the police department if they share it. Isn't that their endgame?"

"I honestly don't know anymore."

Jeremiah shook his head slowly, scratching his neck. "It does sound like Stetson, though."

"What does?"

"The stuff the detectives in that letter said he did. Doing some sneaky shit to look good for the chief and the mayor. Pissing most everyone else off and not giving a single, solitary fuck. Did that letter ever actually make its way to the chief's desk back then?"

"No idea."

"I didn't know Chief Gonzalez, but if he was anything like Stetson, he wouldn't have given a damn about any of that so long as Stetson's arrests made him look good, too." Jeremiah laughed, drumming his fingers on the edge of the table. "At least it makes sense now."

"What does?"

"Why Stetson is handling the investigation the way he is. I couldn't figure it out before." Jeremiah took a drink of his coffee and leaned over the table, lost in thought. "See, he could have just released the report today and ended this. Everyone is treating it like a ransom, but it isn't. He could have just released the report and said that he was going to declassify it soon anyway. Or he could have said that its confidential status was a filing error or some shit. He could have done it. But even if that had stopped the gunman from killing the hostages, it would still mean that everyone knew he had been lying about the contents of the report, and then everyone wonders why the police said one thing and the ME report says another." Jeremiah tapped his chin, a revelatory smile. "But if Stetson could just kill the gunman, maybe people would forget all of it eventually. The media would run a few days of coverage on the lunatic, interview his family, interview his victims' families. Meanwhile, Stetson washes his hands and goes about his merry way, looking to the whole world like the hero he thinks he is."

Marcus couldn't argue Jeremiah's logic. "Well, it doesn't seem likely that scenario will happen now," Marcus said. "The report is out there. Stetson will have to address it."

Jeremiah shrugged. "Stetson's a lot of things, but he's not stupid. I wouldn't put it past him to find a way around it. You know, sweep it all under the rug. What's funny is that if he knew about that letter you got in your hands there, he'd be sweating bullets right now. I can tell you that much. He can only stave off so many accusations before they start sticking. Yeah, if he knew you had that letter, he'd be shitting his trousers."

Marcus couldn't help but smile at the image. "You want to know something I remembered today?"

"Shoot."

"Stetson was the first responder when the call came through about a body in the Chicago River. And he was the one who told me it was the Kingfisher."

"Motherfucker," Jeremiah said in a sort of whispery singsong. "You think it's possible?"

"What?"

"That Stetson helped the Kingfisher fake his death?"

"That's not what I'm saying. I guess I actually don't know what I'm saying. It's just a strange coincidence, if it is a coincidence at all."

"Tell me something, Marcus," Jeremiah said, leaning his elbows on the table. "You think the Kingfisher could still be alive?"

"No." Marcus shook his head. "I really don't. It's possible that the police, or maybe just Stetson, was somehow involved with the Kingfisher's death and autopsy, but I don't believe for a second that the Kingfisher faked it. It just doesn't make any sense why he'd do that. Even if he just wanted to leave, he would have just left. He wouldn't have to make such a spectacle of it. That doesn't seem like something he would have done. He was not theatrical. Granted, I never got close to the man himself, but I think I got close enough to know him in some small way. Enough to know that he wouldn't have faked his death just to retire."

There was the sound of a car passing by outside on the street, the burden of a muffler. Jeremiah scratched mindlessly at his neck, looking at Marcus. A saturated stare, the weight of a world, and a question lingering on his lips, struggling to pass into open air.

"What is it?" Marcus asked.

"If I tell you this."

"What?"

"Something I never told anyone."

"What?"

"Not even my mother. Never told her."

"What?"

Jeremiah hesitated, stuttering over the words, "I had a run-in with the Kingfisher." He smiled, casually, as though inviting Marcus to disregard it. "I was thirteen years old, walking home later than I ought to have been from a Bulls game. They'd just beaten the Bucks. It was a game, man. A good game. Sort of game you remember forever."

"When was this?"

"This would have been December of—let's see—1983. I know that, because it was just a few days before he died or . . ." He paused, shook his head. "I don't remember too much of it. It happened pretty quick." He began to laugh, crossing his arms more tightly. "It's funny though, because what I remember most from that night isn't the Kingfisher, but a woman. Sounds dumb, all things considered. But I was a teenager and this was the most beautiful woman I ever saw in my whole life, I swear. She had this bright red hair like a stoplight, man. I couldn't keep my eyes off her."

"Red hair?" Marcus asked, leaning his elbows on the table. "You said she had red hair?"

"I can see it when I close my eyes, to this day. And the reason I hesitate to tell you all this is because she asked me that night to keep the whole thing between us. Not to mention I don't expect you to believe a word of it. I know that I wouldn't, if I were you. Only reason I would tell it is because I honest-to-God don't think he's dead. The Kingfisher. I never once believed he was dead. Not ever. And now, with all of this"—he pointed back at the television broadcasting into the empty room—"I'm damn near sure of it. And I'm not sure who else can fix this fucking mess except for him."

"Tell me the story."

"Well, like I said"—Jeremiah breathed in and out, closing his eyes as though willing himself into some lost past—"I was walking home later than I ought to have been. I'd gone to a Bulls game. They'd beat the Bucks. It was a great game. Reggie Theus was on fire that night."

Jeremiah's story ended abruptly without ornamentation or speculation. Just the drip of a sentence into resolute silence. As he was talking, Jeremiah had been staring down at the grain of the wooden table like a mystic reading tea leaves, but when finished, he turned his gaze up, a sense of wonder that lasts through the years, and Marcus felt as though he were seeing the boy who had sat in the back of that Lincoln Continental on a snowy December's night.

Jeremiah broke from his pensive arrangement and took a sip of coffee. The mug said in plain black type: I GOT ELEVATED IN DENVER, COLORADO. It was from one of the last vacations the entire Waters family had taken together before the youngest went off to college. They'd taken a monorail up to Pikes Peak and smiled in front of a camera, as families often do.

Marcus held a finger out across the table as though tracing Jeremiah's story in the air. "You said the woman's name was Miss May?"

"I'm sure of it. Or I think I am. It's funny, sort of, talking about it now. I've never talked about it with anybody, and I always felt like I knew the story inside and out. But when I'm sitting here across from you, trying to get it all out there—I don't know—it just doesn't feel like I'm doing it right. It's all coming out weird and sounds sort of crazy. It's all trapped up here." He tapped his temple. "Shit, I'm not making an ounce of sense anymore."

But Marcus knew what he meant, even though he said nothing in response. The way that memories of memories stagnated in the mind's still waters. "And you didn't see what happened to the two men in the car?"

"Nothing. No trace. Like they vanished in thin air. But judging by what little I saw, I'm guessing they got beaten bad. I've never seen a thing quite like it."

It was this detail that puzzled Marcus most. He'd never heard of this Kingfisher encounter.

"Well, as far as I know," Marcus said, "they didn't turn up on some street corner like all the other criminals the Kingfisher apprehended. Someone would have called me had that happened. But surely they went to a hospital or, if not there, a police station or morgue. I just don't understand how I could have missed this."

Jeremiah shrugged and then checked his watch. "Shit, it's getting late. Shift change. I have to go check up on a friend." He stood up, drank the dregs of his coffee, and made off to the door.

Marcus cleared his throat. Jeremiah turned around.

"So you really think he's still out there somewhere, Jeremiah?"

Jeremiah paused, reaching his hands into his pockets, jangling his keys. "All I know for sure is that what I saw that night wasn't the work of a human like you and me. I don't know what the Kingfisher was or is, but I'm just about certain he isn't like us in any way except that he could hurt us the way we hurt ourselves." He smiled and shrugged. "He's either alive or he isn't. And if he's dead, then God rest his soul. But if he is alive, well, God forgive him. Because I'm not sure what the hell he's waiting for."

17 LIKE THEY ALREADY ALWAYS WERE

WHEN HE WAS NOT SIMPLY A VOICE in a window, Baxter Bedford was a tall, skinny, sloping man who moved about his home in hurried, lunging steps, as though walking through quicksand. He picked up a few empty fast-food bags in the kitchen, mumbling under his breath angry condemnations, embarrassed apologies, or some mixture of the two.

Tillman sent Jeremiah a quick text: *Baxter Bedford safe. Talking with him. Dad OK?*

A dappled mastiff followed Bedford around at his hip, long nails clicking on the linoleum, casting paranoid glances over her haunch at Tillman, who was seated at a card table in a corner of the kitchen. Tillman returned the dog's uncertain stare with her own. Moments ago, the dog would have torn her throat from her skin like a plaything. But now, the dog's tongue hung from its mouth in a bookstore-calendar pose.

Jeremiah texted her back: *Checking on your dad now.* And then another immediately after: *ME Report was hacked. Long story. Not sure what happens next. Be safe, Tilly.*

Bedford turned around in the kitchen. "You thirsty?"

"No." She set down her phone. "Thank you."

"Good. All I got is water and the water around here is shit."

When he'd sent her the names and addresses, Jeremiah had also sent her one of Bedford's mug shots. The photo was from 1986—possession of a criminalized drug with the intent to sell. And for whatever reason,

Tillman had expected Bedford to look exactly as he had in his mug shot from thirty-some years earlier. An untamed afro and playboy snarl. But she found instead a man with a shaved head and a gray beard that he twisted with his fingers when perturbed, which thus far seemed to be quite often.

Yet the longer Tillman watched him clean up his kitchen, the more she could see his resemblance to his old mug shot. There remained the same unapologetic defiance in the narrowing eyes as he cleared his countertop of McDonald's wrappers and stuffed them into an overflowing trash can.

"So you're not really a cop," Baxter Bedford said in a matter-of-fact tone, his back turned to her. "What are you, then?"

"Why do you think I'm not a cop?"

The faucet was on and he seemed to be searching for a clean glass, slamming cupboards. The kitchen smelled strongly of gunpowder from the shot that still rang in Tillman's ears.

"Call it a sixth sense," he said.

He found a glass and inspected it beneath a light bulb hanging from the ceiling by its wires, turning the glass over in his fingers like a jeweler inspecting a fraudulent stone. He shrugged and poured himself a drink. His Adam's apple bounced up and down in his long neck.

"I'm actually on leave from the force at the moment," she said. "Administrative leave."

"Don't know what that means, but my sixth sense tells me it means you fucked up."

Baxter sat at the card table across from Tillman. The dog pranced around his legs nervously, emitted a repentant bark. Baxter hushed the dog with a snap of his fingers and it lay down on the floor reluctantly. A pink tongue lolled out the side of its mouth, wet and glistening. Its muzzle was speckled with gray.

"Bambi is old, but she's got spunk for days," he said, petting the dog with his foot. "Now, on the matter of my front door, I'll need money for it. The lock is busted clean through. Torn to shit. And this isn't an area you want to live in without a lock on your front door. Bullet hole I could live with. But I need a lock."

She reached for her wallet and slid the fifty she'd managed to save for next week's groceries across the table. "That's all I have."

He stuffed the bill into the breast pocket of his flannel shirt. "I need to go to bed before too long, so I'm hoping this little powwow doesn't last a second longer than it needs to," he said. "But first tell me what you did to get yourself get kicked off the Chicago force?"

"I didn't get kicked off," she corrected. "I'm on leave."

He dismissed the semantics with a shake of his head. "Whatever you did must've been pretty bad, seeing as how I remember you Chicago badges getting away with all sorts of shit."

"It isn't important. I didn't come here to talk about me."

"It's important to me. And if you want me to tell you anything, maybe you should start by telling me what sort of hell you unleashed to get kicked off that hellspawn of a police force. Those assholes could shoot someone that looks like us in broad daylight for no good reason, blame it on arthritis or the wind, and be back on the job in the morning."

She wasn't about to defend those on the force who had done much worse than what she had done and suffered much less, if at all, as a result. "I wasn't kicked off the force—I was put on administrative leave," she reminded Bedford, the words feeling suddenly plastic atop her tongue. Bedford stared back at her, waiting. Tillman thought of a thousand lies she could tell. But instead, she settled on the truth. Or whatever was closest to the truth. "Excessive force. That's what the Police Board called it, at least. But they weren't there when it happened. They didn't see what I saw. If they had, they wouldn't have called it 'excessive.'"

Bedford sat unblinking before her and curled his fingers to coax out the story lingering deep beneath these nothing words.

"My partner and I were responding to a domestic abuse call in Lawndale," she said. "We'd get called there every couple months, always to the same apartment. Always the same thing, every time. Father beating up on his kids. He used a belt, sometimes an open hand. But it's tough with those sorts of calls because, when it's a parent, they can just call it *discipline.*"

"Discipline," Bedford repeated, smiling.

"So I take a report and have to hand it off to DCFS and let them take it from there. But they must have not found much, because every few months I was back down there knocking on that same door. Same thing every time. Then I got the call for a fourth time. I show up and I hear the kids behind the door screaming. A boy and a girl. It was like they were screaming so loud you can hardly make sense of it. Just terror. Pure terror. Even behind the door, I was hearing the slap of a leather belt against skin. Over and over and over. You want to talk about excessive force? What I heard behind that door was excessive force."

She paused. This was the first time she had ever spoken the story aloud since being put on leave. She was frightened by the crystalline quality of the memory of that day, these months later.

"Keep going," Bedford said. "You're not done."

"My partner knocked on the door, loud, and I was just sort of standing there. I must have been thinking something, but I just remember staring at the door. And as soon as the father opened the door with that fucking smile on his face I grabbed him by the neck and threw him to the ground. I wasn't planning on doing it. It just happened. I did it, and I didn't know why, but I did it. And it was like someone else was doing it, and I was only watching."

"And then?" he said.

"And then? I pinned him under my knees and choked him. I felt his heartbeats slowing down. I felt it through my fingertips."

"Keep going."

"I dug my fingers in his neck like I wanted to pop his head off his body. And I might have done it, but my partner wrestled me off. Not until after the father lost consciousness. Of course, when he regained it, he threatened to sue, and I'm placed on unpaid administrative leave for 'an indefinite period of time after review.'" She shook her head. "So, there you go," she said, opening her hands, showed that they were empty, nothing left concealed. "You satisfied?"

"You got off soft," Baxter said after a moment, but there was a new texture somewhere beneath his hardened voice, a softer edge undercutting the clipped words. Fighting a smile. "Me myself, I would have just shot the asshole in the head and been done with it."

Bambi began to kick and yip in her sleep. Bedford nudged her with his toe until she bolted upright, scanning the walls for the apparitions of a dream.

"So if you're not a cop," Bedford said, "what are you doing here? You said something about the Kingfisher, but if you were here to chat about that asshole, it probably could have waited until morning."

She cleared her throat. "Have you been watching the news?"

"No, no, no." He shook his head slow and even like a hypnotist's watch.

"I don't own a television. No phone. I don't like the electronics humming constantly. They'll give you cancer just by thinking about them. But I was visiting my daughter and grandchildren in Indianapolis for the past few days. I got back just this morning. My daughter had the television on while I was there, though. That girl's always glued to whatever screen is nearest to her. She was watching the news and I could hear what was happening. I said, 'Turn that noise off.' Not that she listened to me, of course, but that's what I told her."

"So you didn't actually see it? The video?"

"No. Heard it, but I wouldn't watch it."

"Why?"

"Why?" he repeated, letting the word ring. "Why would I want to watch that? I don't care about that shit. I don't want my grandchildren seeing that garbage neither. No one ought to watch that. Just because you can see something, doesn't mean you ought to. That's what no one seems to understand these days. Whole world open for you. But doesn't mean you're ready for it."

"Does your family know about your connection to the Kingfisher? Do they know that you saw him?"

He seemed unsurprised that she knew this about him and simply shook his head.

"My daughter knows, but she hasn't told my grandchildren. She won't. That girl, she won't even talk about it with me. So, no, they don't know and won't ever know. But one day, they'll learn that I was a criminal. I know that day will come. All they got to do is put my name in their computers, their phones, and see that I got booked for intention to sell in '86. They'll see I spent years staring at a fucking wall. And then they'll know who their grandfather was once upon a time. And I bet they won't ever look at me the way they do right now. It'll change forever, the way they look at me. But they don't know it yet, and I'm grateful for it. I just want to enjoy every second that they don't know who their grandfather really is or was or whatnot."

Baxter stood up and retrieved a framed picture from the kitchen counter. He slid it across the card table as though submitting evidence. Tillman picked it up. Three shining faces, precisely arranged one next to the other. She immediately saw the family resemblance to their grandfather. The same slender faces, up-to-no-good grins.

"The boy in the middle, there"—Bedford reached forward and pointed a finger at a boy wearing a LeBron James jersey, side-eyeing the camera, his sly smile revealing several missing baby teeth. "Name's Jordan. As in Michael Jordan. His dad named him. I was at the hospital when he was born. The first and last time I ever been thankful to God in heaven. It was his birthday a few days ago. That's why I was in Indianapolis."

Tillman smiled and handed the photograph back. Bedford set it in front of him.

Tillman lowered her voice and crossed her hands in front of her. "You need to know something. About that video that was released."

"Go ahead."

She paused, "The hostage who was killed was Walter Williams."

Bedford smiled disbelievingly, like she was holding off on a punch line. "Now I know you're fucking with me."

"It's true," she said.

He stared back at her, the smile slowly dissolving. "Bullshit. Walter got out of the game way back when."

"I'm sorry, Mr. Bedford."

"Don't call me mister," he said sharply. "You don't know what you're talking about."

"I could show you the video."

"Fuck that."

"The hostage killed was Walter Williams. And I hear there was another video released recently." She cleared her throat, hoping to make space for the words she wasn't sure she had. "I haven't seen it yet. But I'm told the gunman is threatening to kill another hostage. Would you mind if I showed you the latest video?"

"What good will that do?" he spat.

"Just in case you recognize the hostage."

"I don't want to see that shit." He pointed at her phone. "Get that out of here. I'm not playing with you. Put that away."

Her training told her to speak calmly in order to relax the person she was speaking to. But she knew men like Baxter Bedford. Men who responded not to calm deference, but to steel resolve. "Mr. Bedford"—she raised her voice and leaned forward—"you are being selfish right now. If you recognize the person in this video, it could save his life. Why wouldn't you want to do that?"

He folded his arms and craned his head. His tongue wandered the inside of his cheek. "You bust down my door, demand to take up my time, feed me all these bullshit lies, and still have the nerve left over to call me selfish?"

"Only because you are."

He reached out his hand. "Give it here, then. Calling me selfish, Jesus Almighty."

She pressed play on the video and handed it to him. She couldn't see the latest video, but she could hear it. She heard the gunman's digitized voice. But she wasn't paying it much mind. Her focus fell entirely on Bedford's face as he squinted at the screen in his hands. She saw his eyes widen, and then his lips part. His shoulders hunched as he brought himself closer to the image, while a tremor passed through his fingers, moving quickly to his arms, as though an electric current were working its way through his body. The phone slipped from his fingers and onto the table. He pushed it back to her forcefully and cracked his knuckles. His lips pressed together so tightly they nearly disappeared.

Tillman let a moment pass before asking him, "Did you recognize the hostage?"

He opened his mouth to speak, but nothing came out.

"Mr. Bedford, who was the hostage in that video?"

He cleared his throat. "Penny," Bedford said finally, his room-wandering voice reduced to a scratchy whisper. He stared forward at the picture of his family in front of him, biting his lips. His foot bounced against the linoleum. "But you know," he laughed, chin trembling, "Penny's going to be fine. He can take care of himself. He'll figure something out. He's a junkyard dog, Penny is. He's fine."

"We have to assume the possibility—"

"We don't have to assume nothing," he said, his voice rising. "Nothing. Penny can take care of himself. Junkyard dog, Penny is. He'll be fine."

"What we need to focus on right now is making sure that you are safe. The man in that video, he killed Walter and he has Penny. He must know the Kingfisher saved you three. He's—"

"He's crazy. That's all he is. I'm not scared of him. I'll kill that asshole if he gives me the chance. Besides, Penny's fine. I know Penny. Penny's fine." And saying Penny's name this last time seemed to release something inside of him. He sensed it coming and bit his bottom lip harder, his teeth digging into his skin. "You said he killed Walter?"

"I know this is difficult."

"Fuck you know," he said, tears forming like morning fog. "You don't know. You don't know. Why are you the one here right now? Why not the real police? Where the fuck are they?"

"Police Chief Stetson has not . . ." she began to say, a diplomatic caution to her words. But she decided to tell it straight. "He doesn't seem convinced you're in danger. But you obviously are in danger. If the gunman found Walter and Penny, then I'm sure you are aware of what that means for you."

Bedford looked out the window into his backyard, the slate-gray night consuming the horizon, nothing in sight save for spindly telephone poles stretching down a long and empty road.

"You said you were in Indianapolis recently for your grandson's birthday?" she asked. "How long were you there?"

"Three days," he said absently.

"And you came back this morning?"

He nodded and she saw him realize what she, too, suspected. Had he not been in Indianapolis, who knows where he would be right now or if he would *be* at all? Had he not gone to visit his daughter and his grandchildren, had coincidence not aligned . . . The frailty of the everyday decision.

"You need to find somewhere safe to stay for a while," she said. "You can't stay here."

"I can look after myself just fine. You witnessed that yourself."

"Whoever is behind these videos is extremely dangerous. He's probably looking for you. Please, Baxter, you need to go away for a while. Call your daughter. Go back to Indianapolis. Wait for this to pass."

A latent tear fell from his clouded eyes and he brushed it away with a thumb. He reached over to pet Bambi, who licked his hand. "You're sure it was Walter in that other video?"

"Yes."

He scratched Bambi's stomach. "Can I use your phone to call my daughter?"

"Of course." She slid it across the table.

Bedford made the phone call in the other room. She heard his voice, a soft and giving whisper as he spoke to his daughter. Tillman heard him say, "I'm fine, baby, really. It's the allergies. I'm getting old, you know that. I'm missing you all. I know, I just saw you. But I'm wondering if—well. Yeah? Good. Good. I'm excited to see them, too."

Bedford reentered the kitchen after a few minutes and handed Tillman her phone. Wordlessly, he moved over to the sink. He straightened up and remained there, unmoving, his spidery frame blocking the light, silhouetted and shadowed.

"Are you leaving tonight?" she asked.

He nodded, refilled his glass. He spoke in a voice detached from the moment, as though speaking backward into the hollow wake of years. "You should know something about that night. That night with me, Walter, and Penny? We emptied our clips into the Kingfisher. Head, gut, chest, legs. I saw the bullets hit him. I swear it, I saw. And that motherfucker didn't even move. And then those years later, the cops say they found his body, shot and stabbed to death? Bullshit they did."

"You're saying you think he's still alive?"

Bedford took another lung-heaving drink and wiped his mouth with his hand. "What I'm saying is that if I were you, I'd be careful if you intend on looking for him. I've seen what he is capable of doing, that man. And believe me when I say you don't want to be on the receiving end of his holy anger. Man like that couldn't do what he did out of the goodness of his heart. It came from something deeper and darker. Something evil. I can tell you that for certain."

"I don't care about the Kingfisher. Dead or alive. My only concerns are the hostages."

"You said the police aren't looking for them?"

"If they are, they're not looking too hard. Or else I wouldn't be here right now."

"You know why, don't you?"

"They might think their time is better spent working on identifying the gunman before he can get to the rest of the hostages. But even then . . ." She stopped. "I really don't know."

Bedford laughed, setting his glass down in the sink. "Those cops really did a number on you, didn't they? You've been brainwashed by the boys in blue."

"What is it, then?"

"It's simple. One word." He held up a single finger. *"History."*

"I don't understand."

"Penny and Walter are two men with criminal records. And I can tell you from personal experience, being someone with a criminal record in this country makes you something else, something lower than the dirt the police scrape from their shoes. Doesn't matter what you've done since, who you think you've become, you'll never escape it. And I promise you—I *promise* you—when that police chief, whatever his name is, saw that video, he knew those men. But they weren't men to him. No, he wasn't watching a man die. He wasn't watching a man with a family, a man who lived a life, a man who paid for his crimes in one way or another. Man with blood pouring out his head. No, that police chief only saw that clown wearing that ridiculous Halloween mask, shooting a gun into nothing at all. Firing a gun into empty space. Because that's all we are to him. Empty space. Yeah." He shook his head, drifting through some unspoken thought. "And when it's all said and done, whole world will know the name of the clown in the mask, but Walter—and God forbid, Penny—will be forgotten about like they already always were. And the world will just keep on"—he traced his finger in the air, a circle—"keep going. Like it usually does." He lingered on the pause, and then walked to the door, swinging it open. "Now, if you don't mind, it's time you got going. I've got a long drive tonight. I figure you do, too. Give my regards to Chicago. I miss it."

She stood up, stepped over Bambi on her way to the door. "If you miss it, why'd you leave?"

"Suppose I prefer missing it more than living in it."

The trip back to Chicago from South Bend trailed through highways she did not remember taking on the way in. Highways without names. The only light for miles around was her headlights, which absorbed into old, buckled roads that wound sharply for no apparent reason. It required all of her attention just to keep moving forward, so every time her mind wandered back to Baxter Bedford's kitchen, the jostling of the gravel shook her back into the present moment behind the steering wheel.

Smoking with the windows down.

She thought of a hundred questions she wished she had asked Baxter Bedford, and then she thought of a hundred more. Was there anyone he knew who might have been there that night who could be responsible for this? Was there anyone he knew who might be at risk? But she rolled down the window of the SUV and these questions and the many others sifted out into the open air of a prairie night.

Bedford was safe, and this was what mattered. It should have left her with something resembling peace, except for the fact that Penny was next. She had tried to find him, she told herself, but this did little to ease her mind. The only thing that would do that is if he were still alive tomorrow. If this nightmare ended tonight.

It would be a long drive. She was alone. She was far outside the city limits, and she could see the stars tearing through the swarthy night. She never saw them in the city. They hid behind a veil of light pollution. Seeing them now filled Tillman with a curious panic. A sense of exposure, of being seen, of being watched, of being known.

Out ahead of her, she saw wind turbines grow up out of the earth, spinning slowly, slowly. Atop each, a red light warned off low-flying planes. The lights pulsed together. Bloodred eyes hungering in the dusk.

18 APRIL 1982

DETECTIVE GREGORY STETSON SAT IN HIS OFFICE, eleven o'clock at night, staring ahead at nothing in particular, biting mindlessly on his thumbnail. An old habit, a bad habit.

His office was larger than the guest room of his house that his mother-in-law slept in during her too-frequent visits from St. Louis, and this fact alone, even on a night such as this, filled him with something resembling joy.

Stetson adored his office. Every square foot, every sea-blue carpet fiber. He loved unlocking his office in the mornings. He loved shutting the door behind him when he went out for coffee. He loved locking it at night, the music the key made in the dead bolt. He loved the painting Mindy had given him after his promotion—a lone hunter in an overgrown forest, double-barreled shotgun slung over his shoulder, staring up at a full and bright moon shining through the trees. He loved the pictures on his desk, pictures of himself and Mindy. In the latest picture they'd taken, Mindy wore a blue dress pressed tightly against her eight-months-pregnant belly. She held her hands over her stomach. And Stetson, standing behind her in a blue sports coat, held his hands over hers, cradling their unborn child.

Most of the other detectives sat in desk-clumps scattered haphazardly about the open floor of the precinct, but not Stetson. And to make it all sweeter, he was also the youngest detective on the force, in possession of what Chief Gonzalez called "exemplary acumen for the promotion to detective." And when he'd requested an office in which to apply his talents in peace, the chief said he'd look into it. The next day, the chief showed Stetson to his new office.

It overlooked a quiet park, ash trees stoic beside a glimmering pond. During the day, a few senior citizens showed up and threw bread into the pond and waited for ducks. The ducks rarely arrived, but the seniors didn't seem to mind. Old folks, old habits.

The other detectives whispered about him when they thought he wasn't listening. He knew this. After all, he had "exemplary acumen." They passed rumors in hushed tones, leaning over their desks. The typical green-eyed, jealous bullshit. One of his favorite idling activities was to swing open his office door and watch the gossiping detectives fall perfectly silent, sitting at their desks and leafing through files like choirboys digging their noses in hymnals. When these rumors made their way back to Stetson, he was surprised to find that some of their speculation was true, but even those that had some kernel of truth were flavored by some crazed conspiracy based feebly on a reality they did not understand, could not understand, would never understand.

Let them whisper, Stetson thought, while I save this city from itself.

On this particular night, though, Stetson was the only detective left in the precinct. The janitor was running a vacuum outside his door. Stetson was expecting an important call at any moment. They had agreed on eleven o'clock, but it was currently five past. He checked his Rolex every few moments just to see if time was still moving forward the way he remembered.

He had nearly chewed his thumbnail clean off when his rotary phone rang on his desk. He sighed, picked it up, and set it back down. He checked his watch.

The rotary phone rang again. He sighed again. He checked his Rolex again. But this time he picked it up.

"Stetson," he said curtly.

"Greg?" Mindy's sweet, sleepy voice whispered into his ear.

"I'm working late, Min. Can't talk right now."

"You didn't tell me you'd be working late. I was worried sick over here."

"Something came up. Can't talk right now. Waiting on a call."

"When will you be home?"

"I don't know. But I really can't talk right now."

"What came up at work?"

"I have to go, Min."

"Are you safe?" she asked.

But he was already hanging up. And just a moment later, the AN/PRC-18 walkie-talkie stashed beneath his desk came alive with a static yawn, followed by a piercing frequency that burst through the speakers. Phone lines could be tapped, but the AN/PRC-18 operated on a frequency that belonged solely to himself and the man hopefully on the other line. Paranoid? Maybe. But he wouldn't put it past some of those lousy desk-clusterfuck detectives to try and crucify him for doing exactly what they all knew he was doing, for doing what any of them would do, given the chance, for doing exactly what had gotten him a promotion and an office with a nice view, for doing something that was helping the city they had all sworn to protect. So he kept the walkie-talkie locked in his bottom drawer in the office that he locked each night.

"Seventy-first and Pulaski," said the deep voice on the other end.

Stetson brought the receiver close to his lips. "Roger that. Stay put."

Stetson knew where to look for him. In two years' time, he'd come to know the way that the Kingfisher's mind worked. He preferred unlit alleyways, gravel drives, construction sites, dead ends, underbellies of bridges. The areas the casual observer's eye naturally drifted over, like the space separating words. These places, Stetson thought, they were reflections of the Kingfisher—you would never see them unless you knew what you were looking for. And the more Stetson worked with the Kingfisher, the more he began to casually notice these spaces, and the more he realized that the city seemed to be built for the Kingfisher. Chicago was an architecture of lost places. A myriad of shadowed corners, recessed secrets. Plenty of real estate for those who wished to remain unseen.

So when Stetson saw construction scaffolding climbing the sky alongside 71st and Pulaski, he knew he would find the Kingfisher somewhere inside the site. He threw the unmarked car into park across the street and was careful to get out of his seat slowly, so as not to raise alarm from any observing party, even though he saw no one. He walked casually across the street, hands in his pockets, and ducked beneath a metal girder meant to ward off street traffic.

Inside the construction site: rebar crawled out from Druidic concrete slabs; backhoes and cranes loomed over a dig site; a bulbous concrete mixer; pallets of bricks and two-by-fours grew up from the ground, the sheen of cellophane wrapping reflecting the full moon hanging overhead.

Stetson heard only the sound of his own footsteps in the gravel, unhurried but louder than he would have liked. He moved forward, farther into the site, looking for the Kingfisher. He wondered if he could have possibly come to the wrong place after all. But then he heard a cough. Phlegmatic, wheezing. And he set off in its direction at an even faster clip, arms pumping at his side, his tie flapping over his shoulder.

Stetson saw him, the Kingfisher, standing in the shadow of a rusted staircase that crawled alongside what looked like an aluminum silo. The Kingfisher's back was against the wall. As Stetson neared him, the Kingfisher pointed at the man lying before him in a heaving mass. The man, as if on cue, coughed. Blood or spit or both dripped in black strands from his mouth like fat raindrops on this cloudless night.

"Jesus," Stetson whispered. "Is he going to live?"

The Kingfisher didn't say anything. Stetson thought he might have seen him shrug, but even that was uncertain.

"Where'd you end up finding him?"

"Address you gave me. He didn't run. Pulled a gun."

"Really?"

"Made it easy."

The man at Stetson's feet coughed again, followed by a low rattle in his lungs that faded as quickly as it had come. He was broken and curled, legs bent backward in some impossible pose, his arms hugging his back. Like a flower in reverse bloom.

The man let out a groan, soft. And then he went silent.

"What the hell did you do to him?" Stetson asked. He couldn't rip his eyes away, no matter how much he wanted to. It didn't matter how many of the Kingfisher's criminals he had seen twisted, broken, reassembled, disfigured—each time it struck him with the same impact, the realization that we are so much more fragile than we think. So easily broken, so capable of bleeding out into the dirt.

"He pulled a gun," the Kingfisher said. "And he fired it at me."

"What do you care? It's not like he's going to actually hurt you, right? Why do you have to do this to them?"

The Kingfisher didn't respond. He tucked his head down into his shoulders, raised them in a sort of lazy response.

Stetson asked, "What was he going to do to you that would make you do this?" When he realized an answer wasn't coming, he turned back to the broken mass before him. "I don't think he's breathing."

The Kingfisher crouched down and laid a hand on the man's neck. He rested it there, this shadow over another shadow, the two temporarily joined, and then he stood back up slowly.

The Kingfisher shook his head.

"Fuck," Stetson whispered. "I've told you. I've told you about this. And you said you'd be more careful."

"He pulled a gun," the Kingfisher said in his same flat voice. "He would have killed me, too."

"And just how the hell would he have managed to do that?"

The Kingfisher turned around with a sigh and paced a few steps. "He would have killed me if he could."

Stetson reached for the flashlight on his belt and shined the white beam at his feet and then passed it over the body. It was worse than he could have imagined. Blood poured down the man's shirt, shining against the fabric. As Stetson passed the flashlight over his face, he saw a black man whose nose lay folded over his cheek, the skin around his eyes swollen to the size of plums, and his mouth opened to a scream that would not come.

"Who the fuck is this?" Stetson whispered, a sick feeling overcoming him. Cold sweat poured down his forehead; his throat went dry.

"That's the guy," The Kingfisher said over his shoulder. "The guy you told me about."

"No," Stetson whispered, and then a shivering pulse ran up his spine and crawled from his mouth at a volume that penetrated the once silent night. "No, it's not the fucking *guy*. Goddamnit, it's not the fucking *guy*. That's not him. Who is this?"

The Kingfisher turned around and traced Stetson's flashlight. He seemed to be looking down at the dead man, trying to make sense of this, but that could have just been an illusion of the shadows, an illusion of Stetson's own sudden sense of vertigo as he folded over, hands against his knees, breathing heavy as he tried to reason the unreasonable.

"What did you do?" Stetson asked. "Tell me exactly what the hell did you do?"

The Kingfisher didn't say anything at first, only leaning closer to the body while keeping a space between them. And when he did speak, it was only a whisper. "He pulled a gun."

"Every time, I give you the fucking name, and I tell you where they might be. I describe what they look like. I give you a fucking physical description. And now this happens?"

A train whistled past in the not-so-far distance. The wheels kissing the tracks, roaring southbound.

"Jesus fucking Christ Almighty," Stetson felt himself shouting. "You fucking imbecile. I just can't wrap my head around what little goes on in your stupid empty head. Every time I tell you exactly what to do. I give you everything you need. And then you go off and do this and now I have to take care of it for you? Is that what this is? I clean up your murder? Because that's what it is. You murdered this man."

The Kingfisher crouched down and looked at the dead man. He ran his hands over the man's eyes, closing them.

Stetson stuffed his knuckles into his mouth, bit down. He felt blood on his tongue. "You're a fucking joke," he said, in a voice as low as he could manage. "That's what you are. I may not be as strong as you or as fast as you or as whatever-the-fuck-you-are, but at least I know how to identify a person. This guy is black, for Christssakes. I told you, the guy you're looking for is a white guy. Caucasian male. White guy. I mean, holy shit. White. White. White."

"He was at the address," the Kingfisher said in a voice that was just a breath, dead in the air. "He had a gun. What was I supposed to do?"

"You were supposed to get the right guy," Stetson screamed, voice straining. "You killed the wrong guy. And now I have to deal with it. Now it's my problem. Mine."

"I didn't know," he said. "I didn't remember. I didn't know."

"The only thing this guy did to you was pull a gun. And can you fucking blame him? Some freak-of-nature came bull-rushing towards him. Anyone in their right mind would have pulled a gun. You killed the wrong guy. He's dead. You did that. You. Only you. You murdered him. This isn't on me."

"I know that," the Kingfisher shouted. He lunged toward Stetson—a movement that was not a movement at all, but rather an instantaneous shift of his body from one place to the next—but stopped just a foot away.

"I know what I did," he said. "I know what I did and I didn't mean to do it." He turned and walked back to the edifice behind him, leaning against it, tucking his head between his shoulders. He was never as big as the newspapers said he was, but here he was, not even as big as Stetson remembered him being. He seemed to shrink with each passing second. Stetson thought he might have seen his wide shoulders shake, but just for a brief second.

Stetson ran a hand through his thinning hair and looked around to make sure they were still alone. "Go home. Get some sleep. I'll figure this out. I'll take care of it."

Stetson could only make out the whites of the Kingfisher's eyes as they stared before him at the crumpled shape of his creation. A mangled body curled into the tortured shape of a question mark at the end of a question unasked.

And now the Kingfisher was saying something, a long and stringing thought, but the words didn't seem to make it past his lips.

"It's OK," Stetson assured him. "Just go home and get some sleep. I'm sorry. You did what you thought was best, right? That's all that happened here." And now he was speaking rapidly, trying to convince not only the Kingfisher, but also himself. "But, listen, no one has to know this was you. Here's what I'll do. I'll call it in. I'll say I saw some guys fleeing the scene. No one's going to think twice. It's going to be OK. Hey. Listen to me. It's going to be OK. And besides, he had a gun, right? Who knows who he might have killed with that same gun? Maybe he was planning on robbing someone or killing someone with that gun. You did something good here. Let's just forget about this whole night, OK? We'll give it a couple days and start fresh. Take some time and get some rest."

But the Kingfisher remained standing there, staring down. He slid down the wall until he was sitting, and brought his knees to his chest.

Stetson had seen this man jump from a seven-story rooftop to the sidewalk, unscathed. He had felt this man lift him off the ground with a single hand wrapped around his throat. And Stetson nearly pitied him now, this man who could perform extraordinary and unimaginable feats. A man with powers and abilities Stetson would give anything to have, now reduced to a child's posture in the gravel. You can give a man all the strength in the world, but you can't strip from him his human weakness.

"There's no shame in this," Stetson said, although he knew there was.

There was nothing but shame. Paralyzing and suffocating shame. A dead man at his feet. An innocent man. Those lifeless eyes. "It's going to be OK," he said, more to himself than the Kingfisher, surprised by the softness of his voice. Softer than he had ever heard it passing from his own lips, softer than he would ever hear it again. He reached out a hand and laid it on the Kingfisher's shoulder. It was bone-hard. Stringed and warm and muscled and cold.

"I didn't know."

"I know."

"I wouldn't have."

"I know."

"I'm sorry."

"You did what you thought was best. That's all you or I could ever hope to do."

19 MINESWEEPER

"**WHAT'S THIS?**" Fester inquired in a sleep-laden, two-packs-a-day drawl.

Wren jumped, fell back against the racks of shoes. For a large man shaped like a deflating beach ball, Fester was astonishingly feline in his movements. She didn't know her boss was at the alley this early hour of the morning, much less that he was so nimble at sunrise.

"What is this?" he repeated, pointing a cigarette-stained finger at her laptop.

Wren herself had woken up only a half hour ago, literally rolling out of bed just in time to catch the L. No time yet to adjust to the new day, squinting at the sun pouring through the handprint-smudged windows of the train car. No time yet to think of yesterday, even. When she'd arrived at the alley a few minutes ago, she flipped on the lights, put cash in the drawers, and ran a vacuum halfheartedly behind the counter. There'd been no trace of Fester, but then again, he was known to sleep in his office sometimes. Though she had never actually seen the inside of his office, she'd heard from coworkers that he had an air mattress and an extensive and valuable vintage *Playboy* collection. How they knew this, though, she didn't want to know.

So she was both dismayed and fearful to look up and see Fester's sunburnt bulk standing in front of the counter, his face reddened like brick with pale circles around his eyes where he often wore a pair of orange-tinted sunglasses.

"This?" Her voice broke like a twelve-year-old boy. Most people made her nervous, but him especially. "Oh, sure, yeah, it's my laptop."

"No shit," he said. "I mean, what're you doing on that thing?" Fester's accent Wren had always guessed to be from Kentucky, maybe Tennessee. How he ended up owning and operating a bowling alley on the South Side of Chicago, Wren would never know, nor did she really care to. He was enigmatic in the least intriguing way possible, a cipher she didn't care to solve, or for that matter, speak to face-to-face.

"I was playing a game." And then she nodded at the empty lanes. "It's a slow day."

"What game?"

It took her a few beats to think of one. "Minesweeper?"

In reality, she had been scouring every corner of the internet—the darkest catacombs populated by nothing more than bones, smiling skulls, and the most egregious of internet trolls—for a final video from the gunman acknowledging the leaked ME report, his promised release of the hostages. There hadn't been one yet, which she took as an ostensibly good sign. Perhaps he wouldn't put out a final video at all and instead, he would simply stop all communication and disappear into the beyond. But Wren wanted a final video. She wanted to know that she had done something good. She wanted visual proof that the hostages were safe. She wanted to know it was over. All of it. She wanted absolution.

"I've played Minesweeper a time or two," Fester said.

"Cool. It's a fun game."

"Yeah."

She hadn't gotten a moment of rest last night. Each time she had tried—curling closer to Parker's sleeping body, closing her eyes—faces emerged from beneath a dark veil. An endless procession of faces. The women from the missing persons directory. The first hostage, with a bleeding hole in his head. The second hostage, staring into the camera, eyes rolling and lips fluttering like the wings of some dead or dying bird. But he would be safe, she told herself. They had given the gunman what he wanted. It was over.

"Actually, I hate Minesweeper, myself," Fester said. "Seems like pure luck, dumb chance. Click and boom." She smelled liquor on his breath, sour and shaped into a slur. "Just click and boom. Click and die. Chaos, girlie. That's why I prefer Spider Solitaire."

"I'm not very good at Minesweeper either."

"Then what's the point?"

"There's a strategy," she said. "I'm not sure what it is, but I think there's a strategy." She regarded his impassive expression. "But maybe you're right—it's just dumb luck."

"Then maybe there are better ways to spend your time." He smiled, revealing egg-yolk teeth. "Maybe you could get the Windex and scrub down the seats out here. Saw some kids doing unspeakable things there last night around closing. Had to chase them out with a broom, I shit you not."

"Sure," she said. "I'll clean them."

Fester thumbed his belt loops, pulled his blue jeans up an inch, and surveyed his minuscule and ill-lit domain with a long, tired sigh. "All right, then, girlie." He rapped his knuckles on the counter and walked briskly away without a sound.

She closed her laptop and rooted around for the Windex beneath the counter. A mindless and needless chore sounded appealing. She could do with the distraction.

Sitting in front of the cash register was the business card the prostitute had accidentally left behind yesterday: MISS MAY PIECEWORK. She had fully expected either for someone to throw it away or for it to dissolve back into the fever dream that was yesterday.

She wiped the length of the counter three times over. Every square inch was polished meticulously, yet it somehow retained the same dull and dirty appearance.

She saw Fester approaching once more from the corner of her eye. She closed her laptop, reached for the Windex beneath the cash register, and frantically began spraying the counter again.

"You got the TV remote?" Fester asked. He pointed at the television hanging above them.

She handed the remote to him. It was dwarfed in his massive hands.

He changed the channel to the channel six morning news. "My buddy just posted something on Facebook," Fester said to her without taking his eyes away from the screen. "I guess something else is happening with all that Kingfisher shit-show."

"What happened?"

"That's what I'm trying to find out." His enormous fingers fumbled with the remote as he turned the volume up.

But Wren didn't need to hear what was happening to understand. She knew the moment she saw the masked man—still wearing the same Liberteen mask—standing in that cold, dark room while a hostage writhed against the ropes that bound him in an office chair. The hostage was the same man from the last video, beaten and dazed, head rolling from shoulder to shoulder, lips moving without sound or reason. The gunman stepped forward to pick up the camera, panning to the far corner of the room where the other hostage remained, and Wren recognized the ring on her left hand.

The bulletin at the bottom of the screen read: NEW VIDEO FROM CHICAGO GUNMAN.

He's going to release them, Wren thought. He's going to turn them loose.

The gunman said in his digitally modulated voice, "We asked for Police Chief Gregory Stetson to release the ME report, but he did not. Instead, we had to take it ourselves."

Wren's stomach sank at the use of we.

"So now it is time for the police chief to admit the truth we have seen with our own eyes in the medical examiner's report and apologize to this city on behalf of the entire Chicago Police Department. Apologize for the corruption and the lies. Tell us the Kingfisher is alive and tell us that you lied. Beg for the forgiveness that you do not deserve. And then resign at once. Until then, lives will be lost." He pressed the pistol against the hostage's head. "And because you, Police Chief Stetson, failed to comply, this blood is on your hands. Don't make the same mistake twice. Tell us the truth." He pulled back the hammer, stalled for a moment.

The news station cut the video short. But it didn't matter. The phantom gunshot found its way into the ensuing silence.

Wren's heart rose to her throat and then crashed into her stomach, dissolving in the acid. She was left with a numbness that was nowhere near numb enough.

Hadn't you known this would happen? she reminded herself. You knew what you were doing, but you did it anyway. You knew he wouldn't stop. You knew you would only make it worse. You knew what you were doing, and here you are. Exactly where you belong. You may as well have been the one to pull the goddamned trigger. And for what? What was it for? To prove that you could do it? What's wrong with you?

"What's wrong with you?" Fester asked, his voice far away and muted, as though she were hearing it from deep underwater. "You look like shit on a shingle. You hungover? Jesus, girlie. If I've told you once, I've told you a hundred times. I swear to God. Stop coming in here hungover. I don't need you puking on customers. They'll write their stupid reviews on the inter-webs and complain about being puked on."

She shook her head slowly. "I'm fine. I just—it's just—it's hard to watch that."

"That?" he laughed. "It's a shame, but this shit happens every day. People killing people for no good reason. No use in letting it fuck with your day. Just be glad it isn't you in that chair, am I right?" he laughed.

She groaned, her vision going black.

He inspected her closely, the stale tobacco on his muddy breath send-ing her stomach into another tailspin. "I've got some TUMS in my office. Let me know if you want any." After he pulled away from the counter and ambled back to his office, she allowed herself to panic. She withdrew her phone from her pocket, fumbling it. Out of reflex, she called Parker.

It rang four times before going to Parker's voicemail. *"This is Parker Dillinger. If you're hearing this, that means you tried to call me. Don't call me."*

"Parker," Wren said to her voicemail, wishing she had thought out an explanation for the hollow ringing in her head that she assumed was also audible through the phone.

She swallowed. Her lips felt dry. When she finally spoke, it sounded like someone else's voice altogether. A stranger, crying softly. "He made another video. Parker, he made another video. The gunman. He killed the hostage. We released the file, and he still killed the hostage. It didn't matter, Parker. We didn't help. We only made it worse." Her voice rarefied as she said this, the words surreal yet immediately true. "I need you to call me back, Parker. I need you. Please, Parker. I need you."

She winced when she heard herself say this, because she knew it to be true.

20 PWOBLÉM PAP FINI

IN THE EARLY MORNING, the total quiet and absolute dark, Tillman emerged from her bedroom—her running shoes in hand—to find her father asleep in his chair and Jeremiah curled on the couch, both of them in the exact position they had been when she arrived home last night from Bedford's. Jeremiah slept bare-chested. He clutched a ratty fleece blanket to his hip like a boy and his blanky, and she thought if she looked at him long enough, she might just wake him up and ask him to stay like this every night so she could see him like this every morning.

So she left quickly, shut the door quietly. She left it all behind her where it belonged.

Still, she half hoped, after returning from her run an hour later, to find them both in the same stilled postures of sleep. But when she opened her door, sweat dripping down her chin, she saw her father sitting in his recliner, rocking gently back and forth. Jeremiah sat pin-straight on the couch. The television broadcasted into the room.

They took no notice of her entrance, both them glued to the television's glow.

"We have a saying for this in Creole," her father said to Jeremiah, finger pointed at the television. "We say, '*Pwoblém pap fini.*' Do you know this?"

Jeremiah didn't answer.

"It means that when problems come, they come like this." Her father snapped his fingers in a steady rhythm, unchanging. "You think that these things will not end, because they come and they come like this." He snapped his fingers again. "But they always end. This is how it always works. This is how it always will work. This will end soon enough."

Jeremiah scratched his neck furiously, which Tillman recognized as his mounting anxiety. Once upon a time, he used to come over to her place after bad days down at the station with claw marks up and down his throat, as if he'd been mauled by a bear. She'd touched them with her fingertips, and he'd let her. It seemed impossible to her now, but so did most things from that past life.

"What's going on?" Tillman asked.

"You can see, can't you?" Jeremiah snapped, nodding at the television.

A news channel banner suspended beneath a moving image of a dim room. She recognized it at once and slowly lowered herself to the ground. The man in the mask, pushing a man in an office chair, his mouth bound by rope, his body constricted. She felt as if she were watching a silent movie, all exaggerated bodily movements. The gunman spoke, but she didn't hear this. All of her focus was on the hostage's face. A hundred-yard stare into oblivion.

The news station cut away from the video before the final gunshot.

"That was Penny," she mouthed.

"How do you know?" Jeremiah asked.

"Bedford confirmed. I showed him the second video."

Jeremiah pointed at the television, which displayed a still image of the gunman's face, the oddly inhuman mask. "The asshole got what he wanted. That fucking ME report. It wasn't enough. He won't ever stop. He'll kill the other hostage. And then he'll just find more. He won't ever stop. This is insane."

She felt panic rising to her skin like sweat. She took out her cell phone and called Paulina's fiancé. It went directly to an automated voicemail. She tried again and then again. But then, as she watched the television, she knew why he wasn't answering.

"We just have received information confirming the hostage's identity in this latest video," the newscaster said. "The hostage's name is Jeffrey Jenkins, a fifty-eight-year-old Chicago resident. We are joined via phone by Ibrahim Rodriguez, the victim's son-in-law, who provided this information. Ibrahim, are you there?"

"Yes."

"Ibrahim, I know you are going through a lot right now, and our thoughts and prayers are with you. Can you tell us about your father-in-law? Had he been missing for some time?"

"He's not my father-in-law yet. I'm engaged to his daughter. And I want to say right now that the other hostage in that video is my fiancée. She's Penny's daughter."

"Penny? Excuse me, Ibrahim—"

"And I got no fucking clue why the cops aren't trying to find her. I got no fucking clue why they didn't try to find Penny. I've been trying to call them, but they're not doing fucking anything."

"Mr. Rodriguez—"

"They should be out there looking for these people. I tried calling them all day yesterday, and the most I got was some fucking secretary taking down my information, but no one fucking came around. People are dying out there and what are they doing about it? They're watching these people fucking die like they don't—"

The line went dead.

"I apologize to our viewers for Mr. Rodriguez's use of language," the newscaster said. "He is clearly and appropriately upset. Our thoughts and prayers go out to him and his family in this very difficult time. However, I should note that Mr. Rodriguez's opinions are entirely his own, and we do not endorse—"

She reached for the remote and turned off the television. Her father immediately protested in Creole—his language of choice for anger—but she wasn't listening. She went into the kitchen. Jeremiah called after her, but she drowned out his voice by opening cupboards mindlessly, searching for nothing. Occupying her body with the motions of a day in progress.

She hadn't had time to look for Penny. That was the simple truth. No, make coffee. There was nothing she could have done. No, start the dishwasher. A day in progress. It was morning, and she could make coffee, start the dishwasher, make a protein shake, take a shower and disappear in the jungle steam. There was nothing to linger on. Ibrahim said the woman in the video was Paulina. No, clean out the refrigerator. But how could he know that was Paulina? The woman in the video was wearing a sack over her head. Maybe he's wrong. Maybe she's safe and on her way home with apologies. And does she look like her father? And if she does, has anyone ever told her this? It's the sort of thing that doesn't mean anything until it means everything. And maybe that is what Paulina is thinking at this moment. Strapped to a chair with the world reduced to a burlap sack, thinking that she does look an awful lot like the father she could not save, and what does it mean anyway except that every morning when she looks in the mirror it will no longer be her own face she sees but the face of a ghost who stares back at her with drooping eyes, the face of a ghost who slept on her couch after he lost his job, the face a ghost she loved beyond comprehension, the face of a ghost she may soon join.

Tillman closed a cupboard and saw Jeremiah right in front of her, leaning against the refrigerator. She dropped a ceramic mug and it bounced across the floor.

"Jesus Christ." She held a hand to her heart. "What the fuck is wrong with you?"

"Listen, Tilly," Jeremiah said.

"No. Just don't. I'm fine."

"You need to understand that this situation isn't your fault."

"*Situation*," she scoffed, bending down to pick up the mug. "You mean that psychopath executing Penny? That same psychopath who has Penny's daughter? You mean *that* situation?"

"There wasn't anything you could have—"

"Don't you have somewhere to be?"

He crossed his arms. "I'm headed out soon. Got a call just before you came. They want me down at the station soon."

"Then you should probably just leave now."

"I'm trying to tell you something. I'm trying to talk to you."

"I know this wasn't my fault," she said, pulling her protein powder from a cupboard. "You don't need to tell me."

"You're saying this. I hear you saying this."

"I mean it."

"OK," he said warily, as though trying to convince himself that he believed her. "I'm glad to hear it. Because you know what? You probably saved Baxter Bedford's life last night. And that's worth a hell of a lot. I hope you know that."

She found a glass in a cupboard and slammed it shut. She ran the faucet and mixed in protein powder. "Whatever this is that you're doing, just save it. I'm fine."

He nodded. "That's what you said."

"What time are you headed to the station?" she asked before taking a heaping drink of the concrete-like mixture that calcified as it passed through her throat.

"I should probably head out in the next half hour. I can leave sooner if you want, though."

"Can you make it an hour?" She wiped her upper lip of the froth, flicked it into the sink.

"You wanted to get rid of me as soon as possible a minute ago." He smiled. "What changed?"

"I've got some things I remembered. Errands. I'd appreciate it if you could look after my father for a bit. Make sure he eats breakfast with his meds. He'll get sick if he doesn't."

Jeremiah stepped closer to her, lowering his voice even though her father couldn't possibly hear them at this distance. "Don't lie to me like that. What are you actually going to do, Tilly?"

"Don't call me that."

"Where are you planning on going?"

She washed her empty glass in the sink, running the water over its surface until it resembled something clean. "I just have somewhere to be. Errands. That's all."

"Cut the bullshit," he whispered, the harsh words somehow taking on the dimensions of affection. "Tell me where you're going."

"I think it's best you stay out of this one," she said, matching his stare. "For your sake, Detective Combs." She pronounced his title as though passing a razor blade from her stomach through her throat. That was what it felt like, at least.

"I know I brought you into all this," he said, "and I'm sorry for that. But don't do this. Please. Whatever the hell it is. You've done all you could possibly do. There's nothing else to be done."

"You know where the spare key is," she said. "Lock the door when you leave. You'll need to make my dad some breakfast. Eggs are a safe bet. He can have one cup of coffee, but don't give him any more no matter how much he begs. Caffeine doesn't mix well with his meds." She pushed off the counter. "I'm taking a quick shower and then I'm out."

"Tilly, just listen." Jeremiah reached for her elbow as she walked out of the kitchen. She spun around and broke out of his loose hold. He held up his empty hands in faux surrender, stumbling over a plea for her to allow him a chance to talk. "You don't owe Penny anything. There's nothing you can do for his daughter. I'm sorry, but it's the truth. You've done what you could do."

"Maybe if you and the rest of the department gave a shit, we wouldn't be having this conversation."

"Are you fucking serious? You think I don't care?"

"If you cared, you'd understand why I'm leaving right now. You wouldn't be babysitting that journalist all day. You'd go out there yourself, no matter the consequences. No matter if it meant losing your job, you'd do it. Because it's what needs to be done."

"Oh, is that what this is? You think you're leaving here because you care?" he asked, lowering his voice. "Are you sure you're not just doing this because it feels good to feel like a cop again?"

In a single, time-stilled moment, Tillman bounded forward and pushed Jeremiah. Pure inertia that grew from her feet, out from her hands. She felt a full release, the transfer of energy that exited her palms and sent him sprawling backward, arms in the air, grasping for nothing. He collapsed against the counter, knocking over an empty pizza box and a few stray glasses that shattered on the floor. He lay against the counter, staring at her. Blank, unbending. Neither injured nor insulted. Just fearful. Of her, of himself, of the moment itself, or of the glass shining on the floor at this feet. In each shard, a thousand reflections of himself, of herself, daring either of them to look.

She didn't know why she'd done it. But it was done.

A thousand things she might like to say to him—a thousand apologies, a thousand damnations, a thousand nothings—but there was never any time for these things. And even if there were, there was no use in dwelling in those histories, each one scattered and sharp.

"There's eggs in the fridge." Tillman pointed over her shoulder. "I appreciate the help."

21 PAUL WROBLEWSKI

MARCUS BACKED HIS CAMRY OUT of the garage an hour after sunrise. A police cruiser was blocking his driveway. Officer Danby—evidently his guard dog for the day—was hesitant to let Marcus leave the house alone.

"Can you at least tell me where you're going?" Danby asked in a slow and clumsy voice, scratching the back of his bald head. He was the shape of a cargo drum, with the skin complexion of a Handi Wipe. Dime-sized beads of sweat rolled down his cheeks. Even while sitting in his air-conditioned car, he had somehow managed to get sunburned on his face and his neck. As he was speaking to Marcus, he was simultaneously applying a generous dollop of lotion to his forehead. "If my supervisor calls me on the radio while you're away," Danby said, slapping the lotion on the back of his neck, "I don't want to look like I lost you. I think it'll look bad on me, letting you go without telling me where, especially with the most recent video and all, you know what I mean?"

Officer Danby spoke of the video as though it were a weather event, a storm system you observe from behind a pane of glass. But Marcus didn't feel at all distanced from it. He'd watched the video just once, though not all the way through. As soon as the gunman had put the pistol to the hostage's head, Marcus turned off the television. Only to later get a text from Jeremiah confirming what Marcus had already feared: *Hostage was Penny. Bedford is safe.* His mind immediately wandered to his meeting with Peter the previous day. He recalled Peter's insistence that the woman from the Englewood apartment, the woman with the red hair, was in danger. Likely the same woman Jeremiah had encountered all those years ago. Miss May. If Marcus could find her, he could advise her to take extra caution, but she might also know something, anything, that could put an end to whatever hell had awoken.

"I'm just going to Livingston Estates, about an hour south of here," Marcus told Danby. He had brought with him his brown leather shoulder bag, a comfortingly familiar weight. Like a child with a blanket.

"Oh." Danby smiled. "I know that place. Yeah, my grandmother used to live there until she croaked. God rest her soul. But real nice place they got there, and the food isn't as bad as you might think. You considering making the transition?"

Marcus was in too much of a hurry to take offense. So instead he smiled, nodded. Officer Danby pulled his cruiser away from the drive, just enough for Marcus to slip through.

As it turned out, Livingston Estates was indeed a "real nice place." Or at least it looked to Marcus like one. Something lifted directly from the glossed pages of a brochure and gently placed into reality. Nestled in a quiet, isolated reach of the far-south suburbs, Livingston Estates was a large, sprawling complex of limestone apartments spread out like a pinwheel. It boasted a soccer field, a basketball court, and an Olympic-length swimming pool. Like some college campus populated only by emeritus professors.

Through the sliding door entrance, a large check-in desk, behind which stood a young girl donning a hundred-dollar smile, which was most likely practiced in front of her bathroom mirror every morning until perfection. She was pouring a bag of multihued hard candies into a glass bowl. Readying the day ahead.

"Welcome to Livingston Estates," she chimed like a cuckoo clock. "How can I help you today? Are you interested in a prospective resident tour?"

"No, no thank you. I'm actually looking for an old friend. He lives here, I think. I wonder if you could point me to his apartment?"

"It would be my pleasure." She smiled widely, a few keystrokes at her computer. "What's the name?"

"Paul Wroblewski."

Her evergreen smile flickered like a light bulb in a thunderstorm, and she looked at Marcus as though waiting for him to correct a misspoken name. "Did you say *Wroblewski*?"

"That's right. I believe he lives here?"

She eyed him suspiciously.

"Is he," his voice narrowed, "still *here*?"

"He's very much *here*." Her smile now fully deflated. The cheeriness in her voice emulsified into a groan. "Sorry, but did you say that you're *friends* with him?"

"Well, we sort of worked together many years ago. I don't know if you could say we're friends, exactly."

"Oh, OK." She nodded, as though this made a great deal more sense. "Let me call a nurse to take you to Mr. Wroblewski's apartment."

"There's no need for that. You can just point me in the direction."

"Mr. Wroblewski doesn't—well—he doesn't respond positively to surprises. You should probably have a nurse escort you."

The nurse who met him in the lobby was an older woman, starch-white hair kept in a short braid that sat squarely on her neck. As they walked outside, she behaved as though she were actually giving him the prospective resident tour, which maybe she was. She pointed out card tables where old men in fedoras traded chips with their shaking, medicated fingers; women gathered in semicircles in plastic deck chairs, talking over each other or not talking at all. The nurse spoke slowly and cautiously, masking an untraceable and vaguely Spanish accent.

"I have a favor to ask," the nurse said over her shoulder as they passed the pool. An octogenarian swam the breaststroke. "Maybe since you know him—Mr. Wroblewski—maybe you could ask him to please finish his breakfast. He's not a very good eater. *Likes to voice his discontent*, we say around here. But really he is just being a pain in the ass. He likes being a pain in the ass."

"I really can't imagine that he'll listen to me."

She didn't seem to care. "He says nasty things about the food. Very nasty. He used to call the kitchen and say those nasty things directly to our chef, but we've since blocked his calls. That's what happens when three chefs quit in the span of four weeks. We block your calls." But then she quickly added in a flat tone, "I don't mean to say he's a bad person, of course."

"Of course."

There was a group of men standing at the shuffleboard court against the rising sun behind them. They were gathered in a closed circle, like some pack of sloped birds. As he passed, Marcus heard one of them saying, "If you aren't interested in learning the rules, Richard, I can't be interested in learning them for you."

"Does Mr. Wroblewski ever hang around out here with the other residents?" Marcus asked, noticing the doubt in his voice.

The nurse turned around to meet his gaze, a sour smile. Marcus took it as a firm *no*.

They arrived at the final apartment. Beyond was nothing but open field, recently mowed. A cloud of insects hovered against the infinite horizon. The nurse had a key on a bracelet around her wrist, but knocked first.

"Mr. Wroblewski," she said loudly into the door. She took a cautious step backward, as though serving a search warrant. "Mr. Wroblewski. You have a visitor."

No answer. Marcus heard the faint sound of a television from behind the door.

"Mr. Wroblewski, I'm opening the door. Did you hear me? I'm opening the door. OK? Here I come."

She opened the door cautiously, as if it might be rigged to explode. When it was opened a quarter of the way, she poked her head inside.

"Mr. Wroblewski," she said, louder. "You have a visitor."

"Good Christ, I heard you the first time," shouted a hoarse voice from inside. "Who is it, Marcy?"

"My name isn't Marcy. I'm letting your visitor in now, Mr. Wroblewski."

"Hope the door hits you on the way out, Marcy."

She backed out of the door and gave Marcus a look—equal parts pity and told-you-so—before turning back to where they had come from. She disappeared so quickly that Marcus didn't even get a chance to think of saying thank you.

Paul's apartment was lit only by the television. The curtains were drawn. The lights were either purposefully kept off or the bulbs had burnt out and not yet been replaced. Hard to say. Newspapers were piled on the floor, on the kitchen table, on the chairs, on the refrigerator. There lingered about the smell of a cat, though Marcus neither heard it nor saw it the whole time he was there.

Paul had never seemed like a cat person. Or really an anything person, for that matter. *Singular* would be the wrong word to describe him, but it was the only word that came to Marcus's mind in the moment as he waded through the kitchen and into the small living space where he spotted Paul, who was already studying him with sharp, slitted eyes.

"You're shitting me," Paul said, his voice, at least, untouched by the years. The same manicured gruffness, like a studio actor playing a Chicago cop. "Is that Marcus goddamned Waters in the flesh?" He wore a thick green sweater even though the apartment was uncomfortably warm, inexplicably humid. A wool-knit blanket draped over his knees, its original color stained a filthy brown.

"Good to see you, Paul."

"Shut up with the lies. How did you find me?" A tube ran from a rolling oxygen canister into his nose, clicking in relaxed intervals.

Marcus cleared a space to sit on a floral love seat stained with ancient cigarette burns. "When I interviewed you for the book a few years back, you mentioned then that you were moving here."

"Right, right, the book." Paul smiled emptily, and Marcus suspected that he had no recollection as to what Marcus was talking about. Paul could probably recite every *Inquisitor* headline from the past year or draw a detailed map of the South Side circa 1985—complete with street names, train routes—but when Marcus had last spoken with him, Paul had trouble remembering his grandchildren's names. Marcus considered it tragic that Paul's lasting memories were so impersonal and detached, but he wasn't sure Paul would see that as a tragedy. "You want something to drink? I got old milk that'll kill you on contact, and then I got some scotch. Be a dear and get the scotch."

"Thanks, but I'm fine. It's pretty early in the day."

"The scotch is on top of the fridge. Be useful, would you? Highballs are in the cupboard there by the fridge. And don't be stingy. Maybe after all these years, you've finally learned how to drink like a man. I don't need you falling over yourself the way I seen you do before. Little yuppie journalist sweating through his shirt, slurring his fancy words."

Marcus poured Paul a double and himself a half. When he handed Paul his drink, Paul pointed at Marcus's nearly empty glass. "Some things don't change."

Marcus nodded at the tray of food placed next to him on the couch. Undisturbed biscuits and gravy, already coagulated. A layer of iridescent grease coated the entire tray.

"Your nurse told me to tell you to eat your breakfast."

"And you know why she said that?"

"She doesn't want you to die?"

"Wrong," Paul barked, taking a large and slow sip from his tumbler. "It's actually the exact opposite, Marcus. Moment I swallow one of those fucking hockey pucks they call biscuits, I'm going to meet my maker. And then they collect my next month's rent and who knows how many other months. It's a fucking Ponzi scheme in here, Marcus. Swear to God. Every day I have to order food from the Chinese place in town. And I'm getting real sick of eating chicken and broccoli every day, but I have to because I don't want to die just yet. I haven't worked out how I'm going to explain a few things to the big man upstairs." His lips parted to reveal smiling rows of grayed teeth, repeating a joke Marcus had heard him use a dozen times before in all sorts of contexts. "Yeah, see, I'm trying to figure out how to explain a few *immaculate conceptions* of my own."

"I'm sure you'll think of something," Marcus smiled, rubbing the glass of scotch between his palms.

Paul seemed pleased by this response. He breathed heavily out from his mouth and gestured at the television. "Your timing was pretty good. Not a coincidence, I'm sure."

Marcus turned and saw that Paul was watching the news, where they were currently broadcasting an image of an empty podium with the Chicago Police Department insignia on the front. The top of the screen read: HAPPENING NOW. And beneath that: CHICAGO POLICE CHIEF ADDRESSES QUESTIONS AMID HACK, SECOND EXECUTION VIDEO.

There was a flurry of cameras clicking as Stetson entered the shot holding a folder. He was accompanied by a few lieutenants, colonels, and the mayor, all of whom stood behind him as he sidled up to the podium and looked down at his comments in his folder.

"My God," Paul moaned. "Old Stetson is probably shitting bricks, but you'd never know it by looking at him. Say what you will about the man, but he doesn't break."

It was true. Stetson was good in the front of the camera. Always had been. He made himself the dominant force in whatever room he was broadcasted into. He looked the camera in its solitary eye and assured the citizens of Chicago that their police force and the FBI were actively pursuing the perpetrator of those heinous videos. They would bring justice to him, Stetson said with a confidence that transmitted across the airwaves. "And concerning the hack that occurred yesterday," Stetson began, "at least one file that we know of was taken from our private servers, though we are actively investigating other information that may have been compromised."

Marcus shifted uncomfortably in the chair, remembering the letter sent to him. The letter that sent him here.

"Everything we know thus far about who performed this attack we cannot make public at this time," Stetson continued, "due to the overlap with the ongoing investigation. But what I can say is that we do have reason to believe that the attack was performed by the hacker group known as the Liber-teens, and that their intentions were transparently malicious towards the Chicago Police Department. Last night they released a statement declaring that they performed their hack in order to put an end to the violence we witnessed yesterday. To this, I point to the execution video just recently released. One in which the gunman acknowledges their hack and perpetuates more heinous violence. To those who have expressed empathy or interest towards the Liber-teen cause, I urge you to consider these facts I have laid before you. Moreover, we cannot, at this time, rule out the possibility that those individuals who hacked our servers were not, in some way, involved in the videos we have witnessed. At this time, I'm afraid that I cannot say much more on the matter since it is still an open investigation. I'll simply close by saying that Chicago does not need more fissures amongst its citizens. Now is a time for unity, a show of our collective force and spirit. I assure the citizens of Chicago that your police are working tirelessly on this matter. Thank you."

He backed away from the microphone and nodded. Cameras flashed, voices rose. He stepped back to the microphone and marched off the platform while reporters lobbed questions at him like grenades.

Paul took a long and savoring drink. "Good Christ," he said, wiping his lip with a shaking finger. "Thank God for retirement, right? Maybe I should wish I could help with that madness, but I'm glad as all hell

I'm sitting here in this dungeon instead. First time in forever I felt that way."

"Why is that?"

"Because this is a sort of mess we never had to deal with back then. Back in our day, you had good guys over here"—Paul gestured to his left—"and the bad guys over here," he nodded at his right. "Sounds simple because it was. But nowadays, all the bad guys think they're good guys and all the good guys are told they're bad guys. Meanwhile, all the normal folks in between don't know which way is up and which way is down. I don't want any part in that bullshit, no thank you. You probably feel the same, though."

"What do you mean?"

"Well, I imagine it would be pretty damn hard these days to write the stories you used to write. Have to tiptoe around every single person's feelings because no one is a bad guy anymore. God forbid you say something offensive, even about the criminals themselves, because nowadays they're just 'misunderstood' or 'disadvantaged' or 'ill.' Give me a fucking break." He gripped the arms of his chair, his long and yellowed fingernails threatening to tear the fabric. "I worked those Chicago streets long enough to know for certain that there are some people who are just plain evil and plain good and that's that. What a fucking world we live in, where we give up telling the difference."

Marcus nodded, if only to acknowledge that he'd heard him.

Paul punched in some numbers on the remote. A baseball game. The first inning, seats mostly empty. A tied score of zero. The announcers agreed that the day was a scorcher, called the next pitch a rocket.

"I'll tell you this, though," Paul said, polishing off his glass. "Stetson sure can talk. He may have been a brown-nose cop, a prick detective, and then an asshole boss, but if I were still slumming at the precinct, there's no one else I'd rather be in charge right about now. Not too many folks could take this bull by the reins and talk the public down from a ledge like that. Because, from what I've seen, people are about ready to jump and see what the hell happens when they hit the concrete. They're talking about protests, these people they interview on the news. They're saying they want to protest the cops. Can you believe it? Citizens angry at the police at a time like this? And let me tell you why, Marcus. These young kids don't know who to hate at a time like this, but they know they like the way it feels to hate someone. So they'll be protesting the goddamned police at a time like this. Just kills me, I swear it does. Because, back in our day, you had the good guys over here and the bad guys—"

"Stetson didn't mention the contents of the ME report in the press conference," Marcus pointed out before suffering through Paul's philosophy of the twenty-first century for a second time. "Doesn't that seem strange to you?"

Paul smiled, as though remembering the stark differences between Marcus and himself that had so consistently flavored their old meetings.

"And you know why he didn't mention that report, Marcus? It's because he didn't need to," Paul insisted. "He talked about what actually matters. He would have only stoked the bullshit fire if he'd gotten into all that conspiracy shit. Because it doesn't matter what he says, people only hear what they want to hear anyway. It'd be a waste of breath. That's the truth, the way it goes these days. Besides, that ME report doesn't mean a damned thing. Smoke and mirrors is all it is. There should be only one focus for the police and one focus for the public, and that is finding whatever piece of horseshit crawled out from hell and killed those people. And then burying a bullet in his head. Right here." He pointed between his scruffy, overgrown eyebrows and smiled gleefully. "Paint his fucking brains on a wall. Then carve out the wall and hang it up next to a Jackson Pollock or whoever at the art museum. I'd pay good money to see that masterpiece."

Marcus wasn't sure how to respond to this particular brand of Wroblewskian macabre, so he withdrew a pen and a fresh legal pad from his leather shoulder bag and wrote the day's date at the top. Old habits.

"So I take it you didn't find anything odd about the ME report?" Marcus asked.

"Barely looked at it."

"But you did look at it?"

"Sure. For a second. Couldn't hardly see it. TV's so goddamned small. Practically a microwave with antennas."

"What'd you think of what you saw?"

"Looked like an ME report." He shrugged. "Nothing out of the ordinary."

"Really? It said that the identity of the body was 'inconclusive.' But the police and Stetson himself have always said that it was a positive identification. Doesn't that seem—well—out of the ordinary?"

"If you're so worried about things out of the ordinary, then let's talk about those kids who stole confidential information from the police. That seems pretty fucking out of the ordinary, if you ask me."

"That's not what we're talking about, though."

"Hey, is that the same bag you used to have?" Paul asked, pointing at the leather bag at Marcus's feet.

"Do you have any idea why Stetson would have kept the ME report confidential all these years?"

"That wasn't his decision. It was Gonzalez, back when he was chief. If you want to ask Gonzalez why he did it, you could go visit his grave and shout into the soil, but I'm guessing he won't answer."

"But Stetson could have authorized a declassification, right?"

"Could have." Paul took a drink, washed the liquor around in his mouth. "Wouldn't be a reason to, though."

"Why?"

"Because none of that matters. No one cares anymore about all that. All that Kingfisher stuff. No one cares."

"Obviously, someone cares," Marcus said. "Or else none of this would be happening. I wouldn't be here."

Paul shook his head ruefully. "And here I thought you came to shoot the shit and mooch my scotch. Speaking of which, how about you be a dear and refill our cups." He glanced at Marcus's glass and smiled. "Or at least refill mine."

Marcus did so. He'd gone easy on his own tumbler after reminding himself that it was not yet midmorning. Paul, however, didn't seem to mind the early start. With his curtains drawn, the only discernible sign that it was morning were the biscuits and gravy, which had garnered the attention of several enthusiastic flies.

"Can I ask you for a favor?" Marcus asked again.

"So long as I can say no."

"I'm looking for someone and I think you can help me out. I know you had a number of contacts on the South Side back in the day. Some folks on the street."

"You're going to have to be more specific. There's a whole lot of types of folks on the South Side."

"She was a working girl. Went by the name 'Miss May'?"

Paul took a drink and wiped a lingering drop from the glass with a mangled finger. He stared at Marcus. "What do you think you're doing here?" he asked, his voice dry and searching. Mildly perturbed. "I thought you'd retired. What are you doing with all this? Shouldn't you be down somewhere in Florida reading your fancy books? I hear Pensacola is nice. Got some friends down there myself. Most of them dead. Maybe all of them."

"I'm looking into something. Old business. Tell me what you know about Miss May."

"No. Cut the shit and tell me what you're doing here."

"I talked to someone who had an undocumented run-in with the Kingfisher back in '83. This was in Englewood. He said that this Miss May was there, along with a couple of guys. A pimp and a bodyguard. He beat them up pretty good, the Kingfisher, but didn't turn the guys over to police. So I was thinking they may be persons of interest, if they're still around. They may be overlooked, since it wasn't ever reported. And Miss May herself, if she had any sort of relationship with the Kingfisher, she may know something. That, and she might be in danger. The gunman might be looking for her, or maybe he already has her."

"Why don't you drop a call to Stetson if you're so worried about all this?" Paul asked, smiling. "Seems like something he should know."

Marcus swirled a tongue-drop of scotch in his mouth, buying himself some time to gather a response. "I'd rather do it myself, for the moment. Besides, it may not amount to much. I figured I could save Stetson the hassle."

"Is that really what you think you're doing, Marcus?" Paul stared somberly into his tumbler and then looked up at Marcus, a neutral expression. "Trying to help out Stetson?"

"Paul, listen—"

"Because I personally think if you were trying to help the investigation along, you'd have turned this information over to the police. That's my opinion. That's what I think. But then again, maybe you're one of the clueless thousands who distrust the cops for no fucking reason other than the baseless claims of a murdering psychopath."

Marcus sensed the shift in atmosphere and set his pen down. "What are you trying to say?"

"I'm saying I think you ought to examine your motivations. That's all." Paul ran a shaking thumb along the rim of his glass. "What do you think is waiting for you at the end of this road, Marcus? You think you're going to stumble on something you somehow missed all those years? Is that what this is? Or are you just trying to rewrite history?"

His oxygen tank clicked.

"Because let me tell you something," he continued, "and I want you to listen real close when I say this to you, OK? You and I, Marcus, we had our time and we retired with grace and there's nothing left back there for us but dirt and bones. Dirt and bones, Marcus. And if you decide you want to start looking at all of it again, you want to pal around with the past and everything that happened back then, of course it's going to look different. It always looks different. And don't expect it to come to you gracefully. Expect a sledgehammer to the head. Too much time has passed for it to look the same." Paul seemed energized by this last sentence, a sudden spryness in his posture, a liquid gesticulation of his arms. "It's a whole different world back there. It's all carnival mirrors. All of it. So my advice to you is this." He leaned in close until Marcus could smell the whiskey on the man's breath. "Everything you remember, just keep it the way it is, because that's the way it ought to be. That's the way that it was. Don't bother digging up old bones, Marcus. It isn't worth it. Save yourself the grief."

Paul threw back the dregs of his tumbler and set it down gently on his breakfast tray. A fresh spurt of oxygen puffed into his nose, and he tapped the rim of his glass the way he used to when they'd meet in dingy dives and talk about things they thought they understood. Marcus stood up and poured Paul another drink.

"I need to do this, Paul," Marcus said. "I just do."

"Is that an answer to a question?"

"You asked me why I'm doing this. I'm telling you. I need to do it."

"For who? A couple dead hostages on television? A street whore you don't even know? Or is it for yourself? Who is it for, Marcus? You tell me."

Paul's eyes were glassy. He blinked slowly, as though falling asleep.

"I don't think I'm asking for much," Marcus said, feeling frustrated enough that he drank his scotch in a single swig, which he immediately regretted as the burning alcohol reached his empty stomach. He winced, coughed. "I'm just trying to get in touch with Miss May. She might be in danger. I don't know. But if I can find her, I'll warn her. I'll talk to her. Maybe it'll lead to someone else, or maybe it'll end right there. Either way."

"Can I tell you something?" Paul asked, eyes foggy. "You can consider it free advice, or maybe just a little story. Depends how you want to take it."

"Sure."

"Back maybe fifteen years ago, I started going to those AA meetings. My son dragged me to them. As you can see," he said, holding up his glass, "they didn't stick. But my son, he took to them pretty good. We'd get dinner after the meetings, just him and I. We'd go to that place down near 34th, the Bosnian place that's not there no more. He'd talk to me like one of those doorstep preachers, the same sort of insistence. All bellow and gas. He'd tell me all about the world as he saw it, and he'd always tell me that we're powerless. We, as human beings. We're powerless. He'd say it again and again. Like he was trying to convince himself and myself in the same breath. What happened was, he said it so often I started to believe him. Or maybe just a little. And then when he died a few years after, I believed it a lot."

"I didn't know that he died," Marcus said. "I'm so sorry, Paul."

"What was I telling you before all that? I can't seem to remember. Old brain is fried like an egg. It's the goddamn medicine, is what it is. They feed it to us by the spoonful."

"You were going to tell me where I could find Miss May."

"Miss May," he repeated, giggled, half-drunk, the onset of a boyish grin threatening to take hold. "I remember her specifically because I liked to call her Miss Ginger. She looked kind of like that gal on *Gilligan's Island*. She'd get brought down to the station pretty often. But that was back before all that Kingfisher shit. Word came down that she was a CI, so she stopped getting booked."

"A confidential informant? For what?"

Paul shrugged. "I never saw her doing much informing. Guys down at the station missed her being around. A fiery one, Miss May. Stetson never once brought her by the precinct, that I know."

"Stetson? Why would Stetson have brought her by the precinct?"

"Because she was Stetson's CI."

Marcus sat forward on the edge of his chair, his mind reeling. "Why would Stetson have a prostitute as a CI?"

"You'd have to ask him, but it makes sense to me. He had enough sense to know that she knew the South Side better than he did. Girl like that, she'd know all the major players."

"Was this before the Kingfisher came around, or after?"

"Don't recall exactly, but I know what you're trying to get at and I'm not going to entertain it. Don't go down that road, Marcus."

"Did she ever get picked up after the Kingfisher died? After Stetson's promotion to chief?"

Paul's laugh was followed by a sigh. "I don't know, Marcus. I don't recall. You're asking useless questions right now."

"It just seems odd for a prostitute, who may have been involved with the Kingfisher, to receive what amounts to immunity for being a CI. And through Stetson, no less. Doesn't that seem strange to you?"

"Yeah, well." He sighed, pausing for a moment. "A lot of strange things in this world, Marcus. You ought to know that by now."

Marcus had been hoping to find an organic way of bringing up the letter from the CPD detectives about Stetson, the same letter that had been cosigned by one Paul Wroblewski. But now it seemed that Paul was anticipating it, maneuvering out from under the question unasked.

"You know what I remembered recently?" Marcus asked. "Stetson was the first one on scene when the call came through about a body in the Chicago River. The body that turned out to be the Kingfisher. Why would a detective be the first on scene?"

"Good Christ." Paul shook his head. "Don't do this."

"Don't do what?"

"Dust and bones, Marcus." Paul finished his glass, wiped his lip with a knobbed finger. "Don't go digging up dust and bones."

Marcus knew Paul wasn't going to divulge what he knew about Stetson, if in fact he knew anything at all. But Marcus refused to leave empty-handed. "Where can I find Miss May?"

Paul sighed, tapped his glass for a refill. Marcus filled it with a sliver of scotch, but Paul stared at him until Marcus poured more.

"I'm going to tell you this because I'm your friend," Paul said. "I consider myself your friend even after all this time. Know that."

"OK." Marcus nodded.

"Last I knew, she lived near Wrigley. But that would have been about fifteen years or so ago. God knows if she's still down there."

"Address?"

"Do I look like a fucking Rolodex?"

"What about the street name?"

Paul thought about it. "No, but I can do you one better, though. I remember her apartment complex. Lindley Apartments, I think they're called. One of my buddies from the precinct passed through there after his wife kicked him out. But this was years and years ago, Marcus. Miss May's probably moved to a shit hole like this by now." He gestured weakly around him. "That or she's croaked. Street whores don't exactly live forever, if you get what I'm saying."

Marcus ignored the provocation. "Do you happen to know if she ever lived in an apartment down in Englewood before that? This would have been during the Kingfisher years."

"No idea," he said without deliberation.

Marcus made a few last notes and then packed his notepad into his shoulder bag. Paul watched Marcus with a blank expression.

"You're leaving?" Paul asked.

"I'd love to stay and catch up," Marcus said, making sure he'd collected all of his things, "but you know how it is."

"Sure," Paul said, lips curled into a genial, albeit forced grin. The oxygen ticked into his nose. "Sure I do. Time being what it is and all that. Good Christ. It doesn't ever seem to stop, does it? Just keeps coming and coming. Doesn't even stop for two old friends to catch up and shoot the shit a little while. Drink some scotch and watch a ballgame." He paused uncomfortably, as though unsure how to continue or if to continue at all. How to end a moment that never really began? "Best of luck, Marcus. Hope you find whatever ghost you're chasing."

Marcus nodded, smiled. He opened the door to leave. "Eat your breakfast, Paul."

"Not if it grows legs and eats me first," Paul shouted back at him, settling into a laugh as the door closed between them.

Marcus walked back to his car, not even pausing to take in the day-lit faces of the residents gathered around the lawn, a future he couldn't imagine. Slow laps in an Olympic pool. The clatter of a game of shuffleboard. Sunglasses so large they masked the face. But then again, at any point in his life, he couldn't have imagined any future he had lived, and so far he had lived them all.

Back at his car, he took out his cell phone. He tried calling Jeremiah, but got his voicemail. Jeremiah texted him a moment later: *At the station. Can't talk. What's up?*

Marcus texted him back. His thumb hovered over each tiny letter: *Have a lead on Miss May's location.*

Want me to pass it on to Stetson?

Marcus didn't need to think about it. *No.*

Didn't think so. Wish I could help. Things are bad around here. Good luck.

He called the only other person who would be able to ID Miss May for him.

One ring.

"Marcus?" Out of breath, scattered and soft. "Did you see the video from this morning?"

Marcus ignored the question. "Peter, I've got a lead on the woman from the Englewood apartment you brought me to. I might know where she is."

"Really? How did you find her?"

"I'll explain later. I only know what I've heard about her, but you've actually seen her. I don't have an exact address, just an apartment building—Lindley Apartments. I'll need you to come with me. I need you to help me spot her."

The phone rustled in Peter's hands. Marcus heard him breathing, hesitating. When his voice came back, it was nearly a whisper. "I don't know, Marcus."

"What's the problem?"

"I just don't want to get wrapped up in all of this. If it's OK with you, I think I'll stay out of it. I'm sure you'll recognize her when you see her. You don't need me there."

"You said yourself that you're worried she may be next," Marcus said. "If you mean that, then you'll help me find her. I don't know who I'm looking for."

Peter sighed through the phone. "OK. Fine."

"Give me your address. I'll be back in Chicago in about an hour. Be ready to go."

22 LUCKY

LUCINDA TILLMAN'S SUV GROANED as she turned the key, the engine whining like a gutted animal. The check engine light flared for the last time before the vehicle yawned a sad, sputtering death.

There wasn't time to grieve, even if she had wanted to. Tillman threw the door open and slammed it shut behind her, making off down the street to catch the next L to West Lawn. There was a bar in that corner of the city by the name of Lucky's. When Tillman had met with him yesterday, Paulina's fiancé had scratched the name of the bar on the back of an envelope Tillman had folded in the back pocket of her jeans, along with the names of some of Penny's drinking companions. Tillman knew that Lucky's would be the best place to find them. Drunks don't too often stray from the barstool they've adopted as their second, or in some cases *first*, home. She only hoped that they would know something, anything that would help her locate Paulina.

She hadn't taken the L in months. In that time, she had nearly been able to forget the acrid smell of piss, cigarillo smoke, and industrial cleaning products. The windows scratched with apartment keys into the shapes of names and phalluses and hearts—initials added to initials, symbols of unending and indelible love. Passengers sitting like antiques shop statuettes, clutching purses and backpacks, staring forward into some hopeful future that lurked always beyond the next yawning turn.

She got off at the West Lawn station and bounded down the concrete stairs into the street. Half walking, half running. Sidestepping the slow crawl of sidewalk traffic, sliding through clustered bodies stopping in their stride to take a call or simply stare at the steeple of some Unitarian church they'd never noticed before, a grocery bag slung into their elbow, twisting in the wind.

Lucky's protruded from the neighboring buildings as though it were taking a step toward the street. A green awning adorned with painted-on shamrocks scattered around the Gothic typeface name of the bar. Two men in Day-Glo construction vests stood against the entrance, pulling lazily on their cigarettes, nodding in agreement at something neither of them had said.

Inside Lucky's it was dark enough that Tillman had to pause in the entryway to let her eyes adjust. The only sources of light spawned from beneath the liquor bottles at the bar and the lights hanging over the deserted pool tables. As her eyes gradually focused, she saw four people seated at the bar, a few more in the booths lining the walls. Older folks, crusted from a day just beginning. Speaking in low, conspiratorial volumes, followed by sporadic bouts of laughter loud enough to scare away any and all pigeons within a one-block radius.

Tillman approached the bar. She took out her wallet and removed her credit card, tapping it against the wooden counter for the bartender's attention. The bartender was young. Or at least too young to be working at a place like this. Hair in a tight ponytail that pulled her eyebrows back in a look of constant surprise. She wore a low-cut top that revealed a tattoo over her right breast—a shamrock wearing sunglasses with arms and fingers giving two thumbs-up.

"What can I get you?" she asked.

"A ginger ale."

"Sure." The girl nodded, scooping ice into a glass. "Are you driving someone?"

"What?"

"It's just, you're ordering a ginger ale at a bar. I figure you're driving someone."

"No, I'm actually looking for someone. Maybe you can help me."

"Who you looking for?" she asked, cracking open a ginger ale and pouring it into the glass.

Tillman withdrew the envelope from her pocket, unfolded it. She read

T. J. MARTINSON

the names. "Abe Dawkins, Chuck, Wanda, Tank, and"—she squinted to make out Ibrahim's scratchy handwriting in the scant light—"*Slimskin*?"

Some of the regulars at the counter overheard this particular name, laughed into their empty glasses.

The bartender took her credit card to the register. "Slimskin got arrested a few nights ago," she said over her shoulder, smiling. "Pissed on a cruiser with the cop still inside."

The men at the bar listening in on the conversation laughed once more, relishing the memory. One of them said, "Ol' Dumbfuck Slimskin."

Another—an older man with a John Deere ball cap, staring longingly into a half-empty pint—replied, "Wasn't Slimskin's fault. That asshole cop was baiting him. Infringed his rights. It's right there in the Constitution."

The bartender ignored the commentary, turned back to Tillman. "Tank and Chuck won't be in for another few hours, I'd guess. Wanda's in the hospital with walking pneumonia, last I knew. But Abe"—the girl brought Tillman her receipt to sign—"was right over there somewhere last I saw him." She pointed across the dark room, squinting through the din. "May have gone out the back for a cigarette, though."

"Abe's making a call," said one of the men to Tillman. "Wouldn't bother him if I were you."

"What are you looking for them for?" the bartender asked Tillman, setting the ginger ale down before her.

"Just business," Tillman said. *Business,* she knew, meant nearly anything in a crusted bar this time of day, not even noon. A word that flagged itself as a sort of warning shot.

The bartender nodded and went back to talking with her regulars. Tillman took her ginger ale and sat down at the bar, keeping her eye trained on the back door.

"Back to what I was saying," said one of the men to his half-drunk comrades, huddling over the bar, punctuating his words with thrusts of his whiskey. "What happened to Penny was a goddamned shame, no matter what you think of the man. But if it's true the Kingfisher is still alive like some of them are saying, then he's going to unleash holy hell pretty soon. Mark my words. Won't be a second too late, either."

"Oh, please," the bartender said. "If he's alive, he doesn't give a damn about any of this."

"Or he's just old and tired," said another. "He's done with it. Can't blame him."

"Man like that doesn't get old and tired."

"Bullshit he doesn't. We all get old and tired."

"He's not like us. He's not one of us. I've said it before, but I'll tell you again. He came from somewhere else. Some alien visitor. Maybe he ascended back to wherever planet he came from."

"Don't start with that again."

"I don't feel old, and I don't feel tired. That make me an alien superhero?"

"Take a look at yourself. You look like you stumbled out of the morgue."

"Fuck you."

"You'd have to buy me a drink first."

Tillman decided that waiting on Abe wasn't an option. She took her drink and walked through the bar toward the back exit. Stained glass Budweiser lamps hung over grass-green tables. A dartboard hung askew on an empty wall, surrounded with Sharpie graffiti. Faces emerged in the shadows of booths she thought were empty, whites of eyes tracking her movements. Each step forward felt less certain than the last, a growing malignancy in her periphery, and slowly, so as not to warrant suspicion, she reached behind her back and touched the stock of her pistol. Just to know it was there. Its familiar heft, the coolness of metal pressed against skin.

She opened the back door. It fed directly into a narrow alley, two body length's wide. A rat stood on its haunches across from her, working its way through a trash bag. It regarded her with bored indifference before resuming its immovable feast. Tillman turned and saw a man standing at the end of the alley, facing the street. He wore a black T-shirt, dirt-stained jeans. Long-limbed, but muscular. A shaved and sweating head. His phone was tucked between his ear and his shoulder, freeing up his hands to hold a cigarette and a beer bottle.

She lit one of her few remaining cigarettes, leaned against the brick wall.

He hung up his phone and started toward the back entrance. As he approached, Tillman saw tattoos crawling along his pale-white skin. The tattoos were smudged, fading, as though evaporating from his skin. Prison ink. He took a swig of his beer and flicked his cigarette at the wall.

When he passed her, she asked, "Abe Dawkins?"

He froze, slowly turning on his heels to face her. He looked her up and down, a carnivorous grin. "Who's asking?"

"My name is Lucinda Tillman," she said in a cloud of smoke. "I was hoping I could talk to you."

"That right?" He smiled, revealing a row of grayscale teeth. "About what?"

"Penny."

He nodded once, paused, and then took off in a sprint down the alley. Tillman went after him, dropping her cigarette and ginger ale, no time to question the moment. Abe was surprisingly fast for such a large body, but she was faster. He turned his head over his shoulder and saw her gaining on him. He spun around, planted his feet, and threw his beer bottle at her head. She sidestepped and stumbled over a fallen trash can, landing on her palms. By the time she regained her footing, Abe had exited the alley into the street. She turned in either direction and spotted him running toward an intersection, barreling through wandering crowds. She chased after him, pushing through pedestrians amid a flurry of curses and shouts. Half a block ahead of her, Abe ran through the open intersection. As she neared, the light had changed and cars were incoming, but she only quickened her sprint, willing her strides to widen beyond her anatomy. A chorus of horns, squealing tires. From the corner of her eye, she saw a black town car screeching toward her, unable to stop in time. She hurdled, feet forward, and slid across the hood, landing on her feet. The driver leaned out of the window, shouting nonsensical damnation. She made off down the sidewalk and darted after Abe into another alley. He was slowing down, ambling in his run. She summoned whatever energy remained and took off full-speed. When she was within range, he whipped around, brandishing a butterfly knife that he flourished deftly in his fingers.

Red-faced, eyes bulging, heaving for air. "Get the fuck away from me."

In a single motion, she pulled her gun from her waistband and leveled it at his chest. She gestured at his knife. "Drop it."

She saw him calculating the distance between them. He was within distance to strike, but in the time it would take him, she could bury two shots in his heart. She worried he might not know that, but she would be willing to prove it if push came to shove.

"Drop it," she said again, keeping her voice low so as not to attract the attention of the passersby on the nearest street, just twenty yards away.

He opened his hand and let the knife clatter to the ground.

"Step back against the wall."

He held up his hands and took a step back behind a dumpster, which effectively concealed them both from the sight lines at either opening of the alley. She kicked his knife beneath the dumpster.

"I didn't fucking do anything," he panted.

"Then why run?" she said. "The moment I mentioned Penny."

"I didn't kill Penny," he spat. "I had nothing to do with it."

"So you ran?" She kept her gun pointed at him.

"Because I know what you assholes think."

"Who?"

"The cops," he sneered, still catching his breath. "Yeah, go ahead and look surprised. I know a cop when I see one. And I'll tell you right now, yes, I was with Penny the night he went missing, but I swear to God I didn't do that to him. Penny was my friend." His voice shook, either from exhaustion or something else entirely. "I was at Lucky's all last night. You can ask anyone."

"Then tell me about when you last saw him."

"I don't have to tell you anything. I want a lawyer."

She raised her pistol and aimed it at his head.

He stared down the barrel, a smile widening. "You cops might get away with a hell of a lot, but shooting an unarmed man in the head in broad daylight may be pushing your luck."

"Good thing I'm not a cop," she said, finger on the trigger. "Tell me when you last saw Penny."

Abe's Adam's apple bobbed in his throat. "Lucky's. Two nights ago. Penny left and that was the last I, or anyone else, saw of him before those fucking videos. I'm telling you the truth."

"What time did he leave that night?"

"Earlier than usual. Maybe ten or so."

"Why'd he leave early?"

"Said he had a job interview."

"At ten o'clock at night?"

"Yes, now would you please put that thing down?" He nodded at the gun. "It's making it pretty fucking difficult to think."

"Are you going to answer my questions?"

He nodded. She put her gun in her waistband. A show of goodwill she hoped would be reciprocated.

"Penny said he had a job interview to be a doorman at some yuppie hotel," Abe said, releasing a heavy breath. "The Armada. His daughter was going to take him there when she got off her shift at the hospital."

Tillman's worst fear was confirmed. If on the night of his disappearance Penny had left Lucky's with Paulina, then it seemed unavoidable that Paulina was the other hostage in the video. Ibrahim was right. And whoever had wanted Penny had likely attained another hostage by simple chance. Two for one.

Abe pointed his finger at her, smiling. "I should have known you weren't a cop. No way those assholes would show up around here after all that."

"After what?"

"I called them after I saw the first video. Right after watching the first video. Walter getting a bullet in the brain. I called the cops. Didn't give them my name, but I told them I thought Penny was in trouble. Lady on the phone took down my information. But that's most likely damn near all she did."

"You knew Walter Williams?"

Abe sighed and leaned against the wall. He reached into his pocket. Tillman reflexively reached for her pistol, but Abe held up a pack of cigarettes in the gesture of surrender. "Jesus, relax," he said, withdrawing a cigarette. "I've known Penny a long time. We go way back. I knew him back when he still worked with Walter. That was back before Walter took to the straight and narrow. I knew that if that psycho had Walter, he would have Penny, too."

"How would you know that?"

Abe lit his cigarette, drew on it deeply. "Same reason I knew the cops wouldn't do shit when I called them."

"Tell me."

Abe hesitated, blowing smoke in the space between them. "Penny told me something one night when he was drunk. Told me never to repeat it. Made me promise. Said it would be bad news for both of us."

"Tell me."

"Lady, I don't even know who you are or what the hell you're trying to do here. Walter is dead, and so is Penny. I don't see why any of this matters anymore."

"I'm trying to find whoever is doing this."

"Why?"

"Because he has Paulina. Penny's daughter. He has her."

"What?" Abe asked, but no sooner did the question leave his lips than his face blanched, and the veins in his neck tightened like a cord of rope. "That's her in the video?"

She nodded. "Tell me what Penny told you."

He swallowed. "Paulina is a good girl. She never did nothing to deserve this."

"I'm going to try to help her," she said. "But I need you to tell me what Penny told you."

"I don't like this one bit," he said, nervously eyeing the street. "If I tell you what Penny told me, it could come back and fuck me up. Only reason I'm even thinking about telling you is because I'm choosing to believe you're telling me the truth about Paulina. That she's in trouble. That you're trying to find her."

"It's true. I promise."

Abe held his cigarette up in front of his face, studying the ember. "Penny told me that one night, way back then, he and Walter and some other guy I never met were at their boss's house. The boss had some people over for a party, and in the middle of it he was saddling Penny, Walter, and the other guy with supply. Guess they were his main runners back then, see. Their job was to saddle the corner guys. But when the boss was measuring out the supply, the Kingfisher busted in and fucked the guy up. Beat the shit out of him."

"I've heard the story," Tillman interrupted. "All of that was in Marcus Waters's book. The Kingfisher spared the drug runners. Why would Penny tell you not to tell anyone?"

"Because that book didn't tell the whole story. It missed what happened after." Abe breathed out, looking either way down the empty alley. Tillman saw that he was frightened and not used to the feeling. "That night, after the Kingfisher came in and beat the hell out of the boss, the Kingfisher left as quick as he'd come. Walter stayed behind with his boss, who was in real shit shape. The other runner ran off before the cops came. And Penny took off, too, but, see, he wasn't running away. No, he was looking for help for his boss. The boss was going to die if he didn't get some help. And yeah, I know that his boss pulled a gun on Penny. Godknows I would have let the fucker die, but Penny was just that type of guy who would help anyone who needed it. That's just who he was. He cared."

"So Penny left for help and then what?" Tillman asked.

"He said he saw a cop car parked a ways down from the back door of the house," Abe said, cautiously measuring his words as though they were sworn testimony. "Said he couldn't hardly believe his luck. He knew he'd likely be getting a drug charge by the cops when it was all said and done, but still he ran up to the cruiser, knocked on the window. But it didn't roll down. So Penny started shouting through the window that someone was hurt and needed help. Said someone was going to die and needed an ambulance. But the cop just stared back at him behind the window. Penny kept on screaming over and over again. Said that his friend was attacked by the Kingfisher. Kept on screaming that his friend was going to die. But the cop just stayed right there, pretending like nothing was happening."

Tillman wanted to interrupt, wanted to say that couldn't have been true, but Abe saw her doubt and simply talked faster.

"Penny didn't know what the hell was going on and ran back to the house. Walter was still there, but the boss had died. At that point, there wasn't much reason to stick around, so Walter and Penny made to leave. Moment they walked out the house, the cop from the cruiser was coming towards them. Penny said he screamed at the guy, told him he was too late to save their friend. Told that cop he had let the guy die. Penny said the cop didn't say anything back. Just went inside the house all quiet while Walter and Penny ran off together. Only other person Penny ever told what happened with that cop in the car was Walter, seeing as how Walter was there at the end and all. Doubt Walter would have told anyone either. They didn't need any more targets on their backs."

"That doesn't explain how you knew the gunman would have Penny if he had Walter."

"Then you don't know as much as you might think you do," Abe said. "Because whoever is doing this, he must have been there that night. And he knows damn well what he is doing. He chose Walter and Penny carefully."

"But the other runner from that doesn't have anything to do with the videos. I've spoken to him, and he's safe. Who else could it have been?"

"I don't know. But that doesn't surprise me, that the other guy is safe. He probably wasn't ever in danger. Whoever is doing this, he only wanted

Penny and Walter." He paused. "He must have known what happened that night. Maybe he was there. Or maybe when Penny got drunk and told me all of it, he also told someone else and word spread. Doesn't really matter either way. What matters is that whoever is doing this knew that the police would let Walter and Penny die."

"Why?"

"Because of what they knew."

"That a police officer was on the scene and didn't intervene soon enough?"

"It wasn't just any fucking police officer there that night," Abe said ruefully, his voice laced with the closest thing to pure hatred Tillman had ever heard. "It was fucking Gregory Stetson. Parked right outside that house like he knew what was going to happen before it even happened. And he didn't do shit until it was over." Abe paused, clenching his teeth as though holding in something primal. "And if Stetson would have actually tried to save Penny and Walter when those videos started coming out, folks would have had the chance to ask them why the gunman had taken them. And maybe Stetson thought they would have spilled what really happened that night. And I'd be willing to bet Stetson doesn't want people knowing about that. Not then, and sure as shit not right now."

Tillman tried to condense this information into something that made sense. Stetson had been on the scene of a Kingfisher attack before anyone had even called the cops—perhaps he had somehow coordinated the attack with the Kingfisher. He had intentionally let the drug boss die. If any of it was true, it would be reason enough for Stetson to have lost his job, not to mention it was morally reprehensible, but still it didn't make sense. "If Stetson would be worried that Penny or Walter would say what happened that night," she asked, "then why would the gunman use them for ransom? If Stetson wanted to be rid of them anyway, then why would the gunman barter with them?"

"He wasn't bartering." Abe shook his head. "He was proving a point."

"What point?"

"That the police will do anything to save themselves. Even if it means letting Walter and Penny die." He spat on the ground, then put his cigarette out in the small pool of saliva. "I'm telling you right now that the gunman never once expected the police to send him whatever the hell thing he was asking for. Maybe he knew someone else would do it for him, maybe not. Either way, the fact that he got what he wanted anyway is fucking bullshit. Walter and Penny died just to prove his point, one that didn't need much proving, if you ask me." Abe shrugged, looking down at his feet. He kicked at a chunk of concrete, sent it scattering and spinning. It looked like he started and stopped a dozen thoughts, settling into a somber whisper. "I didn't know Walter well, but I can tell you Penny didn't deserve what came to him." His voice thinned out until it was hardly audible, barely discernible from the din of voices creeping from the street. "And Paulina sure as hell doesn't either. She didn't have nothing to do with all of this. You said you were trying to save her."

"I know."

"Don't you forget it." Abe shook his head. "Whatever else is going on right now, it doesn't matter much. All that police shit. It doesn't matter. Because Penny is dead. And no one seems to care." His voice was rising steadily until he was nearly shouting, his eyes red and glossy. "I've watched the news. They call him the *hostage*. What's so hard about saying his name? I know they know who he was. They must know his name. Why wouldn't they just say his name? What's so hard about saying his name?"

Tillman hadn't considered why the news reports had devoted so little time to the hostages. But she now had her suspicions.

"That psycho took Penny's name from him. And his name was damn near all Penny had in this world, aside from Paulina." His face reddened, fists clenched. "And she's a good girl. Always looking after Penny whenever Penny couldn't look after himself, which was too often, if you ask me. She shouldn't be a part of all this. She didn't have nothing to do with whatever the hell happened that night way back when. She doesn't deserve this."

"I know," she said, turning around.

"Where are you going?" Abe called after her.

"The Armada," she said.

23 DECEMBER 1983

IT WAS WELL PAST MIDNIGHT, those intermediary hours of twilight when Detective Gregory Stetson could practically feel the present becoming the past. The same hours Stetson used to patrol Chicago just a few years back as an officer—it felt like an eternity ago, some other life altogether. A sad life that he had risen above and beyond, back when he was just a lonely pair of headlights licking the pavement, dreaming of this life he now lived.

And in this life, in this moment, he was asleep in bed. Mindy was lying next to him with their two-year-old boy, Bobby, cuddled next to her. It was the same each night. Bobby shuffle-footed down the hall, dragging a blanket, and climbed wordlessly into the bed next to his mother. She pulled the sheets to his chin and patted his chest, and the three of them together slept through until morning.

And if he were awake, Stetson might have noticed how Mindy slid closer to Bobby and farther from himself with each dragging chime of the clock. And if he were awake, this might have bothered him.

When the phone rang next to Stetson's sleeping head, he was immediately awakened. He listened to the ringing, trying to distinguish it from the dreams still swirling in his head. Bobby whined, an almost-cry, and then faded into a sleeping yawn. Mindy kicked, turned over.

Stetson picked the phone up.

"Gregory Stetson," he whispered.

There was no voice on the other end, just the dry whistle of static.

"Hello?" Stetson asked.

And then breathing. Heavy and jagged. "I need help."

Stetson recognized the voice at once. The Kingfisher had never called him over the phone, much less at home. This was strictly against the rules Stetson had set. Stetson stood up from the bed and pulled the phone the farthest the wire would allow. He made it almost into the hall. "What the hell?" he asked, his panicked whisper somehow louder than his normal speaking voice. "You can't call me at home."

"I need help."

"Where are you?"

"Pay phone. Meet me at the alley by the precinct parking lot."

"What's going on?"

A dial tone whined in his ear and he regarded the sleeping silhouettes of his wife and his son for a brief moment before setting the phone down, grabbing his coat and his keys, and running to the car.

Stetson sped his freshly leased Buick into the parking lot at a roaring clip, the tires spinning around each snowy corner. He parked away from the fleet of cruisers near the precinct entrance and walked to the sidewalk. He spun around, looking for any hint of the Kingfisher, or where he might be.

A heavy snow had fallen that night, and here Stetson was wearing recently shined Dockers and his blue-striped pajamas beneath his overcoat.

He made off in a dead sprint down the sidewalk, slipping through the snow like a newborn foal. And then he spotted, nestled between the precinct garage and the neighboring Laundromat, a narrow alley. Barely wide enough for a trash can and barely wide enough for Stetson as he pushed through. Silhouetted against the streetlights of the adjacent street, he saw the Kingfisher. A shadow pressed against the bricks. But as Stetson neared, he immediately saw that the Kingfisher appeared different. Washed in the dark water of a winter's night, this man of unworldly strength seemed to bend with each wind passing through the narrow alley.

Stetson waited until he was close enough to whisper. "What's going on? Are you OK?"

The Kingfisher just stood there before him, his powerful shoulders slackened around his neck like a yoke. He turned and looked at the empty street behind him and then turned back to Stetson. "I don't know," he said.

"What's going on?"

The Kingfisher didn't answer at first. He dragged his feet in the snow beneath him, drawing a circle. "I need help."

"With what? What happened?"

The Kingfisher took a few steps back and squatted down. He pulled something from the shadows. Stetson stepped closer, but instinct told him what it was before he even saw it. The Kingfisher's fingers were gripping a man's afro, pulling back his head. Stetson squinted and made out the man's face. It was waxy and still. Stetson recognized that stillness.

The Kingfisher stood back up, and Stetson saw that his head was hung between his shoulders, staring down at his feet, which continued tracing a circle in the snow before him.

"Who is this?" Stetson asked, pointing at the dead man in the snow. "What the hell happened? I didn't give you a name."

"There's another." The Kingfisher pointed behind him at another shadowed lump, another snow-covered body. "I'm sorry."

"They're both dead?"

The Kingfisher nodded, not meeting Stetson's gaze.

"Who are they?"

"I didn't mean to."

"Tell me who they are," Stetson said, his voice sharp and bounding from the narrow walls like a ricocheting bullet.

"He's a pimp." The Kingfisher pointed to the man at his feet and then gestured behind him. "And that one, he's his driver."

"A pimp and his driver?"

The Kingfisher nodded again.

Stetson fell against the brick wall with a long, winding laugh. He wanted to prolong this sense of relief for as long as he could. "Jesus Christ, you had me so fucking worried. I'll call the station and write up a report. Go and make yourself scarce."

"He didn't do anything though," the Kingfisher said, hesitating. "Neither of them did. I just wanted to hurt them. But they didn't do anything for the hurt. They didn't do anything, really."

"Well, he's a pimp, right? Isn't that what you said? And that's his driver?

They were breaking the law. Simple as that. We'll scrounge up some witnesses to identify them. Shouldn't be too hard. That's it. Case closed."

"But I killed them."

"Did they fight back?"

"Yes."

"Did either one have a gun?"

"Yes. Both of them."

"Then what's the problem? It's self-defense. Jesus, you really nearly gave
me a fucking stroke when you called. I thought, well, I don't know what
I thought, exactly."

"I didn't mean to kill them."

"A pimp and his driver. They're among the lowest of the goddamn low.
These are bad guys, OK? They would have killed you just as quickly if they
could have. Know that."

"I only wanted to hurt them."

"Well, you sure succeeded in that." And just as he said it, he realized
he shouldn't have. The Kingfisher shrunk beneath the weight of the words,
laying his head against the wall, breathing loudly through his nose. Stetson
knew this posture, though he had never seen it from the Kingfisher. It
was a posture reserved for criminals when they'd been found out, cor-
nered, nowhere left to turn but within themselves—retreating to their own
private prison.

"Hey, relax," Stetson said. "I'm just kidding. What I'm saying is, you
don't need to worry. This is an easy fix. These were criminals. You found
them all by yourself, right? And when you found them, they pulled weapons. And when they did so, you responded appropriately. But these are
just details for you and me. The newspaper headline doesn't care about
these details or if they're alive or dead. They were criminals, bottom line.
And you took them off the street. This is what matters."

The Kingfisher shook his head violently. Whispering beneath his
breath.

"What?" Stetson asked. "What's your problem?"

"No story on this," the Kingfisher said louder. "I don't want a story on
this."

"Why the hell not?"

The Kingfisher kept on shaking his head like he was trying to loosen
something out of it.

"So you just want me to drag these bodies into the precinct and tell them it's nothing?" Stetson asked. "Tell them to keep it a little secret or something? It doesn't work that way. If there are bodies, there will be a story. Especially when they're your bodies."

"No story," the Kingfisher mumbled. His voice was not the booming thunder Stetson had come to know as the Kingfisher. It was simply the voice of a man. A man reduced to something that resembled humanity. "I don't want a story on this."

"Why?" He cocked his hands on his hips and stepped forward. "Tell me why."

"No story."

"Yeah, you said that already. So just what the hell do you expect me to do with this fucking dead guy? And that other dead guy? Anyone with half a fucking brain is going to know this was you. This has the Kingfisher written all over it."

"Don't call me that," he screamed. Stetson had never before heard the Kingfisher raise his voice. It filled the narrow alley like a bomb burst. Stetson clutched his ears, blocking out the echoes. When his voice ran dry, the Kingfisher stood still, his head tilted to his shoulder. "Don't ever call me that name."

"Look, let's just relax—"

"I didn't mean to kill them."

Stetson's ears still rang. "Yeah," he said, "I get it."

"I don't want this anymore. I wanted to help everyone. The city. I wanted to make things better, but I don't want this anymore. I wanted to help Chicago. I wanted to make it better. But I didn't."

"You have." It was Stetson's turn to shout. "What are you even talking about? Think of the filth you've gotten off the street. The fucking cop killer who's eating through a tube now. Drug dealers who would have sold to kids, little kids, who would have killed anyone who stood in their way. Murderers who gunned down the innocent citizens simply trying to go about their days. You put those evil people away. That was you. Only you could have done all of that. I can show you the statistics, if that means anything to you—the crime in Chicago has dropped to an all-time low. The criminals are afraid of you. You haunt their dreams. They're terrified to even leave their ratholes. How can you possibly say you haven't helped this city?"

Snow began to drift down, rooftop remnants or fresh-fallen. Either way, it clouded the space between the two men.

"Because I liked it, Greg," the man whispered. "I liked all of it. I liked hurting them. I liked breaking them. I liked watching them in pain. But that doesn't mean that they deserved it." For a moment, he seemed to flicker in the space in which he stood, a rapid movement or simply an illusion of the falling snow. "And if I stay, I'm never going to stop. It's in me. It's what I am. It's what I've become. I need to stop. I need to stop forever."

"What are you talking about? What is this *forever* bullshit?"

"I don't want it, Greg." His voice broke, but then galvanized. "I won't do this anymore. I won't. I'm done. All of this. I'm done. I can't keep going. I only hurt her."

The thought came to Stetson slowly, slowly, until it materialized on his tongue. "This is about that whore, isn't it?" Stetson sneered, fighting back laughter that arose like bile. "These were her guys?"

The Kingfisher fell silent.

"Don't tell me you're still with her." He paused for a reply he knew wouldn't come. "Jesus Christ, man. Have some fucking self-respect."

"Don't."

"Don't what?" Stetson barked. "What am I doing? You're the one that killed your whore's pimp and driver. Why? You get jealous? You get angry? Did you finally realize she was fucking other men? Are you that stupid you didn't know it was happening? That's her job, buddy. She fucks other men day in and day out. She's probably fucking some random john right this second."

"Don't."

"I'm just telling you the truth, since you clearly don't understand."

"She was there when it happened, Greg. She saw what I did."

"It's not like she's going to tell anyone, right?"

"You don't understand," the Kingfisher shouted. "She knew I couldn't control it. She knew I couldn't control myself, and I told her she was wrong. I promised her she was wrong. But I've only hurt her by proving her right." The man's thundering voice broke into something recognizable, something familiar. "She doesn't ever want to see me again. She told me. And I believe her. I don't know why I did it. I don't know why. I couldn't stop myself. I couldn't. And now she doesn't want anything to do with me."

"Who gives a shit? You're"—and here Stetson sought a word that didn't exist—"*you.* My God, man. If you let her ruin you like this, that's a giant mistake. You can do so much good for this city. You already have. You can't stop now. There's so much left for you to do. There's so much left for *us* to do. You can't let her ruin you like this. She's a fucking whore. Nothing more, nothing less. You're so much more than that whore."

Only after the Kingfisher had bolted upright to his feet and pinned Stetson against the wall, his hand wrapping around Stetson's throat, did Stetson realize he had once again fucked up. The Kingfisher squeezed so tightly that Stetson, as consciousness quickly waned, realized he was going to die. And to die here, to fall lifeless into the snow, at the hands of the man whom he believed to be the answer to every question Chicago had ever asked.

But he felt the hand on his throat slacken, slowly, and then pull away. Stetson fell to his knees in the snow, coughing.

"You don't know her," the Kingfisher said above him. "And you don't know me."

Stetson tried to speak, but the words couldn't pass.

"I'm done," the Kingfisher said.

Stetson coughed again. His voice came out like a damaged record, stuttered and scratched. "You can't be done."

"I am."

"They won't understand. They need you."

"Who?"

"Everyone. We need you."

"I don't care. I can't help everyone and I can't help you. I'm going to end it. I'm going to end this."

"You're the Kingfisher." Stetson looked up, meeting the man's shadowed face. "I don't care if you don't want me to call you that, but that's the name they call you. That's the only name they know you by. That's the only name that gives them hope. Don't you see? You mean everything to them. You can't just quit like this. You're not a coward. You can't quit."

And now the Kingfisher's voice was roaring from the walls again. "I don't want it anymore. I don't want it. I don't want it." Over and over. The words thundered and blurred into one another as a single breath without beginning or end, climbing upward and outward like a symphony of scattered pages, and Stetson could have sworn, many years later, that in this exact moment, he felt his all-too-human body shaking beneath the brute force of this otherworldly voice—his organs and bones and muscle fibers and veins all vibrating to the tune of superhuman cries. Whenever Stetson remembers it, which he often does, even thirty years later, he feels a phantom tremble pass through his body once more. And he concludes, these years later—now an older man, a wiser man, a police chief, a man who sits in an even larger office with larger windows with a larger view of the larger city that never ceases to amaze him—that these things never truly end even when they're over, and they come back to you in those moments when you're least ready for them.

24 WHATEVER DAYS MIGHT FOLLOW

THE LIBER-TEEN FORUM had been a ghost town since the release of the second video. Digital tumbleweeds. The celebration of Wren's Herculean hack the day before had been cut short, a memory no one seemed in a hurry to revisit, least of all Wren herself. She had watched on television that morning as the police chief stood in front of reporters, implying that the Liber-teens' release of the ME report linked them directly to the gunman. She wished she could say that he was wrong—that she hadn't inadvertently helped the gunman, that she hadn't made everything exponentially worse. But there was nothing to say, no lie she could tell that would make her feel less guilty as she stared at the empty forum.

But Wren still refreshed the page every few anxious seconds. The bowling alley was empty. She was supposed to be vacuuming the carpet, but the carpet was beyond salvation. Instead, she was watching the forum, waiting for Parker to post something, anything. Parker hadn't returned any of her many frantic calls and texts. Nothing. Not from her, not from anyone. Perfect and unsettling silence.

Finally, someone posted something. But it wasn't Parker. It was Proleterrier, posting a link that led to a Twitter hashtag: #LiberteenSolidarityMarch. Proleterrier wrote beneath the link, *Whoever is organizing this saw the police chief's conference and wants to protest the investigation into us. They want the police to apologize publically for blaming us. I know it's a bad time right now, but we are not defeated. Something good will still come of this.*

"Something good," Wren repeated.

And that was the moment, four hours left in her shift, that Wren vomited on the counter the contents of an empty stomach. A sort of watercolor, yellows and browns and a mix of other colors not easily named.

Wren opened Fester's door without knocking. She found him seated behind his desk, half-mindedly eating a hamburger while playing a game on his phone. He held up a finger while he finished the game and then stared back at her, taking a large bite of the burger. Mustard dripped onto his shirt.

"Knock next time," he said, mouth full.

"I'm not feeling well. I need to go home. Right now."

"You got something on your chin," Fester said, pointing at his own ketchup-stained chin for reference. "Is that puke? That's disgusting. Get out of here. I'll call Melinda in to cover for you. Consider this the final warning. No more coming in here hungover. Makes us look bad."

She arrived at her apartment building. The warm, sweltering air gathered in the hall pressed into her skin like a hand, gently and then not-gently constricting her throat. She fumbled with her keys, a shaking hand struggling to turn the lock.

But it was already unlocked. Their door was never left unlocked. And that should have been her first sign that something was wrong, but maybe she knew already. Regardless, she opened the door, standing frozen in the doorway. Her keys dangling in her numb fingers.

Staring back at her were two men in dark, matching suits. Iron-pressed, pleated pants like knife-edges. Both of them, the same granite expression, like park statues, as though they had been standing there in her entryway forever and she had simply never seen them before until just this moment. And even now, Wren looked beyond them, through the cracks of their bodies, and she saw a glint of aquamarine hair. A body curled into the couch. Parker's face was masked beneath her hands, but what or who she was hiding from—or if she was hiding at all—Wren couldn't understand. There are no lines of code, no sacred chain of algorithms that can decrypt a lived moment.

"You must be Wren," said one of the men, a diplomatic friendliness.

But Wren heard his voice only as an echo, emerging from a moment already lost. She had her eyes fixed on Parker, silently pleading for her to look up. She needed Parker. She needed just one look. One dare-me-not smile. One fuck-it-all shift in her cosmic-black eyes. Something to give Wren whatever it was she needed so desperately in this impossible moment. Something to bring her back to whatever moment was unfolding. But Parker only bent further into herself, hair draping over her hands, over her face.

The man who spoke produced a badge from his pocket—Federal Bureau of Investigation. "My name is Special Agent Jorgensen, and this"—he nodded at the man behind him—"is Special Agent Fredericks. I'm going to ask that you come with us Wren," he said.

"Just to talk," said Fredericks.

"That's right." Jorgensen smiled. "We just want to talk. We have some questions we'd like answered."

"Questions," Fredericks repeated. "Just questions."

"Parker!" Wren shouted, the brute force of her voice surprising her. Unbending, unyielding. "Parker!"

"Wren," said Jorgensen, stepping forward and reaching out for her. "Let's just take a moment and talk. There isn't a need to make a scene."

She slapped his arm away, backing into the hallway. "Parker!" she screamed even louder.

Both men followed after her into the hallway, holding their arms out like scarecrows, forcing her back to the wall. One of them was saying something, something meant to calm her down, but she didn't hear him. She felt herself coil like a spring, studied the spaces between their bodies. She saw Parker behind them, balled up on the couch, lying on her side.

Wren rushed forward, pushing through the men's open arms. She rushed into the apartment and grabbed Parker by her shoulders. She pulled Parker upright, wrestling her hands away from her eyes. "Parker," Wren whispered, both hands holding Parker's face. But this was not Parker. It was someone else; it could only be someone else. She looked like Parker. She had all the same features, but was lacking something so essential that without it, Wren couldn't recognize her as the woman she knew she was. The face held in Wren's hands was fearful. Tear-stained, with lips quivering, parting with the onset of a word that rested somewhere inside her, finding its way out.

But not fast enough.

Arms locked around Wren's waist, pulling her away, picking her up off the ground and lofting her into the air. Weightlessness, nothingness. Receding from the walls, the doorway. Wren threw her weight against the bodies holding her own.

"Parker!" Wren screamed. She wanted to communicate a thousand thoughts at once—she should have been there when the men came, she should have known they would come, she never should have taken the police files, she should have kissed Parker when she had held her face a moment ago, she should have done and not done so much, she should have been someone else in some other life altogether—but all that came out was, "I'm sorry."

She kicked her feet against whichever of the men held her. She jabbed her elbows into his ribs. She dug her nails into the skin of his hands until she felt the skin peel. He cursed beneath his breath and squeezed her tighter. She felt her breath come to her slower, and she writhed against the grip of whatever hell was dragging her further and further away from the only person in the world who she needed right now, who she needed tomorrow, who she needed for whatever days might follow. She shouted Parker's name again. Not for an answer, but just to hear it. Just to hear something.

25 MISS MAY

MARCUS WATERS TURNED OFF his Camry's engine and rolled down the window to let in the outside air. Peter shifted uncomfortably in the passenger seat, gently massaging his back. He had withdrawn into his turtleneck as Marcus piloted the Camry around each corner. Peter hadn't said much, if anything, since Marcus had picked him up outside his apartment, offering only a wordless stare outside his window. The entire drive, a sort of silent exchange. They knew why they were here, and there was no reason to speak beyond the courtesies of two old friends. But still, Marcus could sense Peter's anticipation each time he shifted in his seat, his vacant stare out the window at the passing streets, the opening possibilities of a story previously concluded, finished, over.

Marcus had been hesitant to drive to Wrigleyville to look for Miss May, much less park on the street for any extended period of time, even in the light of day. Though he couldn't recall the last time he'd been to this particular corner of the North Side, he remembered it as a place where oil drum fires cast shapeless shadows on buildings that had been reduced to hollowed-out playthings. He was surprised now to find it rejuvenated—deliberately quaint and forcibly charming. The light poles were refurbished antiques, molded iron that reached across the street like tree branches. At the end of the block was a new café, where servers in pressed black uniforms carried cocktails to young businessmen chatting with young businesswomen, faces frozen mid-laugh.

In contrast to the rest of their surroundings, the Lindley Apartments on the left side of the street looked as though they would crumble at a cough or a sneeze. Marcus had parked across the street, and from his vantage point he could see that the building leaned drunkenly. The bricks were arranged slipshod, decades-old mortar spilling like drool. Lindley Apartments had managed to be passed over by the angel of gentrification that had evidently swept through this corner of the city, and it seemed appropriate to Marcus, even unavoidable, that Miss May might live in this residence. A lost name dwelling in a lost history.

"You think she's inside?" Marcus asked Peter. He had considered knocking on every door in the place until he found her, but decided against it. If she was the same woman in the apartment that Peter had found and the same woman with Jeremiah as a boy—his heart raced at the thought—then she would be worth the time spent waiting.

"No," Peter replied. "Or, maybe. But let's wait. Let's see. Let's give it a little while."

As they waited, Marcus's car radio broadcast coverage of a few small protests that were occurring throughout the city. Evidently, a few had turned ugly when pro-Liber-teen protestors wandered into pro-police protests—*protests*, in this case, being something of a loose and lost term. The newscaster spoke solemnly of riot gear, as though reading from a dictionary. There had been two arrests, the newscaster recited.

Marcus had not seen any of these protests on his way to Wrigleyville, and he was thankful for it. Protests made him feel physically ill. When he was in high school, he had been glued to the television during the coverage of the 1968 Democratic National Convention, as was his tenured philosopher stepfather, Corn, who sat on the couch like a sitcom patriarch—legs crossed, straight-backed, posing for no one in particular.

Corn had recently published his fourth monograph—*The Epistemology of Schrödinger: Empirical Inquiry into Unobservable Phenomena.* Though by no means a best seller, it had done well enough that he was granted sabbatical from Northwestern. With his newly found "*free time*"— words he pronounced as though they were a foreign, slightly unbearable phrase—he chose to watch the nightly news with his stepson while also reading from an array of books on ornithology.

Corn loved birds much more than he loved philosophy. Or anything else, for that matter.

"Snowy owls typically live much further north," Corn had explained to his uninterested stepson in a whispery, awed voice. His voice competed against the news broadcast, where the collective roar of protestors grew muffled on the television speakers. "They prefer the northern climates, of course. Hence, the northern border. But they sometimes roost in Minnesota. We should go sometime, just you and I. Maybe quite soon? What do you say? You would love them. I hear they're lovely, the snowy owls. Just lovely, perhaps even regal. *Sublime* is the word I'm looking for, though that isn't entirely accurate if we're being faithful to the origins of the word . . ."

The only times Corn's spoken thoughts were even semi-coherent were when he discussed ornithology. The rest of the time, his erratic speech often intersected and crumbled in the twisting chambers of his mind. His sentences trailed off like cars driving off cliffs or ended abruptly like cars driving into walls.

When Marcus did not offer a reply, Corn joined him in watching the black-and-white broadcasts of protestors spilling and swirling in the Chicago streets. It was all happening just miles from where they currently sat, but that fact did not seem even remotely possible to Marcus, who periodically turned away from the television to glance out the window, as if in doing so he might be able to reconcile these plainly irreconcilable worlds.

He had remained in front of the television for the next few days, watching the ascent of protests, gradually becoming aware of a sharp pain spreading throughout his stomach. He winced, clenched his teeth. His mother had noticed and told him to turn off the television, but he didn't. He dabbed a napkin to catch the sweat that poured freely down his forehead. He took medicine his mother scooped into his palm.

The miniaturized protestors on the screen had chanted, "The whole world is watching." This, more than anything, piqued Corn's interest.

"Correct me if I am wrong," whispered Corn, clearing his throat. "But are they chanting, 'The whole world is watching'?"

"Yes."

He smiled. "That's magnificent."

By the final day of the convention, the pain in Marcus's stomach was too much to handle. His mother had rushed him to the emergency room, where the doctor said he needed his appendix removed immediately. They put him under for the surgery. He remembered only the doctor's face hovering over his own, dissolving into nothing, and then awaking in a hospital room with his mother at his side, her hand holding his.

Marcus turned down the radio in his car, these many years later, and strained to listen for the voice of a not-so-distant crowd, the organized incantations, but he heard nothing save for the clank and crash of dishes from the café bar at the end of the block. He was glad of it. And yet, he wondered what it was that the protestors were chanting, or if they were chanting anything at all. Maybe chants themselves belonged to a lost millennium, a turned page. Or maybe there was simply nothing left to proclaim in unison. Because these days, of course the whole world was watching. That might be the one thing that all the protestors and nonprotestors alike could now agree on. It was no longer worth the breath required to make it known.

"Protests?" Peter asked, repeating the radio broadcaster.

"I guess so."

"Against what, exactly?"

"That's what I'm wondering."

"I'll tell you what I think." Peter shifted again in his seat. "They are protesting the fact that they are protesting. They are angry that they have to be out there. Out here. Why should they, citizens of the twenty-first century, have to protest information that was hidden from them to begin with? They have every right to that information."

But Marcus wasn't convinced. He refused to believe that the protestors cared about whether or not the Kingfisher—a man whom the city had been content to forget thirty years ago—was alive or dead. Perhaps it was wishful thinking, but Marcus wanted to believe instead that the protestors were out there because they had witnessed two men die senseless deaths, and, in response, the police had done nothing but shield themselves. He thought back to his conversation with Paul Wroblewski that morning, remembering Paul's insistence that the boundaries between good and evil had dissolved with the new millennium.

And suddenly Marcus was inclined to agree, though not for the reasons that Paul expressed. Maybe good and evil were no longer reasonable categories to contain the breadth of the twenty-first century. Too subjective, too malleable, too easily weaponized. Perhaps instead, in an era of Occupy Wall Street, Black Lives Matter, women's marches in D.C., there were simply those who spoke out and those who remained silent.

And the whole world was listening.

Peter continued staring out the window at Lindley Apartments. He cleared his throat. "What are you hoping comes from this, Marcus? You find Miss May and then what?"

"Well," Marcus said, removing his seat belt so that he could scan the street more fully, "assuming that she knew the Kingfisher in some way, then I'm worried she may be in danger. Like you said, maybe the gunman is looking for her."

Peter turned to face Marcus, dialing down the volume of the radio. "Don't get me wrong, Marcus, I'm glad we're checking on her, but is that really what you believe you're doing here?"

Marcus remembered Paul Wroblewski asking him a variation of that same question, and if it had annoyed him then, it infuriated him now. "Why else would I be here?" Marcus heard the sharpness in his voice and wished he could retract it. "I'm retired. I don't have any other reason to be here."

"I was just asking."

"I don't want to wake up tomorrow morning to another execution video of a person I might have warned."

"So you don't think . . ." Peter said, voice trailing into a hum.

"What?"

"You don't think he really is still alive?" Peter asked. "You're not here because you think she will tell you that he's still alive? That he's still out there somewhere?"

"No," Marcus said. "I'm not interested in all that nonsense. The Kingfisher is dead, not that it really matters anymore one way or the other."

"OK." Peter nodded. "I guess I was just surprised when you called me today. I didn't get the impression yesterday that you were too interested in delving back into the past. But then you called. I assumed something had happened. Maybe you'd heard something that changed your mind." He shifted in the passenger seat. "That's why I asked."

Marcus spotted from his periphery a flash of red in his rearview mirror. He turned in the driver's seat and saw a wild mane of red hair bobbing along the sidewalk, accompanied by the click-clack of high heels, like diminutive gunshots. He pointed at her, muted words collecting in his throat.

Peter turned, squinted. "That's her," he said to himself. "Oh my God, that's her. Marcus, that's her. It's really her."

"You're sure?"

"Absolutely sure."

Marcus waited until she passed to get out of the car. He shut the door quietly behind him and followed her across the street toward Lindley Apartments. Peter followed after Marcus, body bent, minimizing the space he occupied as he crept forward.

Miss May's head swiveled as she walked to the apartment building's entrance, curious, as though seeing everything around her for the first time. Marcus was worried she might turn around and see them following after her, but she didn't. She never once looked behind her. Her purple-sequined tank top burned in the light of a waning day.

She was tall, but her height was exaggerated by the hand-high skirt that barely inched over her thighs.

When May reached the entrance to Lindley, she stopped and began digging around in her purse, swearing softly under her breath. Marcus froze where he stood, pretending to be lost, which in some sense of the word was entirely true. Peter froze behind him. Marcus listened to May's string of whispered curses as she dug in her purse for her keys.

She passed into the building. Marcus waited, cautious. Three seconds. And then he lunged forward and caught the door before it closed, held it open for Peter, and followed after her. They turned a corner and peered down a hallway. Nothing. Marcus turned the other way and saw May disappearing into a stairwell. He hurried after her, trying not to make too much noise. It was hard for him to walk briskly. He'd been under abnormal stress, hadn't been sleeping well. It was all catching up to him. He felt like cement had been poured into his bloodstream. His legs were stiff, uncompromising.

Peter followed after him, trying to keep up. He hadn't brought his cane.

Marcus turned into the stairwell and paused. He heard her footsteps maybe a flight or two above him. He started up the narrow stairs, wincing at the loud, thunderous echo of Peter's uneven and limping footfalls behind him. But all that mattered now was that he didn't lose her altogether. Marcus ascended four flights of stairs, struggling for each breath, and when he turned onto the next flight, he stumbled backward, nearly falling down the stairs into Peter, when he saw Miss May standing at the top of the next flight, pointing something directly at both of them. A black canister. Upon closer, panicked inspection, he saw that it was pepper spray.

Marcus raised his hands, open-palmed, and felt foolish. Shamefaced. He was sweating, heaving for air, unable to put together the most basic apology, but that didn't stop him from trying. Peter centered himself behind Marcus.

Miss May appeared perfectly calm. Steeled and poised and still, her pepper spray held in an unshaking hand. She waited for Marcus or Peter to put together a sentence that might excuse themselves.

"I'm sorry." Marcus caught his breath. "Are you Miss May?"

She lowered her ready arm a fraction. "Who gave you my name?"

"Sorry?"

"Who referred you?"

It took Marcus a few seconds to understand.

"No," he said quickly. "No, it's not like that."

"Then who told you about me? Because they ought to know I don't do threesomes." She nodded at Peter. "And they should damn sure know that you don't follow me to my home. I have a nine-millimeter handgun in my front bureau. Had you made it to my apartment, I would have buried a bullet in both of your foreheads. I swear to God I would have. You don't show up at my place of residence unannounced. You call me like a normal human being if you're looking to make an appointment. I could have spared you the embarrassment."

"We're not here for that," Marcus assured her. "I was just hoping we might be able to sit down and talk with you." He motioned at Peter's frozen body behind him. "We're worried about your safety, honestly. Just let us explain."

"Who are you?" she asked.

"My name is Marcus Waters. And I really need to talk to you."

"Marcus Waters," she repeated. Something in her expression changed. A glimpse of recognition, revelation. She lowered the pepper spray to her side. Lips pursed, considering the answer to a question he hadn't asked. She looked around at the white walls surrounding her, as though looking for a way out of them. "I don't have anything to say to you, Marcus Waters," she said, her voice hollowed out. She looked briefly at Peter before turning back to Marcus. "I'm not interested in whatever the hell you're here for."

"This is about your safety. Just please let me talk to you."

"I'm not telling you two anything," she fired back. "Nothing. Now, please, both of you, go away."

"It's important," Marcus said. "You are in danger."

"I doubt that."

"You've seen the news," he said in an imitation of calm. "You know what's going on out there right now. Please just talk with us. I just want to make sure you're going to be OK."

"I'm just fine. I've got nothing to do with all that's going on."

"OK. But maybe you could help me find someone who does."

She stared back at him, unblinking, unfixed to the moment. "Who?"

"The men you were with the night the Kingfisher attacked a car you were in."

To Marcus's surprise, she laughed at this, dismissed it with a tilt of her head. "Are you talking about Richie and Olander?"

Peter turned away from May, and Marcus felt his stare. These were clearly names Peter had never heard.

"They're both long gone," Miss May said. "Now please leave me alone. Because I'm about ten or so steps from that pretty little nine-millimeter of mine. And it would sting a whole hell of a lot more than this." She waved her pepper spray in her hand.

"Please, just let us speak with you," Marcus said. "It's important."

"Trust me, it's not important." She turned and walked through the stairwell door into the hallway.

Marcus and Peter followed after her, maintaining a careful distance.

"The man you're searching for, Mr. Waters," she said over her shoulder as she passed through the hallway in an easy bounce step, "is a dead man. You and I, we ought to damn well know that."

"I'm not looking for the Kingfisher."

"Sure about that?" she asked, unlocking a door near the end of the hallway.

"I know that you knew him," Peter said.

Marcus and May turned to face him, both of them equally surprised to hear his voice enter into the narrow walls.

"I followed him back to your apartment in Englewood once," Peter continued, sheepishly. "I knocked on your door and you sent me away. But I know that he was inside. I know that you knew him. Marcus and I, we just want to ask you some questions. That's it. And if you don't want to answer them, then you don't have to. But you could at least listen. There are people out there right now, and their lives might be in danger. Maybe yours, maybe not. But we're trying to help. And we need to hear what you know. That's all."

In the long silence that followed, Miss May slowly relaxed. She looked back and forth from Marcus and Peter. "Well, there's no use for us to just stand around in the hallway like a few fucking idiots. Here, come on." She gestured for them to follow her inside.

"I take it you won't bury a bullet in our foreheads?" Marcus asked, more as a suggestion than a lighthearted joke.

"I'm not making any promises," she said, locking the door behind them.

26 THE ARMADA

TILLMAN GOT OFF THE L at Hyde Park and immediately called her father's cell phone, which she'd purchased for him after he'd moved in. As she had anticipated, he'd refused to learn how to make calls, and instead kept it atop the stand next to his recliner, where he was able to both ignore its material presence while also satisfying his daughter's insistence that he keep it nearby. Needless to say, she was surprised to hear him pick up when she called. She heard Al Green crooning in the background atop the sharp punctuation of a hi-hat. "Stand Up" from *Call Me*. One of her father's favorites. He had made her memorize it at the age of five and she used to sing it back to him before she went to bed.

"Who?" he asked loudly into the phone. Tillman told him it was her, his daughter, and then she told him she'd be home soon, although there was no way of knowing if this were true. It simply felt good to say, and, she hoped, good for him to hear.

These small, untrue mercies.

Tillman pocketed her phone and passed through a sidewalk crowded with college kids hunched beneath the weight of their backpacks, bodies bent and leaning toward the sun slung low across the University of Chicago campus. A lethargic parade of sunglasses, wiry hair. Skinny jeans, too much cologne. She squeezed between their day-weary, hungover bodies with an easy hand, shifting them aside like passive objects.

She passed a parking garage, the hollow sounds of engines erupting through a narrow tunnel into the street. Next to it, the Armada. A sheer-faced glass structure; a human terrarium ten stories high. It resembled its name only in its violent imposition against the otherwise aesthetically unified buildings on either side—red bricks laid delicately atop each other, rising a modest three stories. The Armada seemed to relish its out-of-place-ness. Sunlight reflecting from its glass walls, blinding anyone so brave as to stare at its surface for more than a second.

She entered the lobby, the chill of the air-conditioned space kissing her skin. Everything about the Armada seemed designed to make sure she understood she didn't belong. She passed a plate of apples and oranges arranged into a multicolored pyramid. The light fixtures were shaped into geometric figures she couldn't name. The floors were marble, polished so thoroughly she saw her reflection tracking her every step. A bouquet of fresh lilacs sprouted from a crystal vase on the counter. A sign beneath them said: COMPLIMENTARY BOUQUETS. Tillman could smell them from across the room as she approached. Much to her chagrin, they smelled incredible.

A young man with his long hair pulled back into a ponytail regarded her, head cocked to his shoulder in a show of hyperbolic hospitality. His name was etched onto a metal pin on the breast of his suit coat: DYLAN Q. Dylan Q. was smiling widely, as though relishing the opportunity to quote her prices of rooms he knew she wouldn't be able to afford.

"How can I help you, ma'am?" Dylan Q. asked.

On any other day with time to spare, she would have eviscerated him for calling her *ma'am*. But on this day, she only said, "I need to speak with your manager. Or your supervisor. Or whoever it is above you."

He was taken aback in the literal sense. He stepped backward away from his computer terminal. But the painted-on smile remained. "What seems to be the problem, ma'am? There is a number on the back of your key card—assuming you are, of course, a fine hotel guest at the Armada—listing the number to register any and all unfortunate complaints."

"I just need to speak with your supervisor. Sooner rather than later, please."

His shoulders sloped inward as he stepped back to his computer. "I am the supervisor at the moment, ma'am. Is there something I can help you with? Are you a guest at the Armada?"

"Have you recently interviewed anyone for the doorman position?"

His eyebrows curled into question marks. "If you'd like a job application to join the Armada family, you can find one on our website. Would you like me to write down the Web address for you? We have a variety of job openings for maid service if you would be interested."

"No." She tapped her fingers, on the desk, ignoring the condescension with enormous effort. "Have you recently interviewed anyone for the doorman position?"

"May I ask why you're inquiring about this matter?"

"I have a friend," she said. "He interviewed here, but he lost his phone. He sent me to check up to see if he got the job or not."

"Well, ma'am," Dylan Q. said, turning his head to look over his shoulder at nothing in particular. "I'm afraid I can't help you in this present inquiry."

"Why is that?"

He nodded at the door through which Tillman had entered. "As you may observe, we do not have a doorman, nor have we ever employed any such doorman."

She wanted to reach across the counter and smash his head into the computer terminal, but instead she followed his gaze to the same glass door she had passed through. Sure enough, no doorman in sight.

His smile parted to reveal his bleach-whitened teeth. "Maybe your friend imprecisely offered you the name of the wrong hotel, ma'am?"

She held up her hand and similarly held her tongue. "So you weren't interviewing anyone for a doorman job in the past few days?"

"As previously mentioned, no, we do not employ doormen. We want our guests to feel completely immersed in the architecture of the Armada, including our doorways, which are imported from a glass artisan in Italy," he said, lingering in his own pretention like a pig in its own filth. "And, I assure you, ma'am, I would know if we had decided to hire a doorman. As previously mentioned, I am a supervisor."

Tillman stood at the counter, unsure of what to do with or think about this information, all the while battling her instincts to throw a vase at this man's head. So she resorted to something more direct. "Have you ever heard the name Jeffrey Jenkins? Goes by Penny?"

He shook his head, ponytail tapping each shoulder. "I'm sorry, ma'am. But I believe you have been misled by your friend. There are a few hotels nearby here. I can give you the names if you do not have access to a smartphone or some similar device which would give you this information very readily."

She imagined strangling him slowly, slowly, slowly. A couple walked through the entrance to the hotel. Gray-haired tourists, man and wife, suit and sundress, saddled with leather luggage. The husband pointed at a stone pillar running alongside the full-length windows. "Look at that," he said. The woman nodded. "Wow."

"That was constructed," Dylan Q. called out to them, "by a French mason named Pierre Giraux. The last great mason of the Giraux family." He turned back to Tillman. "Now if you'd please excuse me, ma'am, I have fine guests of the Armada to assist."

Tillman leaned across the counter. She grabbed his tie, but only held it in her fingers, resisting every impulse except to speak into his ear the words "Go fuck yourself, Dylan Q." And with that, she released him and walked calmly past the unaware couple.

The woman was saying to her partner, "What time is the tasting, Charles?"

Tillman exited the hotel onto the sidewalk, unsure of where to turn, where to go, what to do, what to think. She'd come here. That was what she had done, that was what she had to do. But still no answers. No nothing. A dead end. And how perfect a phrase, *dead end*. Because all deaths are ends and all ends are deaths.

Penny bleeding onto some forbidden concrete floor, face arranged into a sort of wry, sleeping smile. His daughter next. She had picked him up from Lucky's. This much Tillman knew. She had most likely driven him here. Or maybe she hadn't. Maybe they hadn't made it. Maybe they had gone somewhere else. Maybe Abe had misheard where Penny had his interview. Or maybe Paulina hadn't picked Penny up at all.

All ends are deaths.

A man with a sandwich board passed her. He wore a beanie, even though it was at least eighty-some-odd degrees. His sandwich board read: *Sell your used phone for BEST PRICE*. He passed through the intersection without waiting for a walk signal.

Why would Penny say he had an interview here if he didn't? Was he running some hustle? Maybe he was grifting money, promising he could pay back his lenders once he got this fictional job? Or maybe he was just talking. From the little Tillman knew of Penny, he sounded like someone who appreciated the sound of his own voice and didn't pay much attention to the words themselves. The sort of person to isolate your attention, breathe it in, and exhale it back slowly into a forgotten, blackout night. But why would his daughter have picked him up to bring him to a fake job interview just so he could run a hustle?

None of it was right. All of it was wrong.

A horn screamed, tires screeched as a car stopped inches away from the man with the sandwich board. He turned to face the driver, threw up his arms, and yelled, "Watch yourself, asswipe."

Her phone rang in her pocket. It was Jeremiah.

"Yeah?" she answered.

She heard a phone ringing in the background, the jostle of Jeremiah's phone changing between his hands, pressing against the fabric of his shirt, bouncing in moving strides. When his voice finally came through, the background was perfectly quiet. "I need you to listen very carefully."

She was picturing him. His voice was a proxy for the person moving through a life disconnected from her own. She saw him in his tweed suspenders, the collared shirt too tight against his neck, walking down the hall and ducking into a precinct stairwell for a quiet space amid the chaos.

"Where are you?" she asked. "Are you standing in the stairs?"

"Do you trust me, Tilly?"

"Don't call me that."

"Stop. Listen. I need you to answer me. Do you trust me?" Jeremiah's voice was rushed and whispered. Emerging from his throat. She saw him backed into the corner of the stairwell, holding his phone over his mouth, cupping it with his hands, shielding his whispers from echoing down the concrete passage.

"Sure. I trust you."

"Then you need to listen carefully."

"You said that already."

"OK, so . . ." But then there was a rustle, the echoing sounds of footsteps, a holding pause. "I can't talk for long. People everywhere. But OK, we have two Liber-teens. The FBI just brought them in. Stetson's keeping it below the radar. No one knows we have them. I only heard about it through Tom Williams—you know him, right? I guess he's friends with one of the agents that brought them in."

"Jesus," Tillman whispered. "Why is Stetson so hell-bent on these kids? He must know they didn't make that video. He's not that stupid."

"Just listen," Jeremiah hushed. "I'm going to ask again: Do you trust me?"

"Why?"

"It's yes or it's no."

"If those are my only options, then yes, I trust you. Would you please tell me what in the hell?"

"Good. Because I trust you, too. I trust you when you say the Liber-teens aren't responsible for that video. And I trust you when you say that the gunman is using the Liber-teens as a distraction. I trust you when you say these things. Should I?"

She paused to think about it. Did she even trust herself? It was a question that had presented itself in so many different forms throughout the past few weeks since her administrative leave, and actually long before that, if she was being honest. Did she trust herself enough to ask someone else to trust her? It was something she didn't have the space, the time, the energy to consider fully.

"You can trust me," she said. "Now tell me what the hell is going on."

She heard in the background another echoing set of feet bounding down the stairs. Jeremiah waited until they passed and then another few seconds more. "I don't know where you are right now, but you need to be back at your apartment as soon as possible."

"Why?"

"Please. Just do it."

"I need to know what's going on. What I'm getting into."

"Just get there. You said you trusted me."

"What in the hell?"

The phone rustled again, and this time she thought he would hang up. But after a few seconds of pause, he came back. In a whisper that elided his voice entirely, "It's better you don't know. Please be there, Tilly."

"Just tell me what's going on—" she demanded to an ended call, a mute phone held in her unshaken hands.

She saw the man in the sandwich board fading down the street, a shrunken body dissolving into the afternoon traffic of daytime wanderers, blithe and lost, a single static figure losing shape in the moving parts of a day unwinding.

Tillman put her phone in her pocket. She turned back to the hotel doors, caught sight of her reflection in the glass doors. Sleep-deprived and sunken eyes staring back. A woman desperate for something.

She took off in a sprint in the direction of her apartment. An L back to her apartment would arrive within twenty minutes, but this wasn't soon enough. And so she ran fast. Faster than most. Faster than all. She barreled through the lazily drifting passersby, breathing in careful measures, saving each lungful of exhaust and diesel fumes and humid backwash of a yesterday-rain.

Of course she trusted Jeremiah. She was a woman running across Chicago. Yes, she trusted him. History being what it was, what it is, what it always will be. That stubborn object she couldn't move no matter how hard she tried. Throw your full weight against something immobile and impassive, you only hurt yourself. And Tillman had hurt herself enough already to know this to be true.

27 A ROOM MUCH LIKE THE ONE WE'RE SITTING IN NOW

NECTARINE HALOGEN COVERING CONCRETE WALLS painted canary yellow. A metal table bolted to the floor. A camera staring from the upper corner of the walls, the only other presence in the room. She felt it, the intrusive insistence of its curious longing, its vacant stare. A red light blinking below its single eye. Wren shied beneath it, unable to escape the horrifying sensation of being seen, of being studied during the lowest moment of her life.

Agent Jorgensen had brought her straight through the station, past security and past booking. He'd handcuffed her at some point and then had later removed the cuffs. This much she knew. But the moments separating her from her apartment to this place were a single strand of images intermixed into something almost unrecognizable, a schizophrenic film reel. There had been a short car ride at some point. She was sure of that. She had lain in the back seat, the kiss of leather against her cheek, as the car rounded corners, sped through intersections. She swayed passively with each shift of centripetal force, a rag doll rumbling in the back seat, falling to the floorboards.

And now, this room. Aesthetically bare, but purposefully so. She'd seen enough cop dramas in her life to know that everything in this room was arranged painstakingly so as to make her feel claustrophobic to the point of spilling whatever confession might save her from drowning in charges. She knew the detectives or feds or whoever the hell was coming to talk

with her were likely waiting in some nearby room with computer monitors, watching her through the camera, studying each movement she made
for some idea of how best to deal with her, which gambit to deploy. So
she did not move. Static and still. But this in itself, she feared, revealed
more than she'd like about herself.

After what felt like an hour—there was no clock in this room—a knock
sounded on the door. It swung open, and in walked Agent Jorgensen. She
recognized him first by his smell. Musk cologne. He was nearly as tall as
the doorframe, but moved about soundlessly as he dragged a chair from
the corner of the room to the table. He smoothed his black tie as he sat
down.

His entire presence reeked of compensatory masculinity. What girl
from his youth had jilted him so badly that it had led him to reclaim his
manhood by working for the FBI?

"So, Wren," he said, folding his hands in front of him. She saw deep
red fissures spreading from his fingers to his forearm, and she remembered digging her fingernails through his skin. She wished she'd dug even
deeper, scraping the calcium right off his bones. "Is that a nickname or
something?"

She didn't say anything, just stared forward, the camera in her
periphery.

"We know who you are, you know. We have your information. So Wren
seems like a funny name for someone with your given name. I'm just curious, is what I'm saying. Where does the name Wren come from?"

He smiled, a practiced peel of his lips. She could see him staring into
his mirror each morning, rehearsing the face he would wear that day. A
sentient robot trying on human masks.

"Is it one of your screen names? Your tag? Your avatar? Your *nom de
guerre*?" He laughed, leaning forward, inviting her to join. She didn't. Instead, she fixed her stare on the residual trace of blood from his shredded
hands. He pulled his hands away from the table and laid them in his lap.

"Are you a Cubs fan, Wren? Jesus, they're looking good this season,
aren't they? If Martinez keeps healthy, there's no telling."

She said nothing.

"You don't want to talk," he said, leaning back in his chair. "You think
I'm trying to lower your defenses to get you to talk, which you'd be correct to assume. But the reason I'm doing that is because, believe it or not,

I'm here to help you. But the only way I can help you is if you talk with me. So what do you say? Can we have a conversation?"

Wren said nothing.

"OK. Let me guess. You figure you can outmaneuver me with your silence," he said. "But right now, I'm telling you that your silence is only going to ruin you. Every minute of silence is a nail in your proverbial coffin." He paused, letting the words hang still. "But maybe you're not even fully aware of the position you've found yourself in. So let me break it down for you."

"I want a lawyer," she muttered. She hadn't planned to say it. But she was glad she did. It was what she was supposed to say, even though she didn't have a lawyer.

He bobbed his head, bringing a pen to his lips, pressing it against his star-white teeth. "You're certainly entitled to one. And if you'd like that, I won't ask you any more questions until your legal representation arrives. However, if you don't mind, may I just lay out your charges? It might be useful information to pass along to your lawyer, assuming you have one."

She crossed her arms, squared her eyes on the wall behind Agent Jorgensen. The vectors of concrete blocks stacked atop each other. Neat, tidy, built to last.

"I'm taking your silence as an affirmative," Agent Jorgensen said, more to the camera than to her. Checking off liabilities. "You are being charged with two counts of computer intrusion and one count of access device fraud. That's the bill as of the moment. Not too bad, all things considered. However, we're also talking with your friend. What's her name? I honestly don't recall at the moment." He snapped his fingers. "Help me out. What's your roommate's name?"

Roommate. Hearing such a trivializing and reductive word pass the lips of a quasi-alpha, pomade-slick FBI agent was maddening. But it also felt intentional, a ploy to make her speak, so she stopped herself from educating him on what "roommates" are capable of feeling and doing, and instead, she continued to remain silent.

"Well, whatever her name is, we're speaking with her, and she's being very, very cooperative. And I don't blame her. See, we have very good reason to suspect that you, and perhaps what's-her-name, are involved with the criminal group the Liber-teens." He paused, as though waiting for some desired effect from her that did not come. He breathed in sharply, leaned forward. "Are you familiar with the Liber-teens, Wren? Nothing? All right. Well then let me ask you this: Are you familiar with someone by the name of Nikolas Wilson?"

She couldn't help but flinch.

Agent Jorgensen smiled. "Mr. Wilson put in a call to the police this morning. He told them he'd had what you might call a 'run-in' with you yesterday. Don't worry, he offered what I assume to be the whole story. He acknowledged he'd acted like an ass. Seemed sincere, too, if you're asking me. He also said that he knew you back in your college days. Said you were an informatics major. Something of a rising star, as well. But then he said that shortly after this recent occurrence he had with you, he woke to find all of his money transferred from his private account, along with some of what you might call *compromising* personal information stolen from his phone. Mr. Wilson also informed us that not only might you have a motive to perform this particular hack, but you also had, and I'm quoting Mr. Wilson here, 'freakish-good skills.' That's high praise, right? It's a compliment, I think. He seems to think highly of your abilities, even after what allegedly transpired between the two of you."

Wren felt a million buzzing points of electricity beneath her skin. She wanted to shrink into herself. She wanted to leap across the table and dig her thumbs into this man's shining eyes.

"The rest is somewhat serendipitous. The police flagged Mr. Wilson's report and turned this information over to us, since it involves a hack, which I don't need to tell you has become something of a red flag considering present circumstances. We received the information Mr. Wilson provided but, honestly, we didn't think much of it at first. I think you'll be the first to admit that that particular hack performed against Mr. Wilson was rather rudimentary. Nothing too extraordinary."

I did it all in four minutes, she wanted to say. *Let's see any of you—all of you—try to do that.*

"But even though it seemed insubstantial, we did some digging. And come to find out, Mr. Wilson was right. You really are quite talented. Maybe had you chosen a different life for yourself, you could have had a wonderful career working for us. We have wonderful benefits. Good health care. Exceptional dental. But that's beside the point. What I mean to say is that we pored through old case files of Liber-teen hacks, but this time with your IP and your apartment's ISP—both of which were attained with a warrant, I should add. I'm told by some of our techs that you kept your IP encrypted with some pretty advanced software. Rest assured, they were duly impressed, but unfortunately for you, they were able to decrypt it after what I'm told was a strenuous process. Anyway, we found that you—or at the very least, your IP—have been involved in some serious criminal activity that the Liber-teens have since claimed credit for. The most damning piece of evidence, I'd say, was when we traced the ME report hack back to you. Yeah, that's not good. You might call that 'red-handed.' I imagine this is all surprising to you—a federal agency actually knows what the hell they're doing. But it's true, or else you wouldn't be here, would you?"

He seemed to expect a response that he knew wasn't coming. He was enjoying this unilateral interrogation, savoring each word that passed through his bleached smile.

"And imagine our surprise when we find that your roommate—whose name and information we attained with an appropriate warrant, of course—also took part not only in unsavory and highly illegal activities that the Liber-teens claimed responsibility for, but also the very same ME report hack. But here, let me make a long story short for the sake of time. We will soon have enough evidence to charge both you and your roommate with at least four Liber-teen hacks—the ME report included—each of which straddle several federal offenses. To be clear, we're talking at least twenty, thirty, forty, fifty years each, once we've added it all up. Considering we've already charged you for hacking Mr. Wilson's personal data, not to mention your, well, your *aggression*"—he held up his river-red-streaked hands—"you're looking at an additional five years if you're lucky. But here's where this becomes important."

He straightened up, loosened his tie.

"If—actually, no, *when*—we're able to tie you and your friend to this whole Kingfisher mess—you know, the two dead hostages—well, that's going to be get ugly really fast. Because we're not stupid. We know you all had something to do with that video and everything that's happened since. We have your cyber fingerprint on the ME report hack, and it won't take much waxing poetic in front of a court to convince them that you, personally, had something to do with the videos, maybe even the murders themselves. And at that point, Wren, you're looking at a life sentence. Maybe even a death sentence. That's not good."

He cracked his neck, cracked his knuckles. "Now that we have the scary stuff out of the way, let's cut to the not-so-scary stuff. I know for certain you've done a lot of illegal things, but I want very badly to believe that you didn't have anything to do with those videos. Maybe you only provided assistance in some form to whichever of your friends made the videos. I know there are a lot of you Liber-teens. However, I'll be perfectly honest with you—we don't know how many of you there are. And I know you don't know their God-given names. We know enough about you all to know how the Liber-teens do business. No names, no identifying info. And, truth be told, I respect the thought that goes into the way you kids operate. It's impressive. But I'm guessing you know exactly who pulled that trigger. You know exactly who helped coordinate it. You know their screen names, and you know a way to get in touch with them. And here's where you should be listening very carefully: if you cooperate with us, we can work with you. We have some, well, what you might call *leeway*. Maybe we even make your police server hack disappear from your charges. We just want to find whoever is killing those innocent people. Even if it was you yourself, if you were involved with those murders, we can be a little more forgiving in our prosecution if you come forward with a confession right now. Time being something of the essence."

He paused, offering a silence into which she might speak. She didn't.

"But assuming you weren't involved with the murders," he continued, "and you tell me right now, well, then it's a whole different story, right? Maybe it's your friend down the hall. What's-her-name. Maybe she helped make the video. Maybe she pulled that trigger. And if you just tell me, then we figure things out from there. You and I." He wavered a finger at the space separating them. "We do what we have to do. Maybe we go our own separate ways at the end of the day. Maybe you go home tonight. Who knows?" He bit down on the pen like it was a cheap cigar and shrugged.

"I want a lawyer," she said, voice soft but resolute.

"Of course. You are certainly entitled to one. And I'll be sure to let you place a phone call to your attorney, assuming you have one. But in the meantime, I'd encourage you to consider the fact that your friend, what's-her-name, is sitting in a room much like the one we're sitting in right now. She's sitting across from someone much like myself. And, truth be told, he's offering the same deal. Because, and make no mistake about this, it is a deal. It's a good deal. And maybe you want to retain your allegiance to whoever or whatever. That's fine. But—and I'm telling you this as some-one who wants to see you have a life after all this—judging by some of the things your friend was telling us back at the apartment, I think she's going to give us exactly what we want. Sooner than later. And once we have what we want, you won't be of any value to us. So."

She nearly laughed at his transparent bluff. Parker would sooner spit on a face, much like this man's own, than ever cooperate with the feds.

His voice narrowed, stripped of its performative sheen. A whisper tra-versing the tabletop between them. "It comes down to who gives us what we need first. There is no second place. Transparency is the only thing that's going to save you right now, Wren. But if you want to keep tight-lipped about all this, then so be it. But just know your friend may not do the same."

He remained in his posture, settling into his shoulders, staring through her. Waiting for something that would not come. And when he realized this, he stood up, smoothed his tie. "We'll make sure you call a lawyer. You are granted that much. But every second that passes . . ." His voice drifted off, purposefully so. "If I were in your position, I'd think for a minute or two about what you stand to lose and what you stand to gain. That should make things pretty clear."

He opened the door out into the hallway, ushering in a chorus of voices, telephones ringing. It closed behind him. Silence, again. The walls seemed narrower than before, expanding to the center of the room, collecting into a single point without name.

She wished she could tell him that it wasn't the Liber-teens who'd hacked the police servers, who'd stolen the ME report. It was her. It was only she. And though she regretted it, it was important that they knew. These Ivy League college graduates, postgraduates, working in tandem. She wanted to confess to this one crime, not for leniency, but so that they would know. So that they would know she was better than them. She had beaten them. She would always beat them.

But this wasn't true, she knew. Because here she was, captured, revealed, reduced, nearly imprisoned. Here she was, without a clock to tell her the time of day. Here she was, ignoring the eye of a camera staring blankly back at her.

"Fuck you," she said at a volume barely loud enough for even herself to hear, but she hoped they heard it in whatever claustrophobic room they were gathered.

Wren attempted to imagine Parker sitting in a room much like this room, having listened to the same impossible accusations, the ridiculous baiting. But she couldn't even summon the image. Parker did not belong in this context. Concrete walls draped in yolk-yellow paint. Harsh lights. No windows. A camera waiting anxiously above her for a confession that would never come. Parker was a collection of many attributes, none of which could exist in a place like this. Parker was too much of herself— too much vibrancy, too much color. She exceeded beyond whatever walls believed they could hold her. But Wren knew, Parker was here, in a room much like this one, and it was Wren's fault. It was her fault that another hostage had died, because she had given the gunman what he wanted and it had only fed his fury. It was her fault that she couldn't rip her eyes away from the wall. It was her fault that she and Parker were being held as murder suspects. It was her fault that she was who she was. It was her fault that she wanted to lay her head on the table and find sleep in this nightmare. It was her fault that the world spun beneath her while she remained perfectly still.

28, THE WASTELAND

MARCUS FOUND MISS MAY'S APARTMENT to be deeply unsettling in its familiarity. The traces of a life lived alone, the patterns of a solitary existence. A half-eaten bagel on the counter in a scatter of crumbs. Coffee mugs piled in the sink, ceramic rims stained with the palimpsests of rouge lipstick. A checkered sofa and velvet love seat pressed against dull yellow walls that were too close together. Magazines dating back from the early eighties, scattered across the countertops.

Peter stood with his hands in his pockets, half stepping and half rocking, an awkward and static fox-trot. Marcus sensed Peter's buoyancy, his barely bridled anticipation to begin asking questions. Marcus laid a hand on his shoulder, gripped through the thin veneer of flesh to the bone, and whispered, "Calm down."

"Take a seat," May said, falling into the love seat. "And let's get this over with."

They both sat down across from her on the sofa. There was a half-finished puzzle on a coffee table that separated them. Van Gogh's bedroom. May caught Marcus staring at it, twisting his head, as though this motion would bring it into sharper focus.

"I got that from the art museum," she said. "You wouldn't believe how much they charged for that fucking thing. Just a cut-up piece of cardboard."

She plucked and pulled at her skirt. She cracked the window next to her, lit a cigarette, and turned on a small fan over her shoulder. Marcus saw Wrigley Field over the rooftops, several blocks away. The jut-and-rise of stadium scaffolding.

May leaned back into her seat, her cigarette burning in her fingers. She appeared to be about Marcus's age, maybe a bit younger. Her hair was dyed a deep red, the color of blood feeding the body.

Even as she blew smoke through an open window, she carried herself with refinement, meticulous yet unrehearsed poise, projected for no one in particular. Marcus suspected that she would be sitting here, just so, cloaked in her self-assumed regal aura, with or without any watching eyes.

She turned from the window and studied the both of them as if she were the subject of a painting from centuries past, hung in the art museum next to Van Gogh's masterpieces, her acrylic stare radiating directly into future galleries and future faces.

"Now, I know who you are, Marcus. Or at least I know the name. But who exactly is this?" She pointed the end of her cigarette at Peter, who had hopelessly shrunken inside his skin, hands bloodless in their chokehold over each other.

"I'm Peter," he said softly.

"Peter." Miss May tested the name on her tongue. "Are you a journalist like Marcus was?"

"No."

"Didn't think it." She studied Peter. "So what are you, then?"

"I'm just Marcus's friend."

She laughed at this and pulled on her cigarette.

Marcus withdrew his notepad from his shoulder bag and placed it next to the puzzle. "You go to the art museum often, then?" Marcus asked, pointing at the puzzle, looking for any way to take control of the conversation's momentum.

Miss May remained staring at Peter for an uncomfortable second, her eyes narrowing on him, dragging slowly on her cigarette. She broke away suddenly and turned toward Marcus. "No. I don't. Not at all. Not ever, hardly. I got that puzzle a couple years ago. Not sure why I decided to go to the art museum. I've lived in this city my whole life, never went to the art museum. Maybe I thought I ought to go. Maybe I thought I needed to get cultured. So I went, and I walked around. It was stuffy and dull. I decided to leave after about fifteen minutes or thereabouts. It felt like a waste of time, the whole ordeal, so I thought I'd buy something from the gift shop. A memento. Came away with that puzzle, which cost about as much as a week of groceries. But I like it. Obviously I haven't finished it, though. I don't want to finish it. As soon as I do, it'll just be a cardboard picture that cost me too goddamn much." She drank from her glass, and wiped away the water that remained above her lip with a slender finger. "I'm tired with the bullshit chitchat. What exactly do you want from me, Mr. Waters?"

"Well, most importantly, I wanted to come here and make sure you were OK."

She gestured at herself. "Are you satisfied?"

"I'm assuming you've seen the videos."

She shrugged. "Who hasn't?"

"Do you know who the men are in those videos?"

She shook her head.

"They are men that he saved. The Kingfisher."

Marcus was taken aback when Miss May laughed at this.

"What's funny about that?" he asked.

"Nothing," she said, taking a long drag of her cigarette. "It's not actually funny at all. I sometimes laugh when I shouldn't. It's a habit." She exhaled slowly through her nose. "It's just, well, I don't remember hearing about him saving much of anyone. That wasn't exactly his style, you know? You sure you got your facts straight there, Marcus Waters?"

He nodded. "I interviewed one of those men for the book I wrote about the Kingfisher. The other man was with him that night. The Kingfisher saved the both of them."

She seemed suddenly fixated on the open window. The not-so-distant sounds of voices clamoring in a non-rhythm. The protest against whatever there was to protest. All three of them paused to listen. Straining to make out the words of the crowd.

"I don't see what any of what you're saying has to do with me personally," May said.

Marcus sensed Peter next to him, withdrawing uncomfortably into the couch.

"I—or we, rather"—Marcus gestured at Peter—"have reason to believe you might have known the Kingfisher in some way?"

"Is that right?" She was amused, fixing her attention on Peter. "Because you followed him back to my apartment?" She laughed. "I recognized you, by the way. Moment I saw you. Couldn't place your face, but I recognized you just the same. Pretty rude thing to do, knock on my apartment door and keep coming back day after day when I clearly didn't want anything to do with you. What did you expect?"

Peter gaped, his tongue searching for a reply. He turned to Marcus for help.

Marcus graciously intervened. "Like I mentioned previously, I actually heard from another source that you encountered the Kingfisher in 1983—"

"No, Marcus," she interrupted. "I want to hear him"—she nodded at Peter—"apologize for bothering me at my apartment all those years ago. I want to hear him say it. I'm not saying another word until he apologizes."

Marcus turned to Peter, who was holding his hands together, fingers knotted.

"Sorry," Peter mumbled.

"Good. That wasn't so hard, was it? Now, Marcus, you were saying something?"

"Right, well . . ." He retraced his thoughts. "I heard from someone else who came across the Kingfisher in December of 1983. You were with two men on that night. You said before their names were Richie and Olander. One of them was your—well, your *employer*."

"*Pimp* is the word you're looking for." She smiled, threw the cigarette butt out the window, and withdrew another. "I take it you think the Kingfisher was saving me that night? Saving poor Miss May from her scary pimp? Is that what you think?"

"I don't know," Marcus said. "That's what I'm asking you."

"He didn't save me. Don't for a second think he was saving me that night." She pointed at Peter. "What did you expect to happen those nights when you were knocking on my apartment door? The nights after? What were you hoping would happen, exactly?"

Peter didn't answer. He didn't seem to hear her. He unhooked his hands from each other and rubbed them together faster, tighter, as though trying to summon a fire he might hold, something to distract him from her sustained attention.

"If it's true that you knew him in some way," Marcus jumped in, "then both Peter and I are concerned that you may be a target for whoever it is making these videos. And you should be concerned, too. We don't know what that man from the videos knows or what he doesn't know. But you should play this safe. Get out of town for a while, maybe. Just until it's over."

"Well, whoever said chivalry is dead?" She smiled, but her eyes were empty. Two green galaxies. "A couple of do-gooder men show up unannounced outside my place of residence, follow me to my apartment, and then condescend to me after I invited them inside against my better instincts. Warms my cold and worn heart." She ashed her cigarette on the windowsill. "I think maybe it's time you two leave. Go find someone else you want to save tonight, because I'm done with whatever this is. Show yourselves out."

Her words possessed a momentum of their own that sent Marcus to his shoulder bag. He put his notebook back inside and stood from the couch. But Peter remained seated, face twisted.

"What do you know about him?" Peter stuttered. "You knew him. I know you knew him."

"Excuse me?" she asked, her words sharp.

"Tell us what you know about him," Peter said with uncharacteristic confidence. "We want to know. We need to know."

"Peter," Marcus said calmly, reaching for his shoulder. "Let's just go."

"No." Peter hushed Marcus with an open palm. He faced May directly. "There are other hostages out there whose lives are in danger. Tell us what you know so that we can help them. You're the only one we know who knew him."

Miss May looked back at Peter, matching his defiance. "Say his name, then. Why don't you?" She inhaled her cigarette, enjoying the silence that awaited her voice. "Are you scared to say it? You scared to say his name? You worried he'll hear you? Say it."

"The Kingfisher," Peter said, lips curled into a snarl. "The Kingfisher. The Kingfisher. The Kingfisher. Is that good enough for you?"

Marcus stood awkwardly between them, his hands wrapped tightly around the strap of his bag. There was a clock somewhere in the room, hidden from view, and Marcus practically felt its hollow ticks spreading across his skin.

"Well OK, then," Miss May said, amused by Peter's stiff posture, his flustering words. "No need to have a conniption. What do you want to know?"

Peter didn't flinch. "Did he ever come to your Englewood apartment?"

"Yes," she said. "But you knew that already, didn't you?"

"Then I want to know what happened to him. I want to know everything you know about him. I want to know everything."

For a while, she did not move. Not even a blink. Only after a few seconds did she reanimate. She looked around the room as if seeing it for the first time. "Take a seat, Marcus. Your friend here wants to hear about the Kingfisher. Because that was his name, wasn't it? The Kingfisher? I'm asking you, Marcus. That was the name you gave him, right? I never liked it myself. I thought it was too soft for the man. It's the name of a little bird, isn't it? No, that man was hardly a little bird. Christ, that man was hardly a man." Miss May took in a deep pull on her cigarette and released it slowly, slowly. And then she asked them, "Have either of you ever heard of the Wasteland?"

Peter shook his head.

"The Wasteland?" Marcus repeated, the name possessing some significance to him. And then it came back to him in a rush. "That old train depot south of the stockyards?"

She waited for him to continue.

"I've been there," Marcus said, surprised at the memory. "Used to sneak in there as a kid sometimes. It'd been abandoned for a couple years even way back then. I was six or so. I lived in Englewood at the time. A few of us boys would get over there and try to stir up trouble, but I don't think we ever did. We just sort of strolled around, thinking we were cool."

"I used to go there when I was a girl," she said. "All the time. Snuck in through the fence. I even lived there for a while, a few months. I'd just run off from my grandmother's home after she passed. Sleeping in an old train car with a bunch of tramps. Some of them were kids from New York or San Francisco, slicking their hair back like Jack Kerouac. But most of them were just older folks who'd been cast out of wherever it was they came from for reasons they didn't care to share."

She paused to take a deep drag on her cigarette, and then another. The silence was so full that to speak would be to interrupt something in progress.

"What does the Wasteland have to do with the Kingfisher?" Peter asked.

"Everything," Miss May said. She seemed content with this answer. But when she saw that neither Marcus nor Peter understood, she continued. "It's where I met him. It's where I learned what he was." She took a drag, held it, and spoke between the smoke, "Or at least that's where I learned what he wasn't. Because, see, he wasn't like us. No, not like us at all."

29 NO KNOCK

WREN LIKED TO KEEP HERSELF occupied—hands, mind, eyes. She needed input, she needed output. She considered those in-between moments of a day—the idle stagnation of a television, the aimless and mindless drifting through apps on her phone—as moments entirely lost to a life. It was her Protestant upbringing, she knew, that had implied to her that God sooner forgives the industrious than he does the lazy. Even though she considered herself an intellectually curious agnostic, you could sooner lose your fingerprints than you could your upbringing.

And so Wren sat in this empty room, feeling absolutely doomed and damned. Nothing to do but to sit and stare while a thousand concurrent fears fed on one another. She imagined them, synapses cannibalizing synapses, metabolizing into some frightful creature that would eventually consume her altogether from the inside out.

Someone, a uniformed officer, had poked her head in the doorway after Agent Jorgensen left and asked if she'd like to call her lawyer. Wren thought about it. She didn't have a lawyer. And she sure as hell didn't want to call her parents right now to see if they had a lawyer. So she waved the woman off and settled into her straight-backed chair. Besides, she knew what lawyers would tell her. Keep quiet. Don't admit to anything. Even if the lawyer told her to take the deal that was being offered to her, she wouldn't dream of it.

So even with no one in the room, she sat quietly and admitted nothing, not even to herself. They said they had evidence of her participation in the Liber-teen hacks and said they had evidence that she'd hacked the ME report. But she doubted it. She refused to believe that they could have cracked her IP encryption. They were only operating on a hunch. Just sit still. Be quiet. If they're lucky, they'll be able to charge you with hacking Nikolas Wilson's phone and bank account, but that's laughable compared to the charges they're threatening. It's nothing. It's nothing. It's nothing. But still her fingers twitched, looking for something to do, something to hold, some task to complete that might save her from this place.

Ignore the camera. Stare at the table. Count out the digits of pi.

Once again, Wren imagined Parker sitting in a room much like this one, an FBI agent seated across from her, trying to leverage information from her. And Parker, baring her teeth, stringing together inventive curses. Throwing up innumerable middle fingers at the man, at the camera, at the moment itself. Opposing this reality through sheer force of indelible will. And this made Wren nearly smile. Parker would relish any opportunity she had to share her thoughts on the police, the feds, the entire apparatus of the security state with whatever suit sat across from her. She would quote from memory Marx, Foucault, Rousseau, the Marquis de Sade. She would spit in the suit's face and smile. She would stare into the camera hanging in the room without fear. Wanting to be seen, daring to be seen.

There was an electronic blip outside the door before it swung open. No knock. A man entered, shutting the door quietly and quickly behind him. He wore suspenders, tight slacks, sleeves rolled to his elbows revealing veined and muscular forearms that he seemed intent on digging into his pockets. Around his neck, a chain lanyard with a CPD detective badge resting against his stomach. He stood there pressed against the door, eyeing the camera suspended over his shoulder. He spoke in a whisper she struggled to hear.

"Three 'yes,' one 'no,' one 'yes.' Trust me."

She stared at the table. The FBI must be getting desperate for a confession, resorting to theater.

The man stepped from the wall. His stare on the camera turned to her, and he walked in long, casual strides. He pulled the chair out from the table in a quick motion, the chair legs scraping against the cement floor in an ear-piercing screech. He sat down, legs parted, and folded his hands in his lap. He cocked his head at her.

"My name is Detective Jeremiah Combs. But you know who I am already, don't you?"

She raised her eyes to meet his own. They were wide open, magnetic, begging her not to look away. She saw the camera in her periphery and she saw this man's eyes widen even further as a warning.

She accumulated every reason she had to ignore this bizarre interaction altogether. Why should she trust this detective? What was Agent Jorgensen's game here? But she recalled the way this mystery detective spotted the camera from the corner of his eye, a true fear in his stare. If it was all an act, it was a convincing one. And if it wasn't, if he really wanted to help her, then he was evidently risking himself. But why?

"Yes." She nodded. Beneath the table, a closed fist. One finger unfurled. The first "yes." "I know who you are."

"You sent a file to Marcus Waters yesterday, didn't you?" Before she could respond, he added, "And you told him to do what he thought was best with it. Is this true?"

Wren tried not to be impacted by these words. How did this detective know what she had sent to Marcus Waters? Had Marcus Waters sent it to the police? And if he had, why hadn't Agent Jorgensen mentioned it earlier?

"Yes," she said. Two.

"I've spoken with Agent Jorgensen, whom you have had the pleasure of meeting, and I would like to propose something to you," he said, leaning forward, folding his hands on the table. "Forget the ME report and the file you sent to Mr. Waters. Forget all of that. We're worried about who made that video right now. And none of us believe for a second that you don't know who made that video. We want to help you, Wren, but only if you can help us. Now, look, I'm not with the FBI. I promise you can trust me. Because there are people out there right now, Wren, who are in some real danger. But if you can tell me where the hostages are, I can help you. Do you know where they are, Wren?" He paused, waiting for her reply.

She swallowed. "Yes." Three.

He smiled, relieved. "Good. That's good. Now, if you don't mind, I'd like for you to tell me where they are right now so that we can send people to check on them. Time is running out, OK? So tell me where they are."

"No," she said.

He leaned forward. "What? There are hostages' lives in danger right now. This is bigger than you. You need to understand that, OK?" His voice was rising, entering into a shout. "People are going to die if you don't start cooperating with me. Do you understand that? You may as well be killing those people, Wren." He paused, but brought his hand to his mouth, holding out a finger as though shushing her from speaking. He spoke in a convincingly manufactured calm. "Tell you what. You got a problem with the FBI. I get that. You and your Liber-teen friends, you hate the fucking feds. Whatever, all right? You don't want to cooperate in any way with them. That's fine. But what if you come with me, just you and I, and you tell me where they are? How about that? I'll even promise you no one will follow us. It'll be just you and I, OK? I promise it. You'll tell me where they are and then I'll take it from there. What do you think? Just you and I."

She waited until she was sure he had finished. "Yes." The final yes.

He rapped his knuckles on the table. "Let met check with my superiors, but I'm guessing they will allow it. This is brave of you, Wren. You're doing something good here. Hang tight, all right?"

And then he was gone, just so, leaving behind not even a question to be answered.

30 HER BOY

BETWEEN THE WOODEN SLATS of train car paneling, beyond the gaps of twisted and rusted metal sheeting, the stars hang still and patient. A fire burns in the center of the train car, an old, ashen charcoal grill casting lights and shadow puppets of bodies onto the cosmos. Half-drunk bodies slanting, their voices laughing at the shapes of themselves in a greater beyond. There is music from a weather-warped acoustic guitar. The notes, the chords—a bouncy and jousting little tune. Something enough to dance to. But the worn strings have a way of twisting it into something darkly melancholic, and the laughter May hears is also a response to this. To this music that shifts as she shifts against the wooden floorboards, a woolen blanket beneath her.

There is Turnbull screaming. He is the latest arrival to the Wasteland. Just last night, a twilight pilgrim garbed in military fatigues, a rucksack slung from his shoulders like an afterthought. He came to the Wasteland seeking shelter. Maybe he'd heard he could find it here. Fresh out of Vietnam. Eyes dulled to a colorless sheen, body perched midstride like a coil. And here he is now one day later—a wall of a man, naked as the night after stripping down to his skin between songs. Sweat pouring down his hairy chest. Veins in his neck like piano strings, drunk as the day is long, and he's screaming at no one or maybe everyone. He screams, "Don't let it, don't let it, don't let it get you down."

And May watches the scene, smiling at it all, even though it—or something like it—happens every night. The guitar, the dancing, the passing gallons of liquor and wine. The days, the nights. The Wasteland consumes them all, spits them out into a seamless memory.

Her boy lays beside her, throws an arm around her, pulls her close. Closer than she knew two bodies could ever be. He's shirtless, denim-jeaned. She's turned away from him, but she knows the face he wears. She can see it, practically feel it with her fingers. A smile half-cocked. The teenage assurance that each moment is his own. She's told him he does this. In a matter of words. And he smiled right back like he'd known she would say this. Because he always seems to know these things—the words on the tip of her tongue.

He tucks her into his body, which is warm and cold and beating. Even though he arrived just a week ago, she believes he is a body born of the Wasteland. A product of this static, yet itinerant world. He carries himself with the same sharpened edge of the barbed wire fences meant to keep people like him away. The same displacement of the rusted train tracks leading from the stockyards to nowhere. She recognizes it in him, because it is also in herself. In the rare moments the two of them speak, he seems to pause moments to hold to them. To memorize details, here and gone. His eyes record every motion she makes in those dark and rare hours when they are both alone and their bodies are interlocked, joined by a cold wind through the cracked wood and metal walls.

No one here believes her boy is fifteen. He's taller than the men, more powerfully built. His body, an oil drum carved into the shape of a demigod. Arms hang at his side like the limbs of some ancient, time-beholden tree. But she believes him when he insists quietly that he is fifteen, because she knows liars when she sees them. She's seen them before. And this boy, this fifteen-year-old boy, is not a liar. She doesn't know what he is, but he isn't a liar.

She asked his name when she met him. He didn't answer. A liar would have answered, would have made something up if he didn't feel like telling her.

"What do you hear?" she whispers into his ear as Turnbull screams even louder.

"The music," her boy says.

"Past the music. What do you hear?"

Her boy falls quiet, and she feels his muscles tighten as he concentrates his entire being. "A boy," he says. "A young boy. He's crying. In Logan Square. A young boy crying in Logan Square."

It's a game they play. Or at least she once thought it was a game. Her boy told her one night, shortly after he arrived, he could listen to the world if he tried hard enough. She took it as a romantic gesture, but it evolved into these late night back-and-forths, something to simply fill the narrow silence. Of the things he said he could hear, she wondered what was fiction, what was real. Or if it even mattered at all.

"Why's the boy crying?" she asks.

"I don't know," her boy says. "He's just crying."

The music picks up. Turnbull kicks the wooden paneling of the train car in a sudden fit. He reaches a hand into the wooden guts and pulls apart the boards, grimacing and screaming. Rusted nails, shards of wood fall at his feet. Dee tells him to cool off. John Q. keeps playing his guitar, but a different song. Something lighter, but it comes out even darker.

Her boy has dirt in his fingernails. This boy whose name was withheld from her, and this is what she first loved about him. That he kept his secrets. Because she keeps her secrets, too. And because love happens like that sometimes, or so she comes to understand. Or thinks she understands. That love might occur in a moment so simple as a brief instance in which neither of them probe into the unspoken and unasked questions that hum over bared skin like an electric current. And for the first time in her life, she finds beauty in silence.

Her boy squeezes her arm, maybe to let her know he's still there. Just like he was last night. And the night before. And the night before. And the night before. The many nights that she hoped would follow.

Turnbull throws his shoulder against the wood panels. They crack beneath his weight. Wendy leaps back. Landon chokes on his wine. Dee shouts, "Jesus, man. Chill out." John Q. stops playing his guitar. The dancing stops. The shadows fall still. And this, above all else, is what seems to bother Turnbull the most. He spins in a tight circle, raising his hands above his head, challenging the silence he has created.

"What the fuck is your guys' problem?" he shouts, laughing. "Come on. Let's go. Don't let it. Don't let it. Don't let it get you down. Let's go. Play that guitar, boy. Come on now. Play it. Let's hear what song you got ready."

John Q. plays a slow chord, but another doesn't follow. The train car is quiet.

"Fuck, man." Turnbull is laughing hysterically, clutching his stomach. "Fucking pussy. Play that goddamned guitar and we dance. Play it, boy. Do I got to beat the music into you?"

John Q. searches the rest of them for direction. His eyes drift to May, and she wishes like hell they hadn't. But, as she knows, eyes have a way of finding her in these forbidden lapses in time. Turnbull traces John Q's stare and finds May.

"What do you think, girlie?" Turnbull asks, a drunken step forward, but no less uncertain. "Shouldn't this colored boy play that guitar a little bit?" He throws a thumb back at John Q. "Make us happy, wouldn't it? If he played that guitar? Don't you think?"

She lies frozen, manages a shrug. She feels the eyes of everyone in the train car, but she focuses on the hand draped over her shoulder, warm and cold and beating.

"Oh," Turnbull says, another step forward. He crouches down, his naked body just inches from her face. A cloud of pubic hair, through which peeks a half-dormant penis. "You don't like the music? Or is it just me you don't like? What's your problem? Tell that boy to play that goddamned guitar. He'll listen to you, won't he? Pretty thing like yourself. He'll listen when you tell him to play that guitar."

She closes her eyes, wishes him away. She feels her boy's body go tense behind her.

"Girlie," Turnbull says, deep from his throat. A plea encased within a growl. "Tell that boy to play, huh? What do you say?"

Her eyes shut tighter.

"Listen," Turnbull says. She feels his hand reaching out to her even though she cannot see it.

But before she can even open her eyes, the moment erupts. A second split into itself, frozen in a thousand pieces.

The body lying behind her is no longer there. Her boy is across the room, and so is Turnbull. And Turnbull is shouting something wild, incomprehensible. A rustle of feet, flurry of empty and full beer and wine bottles being kicked and shattered and stomped into a thousand pieces. She opens her eyes to see her boy holding Turnbull by the neck against the splintered wooden panels. Turnbull's feet kick, suspended a foot off the ground, weightless in his grip. The muscles in her boy's back press against his skin like hieroglyphs. He is silent, her boy, saying nothing and making no sound at all. Not even a breath. He only holds Turnbull up off the ground like some sacrifice to the holy silence that fills them all.

And she, like everyone else, does nothing except stare in disbelieving belief.

Turnbull grips her boy's wrists, his eyes bulging from his skull like billiard balls. He digs his nails into her boy's skin, throws a left hook that lands on her boy's cheek, but Turnbull only screams as he withdraws broken fingers like sunken fence posts in his crippled fist. "The fuck," Turnbull sputters, face going red, then white. He spits, "Let me go, kid."

But her boy doesn't move, doesn't flinch, doesn't retreat. Turnbull's cheeks expand with a labored, unfilled breath. His eyes gone wild, spinning around the room for a friendly face and then slowly turning back into his skull.

She sees her boy's hands tighten around Turnbull's neck. He is going to kill Turnbull. He wants to kill Turnbull. She knows this the same way she knows she must say something.

"Stop!" she shouts.

Turnbull tries to scream, mouth open, but nothing comes out. His legs stop kicking, his eyes close, his arms fall limp at his sides. His eyes slowly close.

"Stop it!" she shouts even louder, her voice carving rivers into the soft flesh of her throat.

And then her boy releases Turnbull, who falls with a loud thud to the wooden floor. The light of the fire flickers against Turnbull's purple face. The stars somewhere out beyond all of this. Whatever this is. And her boy stands there above him, fists clenched at his sides, staring down.

Her boy steps back, throws his head around each shoulder. And she feels him looking at her, but she is staring down at the wooden floor. She feels him maybe ready to say something, but she shrinks farther away without moving.

John Q. sets his guitar down and crawls forward toward Turnbull's body. Dee watches. Wendy watches. Landon watches. Quentin watches. Everyone watches. Even the names she does not know, they watch. John Q. crawls past her boy's legs and lays a shaking hand on Turnbull's neck.

"He's alive," John Q. says after a pause.

"He's alive," Dee repeats, louder.

Her boy stands there for a moment, maybe two, and then leaps out of the train car. She hears his feet in the gravel, light footsteps that disappear before she realizes she was listening for them.

"What the fuck was that?" Quentin asks.

"Never seen nothing like it," John Q. adds.

And their eyes turn back to May, as though pleading for answers to questions they cannot even phrase. But she isn't worried about them. She's wondering where her boy is going to on this night. She wonders how far he will wander, how soon he will be back. Because she knows he'll be back. Because he is someone with secrets. Everyone with a secret has no home but the Wasteland. And she wants him to come back. Desperately. But after days pass and she comes to realize that he is not coming back, she takes solace when she remembers that he's out there somewhere. Somewhere among it all. And this gives her something resembling hope. Whatever that means. He's out there somewhere.

31 MELTED BODIES

DETECTIVE COMBS BOUNCED IN THE SEAT of the unmarked SUV, clutching the wheel with his knuckles nearly popping from the skin of his hand. His head swiveled shoulder to shoulder. Squinting into the headlights of the cars behind them, the evening march of commuters headed home. He laid on the accelerator, weaved through the tired crawl of cars.

Wren sat in the back seat, hands folded in her lap. "What's going on?" It seemed like a reasonable question. Detective Combs hadn't spoken a word to her since they'd left the station for the motor pool, a thousand suspicious stares accompanying them both. He'd only gripped her elbow, gently, leading her steps.

She asked him again, louder, "Where are we going?"

He either didn't hear her or didn't care. He turned a corner sharply and accelerated quickly, swerving through openings of clustered traffic, eyes oscillating between his rearview and the street itself. He fidgeted as the radio on the passenger side crackled. The words indiscernible to Wren's untrained ear. But Detective Combs plucked it from the leather and brought it to his mouth. "En route."

"Where are you taking me?" she asked, louder. "Do you really expect me to be able to tell you who made that video? Because I really don't know."

He peeled out from beneath a red light, running through the intersection. Wren reached out and grasped the door handle as oncoming traffic darted around them, stopping just inches away from her window.

Headlights everywhere, tires squealing. The SUV turned a corner and screeched to a halt.

"Shit," Jeremiah shouted. "Fucking hell fuck."

Ahead of them, a street filled and overflowing with people. The street was marked off by police tape. Red and blue lights somewhere beyond the crowd. The crowd was so large that at first Wren couldn't make sense of it. It was beyond comprehension, the mass and the swell. She heard, delayed, the distant drone of voices drowning beneath their own echoes. She thought of choirs singing in massive and empty cathedrals, the prophesied end of a world memorialized in church pew hymnals.

"What is this?" she whispered.

"A fucking protest," Detective Combs said, more to himself than to her, as he threw the SUV into reverse and peeled out into the intersection. "We'll have to find another way."

She kept her face to the window, watching the event. She saw growing from the crowd a white banner spanning the breadth of the street. The banner displayed a spray-painted outline, the details minimal yet immediately recognizable. A likeness of the same face on every television— the Liber-teen caricature of Robespierre staring out over the masses, grinning, as though he had known in his lifetime that he would end up here on this banner, this millennium, and this street, wet paint dripping from his chin, smiling and presiding over a growing crowd, all of them chanting a thousand discordant cries. She watched the painted specter of Robespierre and couldn't shake the feeling that his likeness was staring directly at her, thanking her, congratulating her, taunting her. She had given him new life in the twenty-first century, and she wished desperately that she could take it back. All of it.

Detective Combs maneuvered the SUV backward into the street, eyes wide in the rearview. "Oh shit."

"What?"

"They're following us," Detective Combs said in a measured tone as he switched lanes, leaning into the window to peer through his side-view mirror. "Shit. I should have known."

Wren turned in her seat. She saw headlights, outlines. Sports cars, taxi cabs, sedans with mufflers dragging on the concrete in a shower of sparks. Nothing out of the ordinary. Whatever that meant.

"The FBI is following us?"

He didn't answer, speeding through another red light. A sedan crossed the intersection toward them, brakes squealing, and Wren heard the engine of the SUV strain as Detective Combs floored the pedal, streetlights and passersby melting outside the window.

"Where are we going?" Wren nearly shouted.

"Just, please," Detective Combs barked, turning his head over his shoulder, narrowing his focus. "Just stop asking questions for a second."

The SUV barreled forward, shifting and swerving and swallowing the blended world, sprawling corners as if it were not the vehicle turning, but the world that was shifting beneath them.

The next light ahead of them turned yellow, the intersection clustered with turning vehicles. The engine roared as they accelerated. The light went red a full twenty yards out. She tried to shout something, ask him to stop, but she knew that whatever might escape her throat wouldn't be enough to slow the momentum of the moment. Instead, she fell back into the seat, clutching her seat belt. Detective Combs threw his weight on the gas pedal, his whole body thrust against the wheel as though willing it forward.

"Hold on," he said.

Headlights at either side, wheels screaming, horns honking, Detective Combs shouting something primal, the SUV swerving in a lazy side-to-side. A sort of mechanical dance. The wheels lifting off the ground, a moment of weightlessness. The shuttling of a city passing too quickly to orient yourself in its massive spread. Tires screeching against the pavement, a dissonant song for the day blending in the rearview. Detective Combs hung a hard right, the tires slamming against the ground, and then they were speeding down a street Wren thought she might have recognized had it not flown past her window in a flurry of indistinct shapes of sidewalkers bleeding into each other. A static tableau of a city falling to pieces.

32 A FACE IN THE WINDOW

"SO HE LEFT THE WASTELAND?" Peter asked Miss May, an earnest slant to his broken posture. "Just like that? He never came back?"

The sun angled through the open window across May. It reflected from her ghost-white skin like a flashbulb.

"That's right," she said.

"So when did you see him again?"

It was the first day of spring, 1980. A decade that the whole country, including May herself, had seemingly willed into existence. There was a collective, nationwide understanding of starting something new. Forgiving and forgetting. Sleeping dogs of past decades left snoring.

Spring in Chicago. Cold but glowing. Each breath hits your lungs like the first and last you'd ever breathe.

May paused at an empty intersection and waited absently for the light to change. No cars in sight, but still she waited, hips slanted and head swiveling. She'd just used a pay phone across the street to call Richie and tell him she didn't need a ride from the client's home. It was a nice night, she said. The fresh air did her good.

While she waited for the light, she caught sight of a window display to her side. A woman's boutique, closed. She discerned behind the unlit window the slim shapes of mannequins, ghostly white, haunting her own reflection, cigarette in hand. The mannequins behind the glass wore diamond necklaccs and stringy negligees, and she thought they looked like something from a horror film. A faceless army of blanched tarts.

As her eyes wandered over the statuettes—the calculated curvatures of elbows and hips—she saw what she first thought was a male mannequin behind the others. The exact shape and size somehow distorted no matter how much she focused. But still she was drawn to its curious shape, or what she could see of it. A sort of imposing stature, leaning into her stare. She tilted her head and, to her surprise, it walked away. She felt her heart kick in her chest. It was not a mannequin, but a reflection in the window of someone behind her, maybe across the street. She turned around so quickly that her stiletto heel snapped and drew a surprised gasp from a rabbi passing behind her.

"What is wrong?" the rabbi asked, steadying her as she stumbled for balance.

"I saw someone," she said, but she saw no one across the street that resembled what she had seen in the glass.

"Who?"

"I don't know."

But she did know. She'd known immediately. Before she even knew she knew.

The first story she had read in the *Inquisitor* about the mysterious vigilante wandering Chicago at night and wrangling criminals, she knew exactly who this man was. But her first thought upon reading this story was that the name the journalist Marcus Waters had given him was a silly name for who he was, or at least for how she remembered him. It was the name of a small and exotic bird. The person she remembered was not exotic or delicate or small. He was plain as day, hardened, and larger than a fifteen-year-old ought to be. Because she still thought of him as a boy. A fifteen-year-old, denim-jeaned boy smiling in his walk. Even though she was now a woman and he was now a man. But these were just words like everything else.

The L thundered down the street, a screaming rush of air in its wake. She watched its cabin lights fade and disappear.

May walked hurriedly to her apartment in Englewood, her heels dangling from her fingers like Christmas ornaments, her feet freezing on the cold concrete. She scanned her surroundings—alleys, fire escapes, the rooftops on either side of the street. For a shadow, a silhouette, a shape pressed into this dark night.

She drew a bath and stuck her feet in a layer of steaming, rusty pipe water. Her toes reddened as feeling slowly returned to them. She dried off and lay on her mattress, which was on the studio apartment floor—she couldn't afford a frame. Her hands held each other over her stomach, rose with each breath. She turned on her radio and lay awake all that night, staring expectantly at the only window in the studio apartment. When morning came, she crawled over and looked out the window into the alley where a dump truck was pulling out into the street and a homeless man, shivering, smoked a cigarette and exhaled into a beer bottle to watch the spectral smoke spin inside the glass.

He hadn't come to her that night, but she knew he would. She felt it, a weighted anticipation of the inevitable. She considered calling out to him, to become one of the many voices he once claimed he could hear. Her voice would rise above the others, she knew. But she also knew he would come to her when he was ready.

So she waited for him the next night and when he didn't come that night, she waited the next. Tomorrow and tomorrow and tomorrow. Throughout each waiting day, she sometimes caught peripheral shimmers of a body in motion on the surfaces that shined, the surfaces that reflected back to her all the things she couldn't see directly. She knew whose reflection she saw, though. She knew every time. A memory like a vagrant wind.

Sometimes she felt, even though she could not spot him, that he was a shadow to her steps, but always at a safe distance away. A respectful, calculated space between them, one that superseded those of the city's creeps and catcallers and seemed to her more like a distant companion—two people walking through Chicago, their steps in sync, aware of each other the way you are aware of yourself in a dream.

When she met with her clients, she could sense his proximity, and sometimes she left the windows open to the street in case he watched as she slipped from her bra and lay on the bed. She felt his hidden, rooftop eyes roving her bare skin. Some lovers know each other by their touch, their voice, their face, their scent; May knew hers by his gaze, the sensation of her skin bristling beneath a steady, obtrusive, welcome stare. She wanted to bathe in his watching.

One of her clients, as he kissed her neck, asked her what she was looking at out the window, and she told him to shut the fuck up.

How good it felt to be watched, to be known, to be seen entirely and completely, and from a distance safe enough to ignore.

So when he finally revealed himself to her one evening as she was walking home, just a block away from her apartment, she took it as an affront. She had been more than comfortable with their relationship of distances and space. But here he was, a tangible presence once again. Finite and comprehensible. All of these short years later.

She was coming back from a visit to a client named Don, an ex-marine who insisted they listen to jazz records before and during sex on his wife's empty side of the bed. He asked her to cling to him once it was over, which she did. He asked her to hold him even more tightly, which she did. He asked her to tell him she loved him, which she didn't.

And now her teenage lover stood before her for the first time in a long time, an immobile presence fixed to the sidewalk. He wasn't how she remembered him. But of course he wasn't, because she remembered a fifteen-year-old boy. Standing before her now was a man. A towering man. He was wearing a bomber jacket, black, and he kept his hands inside the pockets. But beneath it all, there was the same warm and beating body that had wrapped itself around her in the Wasteland, shielding her from whatever world existed beyond. She tried to get a look at his face, a face she had once known, but she couldn't. Shadows from unknown sources hid whatever expression existed beneath.

It was evening, a few passersby on the other side of the street. Two men were greeting each other loudly, guessing how long it had been since they'd last seen each other.

She wanted to ask him, Why? Which, even if she had asked it, would have only been a one-word question to capture the many that tangled all at once. Why did you leave the Wasteland? Where did you go? Why are you here now? Why these years later? How did you find me? Were you even looking for me at all? Did you ever think about me?

But instead, she stood there, silent, waiting for him to speak first.

"You remember me?" he asked.

"Don't ask stupid questions."

"Well, aren't you going to say something?"

A full moon growing from the clouds. A spotlight without direction. You could feel it if you stood still, closed your eyes.

"And just what the hell am I supposed to say to you?"

"Just like that?" Peter interrupted. "He found you?"

She shrugged like, Why does it matter?

"So he shows up out of nowhere, and then what?"

Miss May cleared her throat as if to continue, but instead she crossed her arms and her legs, settling into the silence between them. The street outside clamored with faraway voices, the sky was growing dark. Marcus's hand was cramped from jotting down monosyllabic annotations in his notepad. He couldn't believe what he was hearing, this bared and intimate account of a man he had spent the most important years of his professional career trying to understand. It was delirium, and he tried to capture it all in scratchy ink.

He heard the echo of some sea shanty played on an organ. He made a face that invited an explanation.

"Guess there's a game." She pointed her cigarette out the window in the direction of Wrigley Field, its stadium lights burning like an atom bomb in midburst.

"You two were together then, after he returned to you?" Marcus leaned forward. "Like, in a relationship?"

"I don't know what you'd call it."

Marcus nodded and massaged his hand. He looked back to his notes. "Well, how long were the two of you together?"

"I don't know if I'd even call it 'together.'"

"How long were the two of you *involved* then?"

"Until he died. So about four years, I guess."

He came in through the window noiselessly at hours lost to night and day, slinking over the windowsill to curl against her on the mattress. The way he used to in the Wasteland. Bodies so close that the plural didn't matter. Warm and cold and beating bodies.

Sometimes he was breathing heavy, jagged. Sometimes she heard him cough, a rumble in his throat.

In the mornings, after the sun rose, sometimes she saw blood—rusty and cracked—on his knuckles or his face, and once she saw the blood dried down the corners of his mouth. She didn't know he was capable of bleeding. But she also didn't know if it was his blood or someone else's. She never asked about it. There was nothing to ask. They kept their secrets like they always had.

She only asked him about what he did on those nights once. He came through the window and lay down beside her, slick with sweat. He kissed her forehead, but she wasn't asleep. She asked him the only question she had, "Why do you do it?"

He sighed. "Go to sleep."

She laid her arm across him, her hand atop his chest.

"Just tell me why you do it," she said. "You could do anything. You are"—she paused, feeling his heartbeat pulse beneath her palm—"whatever you are. You could do anything. You don't need to do this."

"I have reasons."

"What are they?"

"Please."

"You could do something for money. You could get good work."

"I don't need money. I don't want money. I don't do it for money."

"Then tell me why you do this." She paused, feeling the silence deepen between them. "Or at least tell me what made you this way. Because I don't believe you are what you think you are."

"What do I think I am?"

"You think you're more than us. Or you think you're not like us at all. I don't know. But either way, you're wrong. You're so wrong."

"Go to sleep."

"You're this man lying right here. And I don't want—I don't know. They'll kill you. One day they will kill you."

"No they won't. They can't."

She felt his heartbeat quicken. She pressed her fingers into his chest, trying to calm the rhythm. "They'll find a way."

"Go to sleep."

"You think that they can't kill you, but it isn't true. You're strong, but you're not invincible. No one is. I know what you think you are, but you aren't that."

"It's late."

He wrapped his arms around her.

"We could leave here. We could go anywhere. We could have a life away from all this. In a second. We could be gone. We could leave this city. You've done enough. You don't owe them anything. We could have a life together without all of this."

"I don't want to leave."

"We could move to that lake you talk about. The one you went to when you were young. We could go there. We could live there. The two of us. We could have a life that isn't this."

"Go to sleep. It's late."

"I don't want to sleep."

"Neither do I."

She nestled against him. "What do you hear?"

"I hear a hawk killing a mouse."

"Where?"

He pulled her closer against him. "Somewhere else."

In the mornings, if he wasn't gone already, they lay wrapped in a single white sheet, punch-drunk on a few meager hours of sleep, and exchanged small pieces of their histories in a game whose rules were left purposefully undefined—a story for a story, a past for a past. Each one told strategically, so as not to reveal very much, just little odd details that could belong to anyone or everyone or no one—truthful lies. They respected the other's secrets. May told him about her arthritic Polish grandmother who played Bach and Chopin in half-time on the piano, slowing the notes until they almost hurt to hear, the grandmother who read the King James Bible in a heavy accent. And in return, he told her about vacations to Michigan's Upper Peninsula as a child, a cabin along a lake with pebbles that ran up to the shore. Lake Walton, he called it, savoring the words. He said he waded into the waters late at night and fished for bass and bluegill and walleye, his jeans rolled up to his knees, dragonflies humming still over the moonlit surface. He said he'd never been happier. And when he said this, she made a face as though to say, You sure? And to this he smiled, maybe laughed, and wrapped her closer into his warm and cold and beating body, as though to say nothing.

A sun warming in the window. A day yet to begin.

But beyond these fanciful pasts, nothing. They left whatever secrets they'd carried all these years tangled in the sheets between them.

"It sounds nice," Marcus said after Miss May reached a long pause in which she relaxed back into the couch, signaling that she had arrived at the temporary end of her story. "It sounds like you two were very happy together."

Peter sat perfectly still, one leg crossed over the other. Deep in some inscrutable thought.

"I don't know if I'd say that," Miss May replied after some consideration. "We were young and we didn't know how those things worked. I still don't know really what it was. I doubt he knew, either. He was just someone I used to know who crawled in my window most nights and slept in my bed after we had sex. Someone who kissed me when he left. Is there a name for that?"

"A lover?"

She weighed the term as if she'd never considered it before. She shook her head slightly. "I don't think that's it."

"You mentioned that you asked him to leave with you," Marcus said, "and to start a life together somewhere else. But he didn't want to leave."

She nodded.

"I guess that's something I never understood," Marcus said. "Why did he do what he did? What motivated him? He wasn't getting paid. No one even knew who he was. And like you said, someone like him could have done almost anything he'd wanted."

May laughed, softly, her eyes drifting out the window. "He never once told me, but looking back, it seems clear to me. I was too young then to realize that I probably already knew the answer and just didn't want to know. He did it because there was something inside him, eating him from the inside out. Something had been done to him, something awful and unspeakable—I don't know what it was, but I know it was there."

"How do you know that?"

"If you know the feeling yourself, it's not to hard to spot it in someone else, unless of course you don't want to, which I didn't at the time. I didn't want to believe that someone like him could be hurt, because I wasn't ready to accept the fact that I'd been hurt. And while I covered mine up with a smile and makeup, the only way he knew to keep that pain quiet, or at least quiet enough, was to go out on those streets and spread that pain to people he thought were more deserving of it than him. That's why he did what he did. He may have been a solitary sort of man, but one thing I can tell you is that he didn't want to be alone in his pain." She smiled. "Maybe that's the real reason why he came back to find me all those years later. Misery loves company."

Peter mumbled something beneath his breath, his eyes glassy and distant.

"What's that?" May asked him.

Peter sat up straight, blinking, as though awoken from a dream. "Nothing. Sorry." He kneaded his temples with his fingers.

Marcus cleared his throat and turned to Miss May. "Was he ever bothered by your—well—your line of work?"

She smiled. "I don't think it bothered him at first. In fact, I think he liked it. It was forbidden and exciting. But it got to him eventually, the longer we were together. He didn't like sharing. Said he didn't know why I did it. I told him it was my job. I told him I liked it. I told him unless the two of us left together, started a life just the two of us far away from this place, then I'd keep doing it. Because it wasn't ever about the sex for me. I told him that. That's not why I do this job. I explained to him that it made me feel good and free and powerful. I thought he of all people would understand that feeling, and maybe he did for a while, but it eventually got to him. Men being what they are."

"What do you mean 'it eventually got to him'? What happened?"

"Well, he started to follow me more and more often. I knew he was doing it, and I kind of liked it most of the time. At first it was because he wanted to watch. He liked it. I'd leave a window open for him to see through. But whenever I'd ask him about it, he'd say he was keeping me safe and protecting me. That really pissed me off, and I told him I didn't need his help. I didn't need his protection. So finally I told him if he ever followed me again, I was done with him. To his credit, he stopped. But then he only started getting jealous. More and more jealous. And then one night, he threw a fucking tantrum. Showed up out of nowhere and beat the living hell out of Richie and Richie's driver. Not sure why, to tell you the truth. Maybe because I'd mentioned to him that I didn't want to go with a certain john again, but Richie wasn't having it. Maybe he was just fed up with the work I was doing. Personally, I think he just lost his shit. Seemed inevitable. Anyone who lives their life doing the sorts of things he was doing, they're bound to come apart at the seams. But anyway, that's the story you heard from whomever you heard it from. I never saw Richie or Olander after that. I don't know what happened to them. Of course, I wonder sometimes," she began, but her voice narrowed into a hum. "But that was also the last time I ever saw him." She lit another cigarette. "He died just a few days later."

"You never talked to him about that night?" Peter asked.

"No." She shook her head. "Like I said, I never saw him again."

Marcus adjusted his seat on the couch and turned a page in his notebook. "I hate to ask you this. But I have to."

"Go ahead, Marcus."

"Can you tell me about when he died?"

"What about it?"

"Just what you know. What you remember. Anything and everything, I guess."

"Anything and everything," she repeated in an amused singsong. "Well, I guess the first thing I'd say is that it came as much a surprise to me as it probably did to you, which isn't to say it was much of a surprise at all. It was a matter of time, really. But I came to cope with it even before he died. I learned to see him as a ghost when he was still living. A walking chalk outline. I mourned that thick-headed man every morning that he walked out my door, slipped through my window."

"Did that help?"

She thought about it for a moment and pressed a finger gingerly to her lips like they would crack. "No. No, it didn't help at all."

In the days after he'd beaten Richie and Olander, May still expected to see him again. Maybe she even wanted to. She wanted to ask him why and she wanted to hear him apologize and she wanted to look at him when he stood before her. But he didn't come to her. She remembered him those years ago when they were practically children, jumping from the train car and wandering off into the dark and dusk and the coming day. But she was certain he would return this time. She could feel it. The same way she had felt his stare on her skin.

Those short days of waiting had the consistency of a sleepwalker's delirium, nights of half sleep while watching a smudgy window for a face to appear just as she had for four years. So she distracted herself. She began contacting her regular clients. Told them Richie was taking a break. She scheduled appointments and handled the money, saving Richie's percentage for whenever he would return. She walked, took the L, hopped on the bus. She met with clients in hotel rooms with unmade beds. Anything to get out of her apartment, anything to keep her from staring at that empty window.

And when the news broke, it was everywhere. His name on every corner, on every tongue. The newspapers proclaiming his death seemed to come alive and take to the streets—they littered every curb, were folded on every barstool, were displayed in every window. The radio disc jockeys dedicated songs to him—slow, downbeat, synthesized tunes. A children's choir sang "Amazing Grace" on the nightly news and May wept, the tears transforming from grief to sorrow to hatred, because she hated him for dying and she hated herself for hating a dead man, a dead man she loved more than any living person.

She still felt him the way she felt herself. Warm and cold and beating. At night, she continued to wait for his face in the window and prayed for the impossible, if only to be able to ask him if she were somehow responsible for this, all of this. She filled the empty, dragging hours by carefully constructing an elaborate and alternate world that the two of them might have shared in some other life altogether—two lovers living in a cabin along Lake Walton, taking a rowboat out onto the water at night, raising the oars, and falling asleep next to each other beneath layers of quilts and stars as a gentle wind slowly guided them back to shore.

She canceled her appointments for a week. This was the amount of time she gave herself to mourn—seven days. And at the end of the seven days, it was over and hadn't she always known this day would come and what difference did it make, really, if it came now or tomorrow or a hundred years from now?

The first client she saw after her seven-day furlough was a man she'd never met, referred from a regular. They met at a hotel, the fourth story that looked out over a construction project. The skeleton of some new office building, scaling higher than she could crane her head. Rows of scaffolding, girders—vectors all pointing a hundred ways at once. She stood at the window while the man undressed hurriedly, his heavy breathing ringing in the walls, his belt buckle jangling in his frenzied hands. She pressed her fingertips hard into the glass window and it felt cool. Her breath fogged against the glass and she closed the curtains to make the room dark enough to disappear.

The day of the city's funeral for him, May put on her clothes with the stoicism of a soldier headed to the front line. A red tank top, white leather jacket, and denim jeans. She would not wear black. She had already mourned him many times before, she told herself as she exited her apartment into the static-still street. She had mourned his death a hundred times before—sleepless and countless nights perched at her radio when he didn't come over, reciting to herself the many euphemisms for death, preparing herself for the inevitable.

Let the rest of them wear black.

The funeral was along the lake. Promontory Point. The newspaper the next day said that nearly half the city had attended. But she remembers seeing no one. A city abandoned, some vision of a distant future set into motion. She remembers the sidewalk, covered in a fine film of snow, frozen over. She remembers the somewhere-song of a street performer with an out-of-tune guitar—"Don't Think Twice, It's All Right." She remembers ice and dirt scattered along the deserted streets. She remembers the hollow whistle of the Chicago wind pressing through buildings as though the city itself were singing a dirge.

She remembers standing at the lake and she remembers seeing his ashes scattered. She was a long distance away, but she saw it, sure enough, a cloud of black ash. It roiled out over the lake, skittering along the frozen surface until it disappeared. And she left. She didn't turn around. She left. She walked to nowhere. She wandered the city, directionless. This was the only way she felt him, whatever was left of him. She paused and stared into the windows of abandoned shops, waiting for a reflection that did not come.

And she likes to think they were alone that day in the city they'd built in brief and unspoken exchanges.

33 TRANSITORY

MARCUS KNEW WHEN MISS MAY WAS FINISHED. It was in the way her body had nowhere left to withdraw into itself. Throughout their conversation, she had compacted herself within her wooden chair, pulling her legs up to the seat, wrapping her arms around her shins, laying her head against her knees. She had reached the deepest recesses of herself and appeared content with whatever she had found.

She looked like a child fighting sleep. Her head was turned and she was looking out the window where the sun was falling into the outfield of Wrigley.

Peter was pacing the room, wandering the walls, leaning into his uneven and pained steps, processing everything May had said.

Marcus caught Miss May's reflection in the window, and he saw her blinking heavily, and each time he thought that it was her last for the evening, that she would fall asleep in this precarious position, maybe dreaming of someone she once knew.

He saw her looking back at him in the window.

"You're looking at me like I've got six heads," she whispered.

"I'm just thinking."

"About what?"

"About him," Marcus said.

"Me, too." She smiled.

"He found her," Peter muttered to himself across the room, moving like a planetary body in orbit. "He found her."

"It's funny, actually," Marcus said to May, ignoring Peter's ramblings. "It's funny to hear you talk about him, because none of it matches with what I'd imagined. I pictured him as an ascetic, the lifestyle of a monk. I pictured meals of gray porridge every day, meditating on his head in a bare room. I even thought he might be some psychopath, a cruel person who occasionally did good things. But to hear you talk, he was almost like anyone else. I don't know how I'll manage to somehow reconcile these two different people."

"I'm not so sure he has to be one or the other." She adjusted her hand to cradle her chin on the armrest.

"Why do you say that?"

"I've never known anyone who couldn't be cruel when they wanted to be. Only difference is that there are people who are cruel to the wrong people, people who are more cruel than other people. People whose occasional cruelty is written about in the morning paper. It doesn't matter much in the end."

Marcus considered it, but he was too mentally exhausted to work through the logic.

Peter passed by them, his steps slower, whispering inaudibly to himself. He turned on his heel and directed his gaze to Miss May. "You said earlier you saw a man break his hand on his jaw. In the Wasteland."

"I did."

"And there's witnesses who say they saw him get shot, but the bullets had no effect."

"I'm sure that never happened."

"How would you know that?" Peter asked defensively.

"I know what you're getting at." May leaned forward, smiling without affection. "But I touched his skin with my own hands. I felt every inch of his body several times over. And his skin was the same as mine. It was the same as yours. That man wasn't bulletproof. He wasn't like us, but he also wasn't indestructible. He was what he was."

"Which was what?" Marcus asked.

"Not us," she said. "He wasn't like us. I don't know any other way to say it."

"You never once thought he might still be alive?" Peter interrupted. He was sweating although the room was cool, a draft passing through the window.

"Never."

"I don't believe you."

"Peter." Marcus held out a hand.

"You didn't know him," May interjected. Her voice hadn't risen even a fraction, but it still sounded louder as she directed herself toward Peter. "You never met him. You don't know who you are talking about. But I did know him. I knew him better than anyone else in this world ever knew him. And I can promise you that he is dead."

"But how do you know that?" Peter said. "You can't possibly know that for certain."

"I do know that for certain," she said, her chin jutting out, her voice hollowing into a hoarse insistence. "Because one day he was gone and he didn't come back. And I knew him. He always came back." She stabbed her finger at Peter. "He always came back. But one day he was gone and he didn't come back. That's how I know he's gone. And that's enough. Think what you want to think, but he's dead. He's gone."

Peter remained standing there for a moment, shook his head, and continued pacing the apartment. May leaned back in the couch, pulling out another cigarette. She didn't light it. She only held it in her fingers and then laid her head back on the couch, studying the ceiling with a tired expression. Her eyes closed and Marcus didn't know if she was simply falling asleep or contemplating something unspoken.

"Do you miss him?" Marcus asked.

She opened her eyes slowly. "Why do you ask?"

"You don't have to answer it if you don't want to. I'm just asking out of curiosity."

She thought about it and smiled, as if she'd just understood some unspoken joke. "I'm not sure there was a time, even when he was alive and lying there next to me, that I didn't miss him. There are some people like that, I think . . ." Her voice trailed off. "*Transitory* is the word for them. They can be looking at you right in the eyes and you're already feeling the full weight of them not being there. Each time you reach out to touch them, you worry you'll pass right through them. You're always surprised to feel your hand touch their skin. Feel their heartbeat. Maybe this is how it is with all lovers. If that's even the word for what we were." Her voice was softer now, tempered by the onset of sleep. She blinked slowly, each time her eyes shut for a second longer than the last.

Marcus took a few more notes in his notepad, which was by now mostly full of hectic transcriptions. He wrote in the margins: *Transitory.* "I read the medical examiner's report," Marcus said. He heard in his voice a rising inflection, an invitation for her to ask him for details, for his opinion, for hope.

"What happened to your wife, Marcus?" she asked, her eyes still closed, her words slow and long.

He looked up from his notepad. "What?"

"How did she die?"

"How did you know?"

"You're wearing a wedding ring still."

"But how did you know she died?"

"I always know these things. How did she die?"

"It was a brain aneurism," Marcus was surprised to hear himself say. He never talked about it with anyone, not even his children. It was something he left to those dark and total nights when there was nothing surrounding you but things left unspoken.

"Tell me about it," she said. "Please."

"About when she died? Why?"

"It seems fair that you tell me, considering what I've told you, doesn't it?"

"OK," he said, entering into the memory slowly, carefully, like a child entering a dark and unlit room. "She died in her sleep, I think. I woke up in the middle of the night, and she was lying next to me. I knew something was wrong right away, because it was so quiet. I realized then that she wasn't breathing. So I turned to her, saw her outline, but I didn't think it was actually her. I didn't know who it was, but it wasn't her. It couldn't be her. I lay there a whole ten minutes thinking here was some un-breathing stranger lying in our bed. And then I touched her skin and it was cold. It was really cold. Like glass. And all that time it had been her, but I only realized it in that moment." He heard his voice breaking, so he stifled it with a sharp breath. "She died in her sleep, though, so that's good, I guess."

"That would be a good way to die." May smiled, her eyes closed. "From one dream to the next."

Marcus heard the minute-hand clicks of a clock. He saw it on the wall behind him. Quarter after eight.

Peter had stopped his pacing and stood stationary across the room, hands on his hips, head cocked to his shoulders, eyes closed and lips moving silently. His thinning hair was a mess atop his head.

"I still talk to her sometimes," Marcus said to May. "My wife. Before I fall asleep. I talk to her. I say something small and inconsequential. It never feels how it used to feel, but it's something. I tell her I miss her. Something like that. It makes me feel like she's there in some small way, and maybe she is."

"Maybe she is," she murmured.

She breathed softly, quietly, her lips parted in a sleeping grin. "I'm glad we did this. It felt good to talk about him with someone like you. Someone who understands him, even if you don't know it."

"Be safe, May. Promise me you'll be safe."

"No one is coming for me. I'm a nobody. I keep a low profile, more as a professional caution than anything else. But I'm glad I got to meet you after all these years. You're a good person, Marcus. Now get out of my apartment and leave me alone."

On their way down the stairwell, Marcus found a business card, folded four times. He stopped and picked it up: MISS MAY PIECEWORK. It had a phone number on the bottom. He regarded it briefly with a smile before stuffing it into his pocket.

Peter walked in labored strides as they exited the building and stepped out into the wordless night. Marcus's throat hummed like a motor with the full weight of a thousand questions he knew they should have thought to ask, details that they should have followed up on. But it had also been enough. Although there were no more leads to follow, he felt like whatever latent and lingering questions he'd had about the Kingfisher had somehow been answered in the spaces between what was left unsaid. And more importantly, he knew Miss May would be safe.

There was ball-game traffic congesting the street. Headlights overlapping into a dull and setting sun. The casual car horn punctuating his and Peter's footsteps on the sidewalk as they neared his parked car. In the distance, the sounds of a protest—bleary and atonal chants rising through police sirens.

Marcus opened his door and began to lower himself inside when he saw Peter standing on the sidewalk, hands in his pockets.

"Come on," Marcus said. "I'll give you a lift home."

Peter shook his head, looked out over the congested street. "I might just walk. Looks like it might be quicker. You get home."

"You shouldn't be walking around that far. Not on your bad leg. Just get in."

"I appreciate it, but I'd like the walk." Peter smiled, pained and far away. "A lot to think about tonight."

"She's going to be OK," Marcus said, standing against his open door. "She seems like she can take of herself. I wouldn't worry about her."

Peter nodded. And then he said, face shining in the creeping headlights, "She knew him, Marcus. She'd known him since he was fifteen. She's seen him. Like, really seen him. It's fucking crazy, isn't it? It doesn't feel real." Peter was energized, smiling widely. As enthusiastic as Marcus had ever seen him.

"I'm not sure any of the past couple days have felt real," he answered.

Peter shifted his step, easing off his bad leg. "But she knew him, Marcus. Doesn't that mean anything to you? You heard what she said about him."

Marcus wasn't sure what May's account signified. This woman had once known a man who might be dead, who might be alive. "She knew him," Marcus said finally. "And I'm glad we found her. We did what we came to do. We warned her. That's all we can do."

Peter looked as though he were just seconds away from jumping out of his skin. Marcus couldn't remember ever seeing Peter so eager, so unbridled, so ready to spill. "You know as well as I do what this means. Don't pretend like you don't."

"What are you talking about?"

"He's alive, Marcus." Peter raised his arms, as though trying to take flight. He was speaking rapidly, difficult to keep up with. "I know she doesn't think so, but that's because she doesn't want to believe it. He's still out there somewhere. You heard all those things she said about him. You think it's some coincidence that he 'died' just days after he followed her and beat the hell out of her pimp? After she yelled at him, told him she never wanted to see him again? He left because of her, Marcus. Out of guilt, anger, or whatever. He left."

"I know," Marcus said. Because he did know. Even if he did not want to know this, he knew. The Kingfisher had not died that day back in 1984. He was confident of this. The rest, though, was speculation.

"But how would anyone else know? The gunman? Do you think it's possible . . ." Peter began to ask, but stopped.

"What?"

"Nothing. I have a thousand thoughts swirling around right now. This is crazy, Marcus. It's fucking crazy. He's alive. He's out there somewhere."

"He may be." Marcus nodded.

The light changed at the intersection, and a few dozen car horns entered into a dissonant chorus as the mass of steel bodies pulled forward in a slow but certain progression.

"Why don't you care?" Peter asked, with a cautioning smile. "Don't you care? He's out there somewhere. We could find him. He can stop all of this."

"Get in the car, Peter. Let's go home."

"We can find him, Marcus." Peter laughed, mouth hung open in disbelief. "Why aren't you listening to me? We can end all of this if we find him. Why don't you care?"

"Because it doesn't matter," Marcus said firmly. "It doesn't matter that the Kingfisher is still out there, because he's sure not doing anything about whatever is happening right now. He's not here, Peter. It doesn't matter that he's out there, because he's not here."

"Maybe we could convince him," Peter said.

A car pulled up and parked behind Marcus's car. A rusted Volkswagen. A man wearing a Cubs shirt and ball cap got out, cell phone in hand. He walked toward Lindley Apartments, but stopped, his focus drifting to his phone. He walked back to his car and leaned against the hood.

"Let's get home." Marcus lowered himself into the driver's seat. He turned the key in the ignition and saw that Peter remained exactly where he had been, fixed to the sidewalk, hands in his pockets. Marcus rolled down his window. "Come on, Peter."

Peter stood, a rueful smile melting from his face. "What's wrong with you?"

"There's no point in finding him, Peter," Marcus said. "We couldn't find him if we tried. And even if we did find him, there's nothing to say to him that he doesn't already know." He glanced in his rearview. The man with the cell phone was standing on the sidewalk. Marcus saw the man glance over at them, expressionless. "We shouldn't be talking about this right now," Marcus said. "Just get in the car."

"Can I be perfectly honest with you?" Peter approached Marcus's car, seemingly oblivious to the stranger behind them, and leaned his elbows on the open window. "I think you're afraid to find the Kingfisher, because if he is really still alive, that will mean that everything else you thought you knew doesn't mean anything anymore. I think you're scared to re-write history, because you don't know what it will mean. You don't know what it will mean for you and your entire life's work. You were wrong, but so was everyone else. This is an opportunity to do something that needs to be done. You have a chance to write the rest of the story."

"You don't know what you're talking about, Peter. This doesn't have anything to do with my career. I've already explained it to you. You're just not listening." He lowered his voice into a barely audible breath. "The Kingfisher, if he's out there, isn't doing anything about all this, and we can't change that."

"But he'd know that we were on his side," Peter insisted. "Sure, maybe he wouldn't listen to me, but he'd listen to you. I'm sure he'd listen to you. He'd listen to Marcus Waters."

"Get in the car, Peter," Marcus said, raising his voice. He wasn't sure if it was because he was speaking over the hum of engines behind him or if he was simply angry, tired, confused, and ready to return home.

The man with the cell phone took a step toward them, but stopped. His phone rang in his hands and he brought it to his ear. He didn't say a word.

The sky was a premature stone-blue, the color of a television playing to an empty room.

"You used to want to get to the truth," Peter said. "All these years, I remembered you as someone who followed a story to its end. And I re-spected you for that. I always respected you for that, Marcus."

"Goodbye, Peter."

Marcus sat in the car, slammed the door shut, and pulled into the street and into the moving tide of cars. He watched Peter in his side-view mirror, the man with the cell phone next to him, two shadows fixed to the sidewalk, both of them soon consumed by a crowd of late-arrival protestors holding chartreuse posters that proclaimed easy answers to impossible questions.

Marcus sat perfectly straight in his seat as he turned the corner. The street ahead. Nothing behind.

34 A CRIMINAL AT MY KITCHEN TABLE

BY THE TIME SHE REACHED the sixth floor of her apartment building, Tillman was breathless. She wasn't sure how far she had run. The city blocks had blurred together, passersby scrutinizing this evening runner in day clothes, this woman pushing through tourists congested on corners, waiting impatiently for the stoplight. And now, a sweating mess, she ambled down the empty hallway and unlocked the front door with shaking hands.

"Where were you?" asked her father from his recliner in the corner of the room. His eyes were closed and his voice seemed to be coming from the far reaches of a half-dreamt dream. "Who are the people here? Talking too loud."

"People?"

"Tilly," came Jeremiah's voice from the kitchen. "We're in here."

She passed her father. Al Green crooned him back into whatever sleep he had briefly emerged from.

In the kitchen, Jeremiah leaned against a counter drinking one of her father's last two beers from the fridge. Tillman's eyes fell upon a girl seated at the kitchen table, her head collapsed atop her arms. She wore a gray hoodie, the folds of fabric actively consuming her skinny body. The last of Tillman's father's beers sat in front of her. Untouched, sweating on the table. She raised her head and glanced over her shoulder. A castaway stare. Her hair was short, cut jaggedly around her ears. She looked young. Too young for the beer and too young for the somber gravity weighing down the room. Her eyes were swollen with either tears or fatigue or both. She briefly regarded Tillman with a scrunched expression, her eyebrows meeting each other halfway.

Tillman looked back at Jeremiah. He smiled weakly.

"Who is she?" Tillman asked Jeremiah and then turned to the girl. "Who are you?"

"Just take a seat, Tilly."

"Jeremiah," Tillman intoned, remembering her last phone call with him. It came back to her in words she hadn't been given time to consider in their entirety. *The Liber-teens. Arrests. Did she trust him?* Tillman took a step closer to the girl, who leaned farther back in her chair, maintaining her distance. The girl's fear was palpable, emanating from her body like an electric current. "Please tell me this isn't who I think this is."

"Take a seat," Jeremiah said. "Please." He stepped forward, pulled out a chair, and gestured for her to sit across from the girl. He sat himself between the two, a litigator's posture, as he tried to bridge, or perhaps enforce, the space between them.

"Why would you bring her here?" Tillman asked, unable to politely ignore the fact that Jeremiah had brought a wanted criminal into her place of residence while her father slept just ten feet away.

"I'm going to explain—"

"How the hell did you get her out of the precinct? Did you stuff her in a suitcase and walk out?" She waited for Jeremiah to answer, but he was making vague hand motions, trying to calm her down as though she were an animal incapable of human speech. "What have you done, Jeremiah?"

The girl stared at her hands. She looked sick. Face paled to the color of bone. She made a low sound in her throat as though she might vomit.

"This is Officer Lucinda Tillman," Jeremiah said to the girl. "She's a friend of mine from the police department. We're both here because we want to help you, and we want you to help us."

"Actually," Tillman said to the girl, "I don't even know who you are. I'm guessing I know exactly *what* you are, but how about you tell me your name."

The girl uttered something so softly it didn't pass her lips.

"Excuse me?" Tillman asked.

She cleared her throat and repeated it again. "Wren."

"Wren? That's your name?"

The girl nodded.

"Of course it is." Tillman sighed.

"Did they follow us?" the girl asked quietly to Jeremiah. "The FBI?"

Jeremiah fidgeted in his seat, casting a nervous look at Tillman.

"The FBI followed you here?" Tillman asked, her voice rising with each word.

"Yes, but I think I lost them."

"*You think?*" Tillman scoffed, rising from her chair. "Did they follow you here or not?"

"No." Jeremiah shook his head after allowing a pause, a meditation on the silence. "They didn't follow us. I was careful."

"You were careful." Tillman laughed, gripping the edge of the table. "Of course you were careful."

"I promise you," Jeremiah said to Tillman. "It's fine. It's going to work out." The sincerity in his voice was enough that Tillman wanted to test it by dangling him off the fire escape—would it still be fine then?

"What am I doing here?" Wren asked. A Midwestern drawl blended her words into a single pitch.

"That's a great question," Tillman said. "What is she doing here, Jeremiah?"

"OK, let me explain." He addressed the girl. Wren, or whatever the hell her name actually was. "Officer Tillman and I both think the police and FBI are making a crucial mistake in their investigation. They believe that you all, the Liber-teens, are responsible for the video." He paused, collecting his thoughts. "I happen to think that whoever is behind that video wanted to frame the Liber-teens so that you all would hack into the police servers and release the report to exonerate yourselves, which I don't need to tell you didn't quite work out the way you had probably hoped. He was baiting you the whole time to give him what he wanted, and now that he has it, he still hasn't stopped. He won't stop killing hostages anytime soon unless we can do something."

Tillman reluctantly admitted to herself that Jeremiah's hypothesis made sense. If what Abe Dawkins had told her was at all true—the gunman chose hostages that Stetson wouldn't try to save by releasing the report—then the gunman had still found a way to make the report public. The gunman was running a bloody smear campaign against the police. And it was working.

"We want the same thing, all of us," Jeremiah continued. "We want to put an end to whatever the hell is happening out there." He pointed out the nearest window in the general direction of a city fraying like a thread of yarn.

"Is that what she wants?" Tillman asked. "You think she cares about all that? She didn't follow you here because she gives a shit about all that. She's here because you probably said you could help her. When you called me and told me to meet you back here, I thought you had an actual lead. Not this, whatever this is. You think you have an idea that the police and feds haven't already thought of? One that involves harboring a criminal and lying to the FBI? Forget losing your job, you're going to stand in front of a grand jury for this. And me? I'm straight to prison. Do you think she cares about that?" She pointed at Wren. "Do you think we—all of us here—do you really think we want the same thing right now?"

"You said you trusted me." He spoke behind clenched teeth. "So just listen."

"I know what I said. But I also trusted you weren't going to have a criminal at my kitchen table. I was obviously wrong about that. The only thing all of us have in common right now is that we're all going to be spending our lives in prison."

"Stop!" Wren shouted from the end of the table, shrinking beneath the volume of her own voice. "I don't care about my sentencing," she said softly. "I'll turn myself in if I need to. I'll tell them whatever you want me to." She turned to Jeremiah. "But if you know a way to find whoever made those videos, I want to help. I'll do whatever I have to. Just tell me," she said, pulling the sleeves of her hoodie up to her wrists. "I don't think we have much time."

Al Green rang through the chorus of "Love and Happiness." Winding through the words as though he thought they might not end.

Tillman faced Jeremiah, with an expression she hoped carried whatever unspoken words through the space between them. "What's your grand plan here?"

Jeremiah looked to the girl and paused for her tacit approval, which she offered by staring back at him. "Before we get into a plan, I should be completely forthright with you, Wren. The FBI has enough to put you away for a while on some legitimate charges, it sounds like. But they'll also leverage for an even longer sentencing."

She gave a nervous laugh. "No. They can't prove that I took the ME report from the CPD network." She quickly added, "I'm not saying that I did. I'm just saying they can't prove it one way or the other."

Jeremiah leaned into the table, his chest pressed against the wooden corner, until he was just a foot away from the girl. He reached a hand halfway to hers and tapped his fingers against the surface. "Your friend," he said. "The girl they brought in with you. Your roommate."

Wren unwound from her coiled posture. "What about her? Is she OK?"

Jeremiah paused uncomfortably. "She told the FBI you did the hack. She said you retrieved the ME report. Said she could prove it." He paused, cast a glance to Tillman, and then looked back to the girl. "And she said you might have helped make the videos. That's what she told them."

"No." She shook her head, a slanting smile. "You're lying to me."

"I'm sorry, but it's true. They have her on video making her plea."

"You're full of shit," Wren spat. "You're working with them. You're trying to get me to confess. I'm not going to. This is fucked up."

Tillman stood and went to the sink. She felt sick. She turned on the faucet and watched the water pour over yesterday's dirty dishes.

"I have no reason to lie to you," she heard Jeremiah say. "You need to trust me when I say I'm risking my ass to help you."

"I don't need to trust you at all. I know Parker. She would never do what you're saying she did."

"Look, I was talking with one of the agents back at the station. The FBI only let you come with me because they want to bring down the rest of the Liber-teens and they think you know where they are. He said the FBI gave your roommate an especially tough shakedown. They were promising her a life of jail time unless she told them who hacked the police servers and who made the videos. She held strong for a while, but she broke. Eventually. That's what they tell me. I don't think they'd lie to me about that."

"Well, they did lie to you," Wren said. "Parker wouldn't do that."

"I'm sorry."

"Parker wouldn't do that," Wren said. Her short, messy hair whipped across her face as she shook her head. And then, when Jeremiah didn't respond, she repeated it. Softer this time, without edge or shape. A voiceless sigh for herself to hear and to maybe believe. "She wouldn't. I know she wouldn't. She wouldn't do that to me. She wouldn't."

Tillman filled a glass of water. She dropped in two ice cubes from the freezer and set the glass in front of Wren. "Take a drink. Breathe."

Wren reached unconsciously for the glass, brought it to her lips. She took a small drink, the glass shaking in her hands. She set it down, tears falling freely down her cheeks. She ignored them, stared through them.

"I'm sorry," Jeremiah said. "I know this is a lot to hear. Only reason I'm telling you this is because I think we can help you."

"I didn't make that video," she whispered. "I would never. I didn't. I didn't."

"We know that. But the FBI doesn't."

"How do you know I didn't?"

"Because I believe you hacked the server. Even if the FBI doesn't have all the evidence they need, I believe that you played some part in that. Am I correct?"

She shrugged. "If I hacked the report, why would that mean I didn't have anything to do with the videos?"

"Because whoever hacked the server was probably the same person who sent Marcus Waters another file. A very sensitive file." Jeremiah paused, leaning across the table. The girl stared back at him, her lips pressed tightly together. "And that seems like information the gunman would love to share, but he hasn't, because he doesn't have it. That's how I know you have nothing to do with that video, Wren. But if you can help us find the person who actually killed those people, well, you might be able to save yourself and probably save a lot of other people, too."

Wren slumped over and gathered her hair in her fingers. "How?"

"I have some information," he said. "I'd like to show it to you if you would agree to help."

"OK," she whispered.

Tillman glanced between Wren and Jeremiah, inviting an explanation that didn't come. "What are you talking about?" she asked Jeremiah. "There was another file?"

"It's not important right now."

"No," she said. "If I'm going to be a part of this, I need to know."

In the living room, her father snored like a band saw against granite.

"It was a letter." Jeremiah sighed. "From some detectives to Chief

Gonzalez, written during the end of the Kingfisher years. They were saying that they thought Stetson was in cooperation with the Kingfisher somehow." He looked between the two of them. "And if it's true that the Kingfisher faked his death, then maybe that means Stetson was the one who coordinated it."

Tillman paused, passing over the spaces between the details. "So that's why Stetson didn't release the ME report?" Tillman asked, thinking out loud. "He's trying to hide that he helped the Kingfisher fake his death?"

"Maybe." Jeremiah nodded. "And who knows what else he's trying to hide."

She again remembered her conversation with Abe. Stetson parked outside the drug boss's home, as if he'd known the Kingfisher would be there. As if he'd told the Kingfisher to be there. And Penny and Walter inadvertently stumbling upon the same realization. "You really believe the Kingfisher is still alive?"

"It doesn't matter if the Kingfisher is still alive or not," Jeremiah said, "and it doesn't matter if Stetson is trying to cover it up. What matters right now is that people are going to die very soon if we don't do something." He turned to Wren. "So let's talk about what comes next."

35 BETRAYAL

AND HERE WREN WAS in this unfamiliar apartment, seated across from these unfamiliar faces. Sitting erect, deaf to words being spoken at her. She felt like a tourist inside of her skin, watching the world from an assumed and temporary distance. Every transient thought turned inevitably to Parker. Where was Parker now? Was she sitting in the same holding room at the station, held inside the same phlegm-yellow walls? What was she feeling and what color was her hair when she'd last seen her? What dreams would escape her tonight and was she thinking of Wren right now, just like Wren was thinking of her? What did she wear and if what Wren had heard was true, then why did Parker do what she knew Parker did? And why were fears always impossible questions asked to no one and why did she fucking care about these stupid little things in a moment like this one, with federal prison a future certainty? And what would she tell her parents when this was over, if this would ever be over, and had Parker said anything as Wren was dragged away from her?

The only thing Wren was certain of was that she never would have done to Parker what Parker had done to her. The word for this was *betrayal*, but these letters were too soft, too forgiving. There was no word in the world's lexicon for what Wren actually felt. To capture it in a single word would break the spine of language itself.

"All right, Wren. Take a look at this." Jeremiah pulled from his back pocket a crumpled sheet of paper.

Wren heard him as though he were a mile away, a shot ringing in her deaf ears. She focused on his lips as she gradually descended into the moment.

"This wasn't easy to get," he continued. "Had to make some promises to my colleagues, some of the other detectives who got pulled to assist the FBI with their investigation. May have told them I had clearance, so if this doesn't work out, I'm in some serious shit with all this."

"You're in some serious shit no matter what happens," Tillman whispered across the table. Wren had noticed that Tillman's quiet fury had a way of pronouncing itself through small, easily overlooked gestures. She tilted her chin, clicked her teeth together, stared holes through the ceiling.

Jeremiah ignored this as he slid the paper across the table to Wren, "That should be the email address we're looking for. The email address that sent the first video to Stetson. It's encrypted, I think. The FBI didn't have any luck tracing it to an IP. But from what I heard down at the station, you're pretty damn good with decryption. So all you have to do, Wren, is do what you do with a computer and tell me who it is or where it was sent from, and then we can deal with all the messy shit later. We find where that lunatic is and we have some—what's the word?"

"*Leverage,*" Tillman said. Tilting her chin, clicking her teeth.

Wren took the paper. "You said the FBI already tried decrypting this address?"

"Yeah," Jeremiah said. "But no luck."

She unfolded it and brought it to her face in nearsighted study. It was written out in block letters, angular and hurried. The only print on the mostly blank page was a line at the top, a seemingly random sequence of letters and numbers followed by a cursory Web address—"@fmrp.net"

"No wonder the FBI can't use it. It's not an encryption. It's just a random throwaway email."

Jeremiah fidgeted. "You're supposed to be pretty good with a computer, right? Can't you just, like, figure it out or something?"

"Jesus," Tillman whispered.

Wren continued to stare at the numbers and letters as though they might at any moment rearrange and spell out something even halfway useful or usable, a task made considerably more difficult due to a dull, inexact headache.

Parker had always been able to use her so easily. From day one. And for all of Wren's paranoia about being manipulated by culture, government, religion, and late-night advertising, how could she have missed it when it came from just one single person she loved? A body, flesh and bone. A mind and maybe a soul. Standing in her doorway, lying in her bed.

Wren refocused her attention onto the address.

"What exactly do you expect me to do?" Wren pointed at the email address, her voice carrying a hint of resentment not intended for anyone in this particular room.

"Can't you, like, plug the email in somewhere?" Jeremiah suggested.

"*Plug it in?*"

"Yeah."

"No," she said. "I can't do anything with a disposable email. The addresses are generated by a website and erased on a timed cycle. It's not like Gmail or something, where your email is attached to you. These emails correspond to nothing except for maybe an IP address, which, if it were anywhere at all, would be stored somewhere on the host site, which I'm sure the FBI has gotten a warrant for already. But those sites don't organize the IPs in any real order. There's just a mass of IP addresses floating in a massive bank of other IPs they keep in order to monitor their Web traffic. Finding the IP address of this email address would be like bobbing for a single apple in an ocean of apples."

"OK." He nodded. She saw him struggling to feign an air of calm. "So what are our options? Let's figure this out."

Tillman stood up from her chair and began furiously pacing the confines of the kitchen, like a lion inside a shrinking enclosure.

"Do you have anything else I can use?" Wren asked Jeremiah. "Did the FBI get tower records? Maybe the gunman uploaded the video from a phone?"

"I don't know. This is all I could get." He pointed at the slip of paper, speaking through a smile that flickered on and off like an epileptic light bulb. "It needs to work. It just has to, OK? Because if it doesn't . . ." He left the thought unfinished, hanging in the air like an unspoken guillotine hovering over each of their tired heads.

She looked back at the address. The sequence of random letters and numbers remained predictably unchanged. Her face must have reflected the despair, rising like a fever to her skin.

"Fuck." Jeremiah sighed, and then, louder, slapping the table with an open palm, "Goddamnit. Fuck." He laid his head in his hands. "I'm sorry, everyone. This is my fault."

Tillman rushed away, disappearing into the living room, where the windows were settling into a deeper shade of evening. Wren heard the television turn off, followed by the sigh of the recliner as Tillman led her father to bed, both of them whispering as their footsteps disappeared down a hallway. The record player continued spinning, a scratchy song Wren didn't recognize.

"It needed to work," Jeremiah said dolefully. "It needed to work."

A clock chimed from the kitchen wall. Each tone struck Wren as unlikely as the last. How could time continue moving forward when her life seemed to be slowing to its end? In a few days time, she'd be in an eggshell-colored holding cell, in a baggy orange jumpsuit, and she knew now that she belonged there. She had always belonged there.

Tillman reentered the kitchen. She didn't say anything as she walked toward them. She only set the phone down on the table and touched the screen.

"What is this?" Jeremiah asked.

She pointed at Wren. "You need to see this, too."

Jeremiah's phone rang in his pocket, and he silenced it.

Wren shuffled forward and saw a video on Tillman's phone. She knew what it would be, but still she watched as a masked man stood in that same dimly lit room. A swinging light overhead. And behind the man, two hostages in two chairs, burlap masks covering their heads. Wren's eyes immediately focused on the left hand of one of the hostages.

An engagement ring. It was her. The hostage Wren had tried, and failed, to identify.

"It has become clear to me that the chief of police and the rest of the Chicago Police Department will admit to no wrong," the gunman said. "They are content to let their citizens die rather than simply admit that they assisted a criminal vigilante's fake death. It's shameful. It's sickening. And, citizens of Chicago, know that it could be you right here. Your police would rather protect themselves than protect their citizens."

The gunman stepped toward one of the hostages, the one with the engagement ring. He removed the burlap sack on her head with a flourish, a magician's reveal. The girl in the chair was Wren's age. Black hair matted to her tear-streaked cheeks. A rope tied around her head, cutting through her mouth. The gunman raked his fingers through the girl's hair, revealing eyes wide with terror. She writhed against the ropes, twisting and pulling, craning her neck as the rope dug deeper into her mouth. She bit down on it and screamed. The sound passed through the gunman's modulated voice filter, resulting in something unlike anything Wren had ever heard, could ever dream, would ever forget.

The gunman seemed satisfied by this display. He took his time withdrawing his pistol, studying it in his hands. He turned back to the camera. "The police will do nothing to save these people, although all I've asked for is the truth. It isn't that much to ask for, I don't think. But perhaps there is still someone who can help them. And perhaps it is you who I should have been addressing from the beginning. The Kingfisher. Because I know you're out there somewhere. And I know you're watching. I know you'll see this."

The gunman leveled the pistol at arm's length. He turned it to the unmasked hostage and fired into her shoulder. The girl's head dropped to her chest and the chair rolled back. She raised her head, biting the rope, screaming in jagged bursts. Blood crawled across her shirt like a shadow emerging from within, a shadow dripping to the floor.

"The next gunshot will be the one that kills her, and it will come at midnight. Until then, she will suffer through the most painful hours imaginable. I suspect that, by midnight, death will find her willing." He paused, allowing for the girl's tortured screams to fill the space. "But you can save her. The only thing stopping you must be your own fear. But what could the Kingfisher—the great and mighty and powerful Kingfisher— have to fear? Do you fear being revealed? Revealed as what? The hero who left his city to rot? The villain who fled justice? Because you and I know there were crimes you never paid for. Or perhaps you are not afraid at all. You simply don't care about these people. These strangers. But they are not all strangers."

The gunman tore the mask off the remaining hostage.

Red hair spilling over her face as she fought against the ropes that bound her to the chair. The man cast a look at her and turned back to face the camera.

Wren leaned in closer while feeling herself drift further away.

"You know who this is," the gunman said. "I think I know what she means to you." His digital voice paused to linger on the silence. "She will die at midnight after this one dies." He pointed his pistol at the girl, whose head was swaying side to side in the throes of agony. It was evident that she was losing blood. Her face paled to the color of bone. "But her death"—he placed his hand on May's shoulder—"will be slower. So much slower. But there is no need to worry. There is still time. You can stop this. Or you can watch them die. It is very simple: your penance or your punishment. The choice is yours." The gunman leaned forward, hand covering the camera lens.

The video ended, a black screen that seemed to taunt the waiting bends of their bodies to dip in even closer for whatever surprises it held in its circuitry. Tillman finally picked her phone back up in her fingertips, a gentle touch, as though it might reach back and bite her.

Jeremiah's phone again rang. He silenced it.

"That's Paulina," Tillman said to Jeremiah, her voice even but laced with urgency. "The hostage he shot. She's Penny's daughter."

Jeremiah folded his arms. "I know who the other one is."

"Miss May," Wren said so softly she barely heard her herself. She was speaking into herself for herself, and maybe she wasn't even speaking at all, only feeling her lips glide past each other like tectonic plates beneath the pressure of a thousand separate thoughts left unthought. Wren had spoken to Miss May just a day before, and now here she was with a gun pointed at her head. Strangely, this did not surprise Wren, who was beginning to suspect she was chaos incarnate—introduce her into a closed system and watch order disintegrate.

"How do you know Miss May?" Jeremiah asked her.

"Who the hell is Miss May?" Tillman interjected.

Jeremiah's phone rang again and this time he answered it. He stepped backward into the kitchen.

"Yeah, I just saw it," he said numbly into the phone. He held a finger against his other ear to block out the noise of this noiseless room. "Are you serious?" he asked into the phone. He listened, mouth parted, and he looked to Tillman with an expression Wren couldn't decrypt even if she tried. Tillman nodded back at him in response to whatever question he had posed without uttering a sound. "No, I'm not at the station," Jeremiah said into the phone. "It's a long story. I'm going to give you an address. Get here as soon as you possibly can."

He put his phone back in his pocket and crossed his arms, craning his head to the ceiling. "That was Marcus Waters," he announced to no one in particular. "He saw the video. He's pretty shaken up. Said he and his friend spoke with Miss May just an hour ago. He thinks the gunman followed them to her apartment. Said he can't get ahold of his friend, either."

"So the gunman took the friend, too?" Tillman asked.

Jeremiah shrugged. "This is fucking unreal."

Wren felt her voice rise like bile, possessing the same putrid taste as it passed over her tongue, "I want to go back to the station."

No one said anything.

"I can't be here," she continued. "I want to go back. I can't help you. I wish I could, but I can't. I shouldn't be here. I've done enough to make this all worse."

Tillman squatted down in front of her. "We don't have time for you to work through whatever the hell it is you're dealing with right now," Tillman said sternly, allowing the words to burn in Wren's ears for a few uninterrupted seconds. "Because, unfortunately, it's too late for you to skip out on us. You're all we have right now. You saw that video. He's using those innocent people for some deranged purpose. And this man, he's used you, too. You fell into his trap. But that doesn't make you a victim, so stop acting like one. You gave him what he wanted, but you have a chance to make up for that. So get your shit together, stop feeling sorry for yourself, and figure out a way to find him. You can use my laptop. Do what you need to do, download what you need to download."

"There's nothing I can do. I'll only make it worse."

"Pathetic," Tillman spat, straightening up.

"Stop," Jeremiah said.

"Don't you tell me to stop!" Tillman shouted over her shoulder at Jeremiah. "You put your entire career in jeopardy for this girl and she's just going to give up like this? That man just shot Paulina. He's going to kill her and then he's going to kill someone else and then he'll kill someone else after that. He's not going to stop."

"I need to step outside," Wren said, her vision going dark. She felt a cold sweat dripping down her forehead.

"No, what you need to do is figure something out," Tillman said.

"Stop it," Jeremiah said, stepping between Tillman and Wren. "Come here, Wren. I'll help you outside. Get some air." He gripped her shoulder and guided her to the fire escape. He steadied her as she rolled over the window ledge. He began to follow after her, but she stopped him.

"I want to be alone."

"Listen, Wren—"

"I just want to be alone," she said, crying. "Please."

36 BLUSTERY

THERE WERE STARS OUT. The sorts of stars that don't blink, twinkle, or shine, but simply stare with dead-eyed focus from galaxies away. Wren considered it a rarity in Chicago to be reminded of the world beyond this one. And seeing it now, she couldn't help but feel that it was no coincidence that she was here on this fire escape beneath these stars on this night. In fact, she had given up on coincidence, because it was no coincidence that the FBI showed up to her apartment and arrested Parker. It was no coincidence that the gunman made another video, and then another after she tried to intervene. It was no coincidence that Parker betrayed her. It was no coincidence that the gunman shot the hostage Wren had been looking for. It was no coincidence that it was Miss May's face that ultimately passed across that small screen. It was no coincidence that Wren was realizing all of this while watching satellites drift across the velvet-black sky.

Stare long enough, watch them collide and burn to earth.

She heaved over the iron railing. Below, the pavement waited patiently sixty feet beneath the fire escape. Concrete jaws wide open. She imagined the sensation of impact, the brute fission of bone and muscle tissue. It would be so easy. So impossibly easy.

The window slipped open behind her.

"No," she moaned. "I can't help you."

"That's fine." An unfamiliar voice. "I'm not looking for anyone to help me."

Wren turned to see a man crawling slowly from the window in an awkward sprawl of khaki pants, a collared shirt. He wore a leather bag over his shoulder that bounced as he gently lowered himself from the windowsill. His messy gray hair shifted in the breeze.

"Stars are out," he said. "I'll be damned." He tucked his hands into his pockets. "My wife would have called this a *blustery* night," he said, leaning against the railing next to her. "It's a ridiculous word, *blustery*. Sort of nonsensical. But it's about right, isn't it? She read more books in a month than I ever read in my entire lifetime. So she called some nights *blustery* and she called other nights *placid*. Words that really have no place in the language."

"Who are you?" Wren asked.

"Sorry, my name is Marcus Waters." He looked over at her. His face was tired, eyes at half-mast. But he smiled and the gesture seemed to breathe life back into him.

"You wrote that book about the Kingfisher?"

"Unfortunately, yes. And what's your name?"

"Wren."

"Wren," he repeated. "Well, Wren, they tell me you're a Liber-teen." He pointed a thumb over his shoulder at the window. "Assuming that's true, can I tell you something if you promise to keep it between us?"

She nodded.

"I received an email yesterday from a Liber-teen. I don't know who it was, and I didn't ask. I won't share with you the contents of the email out of respect for whoever sent it. I'll just say it was incredibly illuminating, and I intend to act on the information I received from this person. I'm not entirely sure what that will look like just yet, but I'm going to do something. I have to."

"Why?" Wren asked.

A car passed slowly down through the alley below them, the drowsy headlights passing over the narrow brick walls.

Marcus cleared his throat while he watched the car turn in to the street. "The person who sent it asked me to do what I thought was best, and what I think is best is to act on the information. Right some wrongs, if you will. I consider it an ethical imperative."

"I don't think you're using that term correctly."

Marcus laughed. She wanted to call it *genuine,* but she wasn't sure what that word meant anymore. "I blame my stepfather. He was a philosophy professor, so sometimes I use his vocabulary, even though I have no idea what half of it means. I'm pretentious through osmosis. That's what my wife used to say, at least." He smiled at some unspoken memory, and then it faded. "I've been thinking about her a lot tonight. She died three years ago almost to the day. It was a brain aneurism."

"I'm sorry," Wren said reflexively.

"Thank you. But the thing about a brain aneurism is that it's not something you feel coming. There's no visible or physiological or whatever sort of symptoms. It just sneaks up on you. So when she died, she died in her sleep. Peacefully, or so I was assured. But let me tell you something I've never told anyone, if that's OK with you?"

Wren shrugged. "All right."

"In the weeks leading up to the night that she died, I could sense something was wrong. I mean it, Wren. I could sense it. Have you ever just sensed something is wrong even though you can't name it? It's just there and you get used to it?"

"I'm not sure I know what you mean," Wren said, although she knew exactly what he meant—to stare into the face of a lie until it became familiar, to sleep next to the same lie night after night.

"This may sound ridiculous," Marcus continued, "but she had started using words I'd never heard her use before. Maybe that doesn't seem like much to you, but when you're married for forty years, you notice these things. These little, tiny changes in a person you know better than you know yourself. For example, she began to recite these strange sorts of platitudes. We'd be watching *Jeopardy!* and if I shouted out the wrong answer, she might say something like, 'Is what it is.' Just these strange things she never would have said before. Things like that."

"Tautologies?"

"You would have loved my stepfather." Marcus smiled. "Anyway, after my wife passed, I wondered if these words she used were symptoms of her condition. Maybe they were warnings that I chose to ignore, because I didn't want to see them. I even called a friend of mine who's a doctor after my wife passed. I asked him if the words might have been indicators. He told me I was just grieving, told me I was still in the denial stage of things. But still I wonder to this day. I wonder if I'd said something, then maybe she would have gone to our doctor and maybe he would have run a few tests and caught it before it was too late."

"I really doubt that would have happened."

"Me, too." He nodded. "But that doesn't stop me from wondering, and I wonder every day, Wren."

Marcus looked over the edge of the fire escape with a childlike precocity, feeling his weight shift over the six open stories beneath him. He reminded Wren of someone whom, in some other context and in some other world altogether, she would have liked to have spoken to for longer about almost anything at all. He had an easiness to his speech, an intellectual slant to his pauses, and a care to his words that she found immensely comforting. But more importantly, he seemed present. He was here, fully. For the first time since she'd been taken to the precinct, Wren didn't feel alone.

"I know what you're implying," she said. "But I don't want anything to do with all of this anymore. I only make it worse. I don't want anything to do with it." She paused, lowering her voice. "I'm chaos."

To her surprise, Marcus laughed. "Chaos? That seems harsh."

"No." She shook her head. "It's not harsh enough. Everyone keeps telling me to do what I think is best, and I do it. Everything I've done I did to make things better, but it only fucked everything up even more."

"I see." Marcus hummed, low and long. "Well, let me assure you of this one thing: I'm not going to tell you to do what you think is best. Frankly, I think that's a bad idea and even worse advice."

"Why?"

"Well, speaking from experience, what you think is for the best at any given moment is rarely for the best. Because when you think that you're doing what is for the best, you're assuming a future you don't know. And that's a fool's game, Wren. I can tell you that." He straightened up, cast a glance back at the window, and then turned back to her. "No, see, what I'm hoping you do is to go inside that room and try to save someone's life. Maybe it's for the best, maybe it isn't. But it needs to be done."

"There's nothing I can do even if I wanted to."

"What if I gave you some names of the hostages?"

"It's not enough." She shook her head.

"Then what would be enough?"

"If I had phone numbers, I could try some things, but—"

"I can do that."

"It probably won't work, though," she said.

"Forgive me, Wren, but it doesn't really matter." He bowed his head, shifted his step. "There are people who will die tonight if you don't try to do something. I know one of them. Her name is Miss May, and she is in real danger."

"You know her?" Wren asked.

Marcus nodded, gripping the railing and turning his head to the stars overhead. "She's where she is now because of me. It's my fault, Wren. I think the gunman followed me to her apartment. I suspected it, but I didn't want to believe it. I should have said something or did something. But I didn't. And I'm almost certain that another friend of mine—his name is Peter—has been taken, as well. It's my fault that they are in that position. I don't want to live with the guilt of Miss May and Peter's death. I can't. I have enough of that already."

"Then why don't you tell the police their names and phone numbers? They have an entire FBI cyber unit right now."

"I don't know you, Wren," Marcus said, looking at her, "but I like to think I have decent intuition about people. I can tell that you are a brilliant young woman, but you're also fundamentally kind. You care. You have a conscience." He paused, tangling his fingers together as he turned his head to track a satellite passing far, far above them. "What I'm saying is that I trust you. And that's more than I can say for the police right now."

There were sirens emanating out from somewhere, somewhere far or somewhere near, it was always impossible to tell. They sifted through the air like material presences, something she could reach out and touch if they passed her by.

"How did you know her?" Wren asked. "Miss May?"

"She was a . . ." And then he paused in the thought and began to laugh, a low sound that struggled from his throat, painfully aware of its own misplacement in this moment. "Miss May was an acquaintance, I guess. A sort of friend of a friend. You would like her if you met her. One of those people you don't ever forget. And she could sure use your help right about now, Wren."

GREGORY STETSON LOVED CHICAGO more than he loved life itself. And all things considered, he loved life very much. Mindy, his wife, walked alongside him. Wind combing through her half-blond hair, wearing on her round face an expression that captured, somehow, the grim atmosphere of this particular morning.

And he realized on this bone-cold morning—after parking the Buick on 55th and opening his wife's door for her, the two of them seamlessly joining the massive march across Lake Shore Drive—why and how he could love a city so dearly. It was because this city loved itself. So much so, you felt it with every frozen step. Chicago loved its skyline's cut-and-rise into the thick veil of clouds and smog. It loved the bitter winter wind that ran like icy blood through its concrete veins, washing over old and young and immigrant and drunk and gum-chewing street performer and beat cop and drugged-out singer and lonely artist and student and lawyer and the holy forgotten.

And so many of them here and now. Gathered. A silent tribe en route to a funeral.

Across Lake Shore Drive, Promontory Point ebbed out against Lake Michigan, itself a tundra of ice-capped waves frozen in their crests. There were already thousands gathered, by Stetson's estimation. And the crowd continued to pack into the snowy lawn, overflowing out into the streets. Everyone wore black. They did not speak. A silence so thick you could taste it, a shared reverence for something greater than themselves that they had lost. But also, just maybe, a shared joy at having known greatness, however temporarily. And every mourner stood stock-still with subzero wind lapping at their stoic faces, each frozen breath released like funeral incense.

It was the sort of moment you remember as an event of history even as it unfurled around you.

A priest took the stage first and gave a brief prayer. Police Chief Gonzalez followed, looking as nervous as Stetson had ever seen him. He gave a very brief eulogy, or at least something resembling a eulogy. He artfully avoided openly praising the Kingfisher while also citing the crime-rate statistics, which were at an all-time low. It began to feel more like a press conference than a funeral invocation. When the mayor finally took the stage, he read from innocuous notes he held in his gloved hands. But a few minutes into his planned remarks, he dropped his notes to his side, and soon he was speaking directly to the crowd, his words fixed to each of the thousands of faces before him.

"Heroes rise when they are needed. And that's really what I came here to say. I know there are some who would take issue with me even suggesting the possibility that he was a hero. They would be quick to point out the fact that the Kingfisher was a vigilante, thereby a criminal. They would argue that the Kingfisher was no greater than those whom he targeted. But to those people, I say this: Look around you. Look around you at a city gathered and marvel at the sight. Because I am. I am marveling."

As Stetson watched the mayor deliver his eulogy, he spotted in the corner of his eye something that did not belong, a flicker in his periphery. He turned and saw a woman standing at the edge of the crowd, pressed against the edge over the lake. She wore a red blouse, a denim short-skirt. Red hair pulled into a messy ponytail that hung over her shoulder. Her skin was pale-blue in the cold. She was smoking a cigarette and blew the smoke from the side of her mouth, where it rose like a ghost looking over her before the wind took it away.

It took Stetson a delayed second to place her in his memory. And the moment he did, he wished he were close enough to ask her what the hell she thought she was doing here. He wished he were close enough to tell her to have some goddamned respect. Close enough to tell her this was her fault, all of this, and she ought to be fucking ashamed coming here. Close enough for the words to hit her like buckshot.

Of all people. That woman, this place. He felt dizzy with all the curses and screams that sprung and festered in his lungs.

He felt Mindy reach into his coat pocket. She wrapped her fingers around his curled fist and gently squeezed his hand. She had a special gift: she knew when he needed her to bring him back to the moment. And all it ever took was just this, her hand touching his.

He turned back to the stage, but he kept the woman-in-red fixed at the farthest corner of his vision. Just in case.

"Yes, we could argue," the mayor said, his voice rising like a preacher at a tent revival, "over whether the Kingfisher was a hero or a criminal vigilante. But this argument overlooks one fundamental truth. None of us here today can say whether or not the Kingfisher was a hero. What we say does not matter one way or the other. What we say today are just whispers in the cold wind. Because we do not decide who is a hero. None of us here. We do not."

The woman-in-red was standing akimbo now. Stetson saw her face peel back in a grin, like this was just the funniest goddamn thing she had ever heard.

She couldn't do that.

Stetson pulled away from Mindy and began pushing his way through the crowd. He no longer felt the cold as a fury grew like a wildfire in his gut and soon spread throughout the rest of his body. He felt Mindy reach after him, her fingers brushing off his coat, but he was already in motion. Nothing in the world could stop him.

"Heroes are named by history and judged by the future," the mayor said. "We cannot say if history will remember the Kingfisher as hero, criminal, or even nothing at all. It may not matter one way or another. What we can do is stand here, shoulder to shoulder, and marvel at the fact that one man whom very few, if any, of us ever knew, brought us here together on this freezing day in this beautiful, resilient, miraculous city. Whatever you think of him, we are here together, and it is beautiful from where I stand. I wish you could see what I am seeing."

Stetson forced himself through the packed crowd. He saw the woman pull another cigarette from a pack she kept in her bra, and now Stetson felt an electric collision inside his skin, a total holy rage ready to erupt, and my God, how he wanted it to erupt. He moved faster, pushing aside anyone standing in his way, ignoring the shouts and murmurs. His eyes and body and soul dead-fixed on that woman's peevish grin. And suddenly he knew what he would do when he finally reached her. He would push her over the edge of Promontory Point, and her body would collapse on the ice below. She would tumble through the freezing water like the deadweight she always was.

How dare she interrupt a moment in history with her presence?

"We spread his ashes today over Lake Michigan as a symbolic gesture and also a reminder," the mayor said. "This is not the end of a story, but the beginning of a new one. This is the story the Kingfisher has given us to finish, so how will we finish it? This is the question we must leave with. And as I have the honor to spread these ashes, as they disperse and as we return to our homes, I hope that we can take a moment to pause. Remember this day. Because this is the day that Chicago stood silent and together. How will we finish it?"

Stetson was just several bodies away from her, and he saw her turn over her shoulder. He looked at her. She looked at him. And she smiled even wider. But at that same moment the crowd broke formation and began to shuffle back in the direction of the city looming behind them. He continued to push through them, but there were so many of them now. When he finally reached the outskirts of the crowd, he looked around for her. He could not find her anywhere. She had dissolved somewhere into the crowd.

In her place was only the lake, which stretched out before him. Frozen-white and seemingly infinite.

He felt a hand grasp his shoulder and he spun around to see Mindy looking back at him, her cold-pink face equal parts worry and affection.

"Where'd you go?" she asked.

He started to answer, but he stopped himself. She would not understand, because he also did not understand. He felt as though he had just woken from a strange, undreamt dream. He turned over his shoulder and saw a crowd of people lingering along the edge of the lake, looking down at a roiling cloud of ash scattering against the ice.

So instead he said, "I came here."

"I know you always wanted to see him, Gregory," Mindy said, reaching her hand into his pocket, wrapping her fingers around his. "I'm sorry this is the way it finally happened." She joined him in watching the ashes disperse, squeezing his hand tighter.

And he did his best to smile for her, something that had never come naturally to him, even when he felt like it should.

He had never told Mindy that he had seen the Kingfisher. Countless times. He had never told Mindy that he been nearly killed by the Kingfisher, that he had shaken the Kingfisher's hand, that he had seen the Kingfisher reduced to a hollow skein of a man, that the Kingfisher sometimes called him by his first name, that the Kingfisher had called him from a pay phone just yesterday to thank Stetson one last time for what he did for him and Stetson only replied, "Be well." And although Stetson knew that the ashes currently dispersing across Lake Michigan were not the Kingfisher's, Stetson was already beginning to believe what Mindy had said: he had pushed his way through a mourning crowd to see the Kingfisher one last time. Because, Stetson thought, he would never see him again.

"SS7?" Tillman asked. "What is that?"

"It's essentially a metanetwork for cell phone providers. It's where all the data transmits. There's a glitch in the system that makes it possible to get access to the locations of cell phones."

"I take it this is illegal," Jeremiah said.

"Is that going to be a problem?" Wren asked, clearing the laptop's hard drive in hopes of maximizing the processing speed.

Jeremiah didn't answer, which she took as a no.

Tillman's laptop felt foreign beneath her fingertips. Simply navigating through the hard drive, she was striking wrong keys, closing wrong programs. Any of these minor errors would prove disastrous during the actual hack. She wished she had her own laptop, but it was probably already confiscated, locked away, sealed in an evidence bag in anticipation of a trial that would strip her of whatever life she might have otherwise lived.

"Won't the FBI already have done this?" Tillman asked. "I'm sure they already know the identities of Walter Williams, Penny, and Paulina. They may even have identified May by now."

"It's possible," Wren said. "But they're more likely to go directly through Stingray channels with coordination from the NSA. It's more accurate and doesn't require decryption, but it would probably take them longer."

"Gibberish," Jeremiah said, passing in a figure eight across the kitchen tile.

Wren continued, unfazed. "I'm assuming the FBI has already traced the cell phones of the hostages they've identified and not come up with much. But I'm also going to assume they haven't run a trace on May's phone yet, and if it's true that this Peter guy is taken, too, then I'm sure the FBI doesn't know it yet. What I'm saying is that hopefully May or Peter's phones give us a location."

"What happens if they don't?" Jeremiah asked.

"Then that's when we go to Plan B."

"Which is?"

"I don't know. I haven't thought of it yet."

Marcus rose from his chair, gesturing for Jeremiah and Tillman to follow him. "Let's give her some space."

There is headspace and there is cyberspace and only when Wren hacks do the two collide. Her physical surroundings gradually deteriorate while

38 9-1-1

"GIVE ME PHONE NUMBERS OF THE HOSTAGES," Wren said, sitting down at the table. Marcus sat at the end of the table, looking out the window. Jeremiah stood behind her, but she felt energy radiating from his skin like some nuclear reactor ready to blow. Tillman brought her laptop in front of Wren. An old Dell model, processing speed akin to a circuitry of molasses. But it would work. "It doesn't matter if they are already—you know. Just give me the phone numbers."

Tillman retrieved a folded envelope from her pocket and laid it in front of Wren. Phone numbers scratched in black ink. "Paulina's and Penny's numbers."

"Paulina," Wren repeated, holding the envelope. The girl whose face Wren had sought among the city's lost but never found. The girl who somewhere was bleeding from a gunshot wound in a dark room.

Marcus reached in his pocket and withdrew a folded-up business card. He pushed it across the table. Wren unfolded it. MISS MAY PIECEWORK. A number at the bottom in fine print. "I also have Peter's number. I think I also still have Walter William's number somewhere on my phone."

"So what's your plan here?" Jeremiah asked Wren. He was now nervously pacing the kitchen in an oblong and erratic orbit, his head swiveling so as to keep trained on her computer screen.

"I'm going to do a SS7 hack and see if any of these numbers are still traceable."

her fingers gloss over the keyboard. Even so, Wren feels the waiting presence of Tillman, Detective Combs, and Marcus. They are maintaining a respectful distance, all of them congregated in the living room in sort of a para-circle, and she senses the weight of their stares, but she lets them slide from her. Water from a duck's back. She slips deeper into a world that is not this one. A world of digital intensities, stratified in algorithms she creates without thought, because this is a world she knows better than any other.

An SS7 hack is so easy that she's almost disappointed. Like knocking on a door and it swinging wide open. But once inside, it's vast, seemingly endless expanses of raw data lapping at distant, planetary shores. She pictures herself as a single data point navigating a three-dimensional model of the world. Because in cyberspace, history is joined to the future. There are numbers. Columns and rows. And her eyes are connected to her fingers, which are connected to her racing thoughts, which are connected to her lips as she whispers to the world she has fallen into. She enters the first number—Walter Williams's number—and executes the search. She waits as the humming machine beneath her fingertips answers her demand. Nothing. She isn't surprised. The phone must have been destroyed. She enters Penny's number. Nothing. She tries Paulina's. Nothing. All of their phones, severed from the world. A grim, metaphysical parallelism Wren chooses to ignore for the time being. She tries May's number, allowing herself to feel optimistic. But it comes up empty. No location. She types in Peter's number, already planning her next step from here—perhaps braving the NSA systems and trying to hack into Stingray, a veritable suicide mission that probably wouldn't yield anything anyway—but to her surprise, she finds Peter's triangulated location point. If the gunman did, in fact, have Peter hostage, either Peter didn't have his phone with him or it hadn't yet been destroyed. But there is no room for hypotheticals, because even from the subterranean depth of cyberspace, there is allowance to hope. The gilded architecture of systems processing, geolocation maps of the known world waiting, it's all momentarily peaceful and quiet. Because she is merely a data point detached from the voice she hears shouting over all the others as the numbers thin on the screen. It is her voice and she is saying, "I got something."

She was seated in front of the computer, fingers aching. She double- and triple-checked the map on the screen, zooming in.

Jeremiah rushed forward and leaned over her shoulder. His energy was palpable as he rocked backward and forward. He strode over to the window that led out to the fire escape. The window was pitch-dark. She had no sense of how much time had passed. And for a moment, she worried that none of it mattered, that it was too late.

"What time is it?" Wren asked.

Jeremiah checked his watch. "About an hour to midnight."

"What is this?" Tillman asked, joining Jeremiah behind Wren, leaning forward to stare at the computer screen. "Is that where the hostages are?"

Marcus remained in the living room, standing there with his hands in his pockets, watching from a measured distance.

"I can't be sure," Wren said quietly, as if she might scare away the two-dimensional map on her computer screen. "It's an approximate location of Peter. Or at least an approximate location of Peter's phone."

Tillman nodded, the crack of a smile unrealized.

"How approximate are we talking?" Jeremiah asked.

"It's a triangulation of the phone's location based on its proximity to cell towers nearby. In Chicago, I'd say it's pretty accurate. On the safe side, I'd say it's within a two-block radius of this location?"

"It would take too long to search two city blocks," Jeremiah said. "Even with a full police force. Where even is this?" He squinted at the map.

Wren zoomed and readjusted over a bird's-eye view of Chicago, the location marker pinned to the near South Side, six blocks away from their current location. "Hyde Park," she said. The location marker was pinned just six blocks away from her own apartment. If this was where the hostages were, she had been so close and hadn't even known it. It felt sickening that she had slept within a ten-minute walk of a horror she could not yet fully fathom.

"We don't know for sure that Peter is taken, though, do we?" Jeremiah asked.

"Wait." Tillman pushed Jeremiah out of the way and leaned over Wren's shoulder. She jabbed her finger at a point on the screen. "Zoom in right there."

"That's the Armada," Wren said, zooming in on the flattened image of the otherwise towering building. "It's a hotel."

Tillman stood up, rushed into the living room, and returned holding a pair of running shoes. She began untying them with shaking fingers.

"What are you doing?" Jeremiah asked.

"That's where Penny had his interview," Tillman said. "The Armada. Paulina picked him up to take him there. It was late at night. They must have been abducted when they arrived."

"How would they have been abducted in a hotel? There are security cameras, staff."

"Because they never made it into the hotel," Tillman said, tying her shoes. "The gunman isn't filming those videos inside a hotel. He must be filming them in the parking garage next to the hotel. It's where Paulina would have taken her father." She leaned over and pointed at the screen. A gray structure next to the Armada.

Wren recognized it. The train she took to work passed right in front of the very garage. Just this morning, she had probably seen it pass behind the sunlit window while a homeless man hawked tabloid papers in the aisle. He'd read the headlines at full volume, repeating them, as though each iteration would turn over new intrigue. And she'd been there, just a hundred yards away, staring absently at the pallid concrete structure as it faded out of view. But here it was again, a two-dimensional figure before her eyes.

There passed a silence in which Wren was aware of each second. It was how she pictured the moments after pulling a pin from a grenade and twirling it on your finger. Each movement forward, irreparable and distinct.

"It isn't far from here," Tillman said.

Jeremiah didn't say anything in response. He reached calmly into his pocket for his phone.

"What are you doing?" Tillman asked.

"I'm calling the station. I'm going to give them the address."

"How are you going to explain how you got it? They're going to know that you were working with her," she said, nodding at Wren.

He swiped his finger across the touch screen. "I'll tell them she found the location while we were driving or something like that. They won't ask questions just yet. It doesn't matter anyway. We're running out of time."

"Don't," Tillman said, reaching out quickly and prying the phone from his hands, holding it away from him.

"What the hell are you doing?" he shouted.

"I'll call them," Tillman said. "I'll tell them I told you to come to my apartment with her."

"Why?"

"You have a job with the department. I don't. You got promoted to detective. I didn't. Besides, they're not going to call me back to work anytime soon. Not ever. You know it and I know it."

"Tilly, don't do this," Jeremiah said.

She began dialing.

"Jeremiah should call," Marcus said from the living room, where he had been perfectly silent all the while. Wren had forgotten he was even there. He strode forward into the kitchen, head slung in midthought. "He'll call and tell them Wren gave him the address of the gunman. He'll tell them that she hacked the gunman's email address yesterday from Stetson's email when she hacked the ME report. He'll tell them that she was able to figure out his location and she gave him the address after they left the station. It's best that way. It makes the most sense."

Tillman and Jeremiah stood on the fringe of the living room, each of them weighing this hypothetical.

"He's right," Wren said, surprised to hear her voice enter into this discussion. "You'll stay out of it." She nodded at Tillman and then turned to Jeremiah. "And you should be fine, too."

"What about you?" Jeremiah asked her.

Wren shrugged. "Doesn't matter."

Jeremiah made as if to protest, but the words didn't come out. He only scratched at his cheek and looked to Tillman, who stared forward at the phone in her hand. Her father was snoring from down the hall. Finally, Tillman nodded and handed him his phone. She withdrew her cigarettes and wordlessly climbed out onto the fire escape, leaving Wren alone with Jeremiah and Marcus, who stood quietly behind Wren's chair, eyes fixed on the satellite image of the parking garage as a god, removed from the world and its chaos, surely saw it.

Jeremiah dialed a number on his phone. He held the mute mass of circuits and plastic in his hand, his thumb hesitating over the screen. "Here we go."

Wren wiped away a tear that fell unexpectedly down her cheek. She laughed. "Jesus, I'm terrified."

She felt Jeremiah's hand reach forward and grip her shoulder. "It's OK to be a little scared. I'm scared, too," he said, the phone ringing in his ear. "Just also be brave." And then Wren heard a voice over the phone. "This is Detective Jeremiah Combs," Jeremiah said, disappearing back into the living room. "I need to speak to Chief Stetson immediately."

Wren closed the laptop in front of her, felt its dying warmth in her fingertips. She listened as its electric whir died into a static silence. And only then did she wonder what would come next. She saw that Marcus had sat down at the kitchen table. His arms were crossed against his chest, and he was staring absently at a stain on the tablecloth. The energy that still remained in the room, a lasting echo of revelation, seemed to have no impact on him.

"Mr. Waters?" Wren asked. "It's going to be OK, I think."

He didn't say anything. She wasn't sure he'd heard her.

"The police might be able to rescue the hostages," she said louder. "They still have time to save Paulina, Miss May, and Peter. It's going to be OK."

He smiled feebly.

"What's wrong?"

"I just can't help but feel like this is my fault." He sighed into his hands, rubbing his eyes. "Walter and Penny—it was my book that got them killed. It must have been. And now Miss May and Peter." He cleared his throat. "I should have known. I really should have known." He shook his head and sat upright. "But this is no time for self-pity. That can come later. Thank you for what you did here, Wren. I can't thank you enough."

Before she could tell him that he shouldn't thank her, that she'd done it not for him and maybe even not for the hostages themselves, but instead for herself as a sort of penance she couldn't quite define, Jeremiah reentered the kitchen.

"Stetson is sending the force," Jeremiah said. "I'm going down to meet him." He peered through the window that Tillman had crawled out of. He pressed his face against the glass, and then opened the window. He stuck his head outside, looking in either direction. He turned back into the kitchen, slack-jawed, hurriedly looking around the room as though he had missed something, had lost something, had forgotten something.

"What?" Wren asked.

"Where's Tilly?" he said.

"She's not out there?" Marcus asked.

"No," he said, but as he said this he seemed to realize, and his whole body seemed to respond. He turned around wildly, grabbed his keys from the table, and darted to the front door. "She's going to get herself killed," he mumbled to himself as he shut it behind him.

In the ensuing silence, Marcus said, "What the hell have I done?" His eyes were bleary, glossed, vacant.

"Mr. Waters," Wren began, but the thought felt finished. She only wanted him to know she was here. Someone else was here. It felt like the least she could do, and it was.

"Why didn't the gunman destroy Peter's phone if he has him?" Marcus asked her. "He destroyed the other phones. That's what you said. Why not Peter's?"

"I don't know," she said. "Maybe he forgot to take Peter's cell phone. Maybe Peter has it hidden somewhere on him? Maybe he dropped it? There could be a lot of reasons. I'm sorry, Mr. Waters. But I don't think that any of this is really your fault. It's like you said to me—"

Marcus stood up from the table. Wren heard the shimmer of his keys in his pockets as he pulled them out, making his way to the front door.

"Where are you going?"

But she already knew, and she was already following him.

39 UNDERGROUND

TILLMAN STOOD ACROSS THE STREET from the Armada parking garage, taking in her surroundings without moving her head. Shadow figures in her periphery, each a living and moving threat. But she stood still, waiting. For what, she wasn't sure. A gunshot, an invitation, a voice descending from the heavens? She realized she had a cigarette, unlit, dangling in her fingers like an insect in a web, and she put it behind her ear for comfort. Something familiar, something external, something she could touch with her fingers and know was there.

She heard sirens nearing. Jeremiah must have called. But she knew that, even after they arrived, they would need time to coordinate with SWAT, and SWAT would need time to formulate a plan of entrance. They would waste precious minutes plotting. But she hadn't come here to plot. Every second that passed was a second lost to something eternal. She was here, and no one else was. Midnight was fast approaching. She was here.

Down the street, several blocks, a traffic jam. She could hear the call-and-response of car horns and she could make out the glassy outlines of vehicles. She saw, too, police lights spinning, and she knew that what she was seeing was the expanding edge of the protest against the police still occurring. Tear gas rose into the sky like a feathering flower in midbloom. It seemed more distant than it was. A whole other world just several streets over.

She crossed the street, long strides, entering the parking garage, side-stepping the automated lever. Once inside, she reached back and withdrew from her waistband her nine-millimeter, warmed by her skin. Held at the ready, sweeping every unlit corner and around each pillar, it felt less like a mechanical weapon than a natural extension of herself. Metal flesh and blood and bone.

There was a ramp leading up and a ramp leading down, presenting her with a binary choice. Ascension or descension. She didn't need to stop and think. Evil occurs underground. So she descended into the concrete belly of the structure.

She moved quickly, lengthening each step, using the few cars around her for occasional cover in case she was being watched, targeted. As the parked cars thinned out, she stayed close to the concrete edge and half ran with her cell phone's flashlight pressed against the butt of the gun, its electric beam illuminating the dark. She leapt over concrete barriers, letting herself roll over and drop to the next floor down, tumbling several feet through the void and landing hard on her hands and knees. She felt her ankle sprain, but the pain came as a slow and unsubstantial afterthought. As she descended, the dark grew darker, totalizing, a physical presence she felt against her skin. Her cell phone's flashlight reached about ten feet and no farther. It wasn't enough.

Minutes dripping to midnight.

Each descending floor she was sure must be the last, the bottom-most stratum. And each time she turned the corner, the paved ground curved and led to yet another floor. With each floor, her footsteps seemed to shake the concrete walls. The air grew cooler, thinner. Or maybe it was just her trying to breathe quietly, to lessen her presence in the space.

She came to a stop in front of a concrete wall, the end of the descent, slick with dripping water. She touched it, not sure why. The water was cold against her fingers. A pipe leak, maybe. She guessed that she must have been at least five or six stories underground. More than enough to muffle the sound of a gunshot, or for that matter, three gunshots.

She scanned the surface of the wall with the flashlight. And there it was, almost directly in front of her. A metal door covered in a film of burnt-fire rust. It was cracked open, and she saw the beam of her

T. J. MARTINSON

flashlight pass through before she could think to cast it away. But it was too late. If he was inside, he knew she was here. He would be ready for her.

Good, she thought as she aimed her pistol at the door and kicked it wide open.

40 PARK

BY THE TIME MARCUS turned onto the street, there were already patrol cars cordoning off the block. Officers stood in the narrow spaces between the vehicles, wearing full tactical gear, keeping at bay a crowd comprised mostly of those en route to the protests, craning their heads at the symphony of SWAT vehicles clustered halfway down the block.

Marcus did a three-point turn at the blockade, and Wren half hoped he was turning around to take her to the station, where she knew she would end up anyway. But instead, he parked his car along the street in a tow-away zone.

"I doubt the parking police are in force tonight," he said.

Marcus got out of the car and she followed, struggling to keep up with his surprisingly long and fluid strides. His leather bag bounced against his hip with each step, the brass buckle clicking like a metronome.

She realized he was headed directly toward the blockade. His head bent toward the militarized officers on the perimeter, submachine guns strapped to their chests like infants. But this didn't seem to bother Marcus Waters, who only quickened his step the closer they came. He pushed through the crowd of onlookers who regarded him, noting his sense of belonging to whatever was taking place beyond their field of vision, and so they duly parted to make way for him to pass among them.

And as the two of them came closer to the police line, close enough to hear the officers shouting people back, hands on their weapons, Wren began to feel more than a little sick. Like a mouse who'd been dangling over a snake's cage only to be lowered in reach of its waiting jaws. She worried they would shoot her on sight, which, intellectually, she knew was very improbable, but whatever horrific instinct her body was responding to told her it was an inevitability. And so she minimized the space her body occupied, making herself a smaller target.

"Sir, you have to get back," shouted an officer.

Wren realized he was speaking to Marcus, who was standing in front of the blockade. Marcus said something back, but Wren couldn't hear him beneath the sirens, the chatter of an excited crowd throwing about their theories of whatever was happening down the street.

"You need to take a step back," the officer shouted back at Marcus, shoving him backward with an open palm.

Marcus stared down at the officer's hand on his chest and he pushed it away. The officer gripped his weapon tighter.

Now Marcus spoke loud enough that not only could Wren hear him, but she figured the rest of the crowd, if not the entire block, could hear him as well. "Where is Detective Combs?"

"Sir, I'm telling you one last time, you need to step back."

"I need to speak to Detective Combs. My name is Marcus Waters."

A hush came over the crowd, so sudden it made Wren dizzy.

There was a flash of recognition on the officer's face, which up until now had remained impassive. The officer stepped away, spoke into his radio. He held his ear when it crackled with a response. He nodded.

"Follow me, Mr. Waters," said the officer, who stepped aside wide enough for Marcus to pass between the vehicles behind him.

"She's coming, too." Marcus pointed at Wren, who wished like hell he hadn't.

The crowd turned its collective focus her way, and whatever panic she had been feeling up until now seemed childish compared to this. She wished she could atomize at will—her molecular elements drifting a thousand different directions on this blustery night.

The officer reached out and grabbed her by the elbow, pulling her forward. He kept his hand there as he walked them down the vacated block toward the ring of armored vehicles, flashing lights.

There was a helicopter passing far overhead with a dragonfly's hum of propellers. As they approached the cluster of vehicles and uniforms, Wren saw someone coming to meet them in a sort of hurried half run, backlit by the police lights. As he neared, she saw that it was Jeremiah. He dismissed the escorting officer, who began walking back to the blockade.

"I tried to follow her," Jeremiah said. He was out of breath, sweating through his shirt. "I tried to follow her down there, but the police were already here. They wouldn't let me through. I don't know what to do, Marcus."

"Does Stetson know she's down there?" Marcus asked.

He nodded. "They're trying to figure something out. But she only made it more complicated, running down there like that."

"And you're absolutely positive she went down there?"

Jeremiah nodded. "If you knew her like I do, you wouldn't have to ask."

"What's their plan?" Marcus asked, gesturing at the SWAT vans.

"I don't know." Jeremiah shrugged, and Wren saw his fear in the way his eyes danced in their sockets, as though if they were to linger too long, they would behold something unimaginable. "They don't want to send anyone in there until they know where to look. They're worried the gunman might have a bomb or something. But they're drawing up a plan now." He looked at his watch. "Jesus, I sure as fuck hope they're drawing up a fucking plan."

Marcus nodded, stared at the parking garage. A halogen light hung over the street corner: PARK. Wren had passed this very building on the L countless times, but now it seemed alive, waiting, hulking into its shoulders, waiting to swallow the street.

"Where's Stetson?" Marcus asked, still looking out at the building.

"Why?"

"I need to talk with him."

"He's pretty busy right now, Marcus. I'm not sure it's a good idea."

"I think I know who the gunman is, Jeremiah. I need to talk to Stetson right now."

Jeremiah stared back at Marcus, nodding. "Wait here." He sprinted off in the direction of a particularly massive armored Humvee, painted onyx black. The CPD insignia, painted onto the open passenger door, behind which a throng of men gathered, heads bowed into a huddle. Jeremiah broke through the huddle. Wren saw him corner Police Chief Stetson—who appeared to be chastising him—but Jeremiah silenced him. The two men spoke briefly before Jeremiah turned and ran back to Marcus and Wren.

"He wants to talk to you," Jeremiah told Marcus.

Marcus nodded and walked in that direction, leaving Wren out in the open with Jeremiah, who seemed fixed where he stood. He turned to face the building, scratching at his sweaty neck with his fingernails and breathing in loud, short bursts through his nose.

"She is going to be OK," Wren said, surprised to hear herself interject her voice into this space, this time. "I really think she's going to be OK."

"Yeah," he said in a faraway voice.

"She seems really strong," Wren added. She immediately felt stupid for offering a platitude at a time like this. But she meant it. If only words could carry the weight of their meaning.

"Tilly is strong," Jeremiah said. "She is certainly that."

Wren saw Marcus pull Stetson aside. They spoke near the back of the Humvee. Marcus seemed to be punctuating his words with his hands like the conductor of an orchestra controlling the tempo.

"Problem is, though," Jeremiah said, and by the way he spoke into the passing wind, Wren understood he was speaking more to himself than to her, just to voice whatever frantic thoughts were battling in his head, "she knows she's strong. That's why she ran off here in the first place. It was a stupid thing to do, putting herself at risk. And now that she's down there, if she does something stupid . . ." But he let the thought go unvoiced, lost to the wind that passed down the street like some earthly whisper. "Jesus. If she does something."

After a few moments, someone called out for Jeremiah. He shook himself out of whatever trance he'd fallen into and strode off toward the cars. Wren remained standing there, wondering if she ought to simply join the police. Save herself time and take a seat in one of the cruisers. And from there, patiently await whatever uncertain future she had summoned.

A minute later, Wren turned to see Marcus walking back toward her.

"What did you tell him?" Wren asked.

Marcus didn't answer. He looked out over the street at the police blockade, where it appeared that the crowd had doubled in size. Camera phones flashed like supernovas.

Wren turned back to the parking garage. Spotlights flashed across its concrete walls. It was a theater. Final act closing, the moment before the curtains open to reveal the smiling cast of characters, holding hands and bowing to the faceless crowd.

A collection of officers began pushing the crowd back. One of them broke formation and came to collect Marcus and Wren, ushering them to the sidewalk. Beyond what Wren assumed to be the radius of a potential bomb blast.

From behind one of the SWAT vans came a rumble of boots against the pavement, the clatter of magazines bolted into weapons. A procession of fifteen or so armored officers collected behind a police van in front of the garage, and the leader among them knelt in the center of their circled bodies, laying out their plan of action.

"I don't know if you're the praying sort," Marcus said to Wren. "But if you are, now would be the time."

"I don't pray."

"Yeah. Neither do I."

"Then maybe we just hope?"

"Sure. Let's do that."

41 HOSTAGE

TILLMAN HALF EXPECTED, after kicking in the door, for it to reveal nothingness, an absence of everything. Some void of space and time, a final dead end. But instead she found a room. It was startlingly familiar, and it didn't take long to realize why. This was it; this was where the videos were filmed. Here she was, inside the real space she had only ever studied on a screen, and it felt no more real to her now than it did then.

There was the same light hanging from the ceiling. It swung from an extension cord, gently, throwing shadows. Electric humming. Racks of cleaning supplies along the walls. A mop bucket. Gallons of Formula 409. Stacked cardboard boxes. A dizzying smell of bleach. All of these elements within her reach. The only thing missing was the digital veneer, the pixelated crust of the videos themselves.

Every muscle in her body tightened into stone as she swung her gun around each corner, her focus narrowed as she swept the space for any sign of the man in the mask. Even though the room was small, it was cluttered. Plenty of places to hide. She kicked at empty boxes, peered behind a broken filing cabinet slanting across the floor. She swung to her right and immediately before her a video camera perched atop a cardboard box, the lens shining like a single eye beneath the light. Next to the camera, a semitranslucent mask staring back at her. She stepped back, her finger reflexively pressuring the trigger. But it was only the mask, no face for it to hide. It made her sick, the inanimate smile, as though it had been propped up to greet her. But it also gave her some relief. He wasn't here yet. When he came, she would be ready for him.

She turned back to the hostages.

The center of the room was cleared out save for three office chairs, and in each, a hostage. One was Paulina. A large, glistening pool of blood gathered around the wheels of her chair. Her head was rolled back. Motionless. Tillman reached forward to take her pulse. She was still alive. Next to Paulina was the other woman from the video—Miss May. A shock of red hair, brighter than it had appeared in the grainy video. Her eyes were wide, conscious, and she was moving her head, gesturing at the hostage next to her—a burlap mask over his head, black slacks, tennis shoes. Pale hands clutching the arms of the chair as he tried to shake his way out of the ropes. She felt a euphoric wave of relief to hear his muffled screams, to see that he was still alive, squirming against the ropes.

She stepped to this third hostage and removed the burlap sack. She saw his face—twisted, misshapen by agony, colored white and blue. She knew this must be Peter. He bit down a thick cord of rope tied around his head. His waxy blond hair stuck to his sweaty forehead. She removed the rope from his mouth.

"Oh my God," he gasped, spit dripping from his lips. "Oh my God. I thought you were him. Are the police coming?"

His voice was soft, a boyish slur joining each uneven sentence.

"Are you Peter?" she asked.

He nodded.

Miss May screamed into the rope.

"Where is he?" Tillman asked Peter. "The gunman. Where is he?"

"Oh my God." He closed his eyes and threw his head back. "I don't know. He left a few minutes ago, but he's coming back. You have to get us out of here."

"Do you know where he went?"

Peter's nostrils flared and he was thrown into a coughing fit, straining against his ropes. Long spools of spit crawled from his mouth onto the bloodstained floor below him. "Help May and the girl. Untie them."

Tillman moved to Miss May. Although a rope also cut through her mouth, her teeth bared against the cord, her eyes were alert and shifting. They landed on Tillman with a sort of physical force she felt in her chest.

She was trying to communicate something. Tillman tried to pull the rope from her mouth, but it was tighter than Peter's had been. Tillman set to untying the knot with shaking fingers, and finally loosened it enough to pull it down her chin.

As soon as she could open her mouth, May shouted, "It's him."

Immediately, Tillman reached for her gun in her waistband, but not before she turned to see an empty chair where Peter had been just a second ago.

She felt the cold, hard nose of a pistol press into her spine.

"Drop the gun," Peter said.

He spoke in the same soft voice he had before, but it was now unhurried, self-possessed. As though he were asking her to do something she'd known she'd have to do. A stage direction she'd forgotten.

"You piece of shit," May said, spitting at Peter.

And still Tillman turned his words over in her head, unable to make sense of them. The moment was ruptured. She felt like she had just awoken in this cold, dark room. A light hanging and swinging.

Dust hung in the air, frozen.

"Drop the gun," Peter repeated, pressing his own gun harder against Tillman's spine.

Her pistol clattered to the floor like a plastic toy-thing. With his gun still pressed against her, he bent over and picked up her weapon. His fingers fumbled with the pistol.

Instincts.

Tillman shifted her weight to her front foot and, with the other, she kicked Peter in the groin. He screamed in agony, dropping his gun, falling to his knees. She grabbed him by his hair as he reached his hands across her waist, attempting to pull her to the ground. But she remained planted. She jerked his head up by his hair and struck him in the jaw. He sprawled across the ground, reaching frantically for his gun at his side. She reached for her own, but it was not there. It must have gotten kicked away, she realized. She saw from the corner of her eye Peter pointing his weapon directly at her chest, his back to the ground.

"Sit down," he said. Blood formed in the corners of his mouth, staining his teeth. "I'll kill you right now. It doesn't matter to me either way. Sit the fuck down."

She lowered herself into the chair she had found him in. The ropes that had bound him lay on the ground. They were untied. He must have been holding them behind his back. She hadn't thought to check. The leather cushion of the chair was slick with his sweat, and for the first time she noticed the absence of any sort of ventilation into the room. It was stiflingly hot, each breath a material and burning presence passing down her throat.

With his gun trained to her chest, Peter rose slowly. He was smiling. Of course he's smiling, Tillman thought. He had won.

"Who are you?" he asked Tillman, as though he were meeting her at a bar with the chatter of a hundred conversations drifting between them, a man looking to make conversation out of boredom. "How did you find me?"

"You miserable little shit," Miss May spat.

Tillman spotted her gun lying three feet away, in front of Paulina's chair. Peter saw her looking at it. "I wouldn't if I were you," he said, stepping forward to pick up the pistol. "Seeing as how I don't even know who you are, you aren't worth a whole hell of a lot to me alive."

He backed toward the camera and Tillman saw that he had hidden a limp in his left leg. He set her revolver next to the mask and turned on the camera. It emitted a small electronic whine and he seemed amused by it. He turned back to Tillman and cocked his pistol. A small nine-millimeter. She saw in the way he placed his hand clumsily over the slide that he wasn't used to the weapon. The first time he had fired it might have been directly into Walter Williams's head just two days prior, Tillman thought, though it already felt to her like several eternities ago. "Should I expect any other visitors?"

She gestured at the door.

He smiled wider. "You're lying. I heard you coming. Only you. I saw you coming. Through the door. You came alone."

"They sent me first," she said. "They're coming in after me. Police. SWAT. They're coming."

He remained in front of her and removed one hand from the gun to brush his hair from his sweaty forehead. His teeth were yellowed, nicotine-stained. "Yes, because that's the way that SWAT teams operate," he intoned. "They send some woman ahead of them."

"She beat the shit out of you," Miss May said, laughing.

"Is that right?" Peter turned to Tillman. He held his gun out at arm's length. "Did you beat the shit out of me? Because the way I see it, you're the one with a gun to your head."

She wanted nothing more than to wrap her hands around his neck, feel the life force dwindle with each beat of his heart pulsing in her fingertips. It might even be worth taking a bullet for. But she shook it off. What she needed now was to buy time. If it wasn't midnight already, it would soon be. "They sent me to talk to you. To negotiate."

"Who?" he asked, a disbelieving grin.

"The police."

He broke into wheezing laughter, bloody spit forming at the edges of his lips, which he licked away. "You're so full of shit."

"If I'm lying, then how do you think I found you? They sent me here to talk to you. To hear what you have to say. To see if we can work something out. I'm here to help you, Peter."

He looked back at her, stone-faced. He seemed to her like a boy trapped inside a man, a strained sort of innocence trying to break from his gaze. But he was not innocent, she reminded herself. He would kill her if she let him, or even if she didn't let him. He was the one with a gun. He was more than willing to use it, too. He brought one hand to his head and raked his fingers through his hair while he bit his bottom lip so hard she thought he might swallow it.

"You know why he wants to kill us?" Miss May directed her question to Tillman, but kept her stare fixed on Peter Richards. "Because he's a small, nothing man who has to tie someone up to kill them. He's a fucking limp-dick psychotic piece of shit who can't take the truth." But before she could finish the thought, if there was anything left to finish, Peter stepped forward and lifted his pistol high and brought the grip down on her head. The gunmetal connected to her skull with a dull, percussive thud. Her head lolled forward, slumped to her chest.

"Jesus Christ," Tillman whispered, seeing blood pour from the deep wound, spreading down May's face like a rouge mask, just one gradient darker than her hair.

"I told her to stop," he said, almost apologetically. He shifted off his bad leg, turned back to look at the camera. She was maybe four steps away from him. Too far to make a move for the gun. Peter took another step back, wincing as he put weight on his leg. He leaned against the boxes, taking focused breaths.

"You know Marcus Waters?" Tillman asked, hoping to distract him. She feared he would try to pistol-whip her as well, but unlike the woman, Tillman wasn't bound by ropes. If he tried it, she would be able to subdue him. But if he simply shot her, that would be a different story. "The journalist, you know him?"

He ignored the question as he adjusted the camera. "So then it was Marcus that gave you my name? I'm surprised. Didn't plan on that. He's blind to just about everything. It's willful ignorance. Ignores things right in front of him. Sees the world the way he wants to. I'm actually glad he figured it out eventually, though. Good for him."

"So that woman"—Tillman nodded at May—"she knew the Kingfisher, then? That's what you made it sound like in your video."

"I'm done talking with you. I know what you're doing."

"I'm interested in the Kingfisher, too," Tillman said. "I think he's still alive like you do. I always have."

"No, you don't." He laughed. "No one does."

"Did she know him? The Kingfisher?"

He stood up straight and gently stretched his back, face wrought in a pained satisfaction. He adjusted the camera, turned the viewer around, and framed the shot so that both Tillman and the woman were in the screen. He reached for the Robespierre mask and slipped it over his face, adjusting the elastic band over his ears. Once it was on, his entire presence seemed to change. He stood taller and stepped forward to the camera, his bad leg no longer dragging.

Whatever window she had to act was quickly closing, so she took a leap of faith across whatever chasm she had found herself facing on this stolid night.

"He did that to you."

He looked over his shoulder, eyes hidden behind the plastic sheen. His finger hovered over the record button on the video camera.

She nodded at his bad leg. "The Kingfisher did that to you, didn't he?"

Peter didn't move, didn't speak.

"I don't recall your name from the newspapers," she said.

He patted his gun against his hip, shaking his head. The mask only smiled. That was all it knew. "That's because it wasn't written about in the newspapers," he said, his voice dulled beneath the plastic contours of the mask. "I hadn't done anything wrong. I hadn't broken any laws."

He seemed unsure of how, or whether, to proceed, and he busied himself for a few moments by picking up the rope from the floor and setting it next to the revolver, the video camera. Little tasks, mindless rearrangements. He rubbed his leg with his free hand and she wondered if he knew he was doing this.

"It's past midnight." He sighed and pointed at the camera behind him. "And these things, no one ever cared about them before, they don't care now. They don't matter anymore."

"You don't believe that. You're not doing all of this just to cause chaos. You're not killing people just because the Kingfisher may still be alive. You want to tell your story to the world. Maybe you don't know how. So tell me, and then you can tell them." She nodded at the camera. "You can tell them exactly what it was he did to you, and they will listen."

"You're wasting time."

"What did he do to you, Peter?"

He shook his head slowly. "What happened was he severed four of my vertebrae." He turned in profile and pointed at his lower back. "I found him, but I wasn't supposed to find him. He was supposed to be dead. But he wasn't dead. He wasn't dead at all."

"How did you find him?"

"Her." He pointed at May. "I knew he hadn't died. I knew it was all bullshit. And I knew he would come back. For her. I knew where she was living. I sat in my car and watched her apartment. Didn't have to wait for long. The night after the city's funeral, I saw him. He was standing in the alley outside her apartment. Just standing there like he was thinking he might go inside through the window. I got out of my car and approached him. I was excited. I must have been smiling. I'm sure of it." She realized Peter was laughing. But even so, his voice carried with it a dreamlike formlessness, the words blurred and hazy and automatic. "And then all of a sudden, before I could even say a single word, he was dragging me down the alley by my neck. And the whole time, he was saying how he knew I'd been watching her apartment. He said he knew that I wanted to hurt her, but he wouldn't let me. I tried to tell him he was wrong, but then he threw me up against the wall." He mimicked a push, laughter still dripping from his mouth. "I told him I was sorry. I told him I wouldn't hurt her. I told him I only wanted to say something to him. But he wasn't listening. He was out of his mind, kept saying over and over again how he had hurt her. He was screaming it. Said he only ever wanted to protect her, but he only hurt her. Said he wouldn't let me hurt her, too." By now, Peter was nearly doubled over in laughter. "And you know something? I didn't even see him throughout the whole thing. Not once. He was there in front of me. But I didn't see him. I just kept thinking to myself, 'This can't be him.' It's what I told myself. I said, 'It can't be him, it can't be him, it can't be him.'"

"What was it that you wanted to tell him?"

Peter straightened up, the laughter suddenly gone from his lungs. "I wanted to tell him that he was my hero. And I did. I told him he was my hero. I said it like I thought he would understand. I said it like I thought it might save me."

"And that's when he did that to you?" she asked, though it was not a question. "You told him he was your hero."

"It's terrifying, isn't it?" He clicked the magazine out of the gun, inspected the ammunition, and clicked it back into place. "Realizing that your hero is a monster only when he starts beating you within an inch of your life."

Tillman had only half listened, her mind freewheeling plans of action, none of which seemed more likely than any other, but she knew she needed him to keep talking. She thought of Jeremiah, hoped like hell he had put in the call to the station, and if he had, how long would it be until the SWAT team broke in? She thought of her father, sleeping in his armchair. She wondered if it was possible—but of course it wasn't—that the Kingfisher would appear at any passing second.

"So you told the police?" she asked, measuring the distance between where she sat and where he stood. "After it happened. After he did that to you. You told them?"

Six feet of empty space separated them. If she could charge him, she'd be on him in a second. But a lot could happen in a second.

"Of course I told them, but they didn't want to hear it. They never returned my calls. When I started dropping by the station after I was released from the hospital, they wouldn't even file a report. Wouldn't even listen to my story. I'm sure Gregory Stetson had something to do with that. It was his fault. All of it. The Kingfisher may have been a monster, but he was a monster that Stetson kept fed."

The light in the room seemed to dim briefly, an electric yawn. There was some distant sound, a percussive thud. Maybe just a car door slamming shut. But they both listened for a moment to the ensuing silence, and she saw his fingers tighten around the pistol's grip. She hoped with her entire being that the sound signified something, but she ignored it.

"Why didn't anyone file a report?" she asked.

His face fell flat and he strained to listen to the phantom sounds. He poked his head out the door, stared into the darkness for a few moments until he was satisfied. He shut it quietly behind him and began inspecting his pistol under the swinging light.

"Because he was supposed to be dead, and he wasn't dead." Laughter— loud, gut-deep—erupted from behind the mask so suddenly it made Tillman wince. "I shouldn't laugh. But it is funny, isn't it? It's all funny. It's all very funny when you stop and think."

"I'm sorry that happened to you," Tillman said, willing sincerity into her voice. "That must have been terrible."

He shrugged, still laughing. "He hurt me back then. He hurt me very badly, but now I get to hurt him, too. I want him to remember what it feels like."

He pressed the record button on the camera. A red, blinking light stared forward into the room. He walked between Tillman and the woman in his uneven limp. She saw that he was staring forward at the camera, preparing himself for the thousands and millions of eyes that would consume this moment. His gun he held at his side, fingers dancing along the grip in anticipation.

"You did not come forward," Peter said into the camera. "You did not save her."

If the Kingfisher is still out there, Tillman thought to herself, he's out of time. She was going to die. Paulina was going to die. May was going to die.

Tillman tried to say something that might stall the moment, something that might distract Peter's rigid focus on the red light blinking before him. But she felt lost inside whatever it was unfolding around her, as though she were caught in some powerful tide leading her out into a near-infinite sea.

At once, the door to the room parted just enough to allow a small, tennis ball–sized object to bounce across the floor. It seemed so out of place and unlikely, that in that initial fraction of a second, she first thought she was imagining it.

She had just enough time to look up and see Peter looking down at the flash grenade. Without turning away, he held the gun up at his side, the barrel aimed at May's unconscious head.

Tillman launched forward and tackled him, leveling her shoulder into his chest. She brought him down into the boxes and heard his gun scatter across the floor. A lightning flash of white burned straight through her eyes and etched into her brain, followed by a lagging eruption of sound. A ringing that seemed to feed upon itself. All sensation, all direction, all history lost to a ringing expanse of sea and she was now drowning in it. She released herself to it, felt her body roll onto the cold floor. She tried to press herself into it just to feel something solid and unmoving and unchanged.

She tried opening her eyes. It was horrendously painful and she felt herself screaming as the world was silent. Cold dark. Wet dark. Thin air, heavy air, hot air. Lights so bright they burrow. She tried to remember where she was, who she was.

Muffled voices, many voices, emerged from the darkness, softly at first, but growing louder. Ringing, ringing.

She closed her eyes, felt the return of sensation growing in her toes, crawling up through her legs and into her chest.

And then she was on her back, and there were blankets around her. Straps tied across her chest. She pushed against the straps with wild force, screaming. A gentle hand pushed her back down, squeezed her shoulder. There were voices, whispering words she ought to have recognized. She opened her eyes partly. But there wasn't light. There was only total, revelatory darkness. And then there were lights flickering softly in her periphery, halogen and industrial, and then there was the cusp of fresh air and stars, or at least brilliant spots of electric light that could pass as stars on a night such as this. And she heard the wheels rolling beneath her, ambulance lights, police lights, city lights, and there were the words again, and she ought to say something, but what could she say to something she'd never heard?

And there was someone speaking now directly over her. She recognized his voice, even distant and shrouded behind the static erupting from her head. She struggled to open her eyes once again, but she didn't need to see him to know he was staring back at her, smiling weakly, hand brushing her hair behind her ears, and he called her *Tilly,* which was a name she knew she hated to be called and she knew that he knew this, yet he always insisted, didn't he, because he knew she hated it and it made him smile to see her angry with him and he was smiling now and she was angry with him and that was enough. On this night, that was enough.

42 HOPE

MARCUS PUSHED, SHOULDERED, and fought through the barricade of police officers that surrounded the perimeter around the parking garage, twisting his body through the narrow openings between cruisers and ambulances idling in the street. Everywhere, a choreographed state of emergency. His shoulder bag bounced against his hip. He turned and looked for Wren, who moments ago had been behind him. He saw her, flanked by two federal agents, staring at the ground beneath her sneakered feet. As if sensing Marcus's gaze, she looked up and met his stare for a brief instant before a cruiser passed between them. She might have been smiling, she might have been crying, she might not have seen him at all.

He turned and pushed onward, deeper into the thick of the commotion.

A stretcher was being loaded into an ambulance, the first stretcher to emerge from the parking garage. He saw Tillman lying there, blanketed, an oxygen mask strapped to her face. Next to her, Jeremiah was arguing with the attending paramedics. "I don't fucking care what the procedure is!" Jeremiah shouted, squaring up with a young paramedic. "I'm going with her."

"Jeremiah," Marcus called out. "Is Tillman OK?"

Jeremiah turned around, regarded Marcus with a quick nod, and turned back to the paramedic. "I'm going to ride with her to the hospital, and if you want to try to stop me, you be my fucking guest." The paramedics exchanged a glance, acquiesced, and climbed into the back of the ambulance. Jeremiah turned back to Marcus. "They say she's going to be fine."

"What about May? Paulina?"

But Jeremiah was already stepping into the back of the ambulance, seating himself beside the paramedics. Jeremiah leaned over Tillman, his fingers gently touching her own, whispering silently into her ear.

Marcus watched the ambulance pull away, sirens crying into the night. He turned and saw two other stretchers emerging from the parking garage, each of them setting off for respective ambulances. He ran toward them, but an officer restrained him.

"Mr. Waters," the officer said. "Please come with me."

Marcus strained to see over the officer's shoulder as the stretchers were loaded into the ambulances. On one, he saw Miss May. Her red hair lay against the white sheets beneath her. Blood on her forehead running down her cheeks. "She's bleeding," Marcus said. "She's bleeding."

"Please come with me, Mr. Waters."

The officer forcefully guided Marcus away from the ambulances and SWAT vans toward an unmarked town car parked on the opposite side of the street. The officer opened the passenger-side door for Marcus and gestured for him to sit, closing the door behind him. Marcus lay his bag at his feet. Keys dangled in the ignition. A pineapple-scented car freshener swung from the rearview. But all of his attention drifted out the window as the remaining ambulances pulled away, shuttling down the street in a convoy of accompanying cruisers. He turned his focus to the parking garage, where a final stretcher emerged accompanied by members of the SWAT team, their rifles slung around their shoulders. They ushered the final stretcher directly into the back of the remaining ambulance.

The driver's-side door of the town car opened. A musky cologne wafted inside. Marcus turned from the window to find Gregory Stetson sitting in the driver's seat, stone-faced, his head against the headrest. Eyes closed, breathing heavily. He opened his eyes and stared forward at the squall of police lights illuminating the thin layer of fog that crawled over the street.

"She was bleeding," Marcus said. "Miss May. She was bleeding."

"Took a hit to the head," Stetson said with a flat inflection, as though reading from a news bulletin, "but she's stable. The other hostage will be

out of the hospital in a few days, I'd guess, after recovering from the gunshot wound."

"What about Tillman?"

Stetson sighed. "She's fine. I don't know what on earth possessed her
to do what she did, but she's going to be fine."

Marcus paused. "And Peter?"

"He's alive."

"He shouldn't be," Marcus said, feeling no shame in his disappoint-
ment.

"Yeah, well." Stetson sighed. "It's over. That's what matters."

Marcus looked out the window. "This isn't over. People are angry.
They're confused. Whatever this was, it's only beginning."

Stetson turned the car on. Cool air blasted through the vents. "Where
do you live, Marcus?"

"What?"

"I'm going to give you a ride home."

"I actually drove here." Marcus pointed behind them at his car, parked
just a block away.

"Then let's just drive for a bit," Stetson said, pulling out into the road
and passing slowly through the blockade at the end of the street. "We need
to talk. Just the two of us."

"Figured you'd want to talk at the station," Marcus said, but Stetson
didn't respond. He only piloted the car slowly through the streets. With
the cavalcade of sirens and lights and commotion behind them, the streets
ahead were quiet and still. Like driving through a dream. Stetson changed
lanes with a slow, drifting turn of the wheel. Marcus felt Stetson's silence
as a pressure in his chest. Marcus turned to him. "Look, if I'd known—
or even suspected—Peter was the gunman, I would have—"

"Stop," Stetson sighed. "There is a time for all that. And it isn't now."

"You said you wanted to talk."

"I do." Stetson turned the car onto another street. "We seized the
computer of that girl," Stetson said. "The Liber-teen you showed up with.
Evidently, she'd collected more from our servers than we initially thought.
You can imagine my surprise when I hear that she sent a particular file
to you and only you."

Marcus looked out the window. On the sidewalk, stray remnants of
protestors. They held their signs, they held hands. They watched the car

pass them, day-weary smiles plastered to their young faces. He wondered if they knew what had just occurred several blocks away from them or if they even cared. They walked in groups of twos and threes. Friends and lovers, closer for having briefly shared something they thought they understood.

"I didn't ask her to send me anything," Marcus said. "I didn't even know her before today."

"I don't care. I'm not asking you how it came to be that you met her. I'm not even asking how it came to be that she sent you that file. Like I said, that will come later. All I ask for the moment is that you don't do anything foolish with the file that she gave you."

Stetson turned left on another street. Marcus realized they were driving in a large circle, touring a city that was falling back asleep after a nightmare.

"If you're going to threaten me, at least be more specific," Marcus said.

Stetson shook his head, sighing loudly through his nostrils. "I just want you to understand something, Marcus." His eyes trained ahead of him. "You may have always been a pain in my ass back in the day, but fact of the matter is that you and I are cut from the same cloth. I don't care if you don't believe me. I don't care if you think it's *outlandish* or whatever the hell you'd call it." Stetson shook his head. Marcus hadn't ever seen him like this, speaking with desperate insistence over stumbling words. "But you did what you did back then because you knew that what you were doing was important and good. You wrote those articles about him because you knew that people needed to know about him. You knew that people needed to know there was someone out there doing some extraordinary things because once people knew that, they could feel something like hope. They could know that it was possible for things to be better than they were. You knew that this city needed to know what hope felt like when they had long forgotten the feeling. You understood the importance of that just like I did. And I can tell you this, Marcus—everything I ever did in my career, everything I ever will do in my career, has always been to give this city a reason to look forward to the future."

"Look, I'm not questioning your—"

But Stetson interrupted. "Even after he was gone—after he'd had enough, after he'd given up—I never once gave up the fight, Marcus. Never once. Maybe that meant making sacrifices along the way, maybe that meant doing things I've since come to regret, maybe that meant seeing—" He ran his hand over his mouth, wiping away a stray thought before it could pass his lips. He gripped the steering wheel tighter. "What I'm trying to say to you is that I did what I did because it was for the best. And if you want to write some new book about all my misdealing along the way, all I ask you to remember is that you would have done the same exact thing if you were in my position, because you wanted the same exact thing I did. You wanted them, everyone, to know that there was hope in the world. You wanted them to know that there was someone out there doing what needed to be done at all costs. Even if he would one day leave, even if he would one day have to give up. There was a moment in time when he was out there doing something incredible and awe-inspiring. That's why you told his story. That's why you gave him a name. Isn't that right?"

Marcus considered the question, which felt to him more like an accusation. As a journalist, Marcus had prided himself on the belief that he could separate himself from the world he described, that he could distance his feelings as he carefully annotated reality. He believed that he could dispassionately report on a man who once looked over these streets and protected them. A man who ignored due process and whose conception of justice began and ended with his knuckles. A man who bullets could not bring down, a man who heard the thousands of discordant cries rising up from the city he must have loved dearly. A man who ruptured the lives of petty criminals simply making their way through the world, a man who put away some of the city's most dangerous aberrations. A man who killed, a man who saved. A man who cooperated with the law to subvert the law. A man who gave five years of anonymous service. A man who did not return when the city he must have once loved dearly needed him the most. A man who never once asked to be given a name.

"I think I believed he was a hero," Marcus said. "That's why I wrote about him. That's why I gave him a name."

Stetson nodded somberly, relaxing his grip on the steering wheel. "Then I hope you understand what I'm trying to tell you."

Marcus watched out the window as streets passed under dull lamplight. The city seemed quiet tonight, maybe even quieter than usual. But he knew that if you listened closely enough, the world screamed with thousands of stories desperate to be heard, thousands of lives desperate to be saved, thousands of yesterdays clawing to be remembered. A woman pushed a shopping cart up a curb. A man in camouflage pants held his arms out and shouted at an open apartment window three stories above.

"I won't share the file with anyone," Marcus said, his voice trailing off.

"Good." Stetson nodded. "I think that's for the best."

"But I want you to do something in return."

Stetson glanced over, eyebrows raised.

"Don't bring any charges against Wren. The Liber-teen. I know she's back in custody. But she's the one who found the gunman. She's the reason May and that other hostage are still alive. I can attest to it. So can Detective Combs. Don't prosecute her."

Stetson shook his head, turning down another street. "She hacked our servers, stole confidential information, and then released that information for the purpose of assisting a criminal. Even if she did end up locating the gunman, I can't just let her off. The FBI is involved. They're going to bring charges against her. You know I couldn't do anything for her even if I wanted to."

"Yes, you can. And you will."

Passing lamplight cut across Stetson's face like a scar as the car slowed to a halt. Marcus saw that they had parked next to his car, the police blockade ahead of them populated by a crowd of onlookers, news vans, and reporters with microphones raised to catch their words of revelation.

"Is that right?" Stetson asked, an inscrutable mixture of amused and annoyed. "Enlighten me, Marcus Waters. How can I let a criminal walk free?"

"For the exact same reason you did before."

Stetson pursed his lips and looked out the window in contemplation. After a moment, he said, "It's not the same. She wouldn't cooperate with law enforcement. Especially after all of this."

"You're right. She wouldn't cooperate with the cops or the feds. But maybe, if you're lucky, she'd cooperate with you."

"And just why would she do that?"

Marcus picked his bag up from his feet and laid it on his lap. "If everything that you've told me is even halfway true, I think the two of you may be more similar than either of you would ever care to admit." He opened the car door to get out, but stopped. He turned back to Stetson. "But unlike you, she has a conscience. She cares about consequences. You could learn from her. She's not going to simply follow your orders, but she'll do what's right for this city. If she knows that you share that goal, the two of you could accomplish extraordinary things. But she's not the Kingfisher, Greg. If you're going to work with her, then work with her. But don't you dare use her."

"You don't know what you're talking about, Marcus," Stetson said. "Do you honestly think I used the Kingfisher? You think I could control that man? You think I would even want to? No." Stetson shook his head. "Everything the Kingfisher did, he did out of his own volition. He and I, we shared a vision for this city. It was the greatest honor of my life to know that I was able to assist that great man's mission, because he was a hero." Stetson jabbed his finger in the space between them like a knife. "To hear you imply otherwise makes me fucking sick. The Kingfisher gave this city everything he had until he didn't have anything left to give. He was a hero, Marcus. The last true hero."

Marcus looked out the window. An enormous crowd had now amassed around the perimeter of the parking garage. Curious onlookers, witnesses to something that very few would ever fully understand. "There was a time when I would have agreed with you. But I never knew the Kingfisher the way you did. I don't know what motivated him to do the things that he did, but some of those things I would never call heroic." He heard Stetson begin to say something, a fierce challenge, but Marcus continued. "But tonight, I witnessed a girl with a laptop risk her entire future to save the hostages you yourself could or would not save. I met a woman who ran into a room not knowing what she would find, ready to risk her life for the sake of strangers. It was the greatest honor of my life to meet them, because they are heroes. And to hear you imply otherwise, well, you can probably guess how that makes me feel."

And with that, Marcus exited back out into the night, swinging his bag over his shoulder. He approached his car, keys in hand, and imagined walking in the door of his empty home, falling atop his empty bed, and waking in the early hours of morning when the world was still quiet and the day was unwritten.

EPILOGUE

THE LAST TIME MARCUS had been to Michigan, he was in high school. It was during a particularly frigid winter. His stepfather, Corn, had made good on his suggestion that he and Marcus go bird-watching in the Upper Peninsula. Each morning for four days, they set out before sunrise to a tree blind that overlooked an expansive frozen valley sparsely populated with a few wind-stripped trees and dense thickets. Corn brought with him a pair of binoculars, a thermos of coffee, four peanut butter sandwiches, and a field notebook. Marcus brought with him a copy of *Oliver Twist* and two pairs of gloves. Whenever any bird fluttered into view, Corn shook Marcus's arm gently and pointed discreetly at the fluttering creature. Corn passed the binoculars to Marcus to show him whatever bird had crossed into their observable range—a hawk, eagle, turkey buzzard. When Marcus was done pretending to admire the sight, he passed back the binoculars to Corn, who was smiling so widely Marcus barely recognized him. It wasn't even smiling, so much as it was *beaming*, his tongue clenched between his teeth to contain a primal yelp of delight.

"Isn't it just beautiful, all of it?" Corn asked in a barely audible whisper as he watched a gyrfalcon bury its head into its shoulders on a tree branch. His breath curled around his freshly shaven cheeks like a ghost escaping the boredom that Marcus was tasked to endure for several more days. "My God, my God. You can see pictures of these birds, yes. You can see them in zoos, yes. But to see them in their context, their natural habitat, to know of their existence beyond the pages of a book. It is like seeing the face of God in the mirror. Don't you think?"

Marcus, these many years later, pulled off onto his exit for Lake Walton, and followed the narrow highway to a gas station, nestled in a clearing of ash trees. A single light pole radiated a white glow against the pitch-black surroundings. Marcus felt himself turning the car in to the parking lot before consciously deciding to do so. He still had a notch more than half a tank, but he caught sight of his reflection in the rearview and his eyes looked even wearier than they felt. It was ten o'clock at night, and he needed to know if there was any place he might stay for the night. He tried to remember the details he'd worked out in his head during the four-hour drive, but they had evidently slipped out the cracked car window.

May sat in the passenger seat, her hands pressed between her legs. She stared out the window, as silent as she had been throughout the entire drive. She wore a floral dress that came down to her knees. She still had the stitches on the crown of her head. She wore a wide-brimmed hat to hide them. But Marcus knew she wasn't hiding them from him.

The parking lot of the gas station was strewn with gravel. A few small puddles scattered haphazardly. The night's rain hung in the air, a frozen tableau.

"I'll be right back," Marcus said.

May stared out the window.

Inside, rows of packaged junk food, beer, coolant, and air fresheners in the shapes of pine trees. A small, bearded man wearing coveralls leaned on the counter with his knuckles, midlaugh with the cashier, a woman with her long hair, gray at the roots, tied into a bushy ponytail. She managed a "Hello," through laughter, when Marcus walked in. The other man turned, nodded at Marcus, and then turned back to the woman. "I told Jake, I told him you can't expect to pull a dog's weight with that thing."

In the back of the store, Marcus found a single coffeepot simmering on a warmer. Its surface was gilded with an oily sheen. He poured it into two Styrofoam cups and grabbed a small sleeve of doughnuts. He carried them to the counter and the bearded man stepped out of his way. As he checked out, he asked if they might know of a man who lived on Lake Walton, which was just half a mile away. He said the man was an old friend whose name he had forgotten. Stood over six feet tall, powerfully built, probably the quiet type. But neither of the two seemed to know of anyone matching the description.

Marcus nodded politely, managed a thank-you smile. He hadn't had any expectations to disappoint. It was a long shot that he would find the Kingfisher at all, much less at the same lake where the Kingfisher had told May he'd spent his childhood summers. But it was the only place Marcus could think of. He wasn't sure what he would tell May. When he asked her to accompany him here, she had agreed without any further clarification. She wouldn't say it, but he knew she hadn't come here to look for him. She had come here to find him. She had come here to see if it was really true that the Kingfisher had not died those many years ago. She had come here to see him and to know him and to say whatever words can span the length of thirty years. She stared out a window looking out over a highway always receding into the distance.

Marcus left the gas station. His windshield was speckled and each drop shined beneath a single light suspended at the top of the pumps. He saw May sitting exactly in the position she had been in throughout the entire drive. He began fueling his car and as the counter clicked the gallons away slowly, slowly, Marcus walked around to the other side of his car and leaned against its slick hull. All the stars were out tonight. In elementary school, they'd been taught a few constellations and he searched for them now, but he couldn't find a single one. And he wondered if perhaps the stars had shifted at some point in the past sixty-odd years since elementary school or if he had simply forgotten or if there was some excluded middle he was too tired to see.

He wasn't sure it mattered either way.

The pump clicked, finished. Marcus got back in his car and handed May a coffee. She put it in the cup holder.

"They don't know," Marcus said.

"OK," she said.

"But we'll look around, OK?"

"We don't have to."

"We will."

"OK."

As he drove out of the parking lot, he saw in his rearview the cashier standing outside of the gas station, waving her arms over her head, and he heard her muffled shouts. The man stood with her, fumbling to light a cigarette in the wind.

Marcus turned the car around and pulled up beside them. He rolled his window down.

The cashier smiled and pushed a stray hair behind her ear. She gestured at the man. "Chester remembered something."

The bearded man cursed his lighter, his back to the wind. Once he finally got a light, he turned back to them and smoke punctuated his words.

"Yeah, there's a guy who lives down the road a ways. I've only ever seen him once or twice. Only reason I thought of him now was that my buddy lives next to him on the lake. He's an odd one, though. Keeps mostly to himself. Doesn't have what you might call a 'friendly reputation.' But I think he might be the fella you're looking for."

"Do you have an address?"

"No. I'm not sure he has one, matter of fact. But just drive down that road right there for a mile and a half. You'll see a tin mailbox at the end of a drive. That's my buddy's place. Keep driving to the next driveway. There isn't a mailbox, but you should see it anyway. Just keep your eyes peeled. That's the place you want. Good luck."

They drove beneath an arched canopy of mature birch trees, Marcus's headlights wandering across the luminescent eyes of deer tucked beneath the dense walls of foliage. He spotted a tin mailbox and drove slowly past it, squinting carefully for the hint of a driveway amid the lush overgrowth of ferns and trees.

He nearly missed it—a gravel path leading into a forest wall. Marcus put the car in park. The hotel was in the other direction. He could turn around, buy both of them separate rooms, and come back in the morning. The light of day. Or he could turn around and sleep and maybe never come back at all. He could drive home all through the night and wake up in the morning and write all of this off as some unwanted fever dream. Even if by some impossible chance the Kingfisher was still alive and this was indeed his home, what would he think of some old journalist pulling in to his driveway at twilight with a once-lover?

And there was May, seated next to him. The patient fold of her body, knees bent to the door. She did not belong in a place like this. But she didn't care.

But maybe, Marcus thought, he needed someone like Marcus to fill him in on everything he had missed. It's a different city than you last left it, he would say. It's a different world. Do you remember May? Of course you do. She's here with me. She's in the car. Why didn't you save her? She said she called out for you, but you did not come. She would forgive you, though. But maybe you don't care about forgiveness. Actually, I don't know what you care about at all. That's why I'm here. I just want to understand you. No, I need to understand you. I have to know why.

He pulled in to the driveway. His headlights sharpened the indistinct shapes of hanging branches, overturned stumps rotting in their own shadows, the reflective eyes of animals in the periphery of the conical light. Marcus let his foot off the gas to be as quiet as possible.

He turned off his headlights as the car followed the soft blue impression of the gravel drive, glowing like Italian marble in the moonlit night.

The driveway led to a clearing, occupied by a double-wide trailer, the tin siding rusting and slanted. The windows were covered by wooden particleboards. Two camping fold-out chairs sat in the small front yard, surrounding a burn pit, which was smoldering. An ember pulsed beneath the charred wood. Barely alive.

Marcus saw beyond the trailer, down a slight embankment, the reflective surface of a lake. He parked his car in the driveway, and when he got out, stood next to it, unsure what should happen next, if he was supposed to wait here or go to the door. He drank from his Styrofoam cup and listened. Somewhere, a woodpecker was pounding furiously away, working overtime long into the night. Maybe there were two or three, or maybe it was just a reverberating echo bounding from the hollowed-out trees.

To his surprise, May opened her door and got out.

Marcus decided to approach the door of the trailer, feeling clumsy in the motion. The gravel grated loudly with each sinking step forward. He held the coffee up near his heart, a calculated pose. A way of saying, I'm not a threat. Just a passing traveler with a question that won't take very long. Maybe you know who I am? My name is Marcus Waters.

May stayed standing next to the car, taking it all in. He wondered what she saw.

Marcus came to the door and knocked, a motion that surprised him. He thought it would take him all night to work up the courage, but here he was with three solid knocks—one to be heard and two more for good measure. He practiced an innocuous smile, and for the first time he became aware of his heart beating like a waltz that was steadily falling into some anarchic time signature.

He listened and heard nothing. No soft rustling. No footsteps. Nothing. He knocked again and still nothing.

He wondered if maybe he ought to wait for a minute longer, and so he did. He consulted his watch and at the end of the minute, he waited for another minute. If he drove fast, he could be back in Chicago before the sun rose. The city would never know he had left.

After several unanswered minutes, he started back for the car. A loon called out from the lake in a long, elegiac croon. He stopped in his tracks and turned around, moving beyond the trailer and toward the lake. He heard May following after him, graceful steps. The embankment angled down to the water's edge, spongy and soft. He came to a dock that reached out maybe fifteen feet into the water. There were posts at either end with white ropes floating in the water. A boat had recently been tied here. He walked to the very end of the dock; each step against the rotted boards creaked.

He heard May approach behind him.

Marcus surveyed the lake, a mirror image of the crystalline sky, giving the illusion that the end of the dock was also the end of the earth, a point beyond which the universe began. The mostly still waters lapped softly against the shore.

He felt dizzy, frightened that he would fall into the water waiting below. Instead, he lowered himself slowly, his limbs stiff and unruly. When he was seated on the dock, he pulled his shoes and socks off and dipped his feet into the water, which was warmer than he expected. He wiggled his toes, feeling the water wrap his ankles.

May sat beside him, unclasped her sandals, and set them at her side. She dipped her feet into the water and watched the ripples span and disappear before her.

"I don't know what to tell you," Marcus said.

"Then don't."

"We don't have to do this."

"Yes, we do."

"We just don't know. Maybe, maybe not."

"He's here," she said. "I know he's here."

"How do you know?"

"I just know." She looked back at the trailer atop the embankment and then turned back to the lake. He saw that she was squinting out across the water. "He's really here, Marcus. I wish I could say I couldn't believe it."

"Where is he?"

"I don't know. But he can see us. He's out there. He's looking at us. He can hear us. And he doesn't know what to think. He's scared, but he doesn't need to be scared." She wasn't talking to Marcus, and he understood this. "He should come here. He should talk to us. Because we're only here to talk. We're only here to say a few things to him, a few things that we wished we could have said a long time ago."

Marcus scanned the water. His eyes adjusted to the dark, the play of lights against the surface. He could make out the tree line on the other side of the lake. He saw two loons in the middle, weaving beneath the surface and reappearing fifty yards away. The lake wasn't nearly as infinite as it had first appeared. He could see where it began, where it ended.

"And if he's here," Marcus began.

"Then I'll ask him," she finished.

"You'll ask him what?"

"What I've asked him countless times before. I'll ask him what he's doing here. And then I'll ask him why he didn't come back. He left me, he left us, and he left everything. I just want to know why. I need to know."

Marcus heard a faraway hum. It grew louder. He recognized it as a motor, a small one, whining at an easy speed. It continued to grow louder and he squinted to see where it was coming from, but he could not. It might have been behind one of the several outcroppings of land that projected from the shoreline. Or maybe he was not looking hard enough. Either way, he knew it was coming to meet him at the dock. He knew this the way he knew everything else he had ever known. He sat there. Barefooted, tired. And he raised his coffee cup to his heart as though to say, I am not a threat. I am a friend.

"He's coming," May said.

And here in the black-light night of another endless summer, Marcus hears a small splash to his side, just a few feet away. He turns to see reflected in the water's surface a small, brightly colored bird flying to the shoreline, wings stilled and frozen, picture-book beauty, and he traces its unlikely shape across the water for as long as he can manage until it disappears once more.

May smiles and points out over the lake where there is only shadow and light and the sound of something coming closer, closer, until it is there.

T. J. MARTINSON

ACKNOWLEDGMENTS

My grandmother, Mary Martinson, to whom this novel is dedicated, believes in the transformative power of words, and I am thankful that she displayed for me the magic of books from an early age. My high school English teacher, Barbara Amster, inspired and encouraged me to begin writing, and she taught me to discern in my own writing the good from the bad from the ugly. My mother and father have always supported me in all of my endeavors and encourage my passions, even when I said I wanted to be an English major. My beautiful sisters, Rachel and Lucy, and my average-looking brother, Tad, all go out of their way to keep me grounded, so, thanks for that, I guess.

The incredibly talented author Ashley Woodfolk was kind enough to read the manuscript; she provided insight and perspective that was extremely useful and very necessary. My friends, Sean Towey and Kenzie Grob, read early drafts of the novel and offered crucial feedback. Maureen McQuillan was a source of endless encouragement, enthusiasm, and Indian food. Steve Nathaniel let me beat him in pool whenever I was stressed out, and I appreciate that. And to my colleagues and professors of the Indiana University English department, thanks for being brilliant and kind; the humanities have never been more necessary than they are now, and all of you give me enormous hope for the future.

My extraordinary agent, Sharon Pelletier, has stuck with me through thick and thin; I consider myself the luckiest writer in the world to have her in my corner. My brilliant editor, Christine Kopprasch, shared in my vision for this novel and helped me develop it into something I am immensely proud of. I also want to thank the phenomenal team at Flatiron Books for all of their contributions.

And finally, I want to thank those who inspired this novel. Though we live in turbulent and frightening times, I am honored to live alongside heroes who, in the face of injustice, speak out and refuse to be silenced. Black Lives Matter, the travel ban airport protestors, the women who marched on D.C. after the inauguration, the counterprotestors at Charlottesville, the Parkland students, and so many others—your bravery will write history.

Recommend *The Reign of the Kingfisher* for your next book club!
Reading Group Guide available at
www.readinggroupgold.com